Forced into hiding after his first encounter with the immortal magicians of the dreaded House Montu, Ash and his young family haven't had long to enjoy their refuge.

Now his enemies have caught up to him, and Ash must choose between keeping a deadly secret or charging headfirst into danger to rescue his loved ones.

With the tenuous peace between the rival Houses of Inkarna in the balance, Ash is the only one who can stop House Montu from a power grab that could forever alter human history.

Thanatos
Copyright © 2021 Nerine Dorman

First published by Ba en Ast Books 2021.

All rights reserved. No part of this book may be reproduced in any form by any electronic or mechanical means including photocopying, recording, or information storage and retrieval without permission in writing from the author.
This book is a work of fiction. Any resemblance to actual events, real persons living or dead, is entirely coincidental.

Cover Illustration by Jodie Muir
Cover Design by Tallulah Lucy
Interior Design by Nerine Dorman
Proofreading by Aleksander Voinov and Kimberly Murphy Wilbanks

This first paperback edition was printed by Amazon.

An e-book edition of this title is also available.

www.nerinedorman.blogspot.com

THANATOS
NERINE DORMAN

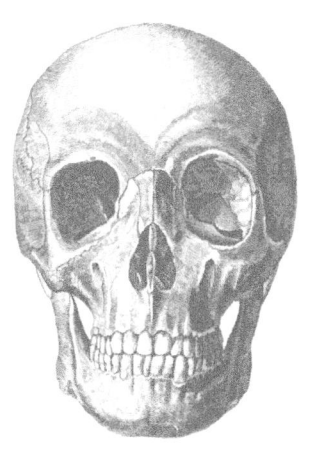

DEDICATION

This goes out to Peter, Shaen, James, and others we've lost too soon. Wherever you travel, my friends, know that you are loved – you are star stuff.

CONTENTS

Acknowledgements	6
Foreword	7
Prologue	9
Chapter One	12
Chapter Two	42
Chapter Three	72
Chapter Four	116
Chapter Five	156
Chapter Six	199
Chapter Seven	233
Chapter Eight	250
Chapter Nine	269
Chapter Ten	280
Chapter Eleven	303
Chapter Twelve	320
Epilogue	325
About the Author	327
Other Books by Nerine Dorman	328

ACKNOWLEDGEMENTS

As always, my friends in Skolion had my back on this project. Without you, I'd have way more typos and the odd 'cup of cigarette' in my novels.

Extra special thanks to Kimberly Murphy Wilbanks and Aleksandr Voinov who lent be their eyeballs and saved me from numerous blunders.

FOREWORD

I always knew I'd write a sequel to *Inkarna*. The story had a 'happy for now' ending, but at the time of completion I had no clear idea what the rest of the adventure would be.

Sometimes a break is all too necessary. The problem with me is sometimes my breaks are more than a few months, but rather years.

I won't lie. *Thanatos* sat on my hard drive for nearly half a decade before I sorted my shit out and got stuck into the edits. Finishing a story is important, and while Ash will no doubt still have many more missions, the origin story started in *Inkarna* attains closure in *Thanatos*.

Thank you for bearing with me. Enjoy the wild ride.

"The United Kingdom has Tanith Lee, the United States has Caitlin Kiernan, and South Africa has Nerine Dorman. An interesting Dark triangle."
– Don Webb

"Nerine Dorman is a master of building a dark and secretive world beneath the one you think you understand. Her writing is lush and seductive, and her characters are flawed and all too human, walking that indeterminate grey line between good and evil."
– Cat Hellisen

"Nerine Dorman's bright clear prose is at the forefront of modern fantasy."
– Storm Constantine

PROLOGUE
A Nice View

THE SUN IS merciless in the Karoo, and I tug my wide-brimmed hat so that it doesn't get blown off. This high up a stiff breeze whispers that's surprisingly chill despite the sun baking the world to a crisp. I've slogged half an hour to get halfway up the flat-topped hill, and I can't help but stop and look about me every few minutes.

Just to be sure.

My burden, though book-sized and insulated in thick layers of builder's plastic I've secured with silver duct tape, weighs more and more with each step.

The Book of Ammit the Devourer. I didn't ask for the responsibility, but the knowledge engraved on this stele, and now imprinted within the core of my eternal *Akh*, is perhaps the most dangerous to our kind. There are those who'd hunt me to the ends of the earth to lay hands on this small, seemingly innocuous serpentine tablet. There are those who have died because of it. I have destroyed with those words that will fly so easily to my lips if given half the chance. What is it like to hold this sort of power, to know that one can wipe away another's true name, or *Ren*, obliterate their *Ib*, and make it as if they never were?

Some would find that sort of power dizzying.

It's up to me to ensure that no one else can use this knowledge.

I can't run any farther. Nieu Bethesda is exactly in the middle of nowhere in this country—the way I like it. *They* won't find me here. At least not yet. We're safe. For a short while my small family has respite.

Under better circumstances, the view from the summit would be inspiring. The verdant loops of the Gat River stand in sharp contrast to the surrounding beige scrub. Where the valley opens, the farmers have laid down a patchwork of lucerne and other crops, but the little village of Nieu Bethesda is tucked away by another hill. I can almost imagine I'm lost in the wilderness. Almost.

The sharp peak of the Kompasberg is an aptly named landmark by which to navigate.

An aeroplane high in the stratosphere is betrayed by a thin wisp of contrail and the muted, delayed roar of its engine. And again, a thin niggle of worry tugs at me. There was a helicopter yesterday. Maybe it was some rich tourist visiting a nearby game farm. Or maybe it was the operatives of House Montu on my tail. Almost a year and a half has passed since that fateful night when I took out House Montu's Cape Town chapter. Only a fool would pretend that he could slip through the cracks. I am a fool.

I bury my burden, there atop that nameless, flat-topped hill, so similar to many of the others in this semi-desert. I dig deep into the stony ground, until my hands are raw, my nails splintered, and I bleed, my essence mingling with the earth to form part of the ward. As always, there is a reluctance to let go of the thing I have carried for what feels like an eternity. How can I turn my back on the cursed object? Yet I know, too, that I cannot take it with me if we are forced to run. Not if, but *when*. A cache is the only alternative I can think of. Who'd even know to look here? Maybe in a few hundred years I'll return, in a new body, with a new name, and I'll dig this up. Or maybe this stone will lie undiscovered until the knowledge required to decode its hieratic script is completely lost and those who speak the forbidden words have passed into eternity. There is always that. Our kind lives a dual existence, and the world of matter is the only one that lends us any sort of enduring permanency. And even that has its limits.

The resting place I disguise with rocks piled haphazardly. No cairn marks the spot. I cast my ward, attuned only to my *Ren*—Nefretkheperi. Any other who comes here will find themselves somehow displaced, "encouraged" by the dryness, the difficult terrain, and the compulsion to cast their nets elsewhere. *The Book of Ammit the Devourer* is buried in a thoroughly unremarkable grave, and I pray that it remains there until the seas rise and the plains of the Camdeboo are once again an ocean floor.

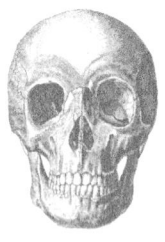

CHAPTER ONE
Disturbance

"EARTH TO ASH! Hello! Are you even listening to me?" Marlise's voice cuts through the buzz of my meditation, as a counterpoint to Alex's hitching cries. He's been crying for most of the afternoon. Until Marlise's interruption, I've been able to block the sound.

"*What?*" I yell back.

"The child! He's your problem. I'm going out."

With a groan, I rise and reach the front door just in time to see Marlise get into the car. She doesn't wait for me but slams the door. For a moment the engine stutters, and I wonder whether the damn Fiat's going to refuse to start like it has the entire week. But before I can raise a hand in supplication, Marlise reverses the battered vehicle out so fast I know she hasn't looked left or right. However, this is Nieu Bethesda. A car might pass our cottage once or twice a day. She's more likely to hit a donkey. All the roads are untarred, and a thick miasma of dust takes half a minute to settle every time a car passes, so she'd have ample warning if there's an oncoming vehicle.

I would like to tell her not to drive too fast, that the municipal workers still need to grade the roads near the pass, but that's pretty pointless. She's gone, and I'm stuck here with that child, and we're nowhere near the 'terrible twos' either. I'll go mad before the little cretin's out of nappies. The fact that I know I should be a better father but seem incapable of doing anything right only serves to make my resentment towards my situation grow by the day.

How much longer will Alex's incessant wailing rip through what should have been a peaceful afternoon? I shouldn't harbour such unworthy thoughts in the first place. I can only imagine women all over lecturing me about condom use. Too late. Of course why the bloody hell Marlise wasn't on the pill back then I don't know. This isn't the first time that I wonder whether she planned to get knocked up all along. The ties that bind. Our relationship is complicated, and I wouldn't put a little conniving past her, considering what my past self put her through. That's the only way to sum up my dilemma. At least Marlise has been in no danger of getting pregnant again for the past six months. We'd actually have to have sex for that to happen. Everything is kak right now. Or if she did get pregnant, I'd know she was cheating on me. Not that she'd do something so unimaginably awful. Again.

She won't let me forget that I wasn't there to hold her hand during the birth, that I was working. My boss, Sonja, was the one who drove her through to Graaff-Reinet to the hospital while I held the fort for her. I'm still paying off the hospital bill, as and when I can.

What makes it worse is that I'm intelligent enough to realise that I'm projecting my resentment onto the child. He didn't ask for any of this. This not-so-small detail only serves to wind me up a deal more. Vicious circle and all that. Fuck that shit.

I sigh and go shut the gate, then go back inside and pull the front door closed. It might be late winter, verging on early spring, but the evening is stretching the shadows, and the nights are still bloody freezing. And that fucking child... Now I know why women sometimes smother their infants.

"Goddamnit, Alex, what the fuck?" I call out to him as I make my way to the second bedroom that's been designated as a nursery. It's Marlise's bedroom, too, now. We haven't shared a bed since his birth.

My name might have been Elizabeth Rae Perry during my past life, but that doesn't mean a single scrap of mothering instinct got carried over into this one. The child looks so small, his face so screwed up and red from the crying. His nappy is dry. He was fed less than an hour ago—which was when I'd tried to go meditate—what more must I do?

Awkwardly, I pick him up and hold him to my chest. Even now I'm not quite certain where to place my hands.

"Will you just shut the fuck up?" I murmur, but most of my anger has been replaced with weary resignation. I don't know when last any of us have slept through a night. The child seems to take his rest in half-hour snatches. If we're that lucky. Then he starts crying again.

Alex smells faintly of milk but mostly of baby powder, and he stiffens as he draws in another lungful of air so that he can continue howling. I could send him to sleep, make up some sort of charm, but if Marlise finds out I've used my daimonic powers on the child, she'll gut me. Even if it means we get some rest. Surely Hathor or Bast would smile on us? The thought is so tempting, and it would be so ridiculously easy. Yet Marlise would know. Her own powers as initiate mean that she's gradually coming into her own and growing more sensitive to anyone wielding their powers around her.

The child tucked securely in the crook of my arm, I scrub at my eyes with a free hand and wander into the lounge. He's still crying, though not as ferociously as when he was alone in his room.

"Want to hear some music, pumpkin?" I try to keep my voice low while suppressing the slightly manic giggle that wants to escape. Somewhere inside this child may reside the spirit of the previous tenant who owned the body I'm currently inhabiting. I'd like to fool myself into thinking that the real Ashton Kennedy did succeed in his bid to own a body again, that Marlise wasn't just imagining things when she told me she'd seen his image superimposed over her own all those months ago when she was still pregnant. Either way, it'd freak him the hell out if I started calling him "pumpkin", and I snort in amusement as I imagine his distaste at the term.

"Ashton, if you're in there…" I say. "Is this your way of getting back at me?"

Yet another reason for me to pile on the sense of obligation. I'm the reason my body's original tenant was cursed to become an angry ghost. He might've been a right royal bastard while he was alive, but no one deserves the hideous limbo of having no body. In a sense, Ma'at has balanced the injustice, and it's up to me to ensure that Her will is done. Sometimes doing the right thing is a bitch.

The child sucks in another breath, but he doesn't put out a yell with as much gusto as before. Alex is as tired as I am. As Marlise is. I lay him down on the couch next to me, wedged between two cushions so he doesn't accidently roll off. Music calms him. Marlise has been learning to play the guitar, and he tends to shut the hell up when she's plucking at the instrument.

I can't play to save my life, but there's a first time for everything. I can fiddle around with a few chords. Maybe lean on some half-snatched structures embedded in muscle memory. The original Ashton Kennedy used to play in a band. He was a singer and sometimes a barman and small-time gangster. He was also a philandering piece of shit with a drug problem. And he'd left me to pick up his tab when he'd gotten himself run over by his ex-girlfriend's vengeful brother-in-law. Who also happened to be a Russian mob boss.

Nice guy. Now he has a second chance in my kid's body, while I try to make do with the tattooed *Kha* he left behind—the body I stole from him. Not to mention his clingy girlfriend I've kinda fallen for. Whom I knocked up because I was a stupid dolt. I have to look on the bright side. At least I am still here. Marlise is still here. Our enemies haven't found us—yet—and we've had a year of peace in an isolated dorpie. Nieu Bethesda is smack bang in the centre of the Camdeboo, an area that once upon a million years ago used to be the bottom of a shallow sea, if my history lessons serve me correctly. A sedate stroll up the stony bed of the Gat River reveals dozens of fossils embedded in the rock, the river reduced to a trickle during the dry parts of the year—which is most of the time. This is the Karoo, after all. I fucking love this place. Or at least my inner twelve-year-old would if I wasn't changing nappies all the time.

But the people... Everyone knows everyone's business here. It's impossible not to when there are fewer than a thousand people living in this hamlet. And it's the perfect hiding place. My enemies haven't thought to look for me here—as far as I know. Marlise and I are yet another slightly artsy-fartsy couple to join the small group of bohemians trying to scrape together a living from tourism. Folks do a little bit of everything to make money: bottling preserves, working at the local pub or restaurant, doing handyman stuff—which I totally suck at—or helping keep an eye on the numerous holiday homes here.

Not to mention that constant worry that House Montu hasn't given up. What small measure of peace we've carved out for ourselves won't last forever, though there's a small part of me that wishes everything would blow up in our faces so that I can feel like I'm doing something potentially earth-shattering again. At present I'm crippled, barely earning enough money to cover rent. There's no gadding about for tea and scones like Lizzie used to, the old duck. Hell, I don't even know which of the other Houses I can get into contact with to ask for help. Or how to even reach them in the first place.

If things are dire on this material plane, even now my brethren in Per Ankh must be in upheaval. That's if my friend Leonora passed through the Black Gate with her souls intact to face judgment and gain *Akh*-hood. My heart hurts thinking of all my loved ones separated from me by this world of matter.

I must protect what I hold, and this inaction is killing me.

The child's cries have abated somewhat. How he manages to keep at it is beyond me, but thank goodness he's quieter now, though I am not terribly impressed with my paltry abilities on the guitar. My fingers are fumble-numb, and I flub more notes than locate the right chords. If I knew what I was doing wrong, then I could coax a better sound.

But surely others have played this instrument with some proficiency in the past? Echoes of this music must remain. Despite the child's whimpering, I push with my daimonic senses, much as I would search for tendrils of the memories of the Blessed Dead. Sure enough, a faint remembering comes to me from the instrument. I can only describe it as an impulse, a snatch of song.

A woman sits beneath the shade of an enormous pepper tree. Sunlight is trapped in the branches, and she hums quietly to herself. Some folk song or Lou Reed, perhaps.

My knowledge of that genre of music is limited, and I can only guess, but it's enough for my fingers to grow less hesitant as I find the correct shapes for chords, and my right hand curls itself so I can pick out the rhythm.

The words ghost onto my lips, something about a perfect day, but these slip from my consciousness before I can fully express them. I want to sing. Warmth blossoms deep in my stomach. This is good. This is right, and dim recollections of the original Ash's times on stage turn over before sinking beneath the surface again. He enjoyed singing. So should I. But the mere thought of standing on stage, with hundreds of pairs of eyes trained on me, makes me swallow my voice, and my playing falters.

I breathe, open my eyes, and revel in the stillness.

The clock on the mantelpiece ticks off the seconds, and Alex is sleeping, his thumb tucked between his lips. That in itself is magic. The house is so quiet I can hear the laughing doves chuckling in the cypress outside. Marlise will be happy, now that I've found a constructive way to bring peace to our home. I rise carefully, then go fetch one of the baby blankets to tuck around the child. Some of the redness has left his complexion, and he's breathing evenly, his eyes flicking behind his lids. The temperature inside the house will drop as soon as the sun sets, and I don't want him to get cold.

If I pick him up now and take him back to his cot, he might wake and start bawling again. What next? I almost don't know what to do with myself in this sudden stillness.

A knock sounds at the door, and I freeze, fingers digging into the couch's upholstery. Normally I'd hear the aluminium gate click, and that telltale clank is conspicuous in its absence. My chest is tight, and I can't help but draw in tatters of daimonic power.

No one visits us. Ever. Not even our landlady. And if my boss, Sonja, wants anything, she usually sends a text message or calls. But things haven't picked up yet since winter's hibernation, so I can't imagine it would be her needing me to take a shift. We've never received an unexpected visitor. If the neighbours want us, they stand at the gate and call us over. All the small hairs on my nape prickle.

Slowly, I rise and go to the front door. Which is unlocked. Of course it's unlocked. There's almost zero crime in Nieu Bethesda. And me and my fancy daimonic powers are more than a match for anything the local miscreants can throw at me. Then again, who'd want to mess with a heavily tattooed male who's well over six feet tall?

I pause at the door but can sense no one save for a heaviness in the atmosphere, as though a presence were deliberately trying to focus my attention elsewhere. An Inkarna trick. One I've used many times before when I don't want to be noticed.

My powers tightly coiled and ready to strike, I pull open the door, my right hand balled into a fist, ready to punch with all my strength.

"Good evening." The man is slight and removes a bowler hat to reveal sandy hair that's cropped short. His skin is milky, his eyes ever so slightly red-rimmed. His charcoal-grey suit, with a fine pin stripe, has most certainly been tailored. The white carnation in his lapel makes him seem as if he's just arrived from a wedding.

"Who the fuck are you?" This is it. They've found us. But I don't detect any animosity from him, so I drop my fist, even if I don't let down my guard.

"May I come in?" He clips his words. British, then. Very, very British.

"Not until you identify yourself." I cross my arms over my chest and glare down at him, well aware that I must be intimidating as fuck. He can't be taller than about five feet and four inches. No muscle tone, and almost effeminate in his delicacy. All it'd take is one shove, and I could have him back on his arse. Damn Marlise for choosing this exact time to hie off. We need to pack and get the fuck out of here.

This man is Inkarna. Of this I have no doubt. It's a matter of which House has found its way to my doorstep that is the crux of the matter.

He offers his hand. The nails are well manicured, and the skin looks soft, like he hasn't done a day's hard labour. I glance at those fingers then make eye contact again, and he withdraws his hand.

"I'm Samuel Forrester, a representative of...House Alba." He says the last two words like he doesn't want anyone else to hear them.

A faint ringing starts in my ears, and my knees want to sag. House Alba. They're the House that started this whole mess by helping found my now-defunct House Adamastor. Or at least that's the case if Richard could have been believed. If House Alba can find me, and even know who they're looking for, that means...

"Look, it's not particularly safe," Samuel says, as though reading my mind. "Could we cut to the chase and continue this conversation indoors? I've driven the whole day to get here and would appreciate a cup of tea. That's presuming you offer real tea in this little village."

I shake my head, as though I could dislodge my misgivings, and against my better judgment allow the man to enter. "We can talk in the kitchen," I tell him. I keep my power at the ready. What if he's lying? I'm letting a total stranger into my fucking house. Of course, he's already found me. What difference does it make? I'll play along, for now. Remain vigilant. Until Marlise arrives, and we'll get him to leave. We'll be gone. Tonight still. We'll figure out where to go once we're on the road.

"Are you alone?" I ask him. Better to let the man think I'm totally calm, collected. That I'm guileless.

"Yes." He watches me with a pale gaze. Those eyes, like he's seen a million ghosts and he's not telling. I go through the familiar motions of filling the kettle with water from the filter.

"What tea do you want?" I ask. "We've only got Earl Grey or rooibos."

"Earl Grey is fine." He sniffs and brushes an invisible piece of lint from his jacket sleeve. His posture is stiff, and he stands as though he's mortally afraid of making contact with the wall or the counter. Samuel's supposed to be the good guy. I shouldn't antagonise him. That's if he's from House Alba. I wouldn't put it past House Montu to lie their way into my home. I have no way of telling, thanks to me being out of general circulation for so long.

"How come the cavalry arrived after the show was over?" I lean against the fridge and keep my arms crossed. "How do I even know you're not some fucktard from House Montu?"

Samuel bares his teeth at me. If he means this to be a grin, he fails hopelessly. "You'd be dead by now."

"House Montu can't afford to have me dead. At least not yet." I regret the words almost as soon as I've said them.

"We know about *The Book of Ammit the Devourer*. You don't have to pretend we're ignorant."

I snort. "So does House Montu. And none of you're going to find it. Killing me isn't going to work either. Why should I believe you're not one of their agents?"

Samuel tips his head, his smile faint. "I told them we should just bring you in. But no, they preferred to negotiate. Don't want to spook you. I'll be frank. A week ago, we intercepted a communiqué. House Montu giving instruction to their chapter house in Joburg to pick you up. An informant located you. We don't have much time. They're moving against you as we speak."

That damned helicopter from yesterday. Worry stabs at my heart.

"Now, you can be compliant, or I can 'encourage'—" He air quotes with his fingers. "—you. But either way, you'll come along to Lanseria Airport where there is a private plane waiting to whisk you and your loved ones to London."

I can't help but laugh. This is ridiculous. "What, you expect me to just drop everything and obey you? A total stranger? Don't talk kak."

He sighs, and only then does he allow himself to sit on the barstool next to the stove. "We lost contact with House Adamastor after Siptah gained control. The chapter house used to be in Rondebosch. He didn't tell us where he moved it late during the late eighteen-hundreds. He was young, brash, and had just taken over from Sethotep."

Unbidden, my hand strays to the silver scarab pectoral hidden beneath my T-shirt. Old memories return. Of Richard's excitement when he brought me to the chapter house in Simon's Town. All those boxes of books we were just unpacking. Suspicion blooms, and I feel my brow furrow.

"Why would he move without notifying you?"

"Sethotep was a traditionalist. Thothmose, too. They looked to House Alba for guidance. Siptah's the one who brought the book to the Cape Colony all those years ago, before he had his second chance here in Africa. Just when the British were angling to oust the Dutch and take control of the colony. Siptah was fresh to his powers. Thothmose had no idea what his companion brought with him. It was supposed to be a secret. House Alba wanted to establish a scion, a new House at the tip of the Dark Continent. There was friction between Siptah and the new initiate, Sethotep. You know how it is."

My mouth had gone dry, and I recall my own betrayal, by the one I'd dared to name as sister. All this makes sense. The moment Siptah—Richard—sensed he could act independently, he'd uprooted. Siptah's name engraved twice on the pectoral, sandwiching

Thothmose's and Sethotep's *Ren*s.

"This doesn't make sense," I say. "Per Ankh... All the others..."

"How much do you remember of Per Ankh?" he asks. "Did they ever mention House alliances and history? Alba or Adamastor?"—his smile is tight when he notes what can only be my expression of bewilderment—"Oh, wait. This is your first incarnation. You're no doubt highly affected by your present *Kha*'s *Ba* and the manner in which you *took* it." He can't quite hide his moue of distaste.

How much of the old Ashton Kennedy am I? Dreamlike images of the Per Ankh taunt me. Meritiset playing along. No one truly connecting with me, the newest, the latest. How keen *she'd* been for me to go back. Particularly. How she'd manipulated to keep me isolated, no doubt. Ignorant. How the older Inkarna did their best to ignore me. Speak over me. And the more I try to snatch at the memories, the less real they seem. All that time between incarnations is dreamlike, a blur. Sometimes the memories are sharp, and I can remember the many-petalled lotuses in my favourite reflecting pool. Other times I can only vaguely recall opalescent pillars in one of the hypostyle halls.

"What are you saying? That the part of Per Ankh I attained is still beholden to House Alba? That the part of Per Ankh where I resided is House Alba's?" And not Adamastor? No one said anything. Not that I can recall. I took it for granted that I was among House Adamastor. I never thought to question. That's the problem. I never questioned.

"You never do remember much the first few times. The *Kha*—the meat, blood and bones—cannot retain the totality of the experience. The *Akh* is an ephemeral thing, water poured into a container that shapes it.

Why do you think so few of us return?" He seems smug, as if he's reciting verses.

"But they said..." I'm not quite sure what they said. The elder Inkarna disapproved of my appearance... Siptah gone. They sent me back because I was the only one who knew where the chapter house was and had a better grip on the culture of the era. They weren't prepared to wait and see whether Leonora—no, I must think of her by her *Ren*, Ankhakhet—would make it across. And Meritiset decided to sneak through on my ticket, so to speak.

"Renegade House. Adamastor wasn't supposed to vanish like that."

"But it doesn't explain why..."

Meritiset and Siptah, lovers... What if she suggested he move the chapter house? Planted seeds of doubt? She just didn't expect he'd take a wife while he was here. Me. I press my hands against my face. I don't know enough, and this man in my space knows far too much. More so than House Montu.

I breathe deeply and glare at him, going out on a figurative limb because I want to needle him and I have the balls to take a chance. "You haven't crossed over yet, have you? You've never been past the Black Gate."

Samuel's *Kha* has maybe ten years on mine; I estimate him to be in his early thirties. His expression remains deadpan in the face of my accusation.

"Herunefer has returned several times. He is a good teacher, and he has looked after his present *Kha*. He hasn't needed to pass through the Black Gate for a long time, though his current allotment of years far exceeds three score and ten." The man's name means nothing to me. No one mentioned him in my presence during my time in Per Ankh. Or while I was still Lizzie. "We have many new initiates. And many more Inkarna have come into being. House Alba is strong in the United Kingdom. And growing stronger still. It makes sense for you to join us. Especially in times such as this, and with the burden you carry."

But there's a reason why Richard wanted the stele out of their reach. I can't forget that. Can't be taken in by Samuel's honeyed words, no matter how attractive they sound.

"I need something with a bit more kick," I say, then turn to let the kettle boil again. I hadn't even registered when it stopped boiling. I pour myself a whiskey. Samuel's manipulating me, but I cannot argue with him. I want him to be speaking the truth. Just over a year of living in exile has left me strung out and tired. It's not easy to admit it, but I want someone else to be in control. Tell me what to do for a change instead of me making one ill-considered decision after the other. I'm adrift. And all too willing to clutch at lifelines.

I pour the water and let the man help himself to milk and sugar. The snotty bastard had better not be expecting me to get out a tea service. We don't even own one. I snort then sip my drink. The whiskey burns on its way down.

So long as *The Book of Ammit* remains hidden, I can go anywhere. That's the thing. Only I know where it is. Only I can retrieve it. Which means I can play along with Samuel's game awhile and like a bird feigning a broken wing, lead him from Nieu Bethesda and the stone tablet no one must see. Things will be easier. For me. For Marlise.

"I'll come with you," I say. "Without the book. And only if Marlise agrees. I can't leave her behind, and I'm not going to force her to do anything against her will." A compromise.

She still hopes to see her family again, but it's too late for me to feel any real guilt about how our lives have progressed. She had opportunities to stay the hell away from me. Countless opportunities. Yet she chose to tie herself to me with blood. I won't feel guilty, but at the very least I will do my best to keep her safe and give her and our son a future. Even if it's fraught with danger. The old Ashton would've forced her to have an abortion. I'm not that man. I also won't leave her vulnerable to the not-so-tender mercies of House Montu, who won't hesitate in using her to get to me. I selfishly started her on this path before she fully understood what she was getting herself into; it's only right that I equip her with the skills and the knowledge to survive in this eternal game.

Samuel lifts his mug and glares at it briefly before he takes a tentative sip. Fucking tosser. I swallow a snigger and imagine Lizzie in his place, how she would react to my behaviour now. For a moment the disjunction strikes me, and I can almost see her. She would most likely put on a saccharine voice and say something along the lines of "That's nice, dear," and pat me on my wrist. She could also be a bitch if she wanted to. *Here, have a biscuit, luv.* I've become more like the old Ash than I'd care to admit. Callous bastard.

"It's not safe leaving the stele behind," Samuel says.

I smirk at him. "Admit it. You tried to find the fucking thing first before you came to me, didn't you?"

He frowns and gives an almost imperceptible shake of his head, but I suspect my assumption is correct. He might be Inkarna, but his *Ka* and *Ba* still need to meld to form his *Akh*, and this only happens after he has passed through the Hall of Judgment. In this I have an edge over him, since I've paid my dues in Per Ankh. I am stronger than most, though I am relatively inexperienced. As for the rest, unless they know exactly where to begin their treasure hunt, they could spend the next twenty years scouring the Karoo without any luck. Nothing like living with the spectre of desperation to strengthen a ward.

"You think you're awfully clever, don't you?" he asks.

I shrug. "Attitude's about all I got left to me." That, and the knowledge to destroy his souls. For all eternity. I don't need to say that. I have something everyone wants, and while I'm at a disadvantage, I don't need to parade this fact about in public.

Samuel narrows his eyes at me, but apart from a faint huff of breath, doesn't say anything for a few moments. He takes his cellphone out of his pocket and makes a show of examining the screen—a bid to hide his discomfort. Good luck to him. There's almost sweet bugger-all cellphone reception here.

"So, dude, how do I know you're not secretly from House Montu? I mean, if force has failed, why would playing the nice guy succeed instead?" There. The question I should've asked all along.

"Do you honestly think House Montu would stand for subterfuge? That's not their style, and you know it."

"I shouldn't put it past them to try a different tack other than bludgeoning their way in."

"Does the fact that I've not drugged you or held you up at the business end of a weapon not mean anything to you?"

I shake my head.

He sighs deeply. "You have a valid point. I suppose there's nothing for it but for us to share more than a handshake. If you'd shaken my hand earlier, you would've known my words for truth. Here." He holds out his hand.

What could possibly go wrong? I stare stupidly at his fingers for a few heartbeats then gingerly accept the gesture.

Our daimonic essences flash against each other with the equivalent of a cosmic exchange of business cards. His bland exterior obscures a lively mind, and the daimonic taste of him, for lack of better description, isn't the fiery force of Montu. The signature is familiar, a shadow of Richard's. House Alba. A white lion, rampant, to my storm clouds.

A signature I've encountered before, many, many years ago when my name was Lizzie.

I withdraw my hand, unconsciously wipe my hands on my shirt. "Oh." Now who looks the fool?

Samuel's snort of amusement is subtle. "Do you trust me enough to come with me?"

"I don't trust you, but I'll come with you. The book you want stays where I've hidden it."

"That is unwise."

"So's taking it with me. There's a reason why Siptah hid it so well in the first place. I don't see any reason why I shouldn't continue the trend. No one but I knows where it is."

"Very well," he says after a pause.

I glance out the window, and a small shudder of concern brings me up short. The sun's gone behind the mountain, and the sky has turned the colour of doves' feathers. What time did Marlise leave? Shortly after three, by my reckoning, and then I messed around on the guitar for how long...and it's now... Half past five. And I've done all this jaw-flapping with Samuel. I do the maths because I know she doesn't like driving up Rubidge pass after dark, and she loathes shopping for groceries on her own that late anyway—it was her desperation to escape our home that drove her out in the first place.

She should be here already.

"'Scuse me a moment," I murmur, then step into the lounge where Alex is still sleeping and where our reception for some bizarre reason is better than in the kitchen, so I can call Marlise. Well, thanks be to the gods the little chap's still down. His continual howling up until today must've taken a lot out of him.

Marlise's phone goes straight through to voice mail. Perhaps she's at the part of the route where cellphone reception isn't that hot. But I can't shake the sense that something's gone wrong. Her phone is always on.

Samuel raises his brows when I return to the kitchen. "She's not picking up?"

I shake my head. "I'm worried. We...we had a bit of a disagreement the past few days. The child's... We've been having difficulties adjusting. You know how it is."

The man's expression suggests he doesn't, but his features soften. The heartless bastard possesses a measure of empathy, then. "I'd like to tell you not to worry, but your wife didn't exactly choose an opportune moment to storm off in a huff."

"She's not my— Never mind." So, the bastard was watching us for a while, then. I bristle at this but refrain from saying anything on the matter. The thought that he's been privy to our domestic non-bliss rankles.

His expression darkens.

"Damn." Maybe the douche can make himself useful. I eye him. "You've got a car, right? Knowing you, something larney."

"We need to leave here for Joburg, Ashton. *Now*. We don't have time to still concern ourselves with your missing girlfriend. House Montu is closing in on us. We can set up a team to keep an eye out, but if anything's happened to her now, there's nothing we can do. We need to leave. Tonight still."

"What the fuck? You expect me to just pick up and leave with you? Abandon everyone here? Are you mad? And what about the kid?"

He gives me a meaningful look that suggests it's better I don't argue with him. Like he's already in charge, the cunt.

My chest tightens, and I ball my hands into fists. Bastard. "She's an initiate, you daft fuck. We don't leave without her. She's my House. After all I've gone through, you don't get to dictate anything." My daimonic energy uncoils, fills the room, and a buzzing starts in my ears.

To give Samuel some credit, he puts down his mug of tea and steps back. But I can feel him dragging at the edges of my awareness with his own powers. Smooth. Perhaps not as raw as mine, but still deadly. I am a kraken to his shark, though.

"We don't need to do this." The man swallows. He's aware of how outmatched he is.

He might have backup. That keeps me from letting loose. I don't need more enemies right now. And this is a stupid way to engage in a daimonic dick-measuring contest, especially with a potential ally.

"If I'm so fucking valuable to your cause, then we do things my way, or not at all." My voice has a hollow, dangerous echo to it.

"There's not much time. I don't know where the House Montu operatives are. Nor how long before they strike."

"I'm willing to take that chance. I'm not leaving her at their mercy." I did that once before, and I still hate that sense of helplessness, of being put in a spot by enemies who are one step ahead of me. "Do you have allies in the area?"

He shakes his head. "To give you a measure of how delicate this situation is, there have been a few incidents this past week. Nothing that can be pinned on House Montu specifically, but your current location is known. We're just lucky I was the first to reach you. The rest of my team...not so lucky."

His voice has become raw, and with my senses outstretched, it's easy to pick up on the ragged contours of his exhaustion. He hides it well, but he's on edge, and it's beginning to set off my deep-rooted paranoia.

"Fine then," I mutter. "I need a few minutes to get the kid sorted. Can you give me that much?"

He nods. "I'll wait for you in the car."

Even as I stuff a bag with Alex's things, I call Sonja, my sometime boss over at the pub.

Thank the Neteru Sonja answers on the third ring. "What's wrong?" Not "hello". What's wrong? Damn witch.

"I need you to watch Alex. Just for this evening. Marlise has run into a spot of trouble with the car, and I need to go help her out." I'm amazed I can string words together in a coherent sentence. The lie is silk on my tongue.

"You should have that car seen to. It's a liability. Need Szandor to give you a ride?"

"I'm good. I've... I've got a friend here. So I can bring the sprog round?"

"Sure." She doesn't sound like she believes me, but jawellnofine, she didn't say no either.

Predictably, Alex begins crying the moment I lift him to place him in his carrycot. Samuel's car is a big silver Mercedes-Benz GL-Class like what the tourists from upcountry drive. It is completely out of place standing across the way from the community art centre's zebra-striped façade.

"You're going to Auntie Sons's place now, pumpkin," I say to the child.

Alex sucks in a deep breath so he can push out another shuddering wail. I should check his nappy but reckon I'll pretend it's all fine and leave it up to Sonja. I'll owe the woman bigtime for dumping the kid on her like this, but it's only long enough for us to retrieve Marlise. I don't want to go look for her and end up in a conflict situation with a kid vulnerable in a car. Dirty nappies are the least of our worries right now if House Montu is breathing down our necks. Now's not the time to reflect on the fact that most heroes don't have babies in tow when they embark on their adventures.

I grab my leather jacket and a scarf before I lock the front door, the screaming child in his carrycot, properly insulated against the chill wind that slices my exposed skin with its ice.

The interior of the SUV is toasty. Samuel has had the presence of mind to run the engine so the heater can kick in, and I give him terse instructions to drive up Hudson Road, over the bridge to Pienaar Street where Sonja has her place near the brewery. We don't have much in the way of conversation, thanks to Alex. The queen of the night cacti form a thick barrier in front of Sonja's small cottage, and the woman is already waiting for me at the door. Her shock of white-blond hair creates a halo against the warm interior of her home.

She takes the child without argument. "Something's terribly wrong, Ash. I'm worried. After you called…"

"I know," I tell her. We've been living an uneasy truce for the past year. Sonja's family is a close-knit clan of hereditary witches. They need to stay under the radar as much as I do, and here I am, bringing all unholy hell down on their heads.

Her features are pinched, whether from the cold or fear, I don't know. I don't have time to worry about her.

"Just look after the child. I'll be back in a few hours."

"Be careful." Her concern is genuine, and if we weren't under pressure to find out whether Marlise is in trouble, I'd hug her.

"Thank you. Don't allow anyone into the house."

I spare a last glance at the boy, who's stopped crying now that Sonja has his cot in a death grip. Before I mumble inanities, I sprint to the waiting car. I don't look back. The witches will look after him better than most. I hate having to do this, but I don't have any other options right now.

Samuel raises a brow as I slam shut the door.

"Just drive," I tell him.

"I thought the last witch cults were put down a hundred years ago."

"One word of this beyond this car, and I will personally hunt you down if any ills befall that woman and her family."

My glare, underpinned with the crackling of my daimonic powers, must be enough of a threat for him to put down his foot. By the time we cross the small dip, he turns on the CD player. Ugh. Mozart. I despise Mozart. I don't know what sonata it is, but I'd recognise that particular trite style anywhere. I stab the power button so all we hear is gravel spattering against the undercarriage.

"How're you going to find your woman?" Samuel sounds resigned.

"We're going to see whether she's parked outside the store and try phoning from there if she isn't." Okay, I have no idea how to go about this, but I have to do something. If needs be, I might even attempt to locate her through the aethers; the Neteru know we share enough of a connection. I've just never needed to lean on it so hard, and considering our current communication breakdown, she might even be shutting me out. Which won't help one bit right now, when I need to reach her as a matter of utmost importance. While we tear up the pass, I keep an eye out for the familiar green Fiat. I'd sooner see her car broken down at the side of the road than have her just up and vanish. Taken.

What if she's decided to return to Cape Town?

Not bloody likely. As much as she has bitched about Alex's crying during the past few weeks, she's fussed over him, taken him through to the doctor a number of times though we can't really afford the bills. The way she dotes over the little one suggests she won't be separated from him for longer than a few hours. It's more concerning that she's not returned yet. Even if she's constantly harping on about contacting her parents, she understands how dangerous that will be.

We have one scary moment when three kudus ghost across the road, almost as grey as the evening and the dust on the road. One, a bull, has impressive spiral horns and turns to watch us. I lose myself for an instant in the impossible blackness of his liquid eyes. To give my companion some credit, he doesn't even flinch, but swerves, and keeps us going. The antelope vanishes into the gloom.

No more suicidal wildlife crosses our path, and soon enough we hit the tar of the N9, and Samuel can take the vehicle up to a hundred and eighty kilometres an hour. He won't go over a hundred and ninety.

"You'll see. Everything will work out once we get to the UK," he tells me.

"That's if we get there," I grouse.

"We've got a chapter house in Oxford. We can see about getting you some qualifications and then set up a nice research position for you. Schooling for your child will be paid for. We'll assist in visas and all the necessary paperwork so that you and your partner can stay."

"So you can keep an eye on me and make sure no one else gets their nasty little mitts on the book."

"Despite what you think, you are a valued member of the House."

"Which House is that? Adamastor or Alba? Sounds like you're poaching."

"Look, just be gracious and accept assistance when it's offered. I believe we are both in agreement that we have a common cause."

I can't argue that and allow our journey to lapse into an uncomfortable silence. All the better to worry about Marlise and mull over the swift horror show my life's turned into after the few months' respite we had. The bastard's offer sounds so damned attractive, and I'm caving fast. No more running, no more looking over my shoulder. No more worrying about medical expenses or having enough food to eat at the end of the month. We sat without electricity for a week last month because we simply didn't have the cash for credits. I do not want to go through that again.

He wants that fucking book. I don't want to give it to him. He doesn't mention it, but it's implied. Samuel's doing his level best to assure me of the security he's offering. Yet there's a very good reason why the book was brought to the southernmost tip of Africa in the first place.

Marlise needs to have a say in this, too. It must be her decision as well as mine, though I'm pretty certain what she'll want for us. Every few kilometres, I try calling Marlise's cellphone, and each time the call goes through to voicemail.

"Sorry, I am not available to take your call right now. Please leave a message, and I'll get back to you at my earliest convenience." Marlise sounds so goddamned cheerful. Almost like one of those teleconsultants I hate talking to when they occasionally get a hold of my number.

I don't leave a message, although some small part of me feels the impulse to apologise for being a complete jerk not only this afternoon, but the past few months, and to explain that I've made a mental turnaround.

Nothing much happens in Graaff-Reinet on a Wednesday evening. The Spar is open until eight, and the last few shoppers come and go, but most of the parking spaces are empty. We stop at the side of the small shopping complex, outside a church built in the angular style so popular during the 1960s. The jacarandas' naked limbs shiver above us, and the wind will no doubt be frigid the moment I step out the vehicle.

"So?" Samuel asks, unclipping his seat belt. To give the guy credit, it looks like he's going to help. Which is something, I guess.

"Gonna go out and take a look," I say, although the darkness is uninviting. I try to call her one last time, but of course her fucking phone goes through to voicemail, further sealing my guilt. She wouldn't leave without the child. Something's horribly, horribly wrong. Deep breaths, Ash. Don't panic.

"We're wasting our time," Samuel says. "Unless she's dumped the baby on you and run off, which I suspect is more likely, she's probably been taken."

My anger is sudden and violent. "Shut the fuck up! You don't know jack shit about our situation." Yeah,

yeah, I know. I'm not exactly up for supportive partner of the year award, but Alex and Marlise are still my responsibility. Though I won't admit it to this smug bastard, House Montu snatching Marlise from right beneath my nose is a massive dent in my pride, too.

He blanches. My fist is right beneath his nose, and I withdraw it, shaking. The ringing in my ears is heavy, persistent. My daimonic powers tighten my skin, make me feel like I'm about to boil over. Way to go, losing my temper with the one person here who's standing by me.

"Look for a late-model Fiat Uno. Quite rusted but dark green. There's a small wirework chameleon hanging from the rearview mirror. What's your cellphone number?"

"Are you suggesting we split up?" Samuel glares at me.

"We'll cover more ground. What, are you afraid or something?" My heart is hammering like I've just taken a hit of amphetamines.

"That's got to be the most stupid suggestion I've ever heard. You've got Montu on your tail, and we simply don't know if they're not setting us up with Marlise as bait."

"I need to find her, damn it! It's not like her to just not respond to calls and stay away from her kid this long." My paranoia is in full bloom, making me feel as if my skin can't contain all of me. I should never have let her go on her own.

He opens his door, and winter sucks all the warmth from the interior. "Well, let's go. We stick together. But I tell you, we're wasting our time."

"Why are you so sure? You know something I don't?" Alex is all alone with the Wareings. How safe is he? I've trusted that family for just over a year, but now

I'm dragging them down with me.

He inclines his head. "C'mon."

Just as I feared, my jacket does little to keep me warm. The onrush of air whips loose tendrils of my hair from the elastic and stings my face and sears down my lungs. Next to me, Samuel is business-like, dapper in the charcoal fitted long-coat he shrugged into when we left Nieu Bethesda. Sensible. My jacket doesn't even have a working zip. Still.

We make an incongruous pair as we stalk down the street, and get a strange glance from an old, wizened man hurrying in the opposite direction. Cars rush past, their occupants no doubt intent on warm dinners and the opiates provided by televised entertainment.

We don't search for long. The green Fiat is parked close to the entrance, and a shock of recognition slams into me. What, did I want things to be more difficult? Obviously Marlise would have parked as close to the entrance as possible. Weather's crappy. She meant to get in and out so she could get back home fast.

"This it?" Samuel asks.

I nod, stricken, my mouth dry and knees weak. There, glinting by the driver's side, lies her cellphone—crushed. The car's door hasn't been closed properly. Inside, scattered on the floor on the passenger side are the contents of her handbag. Such is the nature of a small town that no one's thought to steal anything. Yet. Marlise would never in a million years go anywhere without her handbag.

I glare at him. "You knew, didn't you? All this while you had your people go pick her up so there'd be a hostage."

"Are you quite mad? Why would I go through such an elaborate scheme when I've barely got the time to meet with you?"

I grab him by his lapels, shove him up against the car, and lash out with my daimonic senses. His own power frays against the onslaught. Our common bond through our Houses is present, and I can sense no subterfuge. He's not lying.

Angry and helpless, I shove him away from me and stride several paces along the sidewalk until I turn to face him. "What now?"

Dazedly, he straightens his clothing, his complexion ashen. "We need to go." He says this quietly, firmly, even though he's visibly shaken by my show of strength.

I curl my fingers into fists. "No."

"They're probably long gone by now, or on their way to your house. It's not safe. They most likely already know everything you don't want them to."

I'd like nothing more than to throw him to the ground this time, but I hold myself in. That's the sort of behaviour in which the old Ashton would delight. I'm more than that. I can't alienate the only possible ally I've found since Leonora transitioned.

"Fuck!" I turn and stride from the abandoned Fiat. I can't drive, at least not well. I need to do something, but what? Dimly, I'm aware that Samuel follows, but his shorter legs mean he can't quite keep up as we make our way back to where he's parked around the corner. My helplessness simmers just beneath the surface, feeding the embers of my anger. I draw hard on the daimonic powers around me. I need to lash out at something, anything. The streetlights flicker. Then the world goes bright, and a roar of flames engulfs me.

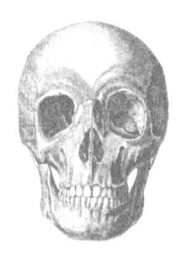

CHAPTER TWO
Burning Man

FOR A MOMENT, as I stagger under the force of the light and heat, I fear I'm on fire, but there's no pain. Then the stench of burning meat hits me, and even as I blink back the brightness to register the smoking corpse that once was Samuel, a wave of daimonic energy smashes me halfway into the road so I come face to face with twisted, blackened bones and smouldering tatters of fabric billowing thick smoke. My stomach convulses at the sight.

I lie sprawled, my head throbbing thanks to its catastrophic connection with the tarmac, trying to overcome the pain and regain my breath. My limbs don't obey my screaming need to get up, turn, and fight. The streetlights dim—a sure sign one of my own is drawing power. With a groan, I manage to roll onto my knees, only to suffer a blow to my left side. Whether this is unleashed daimonic power or someone kicking me, I don't know. All I can do is retch and gasp for breath.

Stupid. Should have listened to Samuel.

And abandon your child and your woman? Chickenshit.

"Don't let him get up!" a man shouts.

Weak, I tilt my head to see a figure approach, silhouetted against the flickering streetlight.

"Watch out!" another man cries. "There's—" A thud follows, like a sack of potatoes falling, then a grunt.

I succeed in drawing a wheezy lungful of air, then release my own attack at the man who's paused near me. He flies from my field of vision, limbs flailing, to thud against the trunk of the jacaranda near the church's gate. Then I lurch to my feet in time to see a woman release a man from her embrace. He drops in a bundle of stiff, stick-like limbs too thin for the clothing he wears. Like all the mass has been leached from his body.

His mouth gapes open, jaw loose yet skin drawn like parchment—too tight on his bones. Eyes stare into eternity. Like a mummy.

The woman is poised to strike, her black hair crackling with daimonic energy barely held in check. Faint sparkles of blue-green motes dance at her fingers, the bones glowing beneath the thin covering of flesh. No Inkarna should have the power to draw life from another...unless... Oh, gods.

"Thanatos!" I hiss. Death-walkers. Lords of the Living Dead. I'd hoped to never encounter these accursed among the Inkarna. So far, they'd only ever existed in rumour, but where there's a rumour and tales of horror, there's usually a measure of truth.

She flinches, then straightens. "What of it?"

A car slows as it rounds the corner. The man rolls

43

down his window and leans out. "Hey! Hey! What's going on here?"

I glance wildly between the driver and the Thanatos woman, then pull a one-eighty and run. At this point I don't care where I go, so long as I can put enough distance between myself, the woman, and the scene of gruesome death. The police detectives of this otherwise sleepy Karoo town are going to think it's Halloween.

What can I do? I pelt down the shadowed streets, my lungs searing with each gasping breath. I must run. And run I do, until I stumble over railway tracks and into an acacia thicket. Here, safe from prying eyes, I lean over, gasping and trying not to upchuck the contents of my stomach. The wail of distant sirens starts up. So much for me and mine staying under the radar. Forget the pigs. What in the hell will the news reports make of a mummified corpse, a crispy-fried skeleton, and a man who's no doubt been pulverised against a tree trunk? Way to go.

That's if my mysterious saviour doesn't chase after me to finish the job. Evidently, she was keeping me for last because of the juicy intel she could extract. House Montu on its own is bad enough. House Thanatos added to this almighty clusterfuck my life is rapidly turning into doesn't make me any happier. I had it so easy when Ashton's angry ghost was with me and I could use him to do my recon. I feel his absence keenly now. A smart-mouthed early warning system back then was better than none at all now.

Oh, the chaos I've left behind. My lungs are on fire, and my skin alternates between hot and clammy as I try to recover from the ordeal. Have I managed to escape the Thanatos woman? The police are easy enough to avoid. A little bit of good old-fashioned Inkarna subterfuge should work wonders. The pigs are none too bright at the best of times.

I snigger at a half-remembered line from one of Marlise's favourite movies and apply it to my situation. This is not the Inkarna you are looking for... The looks of puzzlement on cops' faces as their gazes slide past me. Oh, I can so do that.

My choked laughter turns into a sob, my chest tight. Marlise. Where the fuck are you? I'm too on edge to push outwards with my senses. I'm too vulnerable and emotionally scattered. What if the death bitch finds me while I'm doing a bit of extrasensory recon? No. Not good.

But House Montu is now sans one pyro—what a waste. Fire starters are rare enough as it is. The other luckless bastard got what he deserved for cooking Samuel. This carefully baited trap hasn't worked out quite the way they wanted it to. Now the question remains, how the hell did House Thanatos get involved in the mix in the first place? Their reasons for hunting me down aren't that difficult to surmise. After all, the power to destroy the eternal *Akh* and its *Ib*, the heart, is precious indeed—to erase an individual's existence as if it never came into being in the first place. The world is bad enough with their kind in it; pity the rest of us if they ever lay hands on the information.

Perhaps the dumbest idea I can have is to kill myself. A simple solution to remove the knowledge of the book from this world, but I'm not *that* pragmatic. At least until I am sent back here, which is doubtful, considering my track record. But I'm not that desperate or stupid. Besides, suicide will weigh down my *Akh*.

My training hasn't told me anything about what my souls' fate would be should I seek to end my own life. Suicide goes against everything I've been taught. One's *Kha* is a living temple, to be nurtured, grown, and guarded against the storms of time. There was a reason why tomb-robbing was frowned on in ancient Egypt. Granted, during contemporary times we don't get buried with as much pomp and ceremony, but it's still a pretty big deal when an Inkarna kicks the bucket. Especially considering how many of us meet with untimely, brutal ends. Or at least the Inkarna I've run into have.

Samuel. Stuck-up bastard that he was...his loss hits me afresh. I didn't know him long enough to mourn his transition; he was just my free pass to something better, and it's because of my insistence that we've sprung the House Montu trap. He warned me. Repeatedly. I shake my head. Things are moving too fast. Too late.

When, not if, I meet Samuel again, I'll see what his full story is. All I know is that he wanted me to go to the UK, that a certain Herunefer is building up forces I could possibly consider allies. A cushy pad in Oxford. Of course, me getting to that side of the world now when I don't even have a valid ID, let alone a passport, and have one of the most warlike of the Houses after me... I stand a better chance of getting to the British Isles if I start walking across the African continent. I'd sooner take my chances with the intervening Muslim extremists, child soldiers, corrupt officials, and warlords than face House Montu's ire.

And then there's Marlise.

I need to save her. I can't let them drag her into the depths of the House Montu hornet's nest. But how will I find her? First, I need to get back to Nieu Bethesda. Sonja needs to know. She can still help, maybe look after the kid while I'm gone. Worse comes to worst, I can give her Marlise's parents' phone number, and she can arrange to send the kid to them, where he'll be safe. I hope. Desperate thoughts, and I'm clutching at metaphorical straws here, but I don't know what else to do.

I can't huddle here in a thorn ticket and wait for better days.

"You're not making this easy." The woman's breath is warm on my neck.

I yelp and turn, ready to unleash whatever power remains in me, but a cold hand is pressed to my chest, and my body freezes. I'm unable to move. Don't panic. If she'd wanted me dead, I would've have known that by now.

She's short—about five feet four, her face oval, eyes expressive and throwing back the gleam of nearby orange streetlights. Glossy black hair falls in waves past her shoulders.

"I know you have absolutely no reason to trust me, but give me a moment." The Thanatos woman speaks with a soft British accent, a familiar way that she pitches her vowels, almost breathy. Achingly familiar, yet I can't place her manner.

I can't respond. Her eyes hold me, contain darkness itself, to which I'm irresistibly drawn. Snake eyes. Cold.

"I'm going to relinquish some of the hold, and you're going to promise me you'll be calm and take my hand. Understood? I won't hurt you." She sounds so damned reasonable.

Some of the warmth returns to my body, but my heart feels as if it's about to explode. I'm able to nod.

"All right?" she asks.

It's not all right, I want to say. "Yesss."

I manage to stand when she lifts her hand from my chest. Sensation returns to my extremities, and I take a step back, my spine pressed against the wall.

"Who are you?"

"Bethan McLachlan. House Thanatos, as you already know. But..." Her smile is filled with mischief. "Just take my hand, you dolt."

She could turn me into a dried husk of a mummy in an instant. She's had every opportunity to do so, so far. Bethan could have knocked down my mental shields. She didn't. Besides, she saved my arse minutes ago.

Glaring at her, wary like someone expecting a scorpion's sting, I tentatively extend my hand.

The skin of her palm is smooth and cool, and our daimonic essences rise to meet each other with joy, familiarity. The *Kha* may be unfamiliar, but I'll know the particular signature of that *Akh* anywhere. A wash of joy, recognition, instantly erases the shroud of fear.

"Siptah?" I whisper, my eyes unaccountably blurry.

"I've found you!" she says, even as I drag her into a fierce embrace and crush her to me. Her hair smells of vanilla, and I breathe in the scent and try to trap it forever.

All the intervening years crumble between us: I hold my other half, my great love made flesh once more. After a while we separate, but I grip her shoulders, and she has her hands placed on my hips. It's an intimate contact; it feels right despite our changed circumstances.

"The book..." She wets her lips.

A shadow falls over my heart. "It's safe. You don't... need to know where it is."

Bethan nods. "It's for the best." Then she laughs. "Of all the *Kha*s you could have chosen! This is so not like you."

She reaches out to cup my cheek, and I place a hand over hers, unable to hide my grin.

"I didn't have a choice, and I could say the same

about you."

Her smile is balm to all the awkwardness. "Anpu Upuaut has a funny way of bringing us together again."

"Where were you?" I ask. "When I reached Per Ankh and you weren't—"

Bethan places an index finger on my lips. "Shhh. We need to get out of here. I'll tell you once we're en route. We still have House Montu on our tails."

Only now do I recall the frightening powers she wielded. House Thanatos? "But you—"

"Hush. I'll tell you in the car. Come." Bethan grabs my hand and tugs me out into the chill night. We step over the railway line, scramble down the gravel of the embankment, and slip quickly back into the streets. Bethan's black trench coat flaps like the wings of some great bird.

"You didn't return to Per Ankh while I was there," I tell her.

"I didn't return to Per Ankh." She sounds matter of fact.

Of course, idiot. Technically, that makes her an abomination. Those who don't go through the process. I stop, but she doesn't relinquish her hold on my hand, and I jerk her to a halt. Bethan turns to face me.

"I promise I'll tell you in the car. We really need to go."

"Go where?" This all feels so unreal.

"Away from here. In case you haven't noticed, they're onto you. Not just House Montu. Thanatos, too."

"But..." Do I need to say the obvious?

"Lizzie!"

"Ash. My name is Ash, and we need to go get the child." I can't leave Alex to his own devices, as much as playing absent father is tempting if it means keeping him out of danger.

"The little one. Of course." Bethan doesn't even bother trying to disguise her annoyance.

I nod. I could mention Meritiset, that they had been lovers in a previous lifetime, but I don't. Not yet. The conventions that apply to mortals shouldn't matter to Those Who Return, but it's one thing understanding a reality, and quite another trying to bring ease to one's heart. I'll tell her later. She and Meritiset. Me and Marlise. Even Stevens and all that.

"Where?" Bethan squeezes my hand painfully.

"Back in Nieu Bethesda." Silently, I curse myself. I'm giving away too much. Yes, there is a child, I want to say. What of it? Anger wells up. Misdirected anger. Now's not the right time for petty emotions.

"Shit." She bites her lip then tugs on my hand again. "C'mon, then. We must go. Make a plan somehow."

"What, you're not going to say 'leave the child behind'? I have a girlfriend, too. Or did you know everything else about me?" My bitterness flies past my lips as we hurry.

Bethan frowns. "We can talk in the car. The House Thanatos operatives are going to figure out things haven't quite gone according to plan."

"What plan? You in on it?"

"Let's just say I figured things out when they started talking about the book." She doesn't have to say which book.

"How'd you figure out it was me?"

"Don't be a dolt."

This could mean anything; I suspect that she'd only pulled her punches when she'd first seen me. Take out the two House Montu bozos first, then capture the prize. Richard had always been better at reading daimonic signatures than Lizzie.

Bethan's car turns out to be a gunmetal grey BMW

X5. Nothing but the best for these other Houses. So much for that abandoned Fiat Marlise and I used to drive.

"I need to find Marlise. Someone's taken her," I say as I strap myself in.

The woman doesn't answer at first, intent as she is on our getaway. "House Thanatos hasn't got her. We tailed a group from House Montu. They drove in convoy then took lodgings at one of the guest houses. They sent out sorties every day for the past week or so to try get ahead of the House Alba folks. All directions. They had a sensitive with them. Guessed they must've lucked out when Marlise came in to do the shopping."

Blue lights flash ahead as we near the edge of the town limits where the big informal settlement starts. Crap, crap, crap. Which House has the cops in its back pockets now? One can never be sure.

"Shit, roadblock," Bethan says somewhat unnecessarily.

Two cop vans are parked on the side of the road, and two officers in reflective vests are placing cones, while two stand in the road, flagging down cars.

There are three vehicles ahead of us as we slow down, and all I can do is dig my fingers into the upholstery and pray. It doesn't help that I notice the small beads of moisture forming on my companion's forehead and upper lip, and the air about us vibrates with the hum of her power. She's drawing, preparing, but for what, I'm not sure. Please, oh gods, no more DIY mummies. The cars before us are pulled over, but the officer waves us through with unseeing eyes. Good to know I'm not the only one with mind tricks. Then again, Siptah's the one who taught me to evade notice in the first place.

"Where do you think they've taken Marlise?"

"Probably to Joburg," Bethan answers. "Headquarters

there in the Midrand."

We're going in the correct direction, then, but I can't figure out the right course of action: check that Alex is all right? Insist that Bethan drive straight through? Apologise profusely to Sonja and send money when I next can?

Fuck it. "We need to hurry, make sure my kid's all right."

Bethan sighs. "I heard you the first time. We're going there now. This is ill-advised, but I appreciate your predicament."

Do you now?

Relief allows me to sink back in the seat. I can't help but look behind us. No telltale headlights. Bethan relaxes into the drive with a small sigh.

"You going to tell me what's going on?" I ask. "You never returned to Per Ankh." *Abomination*. I don't say the word. For some reason my relief at having Siptah back overrides my horror at the mere thought.

"There was an ambush. Somewhere before my *Akh* passed through the Black Gate." She sounds resigned, as though she doesn't really want to tell me this. "House Montu operatives were waiting for me. Thought it would be a shortcut to getting hold of the book."

"Is that even possible?"

"You should know by now that almost anything is possible if you put your heart and mind to it."

"And?" I watch her, but she keeps her gaze locked on the road ahead.

"House Thanatos. They were after the stele, too. Intervened. They kept me trapped for many years within a realm not quite part of this world nor that of the Tuat. That was until about a decade and a half ago, when a promising young initiate by the name of Bethan accidentally released me." She chuckles quietly to herself.

I try and fail to absorb what she's just told me. Then I think of my angry ghost. "You possessed her?"

"The *Akh* is always stronger than the *Ka* and *Ba*. Let's just say that Bethan became subsumed. It was not…very simple. She resisted. At first. Now it is very difficult to tell where her souls end and my *Akh* begins. Not an enviable situation."

Abomination. Cold fear thrills through me. But thinking of it, I'm not much better, am I? Except Ashton has moved on. If anyone's an abomination, it is he.

I almost tell Bethan about my experiences with Ashton, but she speaks before I can find the right words. A young woman is trapped somewhere deep inside this female body, and I doubt Siptah is as kind as I was to the original owner of my *Kha*. Siptah would be pragmatic and strip the soul of all identity. The original Bethan has no doubt been reduced to the merest whisper of her former self.

Bethan continues, "I warned Ankhakhet. As a past keeper of the book, I am joined to all those who have carried the burden. I had a very brief window of opportunity and even there almost got caught out."

"You did not come to me sooner." I can't help the bitterness that bleeds through.

"You were well hidden. Very well hidden. Some sort of daimonic interference. I could only find you once Forrester had. Thanks to House Montu, we knew enough that you were in the area, but not where exactly."

"But someone tipped off House Montu. How the hell did they gain that information?"

She shrugs. "They have their ways and means. They monitor the phone lines, emails."

Did Marlise phone her parents or attempt contact? There's a chance.

"How did you know?"

"We watch them. Always. We have to watch everyone. Thanatos isn't exactly the most popular kid at school."

"Ha-ha. Funny. Not. That still doesn't help my current predicament," I say. "What the hell do I do next? The woman I'm involved with is in the hands of my enemy, here I sit with you, and you're supposedly also my enemy. I now have not one, but three Houses all looking for me. And I'm not sure I even know whom to trust anymore." I'm disquieted by the sense that I'm not sure I can trust who Siptah has become. How the hell do I even explain this familiar stranger sitting next to me? The entire situation is too confusing.

"You're right on that count. Of not trusting. Richard didn't initiate Lizzie to be gullible." Ouch.

"Richard died when Lizzie'd barely come into her own powers. What was she supposed to do? She had no basis nor model upon which to build her approach. She did as best she could, with the limited resources at her disposal." I feel a nasty smirk form as I lapse into the way Lizzie used to speak. And it's weird talking about my past life as if it had happened to someone else. I can well imagine the old Ashton rolling his eyes at me and making some sort of disgusted sound at my choice of words.

"True." She lets the silence play out between us.

"So now, you're taking me to House Thanatos?"

"We'll stick to Forrester's plan for you."

"You're a double agent now?"

"Something like that." She flashes me a grin.

The steady buzz of her daimonic power runs through the car, encapsulates us. I can only describe it like standing within the influence of a substation—a constant subsonic hum that makes me ache to my bones.

I need to do something, anything, to feel less helpless, so I call Sonja.

"All sorted?" Sonja's voice is crackly over the bad reception.

I hiss... "Yes and no. I'll talk when I'm there. Is Alex all right?"

"He's fine. Hasn't made a peep."

That's far too unusual. Especially with him being outside of his usual environment. "Go look," I tell her.

Sonja sighs, and I hear a door creak. "He's fine. Still sleeping."

"Okay, we'll be there in about twenty to thirty minutes."

"What's up with Marlise?" Sonja asks.

"I'll speak to you when I get there," I tell her.

"Ash, I can hear by your tone of voice that something bad has happened. And I've had a—"

"Later." I kill the call and clench the phone so hard the plastic creaks. Sonja doesn't call back. Good. I don't know if I can deal with telling her the truth over the phone. Or whether I even should. The SUV's headlights slice into the darkness, and I have to blink against oncoming traffic. The N9 is still busy at this hour. Then I bite back an expletive when two cars overtake us. I hadn't even noticed them creeping up behind us.

"Drive faster!" I snipe at Bethan.

"I'm doing a hundred and sixty. What, you want us to get killed?"

"You're driving like a poes."

She looks away from the road long enough to glare at me. "I'm not driving any faster. I'm sorry. I don't do well with the lights of oncoming vehicles shining in my eyes. Oh, and language. Lizzie would be revolving in her grave."

"For fuck's sake!" Enough procrastination. If I get out of this situation with my *Kha* and *Akh* intact, I'm going to get someone to teach me to fucking drive a car. Properly. "This isn't exactly a garden party."

"You don't think I don't know that?"

"How the hell are you going to handle the dirt road, then, when we reach the turnoff?"

"I'll deal. But I'm not making it so that we're stuck in *Kha*s damaged in what could have been an avoidable accident, and that are physically handicapped for the next few decades either."

A memory returns to me, of times Richard and Lizzie used to fight about his driving, and I can't help but laugh.

"What's so funny?" Bethan snaps.

"Remember that time when we went on tour in the Sabi Game Reserve?"

"And I persuaded the ranger that I should drive... and I took a wrong turn and we ended up in the middle of the herd of elephants?"

"Yes." I can't help myself. I'm laughing at the memory of Richard's ashen complexion. No amount of Inkarna mind tricks would work on an enraged pachyderm. Somehow, we escaped that tense stand-off unscathed. "And who told you to keep on going and not take that left?"

"You did." Bethan's voice is quiet. "Damn. We had some good times."

"That we did." A chasm of more than just time yawns between us. "What now?"

"We go get your child," Bethan says with a sigh. "We'll plan from there."

"What about Marlise?"

"We'll need to regroup. Getting you to House Alba is of primary importance."

"And what about House Thanatos?" I ask.

"Some of them want you dead. As in permanently dead. After they've pried the stele from your cold, stiff hands. As for the others, they want the stele. They probably won't care much who gets hurt in the process of trying to retrieve it. We shan't dwell on why the stele is so important, shall we?"

Well, that's hardly surprising. "Where do you fit in the picture? What if they find out you're working against them?"

"My loyalty remains with House Adamastor, and by default House Alba. So far none know I've defected."

"House Adamastor is finished. It wasn't a true House." I'm struck then by the idea that Richard has been agitating for this House to stand for all these centuries, chafing beneath the yoke of his elders.

"All Houses have to start somewhere. House Alba out of House Aquila. House Aquila out of House Ptolemy. And so on. It's not a static thing, and it takes strength from its genius loci. Why do you think we're named for the Cape of Storms? There's a powerful magic attached to the name, a strong egregore. So long as you and I exist, Ankhakhet exists, we can build the House because *we* are its foundations."

"Building on a sleeping giant," I say. "And you want us to go up against Houses that have existed since the time of the pharaohs?"

"We have what they don't," Bethan says.

"And what is that?"

"Flexibility. We're able to adapt, change. We're pioneering spirits, whereas they're mired in centuries of stasis."

"We have no chapter house anymore, in case you

haven't noticed."

"Fool! We *are* the House, not some bricks and mortar pasted together. We are the living temple. Did you absorb nothing while you had your nose buried in books?"

"But we have no place truly our own within Per Ankh, then. We still fall within House Alba's sphere of influence."

"And your problem with that is? Think."

"In the beginning, there was Amun, blah-blah-blah..." I wave my hands vaguely.

"All Houses are basically permutations of one House. We're just different expressions of Inkarna. Like the Neteru, so the Inkarna. Some have closer associations with others."

"I guess you have a point. So the Inkarna that have allied with non-Egyptian ideals?"

She snorts. "What difference does it make? Once the theory's there, it doesn't take much to elaborate on fresh themes. What's a cosmology but one way of looking at the totality of existence? You haven't met the Children of Quetzal yet, have you?"

I can't help but groan. "Mesoamericans?"

"They came into being without the knowledge we had in ancient Egypt, despite what your crackpot conspiracy historians want you to believe. Not many are left, thanks to—"

"Wait, let me guess..." I hold up my hand. "House Montu?"

Bethan gives a sharp bark of laughter. "House Montu isn't the only House that's been responsible for the ills of modern society. House Alba has created more than its fair share of chaos here on the African continent. Colonialism, much?"

With a guilty pang I consider Richard's work, which

no doubt contributed to much of the exploitation. "Now what? We're kinda fucked."

"You've certainly developed a way with words since we last spent time together."

"What can I say? Goes with the territory." This tall, muscular tattooed male body with its mane of straight black hair is a far cry from the petite blonde Siptah last knew when he walked as Richard. Nevertheless, a certain degree of shame blooms through me. What must Bethan think, seeing me wear such a raw façade compared to my past *Kha*?

"Oh, it's not so bad." Bethan laughs and quickly squeezes my thigh, just above the knee. It's an oddly intimate gesture, and I'm not quite certain what to make of it, as it echoes a mannerism Richard easily shared with Lizzie all those years ago.

I should ask about Meritiset, but I still can't. Recollections of that last horrible encounter with her flash through my memories, of the visions she impinged on my mind—of her and Siptah together in a past life, lovers swept away in passion. Before my mortal *Ka* and *Ba* were even formed from the Sea of Nun.

We ride in companionable silence awhile, and some of the tension leaves my body. The sensation is that of weary resignation, and the certainty that I must rest now while I can. My muscles cramp, as though I've recently been electrocuted. When last did I use my full powers in self-defence? Hell, *offence*. Not since that showdown with House Montu, well over a year ago.

Oh, I've spent months reinforcing the wards hiding the stele engraved with the *Book of Ammit*. I've flexed my daimonic muscles with small acts here and there, but nothing to the degree of what I've survived this night. I'm jerked out of my musings as the car makes a sharp left turn onto the familiar gravel road to Nieu Bethesda.

Bethan's biting her lip something fierce, and the tingle of her concentration makes the air in the car feel almost tight, for lack of better description. She glances my way before returning her gaze to the road ahead. "You certainly know how to pick your bolt hole."

"It seemed like a good idea at the time. It has been good."

"I'm glad...that you had time to rest. And adjust. I don't think things are going to be easy for a while. Not with House Montu and Thanatos after you."

"I can't see a way out of this." I sigh, and the full weight of my predicament bears down on me. "I'm so fucked. I'm going to spend the rest of my existence running, both here and in the Tuat."

"You just need to get better allies," Bethan says. "Right now, House Alba is your best bet—they're the only people who can offer you a shield from the others—and we're going to figure out a way to get you there without letting House Thanatos and Montu know."

"How? They're probably watching all the airports by now, most likely have their fingers in all the security systems, waiting, watching. Fucking spiders."

"We're not going to fly." Her tight grin is only just visible from the glowing lights of the dashboard.

"How so?"

"Have you heard of the pylons?"

I rack my memories but can only come up with the architectural references in temples, and I somehow gain the impression she's not getting at the literal meaning.

Bethan sighs again. "Did they not teach you anything

in Per Ankh?"

"I don't remember much. It's like a dream. Snatches of it come to me. Some of the elders, and others. A garden. Magnificent hallways. To be honest, I spent more time communing with the spirits of the Blessed Dead before they sank into the Sea of Nun. For the most, the others kept me in splendid isolation while they figured out what to do with me."

"Free TV," Bethan mutters.

"What?"

"Never mind. It's easy to get caught up in the lives of those who've just passed, to see their last memories as though they are ours. And, yes, you can learn, and no doubt become very wise in the ways of the world of matter, but you've missed out on some of the teaching the elders guard. Next time you should seek out one of those. But to get back to what I'm trying to discuss with you here. Pylons. Gates. Portals.

"Some of the elders have found a way to bend the world of matter to our will, to shape it, as it were. All this—" She taps the dashboard. "Is illusion. A matter of perception. All is nothing, all is infinite. We can use the pylons to move the *Kha* from one place in time to another. Sometimes yes, there are aftereffects. Time displacement. But most of the time it works. A pylon exists between Cape Town and London. So far as I know, no one has used it in a long while."

"If no one has used it, how sure are you that it will work?"

"I'm not."

I groan quietly. "Let's just collect the child. Though I'm not sure I want to subject Alex to anything that hasn't been tested."

"What's it like living out here?" she asks. Way to go, change the topic of conversation.

"Blessedly quiet."

We lapse into silence. I want to ask so many questions, but I can't, and if she continues gnawing on her lip like that, she's going to bite it clean through.

"I regret that Richard didn't live, Ash. I really do. I regret that he and Lizzie didn't have a long, happy time together. That they maybe adopted children, that they could train initiates together and build something lasting. For what it's worth, he really loved her." Richard was another person, a relationship past, and to hear him spoken of like that causes a singular, exquisite pain for everything that never was, everything that was cut short.

My brain hurts trying to see our past selves as other people, kinda like watching a movie. Stuff that happened to someone else. "Well..." I shrug. What else can I say? "It's kinda shitty that you wouldn't even let me sit by your deathbed. At least let me do that much for you."

"Richard was a proud man. He despised weakness, especially in his own situation. Dying for him was a very private matter."

The way she's compartmentalising the past makes me wonder what her feelings towards me are. "You speak as if Richard is someone else."

"Isn't Lizzie dead to you?"

My feet prickle, and I shift them to ease the blood flow. "I suppose, but it's also so strange to be having this conversation. We never discussed your past lives. I always saw you as Richard."

"And before that I was David Miller, and before that William St Cross."

"And before that?" I ask.

Bethan offers an almost imperceptible shake of her head. Secrets upon secrets.

"How old are you, really?"

"How far is this road still?" Bethan asks.

We've reached the plateau that goes on for a good few minutes before it dips abruptly into the pass leading to Nieu Bethesda. This far off the tar and into what seems to be mountainous veld, it's easy to believe the road goes nowhere, that we'll just keep driving and driving until the car runs out of fuel. The road surface is rutted, but the SUV handles the uneven ground well. Marlise probably didn't have it this easy in the Fiat, with its smaller tyres, and it's a miracle the car hasn't been shaken to pieces after her weekly excursions to civilisation for supplies.

Above us a naked sky gleams with countless stars—cold and distant in the void. I know without having to roll down my window that the air is almost below freezing, the wind sharper than a butcher's knife. The headlights reveal only the pale route ahead of us and the scrub lining the verge.

"Only a little longer now," I say. "But be careful. The road takes a sudden turn to the right and descends sharply."

Bethan nods. I'm not going to press her now about her past. Do I really want to take the chance that I'll hear something I don't want to?

The descent consumes all of Bethan's attention, for which I'm glad. How do I explain to her, to someone I shared my life with more than a century ago, that while I'm glad to see her, I don't fully trust her? Hell, I don't even trust those I left behind in Per Ankh. Yes, there'd been reference to the other Houses, but now that I snatched at the memories, the specifics are dim. Other Houses. References to those who'd been betrayed and lost for aeons in the formless grey miasma that is the Sea of Nun.

Not for the first time I worry about Leonora, my old companion, and what she must have found after her passing. Be safe, dear heart.

If only I could contact her. For her to contact me. Siptah had found a way to warn her. Perhaps she can do the same, though now I realise I'd been so wrapped up in the totality of the novelty of my experiences in the Tuat that it hadn't really occurred to me to even try reach out to Leonora. She must've been so alone, and I'd been so foolishly complacent in my own abilities. Only to be betrayed.

I clench my hands. The SUV's tyres grind on the gravel, and the vehicle slews slightly as Bethan takes the hairpin bend near the bottom. Cars have careened off the edge here in the past, to plunge into the riverbed. Once the road flattens out, Bethan gives the Beemer gas, and we lurch forward, only to be nearly blinded by the headlights of an oncoming vehicle. Bethan wrenches us to the side of the road to avoid the Land Rover that roars past us.

She gives a small shriek. "Shit!"

"Who the fuck is driving like a fucking lunatic at this hour?" I ask even as I wrench my head around in an attempt to see the number plates with the telltale GP for Gauteng. "Fucking typical. They're going to hit a buck or something if they drive like that."

Just then Bethan takes a ditch too quickly, and I'm jerked so that I hit my head against the side of the door with a resounding crack. For a moment I'm blinded by the pain and draw in a hiss as I rub at the affected part of my scalp.

"You okay? That was quite a bump."

"Just drive. You're going to take a sharp left just after the dip." I squint at the road ahead as some of the pain subsides to a dull throb. Just great. I'll have a bruise from being careless in the car rather than having been locked in mortal combat with another of my kind.

Bethan gives a soft snort of laughter.

"It's not fucking funny!" I glare at her, but she keeps her eyes dead ahead.

"Sorry, I'm just imagining how Lizzie would never have been so undignified."

My only response is to growl, but by then we slow down, and I give Bethan directions to stop in front of Sonja's home. The lights are still on, spilling warm yellow stripes between the palisade of cacti outside. Two cement owls, made by one of the workmen responsible for the upkeep of the Owl House down the road, stand sentinel at the gate, their glass-bottle eyes reflecting the lights of the house opposite.

"Mmm, weird," Bethan says as she kills the engine.

"It's a pity you aren't here under better circumstances. I'd show you the Owl House. The place is the only reason Nieu Bethesda is still going."

"Owl House?"

"Helen Martins, some outsider artist who was active during the mid-nineteen-hundreds. Filled her yard with cement sculptures of owls, camels, and stuff. Pretty neat. Tourists love it. Place is haunted like shit, though." A delicious shudder passes through me at the memory. "And not just by the dead."

Bethan raises a brow at me. Her expression is only just visible in the low light. "You really like it here."

"Yeah. I'm sorry I have to go."

"You do realise it was only a matter of time before they found you, right? This little slice of paradise would've been snatched from you whether you liked it or not."

A sigh escapes me. "One could hope that wasn't the case."

She reaches over, places a warm hand over one of mine, and squeezes lightly before gathering her cellphone and bag. "C'mon. Let's get this show on the road. I'm sorry it's come to this."

"Right." I draw a deep breath before I open the door, and the shift in atmosphere from warm to utterly freezing is so sudden it steals my breath.

Fortunately for us, Sonja, in possession of her usual uncanny witch's sense of impending doom—or purely aware of the strange vehicle stopped outside her house—waits by the front door to usher us into her lounge.

The place is cosy, the walls painted in various shades of earth tones, the furniture antique ball-and-claw imbuia and stinkwood, liberally covered in pillows and throws. Lucifer, the resident geriatric wolfhound, lifts his large head at our arrival. He thumps his heavy tail twice before sinking his head back on his paws and returning to whichever rabbits he was chasing in his sleep.

Sonja locks up behind us, her expression pinched when she turns to face us. "Where's Marlise?" Tonight her unruly mop of white-blond hair seems wilder than usual, and her eyes glint hectically as she darts her gaze between me and Bethan, before settling on me. "She's like you. One of Those Who Return."

I nod. "Is Alex all right?"

"He's fine." She holds up a hand to prevent me from moving through to the bedroom. "Don't go in just yet. He needs as much rest as possible. He is a very troubled soul."

No shit. I don't dare speak those words. Sonja will keelhaul me. She might be a mortal, but she's got an uncanny way of laying bare all one's weaknesses in an argument, and I have no desire to show Bethan any more of my vulnerabilities than she is already privy to.

"We couldn't find Marlise," I say, hating those words. "I think she's... She's been taken by the people we were trying to avoid."

Sonja presses a hand to her throat, and although I could hardly believe she could grow paler, she does. "No."

"And now our number's come up. We need to run."

"Who's this woman?" Sonja gestures sharply at my companion.

"This is Bethan. We... We are old friends." I don't need to elaborate.

Sonja narrows her eyes at me. "You do not tell the whole truth." She sighs. "But that is not important, and it is neither here nor there. The point is that you must go. You flee into grave danger."

"I know that. We must take Alex. We must find Marlise."

"With the child?"

Bethan steps forward. "We'll take him to a place of safety first." She tilts her head to me slightly. "Then we rescue Marlise."

"I don't like this. Surely you can leave him here? This valley is protected. A great spirit. One of the Old Ones. They will not come here." Sonja gestures about the room.

Bethan coughs delicately. "With all due respect, shadow-weaver, you do not know what danger you are tangling with."

Shadow-weaver? I look askance at Bethan, but her focus remains on Sonja, whose mouth is slightly parted.

Sonja leans against the couch. "It's been a long time since someone has addressed one of our clan by their hereditary title. We do not speak of this outside our hearth circle."

"I met a Stuart Ebon Wareing many years ago. He was a civil engineer. A good man. It was a pity he had been in denial of his...gifts. It proved fatal when he tangled with the magi from Bechuanaland."

"That was more than..." Sonja lets out a hiss of breath.

"More than a century ago. Be at peace. Let the child go with us. You have played your part in this small melodrama, but now the bigger players must depart, and your family will know peace again."

I glare at Bethan, but she remains focused on an ashen Sonja.

The flames crackling merrily in the hearth offer the only sound in an otherwise silent room, where the atmosphere presses down heavily on the occupants.

"Very well," Sonja says as she expels a huff of breath.

I follow her down the short passage leading to the spare bedroom where Alex rests. The small hairs on my neck prickle, as though I'm expecting trouble.

"Nothing amiss, are you sure of it?" I ask.

Sonja pauses at the door. "I looked in on him about five minutes before you arrived. He was fast asleep."

The room is tiny, at the back of the house, and in summer it's cool, thanks to a gnarled vine supported by an equally ancient trellis outside. The vine is bare now, and I can see pinpricks of stars through the windowpane.

Sonja pauses mid-step. "That's funny. I'm sure I drew the curtains."

Her bewilderment is all the excuse I need to shoulder past her to where the cot rests on the bed. The covers are pulled up, and the child's face is obscured. "Turn on the damned light," I yell at Sonja.

She complies, and I blink back the shock of brightness

as I turn down the blanket. My stomach lurches even as I know to expect the worst. Well, not the worst. That would involve a very dead Alex. Instead of the child, or any remains of him, all I find is a bundle of twigs and bones, tied together with black ribbon. The faint smell of earth reaches me.

I'm aware of Sonja standing right next to me, of the hitch to her breath. She half reaches out then gives a small shriek. She jerks back her hand and stumbles. Bethan only just manages to catch her, and staggers under the taller woman's weight.

Bethan lays Sonja down so that she's propped against the bed. Her eyes are rolled back in her head, and she's twitching—another of her 'turns' as she calls it. She usually snaps out of these quickly, and this doesn't look like one of the big ones when she has a full-on vision. Then Bethan approaches the cot containing its bundle. She peers at it for a few wordless seconds then steps back with a grimace of disgust.

"What?" I ask. I'm still struggling to process what's going on. At the back of my mind I know I should be freaking out. Someone's gotten into Sonja's house—a home warded to hell and gone with all manner of her witchy magics—without her knowledge, and they've spirited away my child, leaving only a macabre bundle in Alex's place.

My chest tightens, and I clench my fists, taking deep, even breaths. Perhaps if I blink, none of this would have happened.

Bethan's face is tight with shock. "Thanatos." She barely gets the word out.

With a growl I spin around and grab her, heedless of the way the fabric of her shirt rips as I shove her against the built-in cupboards so hard the wood splinters. "What have they done with my child?"

"I didn't think... I thought we had time." She snatches ineffectually at my wrists. Bethan could do so much more, and it's a measure of her trust in me that she doesn't.

"You *knew*, didn't you? That's why you drove slowly so they could get there first, isn't it?" I curse myself for a fool and consider those cars that roared past us on the N9; of that departing Land Rover that almost took us out as we entered the village.

I could smash her, break her bones, and subconsciously I'm aware of the way my daimonic power zings through my veins, the way the overhead light flickers as I lean heavily on the resources available to me.

The disparity in our sizes strikes me anew, especially since Bethan—Siptah, I must remind myself—does nothing to defend herself. Her bones are fragile compared to the mass of power I can draw upon when I strike. I can mash her into the wall so that every limb and organ is a mangled mess.

And what would that achieve? Her eyes are huge, the pupils pinpoints of fright in burnt umber irises. Eyes I might've found attractive under different circumstances.

"You disgust me." I shove her across the room so hard that she crashes into the wall.

Bethan's breath is knocked in a whoosh, and she crumples to the floor. My immediate concern is Sonja, who moans slightly, uncomfortably half-slumped on the bed. I help her into a seated position.

"Are you okay? What happened?"

She cradles her head in her hands and inhales deeply, and speaks, her voice muffled. "Some sort of psychic discharge."

I felt zilch, but then again, things happened so quickly,

there's a chance I might have missed something. "Are you going to be okay?"

She nods, her hair spilling loosely to obscure her face. A movement from the corner of the room catches in my vision, and I straighten so I can glare at Bethan, who's managed to pull herself to her feet. She leans heavily on the desk by the window, her expression so stricken I'm almost tempted to feel sorry for her.

"Are you ready to explain yourself?" I ask Bethan, unable to hide my anger.

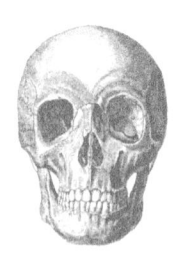

CHAPTER THREE
Keep Your Enemies Closer

"I CAN EXPLAIN everything," Bethan says.

"Sure you can," I reply. "Do you think I'm stupid? I might not have all the pieces, and I sure as hell don't know how the fuck to fit them all together, but I'm not a complete fool. You're a traitor."

Tears run down her cheeks, and she dashes them away with her wrist. "I didn't mean to end up in this situation! With this bloody weak body. A woman's body. How do you think that makes me feel?"

I can't help myself. That's such a fucking Richard thing to say. I laugh so hard my stomach hurts, and I take my time about it, too, before I draw a deep breath and resume my death glare aimed at Bethan. "Fuck you. And you think I haven't had a raw deal trying to fucking deal with this?" I gesture sharply at myself. "If things had gone according to plan, I'd be celebrating my ninth birthday soon, and my name'd be *Catherine*, and I'd consider asking my dad if I could have riding lessons or something equally dumbass. I should be worrying about getting good grades at school, and my friends would still play with dolls! And have time to grow into my abilities so that I don't get a fucking nosebleed whenever I push my *Kha* harder than it should. So don't talk to me about what's fair. You've had it a bit easier since you stole the body of a trained initiate."

Sonja sits perfectly still next to me, her eyes wide as she watches us. At this point I don't care what she does or doesn't know about Inkarna.

Bethan cringes from me, her arms crossed over her chest, all the smug self-assurance gone from her demeanour.

"Can I ask you this much, *Siptah*, how long have you dallied in the Sea of Nun? Answer me truthfully. Have you ever spent what feels like an eternity lost in *hell*?" My voice booms in the close confines of this room. I'm shaking. I want to punch something, the wall, anything.

Bethan flinches at the sound of her *Ren* and glances at Sonja, who's gone taut next to me. Bethan shakes her head, ever so slightly. Fuck her. Right now I don't give a fuck about breach of common courtesy.

"You never did warn me when you drew me into this," I continue. Painfully, I'm reminded of my own omission with regard to Marlise's involvement. The abused becomes the abuser. "And you didn't tell me about Meritiset either." There. I dig the knife in. Twist the blade and hear it scrape on bone.

"But don't worry. You don't ever have to worry about Meritiset ever again." A savage pleasure washes through me with that little revelation.

Bethan straightens, her face pale, pinched. "Not in

front of her." She points at Sonja.

"It's too late for that!" I retort. "She's been dragged into this, thanks to your stupidity."

"We can continue this conversation somewhere private."

"No, we can have this out now!" I roar, and I don't care whether the neighbours or the people across the valley fucking hear us.

Sonja rises and pulls her shawl close. "I'm going to go make some tea." She doesn't wait for either of us to answer and exits the room.

Bethan says, "Are you quite done with your childish tantrum now?" Her anger fizzes in the room, a barely controlled simmer of daimonic power. She's drawing, whether to take the offensive or defend, I don't know. However much she draws, I mirror, and the lights buzz dangerously in the fittings.

"Did you love her?" I ask, my voice little more than a hoarse whisper. "Meritiset."

"Leave her out of this!" Bethan shouts.

"She betrayed me! She blamed me for your disappearance!" I roar.

Her face contorts, but I'm not sure whether it's with anger or remembered pain. "Are you honestly still hung up on your old Victorian ideals of a one true love?"

"I believe in loyalty."

Bethan laughs. "You have so much to learn. *Ash.*" She says my name like it's poison, a bitter word.

"What do we have at the end of it all but loyalty to those we love?" I ask.

"We're beyond petty human squabbles over eternal love. Maybe in a past life we were husband and wife. Things change."

"*Did you love her?*"

"Yes."

Did you love me? My throat thick, I turn away, lean against the wall and sigh. Stupid, I know. Like turning one's back on a tiger. But I'm beyond caring. My world tilts and shifts on its axis and rushes cold water to my belly. My skin is clammy. Meritiset's final moments replay over and over again, the look of dawning horror as she realises she's not just going to die, she's going to end. *Forever*. Her *Ib* destroyed and her name erased from the Djehuty's list. There will be no more returns. There will be no more miraculous reunions after her passage through the Black Gate. Not even the Sea of Nun will hold her. The emptiness is bleak and hollows me out.

Warm fingers brush my wrist. "Ash? What is it?"

My laugh is not a pleasant sound. Then I round on the woman so fast that she takes a step back, her spine pressed against the cupboard door.

"She's *gone*. Don't you realise what I'm trying to tell you? I *ended* her. I really, really killed her, and she'll never come back. *Ever*." I'm sure my expression is absolutely horrific. A leering, evil smile filled with all the past few hours' ugliness. "She stole the body I was supposed to have and tried to kill me. Your lover tried to destroy House Adamastor and hand *The Book of Ammit the Devourer* to House Montu on a silver platter."

Each of my accusations appears to deal Bethan physical blows, and she slides down the cupboard, her hands held over her head as though she could ward against my attack. Didn't see that one coming, bitch, did you?

The kettle's boiling in the kitchen, and Sonja sings a folk song, possibly to drown out what she can overhear of the conversation taking place in this bedroom.

"What? Are you going to sit there on the ground and snivel? Where have your people taken Alex?" I stand over her, shocked not only about this entire situation, but also because this is not how I envisioned a potential reunion with the person who was my life partner. Forever? Yeah right.

"Will you give me some space, please?" Bethan asks.

For a moment I continue to tower over her, then I retreat to the bed and take up the horrid stick-and-bone bundle. Some of the crackling tension in the room dissipates. I'm torn. Rescue Marlise or try prying Alex out of the clutches of the Death Walkers. "What is this thing?" I ask. Anything to avoid discussing Meritiset now that the ugly truth has been released.

"It's a bone cuckoo," Bethan murmurs.

"What does it do?"

"It mimics the target long enough in order to fool others into believing that all is as it should be, as well as creating a loop within any wards so as to suggest that nothing has been disturbed." Bethan sounds tired and keeps her forehead rested on her knees, which are drawn up close and wrapped in her arms.

"What do they want with my kid?"

She looks up, her eyes red-rimmed but dry. "Don't worry. He's safe. They won't hurt him. It's House Montu you'll have to worry about."

"So House Thanatos would kill me, and possibly Marlise, but Alex remains safe. Why don't I buy that?"

"Please believe me. They'd set their sights on him from the moment he became host to Ashton Kennedy's *Akh*. He has come into being as one of us. I don't need to explain that to you."

"Why take him? What do they want with Alex?" I clench the bone cuckoo so that the bones and sticks grind together. A spicy scent, camphor mixed with sandalwood, fills the air as small specks of matter fall to the ground.

Her words come out as a whine. "They want him alive! I'm not privy to all the details! Believe me when I tell you he's safer with them than he is with us. He will get the care he needs. And don't be dumb. He's leverage. What you know, he knows too."

"He is my son. Not some bargaining piece. What do I tell Marlise when we get her back?" How much did my angry ghost learn from me during our brief association? My stomach clenches painfully.

We stare at each other for a while, and I'm the first to look away, my chest heavy. "Now what?" I mumble.

"We get you to House Alba headquarters. We can figure the rest out later." Bethan sighs and pulls herself up onto her haunches. She clenches at her thighs. "If I wanted to lead you to the faction that wants you dead, you'd be dead already."

"Factions?"

"Must I fetch a dictionary? Has your new *Kha* addled what I used to consider one of the finest minds as initiate material? Yes, *factions*. Are you honestly so naive to think that the Houses themselves don't have internal issues?"

"And there I thought you married me just because I had a pretty piece of ass."

She winces and bares her teeth at me in a pained grimace.

"So what you're telling me there's a group that wants Alex alive, and then there's another group within the same House that wants me dead? And there's House Montu that wants me a whole lot dead, and House Alba who're obviously recalling me so they can keep their secret weapon safe now that the cover is blown.

They at least want me alive. For the present."

Bethan nods. "And I need to re-establish contact with House Alba. For both our sakes."

"And then what about Marlise? I can't just leave her there. It's my fault she's been taken."

"They're going to use Marlise as bait to get at you. We can't play into their hands. We need reinforcements, a plan."

"Well, duh."

"Don't fall into their trap. If we go to House Alba now, I promise you I'll personally help you get Marlise back. We'll have better resources at our disposal."

"What about House Thanatos? Can't your friends who don't want me dead give us a hand? Just until we get sorted? And what's to say House Montu won't kill her anyway?"

"If they wanted her dead, there'd have been an accident with a body, don't you think? And even now they're going to trace the car's registration number back to an address here in Nieu Bethesda. After that, it won't take them long to figure out where you've worked and find out who your boss is. By staying here you're putting your witchy friend in danger. That's if they didn't already work out what the others have."

She has a point, and I massage my temples to rid myself of the tension headache lurking there. My previous attempt to rescue Marlise from the now-defunct chapter house of House Montu almost ended in complete disaster, and then we only just succeeded because I had the help of my *Kha*'s previous tenant—a disembodied spirit I'd only just managed to gain control of. Sure, now I have another Inkarna at my side, but the odds are still stacked against us. Two of us going up against House Montu headquarters in this region? I do not relish the prospect, especially not since they clearly expect me to rush in blindly. Just like last time. Disappointment stings at the corners of my eyes.

"Marlise, forgive me," I whisper, then look across at the woman crouched opposite me.

"I found you as soon as I could," Bethan says, as if that would make it all better. "Is that not proof enough? I'm helping get you to safety."

Yet you betrayed me in any case, by allowing them to overtake us on the highway and steal my child. I run my fingers through my hair, which has mostly pulled loose from its band. Before Alex came, Marlise would often fuss over me, brush my hair. Now my fingers encounter snarls. I have not been looking after this *Kha* as I should, and I can almost imagine my angry ghost berating me. Almost. Vain fool.

With a sigh, I stand and hold out a hand for Bethan so she can get up. For a moment she hesitates, then accepts, her fingers warm and soft against mine. Our *Akh*s brush against each other as static buzzing at the edges but recognising each other. No anger. Known territory. Only the need for contact at a time like this. Before I can withdraw my hand, she clasps it in both of hers.

"Trust me, Ash. That's all I ask. I know I've given you very little reason to believe a thing, but did I ever do anything to hurt you in the past? You'd be dead now if it weren't for my intervention. I love you, more than you know."

"Just like you loved Meritiset," I murmur and pull my hand out of her grasp. We stare at each other, and a shadow of hurt passes over her features.

Sonja calls from the kitchen, "You guys want to come get your tea?"

Bethan replies, "We must go, Sonja." Then she

shoulders past me, leaving me alone with the accursed bone bundle dangling from my left hand. Useless.

Although it's a pointless gesture, I drop the thing on the ground and trample it, just to hear the satisfactory crackle of bones and sticks snapping beneath my boots. Fucking House politics. I kick the remains so that they clatter against the wall, then follow Bethan to where she's speaking to Sonja in a low voice, already by the door.

"I'm so sorry we dragged you into this, but we'll be going now." The damnable woman is holding Sonja's hand just like she held mine a moment ago. Bethan casts me a meaningful look, almost as though she's willing me to just shut the hell up.

Sonja makes eye contact with me. "Ash?"

Every moment that we linger here spells more danger to Sonja and her family. They never asked for any of this, and it's my own pure selfishness that brought me here. I knew this day would come. "Gotta fly, Sonja. Thank you for everything."

Sonja wavers and rocks back slightly on her heels, and I rush to catch her just before she topples. This is a big one.

Bethan gives a small shriek. "What's happening to her?"

I grip Sonja's convulsing body to my chest and drag her over to the couch. "She's having one of her little episodes. She sometimes has visions." Now's not the time for this, I want to tell her, but instead I lay her down on the couch until the tremors pass. Her teeth are clenched tightly, her eyes rolled back as she shakes, and her body is stiff. A thin line of saliva trails down the side of her face.

Bethan and I stare at each other with wide eyes until the worst of the seizure passes. Mute, I stroke back the strands of hair from the woman's forehead as she slowly relaxes. She's had several of these in my presence before. The first time it happened it scared the living crap out of me. She'd started babbling about many stars that had burnt out and fallen from the sky. Later that day we found out about a head-on collision just outside of Graaff-Reinet. A truck ploughed into a long-distance minibus taxi filled with folks headed to Port Elizabeth. Seventeen dead.

Another time it happened was in her bistro. Some old lady and her husband had been paying their bill, and much like today, I'd only managed to catch Sonja in time before she cracked open her skull on the way down. That time she'd spoken of the woman's son, that he was tied to a pillar and pierced through with many arrows. The older lady had scoffed as she'd paid and left, but I'd been the one to take the call when her husband phoned a week later to tell us their son had been murdered in a hijacking gone wrong.

Her eyes still glazed over, Sonja reaches a shaking hand to caress my face. "So beautiful, so alone. Beware lest the stooping falcon devours your burning heart." With that she falls into unconsciousness.

I stagger to my feet and make blindly for the door. Better to go outside. "I'm so fucked. That's it. It's game over. I'm so very, very dead." I have no doubt of the meaning of that prediction.

"Wait! Ash!" Bethan calls behind me, but I unlock the door and rush outside. I need the cold air against my skin and filling my lungs.

Bethan shuts the door behind me but hesitates in touching me. "Ash?"

"She's a seer," I tell her. "Sonja's never been known to be wrong." Neither of us needs to discuss that a falcon is the emblem of House Montu—a warlike Neter of ancient Egypt.

"Ever thought that this is just a warning?" Bethan's hand is warm in my own. "Come, we must go. Now. And let's not go where the falcon will expect you to fly."

I turn back to the house. "What about Sonja? I need to check whether she's okay."

"She'll be fine. I've laid a compulsion on her to rest. She will forget everything that transpired this evening. We need to go now, and take another route out of this place, if we can."

"The back roads," I say.

"Let's get you to safety, get backup, then we can plan to get Marlise out of their clutches."

She tugs on my hands, and at first my feet won't obey, but it's easier for me to go along with what the woman wants. Lizzie always found it easier to be agreeable when it came to Richard. He always had a better argument, spoke more sense, and had more experience.

The problem with an isolated hamlet like Nieu Bethesda is that there are only three roads to take to get the hell out of Dodge. Any or all of these could be watched, but we select the road to Middelburg, and hope for the best, that House Montu still needs to marshal its forces.

Bethan doesn't ask about the stele, and I don't volunteer information. The damned thing is as safe as it's ever going to be here. I also haven't told her my *Ren*. I simply can't. It's not a case of won't, it's can't. That knowledge is my last defence. Every kilometre we leave behind us my heart grows heavier. I've failed. I've failed so fucking badly. I should be happy that I've found Siptah, but instead this knowledge brings with it a gall-bitter taste.

I try to reconcile the smiling, laughing young woman I know as Marlise up until Alex's birth with the sullen creature who slammed the door on me earlier today, and I can't. It's my fault. I shouldn't ever have slept with her, shouldn't have dragged her into this mess in the first place. But then again, it's not like anyone was holding a gun against her head now either, was it? There I go, justifying my actions to myself again.

Samuel Forrester. Now there's a problem. He's dead. Whether he'll pull through to Per Ankh is another matter entirely. This is the first time he's died, and for all his smart, smug talk, there's absolutely no guarantee he'll make it. Not your problem. Or will I be blamed for this, too?

I fumble at memories of my own first death, but those thoughts are as drops of mercury between my fingers. Perhaps it is for the best that we don't really remember what happens when we transition. I have a sense of great depth and breadth, bigger than the human consciousness can conceive, a vast abyss that threatens to completely swallow me. Visions of Per Ankh keep morphing. Hallways. Bright faces. Love. Companionship. Ethereal music. Neith's star-studded underbelly.

Get back to reality. If Samuel was so sure he could bring me to London, does it mean I'll have a positive reception upon my arrival? That they're counting on someone to get me there? I glance at Bethan next to me, at her face illuminated by the dashboard. I'd like to reach out and touch her, the way Lizzie would draw comfort from being with Richard, but I can't. We're two strangers, and yet...

There's no turning back. Lizzie's dead, as is Richard. The two individuals sitting here share past experiences, distant, as if having watched the same films together once upon a time. But for once I don't feel so achingly alone. Bethan understands what Leonora or Marlise didn't. She's been through the Black Gate. She's returned from Per Ankh, and many times, at that.

"Tell me about Bethan." I need a distraction.

The woman gives a short snort of laughter. "What's there to tell?"

"You said you can't readily tell where you end and she begins. You didn't displace her souls, did you?"

"No." She shakes her head.

"So, what happened when you took her body? Did you meld with her, or did you shove her so far down she's a ghost inside herself?"

"Why're you asking these questions?"

I look out the window so I don't accidentally make eye contact. "Oh, just wondering." I won't tell her about Ashton Kennedy, the wastrel bastard whose body I now inhabit. How I dominated his spirit with mine. How we were eventually like two horses hitched to the same carriage. I realise with a pang that I miss him, sod that he was. And I hope Alex is okay. I owe the little tyke that much. Bonds of guilt.

"How much of you is you after a while?" I ask.

"It doesn't get any easier. You hold onto your *Ren*. You try to maintain the fleeting memories of Per Ankh. There are some meditations you can practise to rekindle that knowledge of the Tuat, but you are never sure. That's why we should only take the young ones. Their *Ba* and *Ka* are not as developed. There is less to displace." Bethan sounds exhausted.

Not so much guilty conscience about murder, is what she means, I'm sure. "What do you remember of the Tuat?"

"Enough to know that I don't remember all that I should. I haven't been there in more than a hundred years. To be honest… I don't know how I will fare when I pass through the Black Gate again." Her voice shakes, and her fear paints the air between us. Her *Akh* is just as stained as mine. How will it measure against the feather of Ma'at? We don't talk of those whose hearts weigh heavier upon their return.

We drive in silence awhile. Bethan tries to find a radio station but only static hisses through the speakers, interposed with the occasional snatches of voice or music. The pale, dusty road ahead of us flows into an eternity of void. Once or twice lambent eyes are picked out in the headlights, but whatever creatures cross our path we don't find out as they flash into the bushes before we can get a proper look.

"Do you know where we're going?"

"Backroads to the N1," Bethan answers. "We have enough fuel. Get to Beaufort West before dawn if we're lucky."

"I'd offer to drive, but…"

"You can't. Didn't expect you to have sorted that out by now."

I grip my hands in my lap, hating the way there's no recrimination in her tone, only resignation. As if she'd expected me to not have bothered with something as simple as driving a fucking car.

"Marlise tried to teach me. We ended up fighting more every time I stalled the car."

Bethan offers a soft snort. "Why did you stick it out with her?"

"I'm responsible for her."

"You always had a way with strays," Bethan says.

"She took me in when I had nothing."

"You shouldn't base a relationship on obligation."

She's right, and my retort sticks in my throat. I sigh. "I started her on the path of initiate. I must see her training through. Besides. The child."

"Ah. Yes. Guess you have your dream now."

Lizzie never could have children. There is that. I hate that she has a point.

A sticky silence fills the vehicle, and I don't want to share any more of what my life has become. Nor do I want to know more about this near-stranger in the car with me. Then again, at times the road is so corrugated I can tell it requires Bethan's complete attention to keep us from rolling into the scrub. No need for talk. On more than one occasion we take a corner too fast, and the car slews. Both of us draw power at the same time, to what effect, I don't know. I've never tried to stop a car that's about to crash. I'm not even sure how I'd go about preventing the disaster.

At some time past midnight, we pause so Bethan can go take a pee. I do the same, but we head in opposite directions. We haven't met a soul during our journey so far, for which I'm grateful, and the stillness lays its heavy blanket over everything. Not a single cricket or night bird. Just quiet. And the ever-present hiss of tinnitus in my ears that'll never go away so long as I inhabit this *Kha*.

The stars form a glittering, dense throng, the Milky Way a puff of smoke. I recall a snatch of San folklore, that the galaxy's arm is the result of some cultural hero tossing a handful of ash into the sky. Out here, without the city's pollution, I can almost believe that. A single meteorite ignites as it arcs across the sky, an almost greenish glow to the falling debris before it burns out. The ancients would have seen this as a portent. I know better and wonder whether this is a chunk of satellite or space station plunging back to earth, the result of a decaying orbit. The cold wind digs in its claws, and I'm only too glad to climb back into the car.

"Feeling okay to drive?" I ask Bethan.

"I'll manage."

And she does just that, even though to me it feels as if we'll never make it back to civilisation. We've somehow driven off the map into a hellish loop. I can't help but keep glancing at the fuel gauge. We've passed one or two sleeping hamlets that might as well be ghost settlements.

Murraysburg, a small Karoo town, barely registers. The petrol station is shut. All good people are asleep and dreaming during this abandoned hour. We're already past the halfway mark headed towards empty, and I trust Bethan knows what she's doing, as we're back on the dirt road. I'm so lost right now I don't even want to consider how we're going to deal with getting stuck out here.

When I'm not peering at the petrol gauge, I'm watching the road ahead. Suicidal rabbits make excellent targets, and though Bethan does swerve and miss the first of these unfortunate rodents, one is not so lucky. We smack into it with a soft whump as the tyres burst its body.

"Shit," Bethan mutters.

I choke back my cry and instead dig my fingers into my thighs. I so do not need this. We're going to get stuck out here in the Karoo desert, and eventually some farmer's going to come along with his truck and make the grisly find of our desiccated corpses, flies buzzing around our gaping mouths.

We almost miss the rusted sign that reads Three Sisters. That's our turnoff, and Bethan takes the left. If my memory serves me correctly, there's a truck stop on the N1. The blessed N1. Then we'll have to make a choice. Turn north and head to Johannesburg, and make a desperate bid to save Marlise, or turn south and embark on Bethan's crazy notion that a magical gateway that may or may not function exists to whisk us to the relative safety of London. Right now, both options weigh up as equally ludicrous.

To top it all, my body aches like I'm coming down with a bug. I last ate more than twelve hours ago, nor have I had anything to drink.

"We should get some rest," I tell Bethan. "Some food and stuff."

"Need to keep going," she says.

"You're going to get us killed if you carry on without taking a break." This is an old argument, one Richard and Lizzie had on more than one occasion, many years ago.

Come to bed, you're sick, you need to sleep.

I need to finish this research.

She clenches the steering wheel with clawed hands, the SUV sometimes on the wrong side of the road. Not that there are any other cars out here this time of the night, but yet...

She's veering. Again. "Bethan!" I say sharply.

"Shut up!" She jerks the car back on course.

"You need to rest."

"We can refuel. I'll get some coffee."

So our conversation goes in circles, as the gauge's needle drops further. By the time we nose out onto the tar, we've only just missed three bunnies, and my nerves are taut, near snapping. The twenty or so minutes it takes for us to reach the brightly lit oasis of the service station extend into an hour. The novelty of being capable of driving more than eighty kilometres an hour makes it feel as though we're flying through the night, the tar smooth beneath the wheels.

Bethan glides the SUV into the service station's forecourt, and I'm only too glad to climb out and head straight for the shop. Before I even think of buying something to eat, I make my way to the bathrooms where I splash my face with cold water. A youth with the faintest hint of a moustache and a sallow complexion exits one of the stalls while I finger-comb my hair back into a messy ponytail. He doesn't bother washing his hands, the dirty little bugger.

Then again, I probably freak him out. For a moment my reflection in the mirror seems alien, and I suffer a sense of disruption, that the face belongs to that of a stranger who needed to shave more than twenty-four hours ago. I search those storm-grey eyes for an answer, then step out into the night.

A lone cricket chirps hesitantly. Wrong season, buddy, I want to tell the bug, but I stride back into the relative warmth of the store and head straight to the service counter for coffee. Bethan's outside, supervising the pump attendant. I place an order for two coffees and toasted sandwiches with fries, then watch her.

Richard use to stand like that, arms folded while he leaned against a wall, head cocked ever so slightly. Just watching. Bethan does that now, waiting for the attendant. The fingers of her right hand tap on her upper arm. She glances up, in my direction, and I feign interest in the contents of my wallet, turning towards the cashier to hand over the notes—the last of my cash. Marlise was the one who held onto the money, paid the rent, went shopping, the excuse always being that I was too visible.

Bethan joins me shortly, while I'm waiting for the food. Her cheeks are flushed, and she smiles up at me. "You didn't need to. I could've paid for this." As if she knows I can ill afford to spend any money.

"It's okay."

"You still do that thing, despite..." She raises a hand and wipes at my brow. The touch is electric, and I flinch away. "You always used to get a frown line just there. Some things don't change."

"Don't say that, please." A queer sensation lurches in my belly, and my face grows warm. I turn and make a show of watching the kitchen staff through the rectangular serving hatch. I'm all too aware of the woman whose hip nudges my thigh. And her scent—a perfume carrying hints of jasmine.

"I make you uncomfortable, don't I?" Bethan murmurs.

"I've got to go buy some cigarettes," I say and shove away from the counter towards the convenience store side of the station. I haven't had a cigarette in more than four weeks. A bad habit, but one I've unfortunately learnt. An act the old Ashton Kennedy enjoyed, and something that brings me a small measure of comfort though I'm well aware it's not good for my health. May as well blow the last of my small change on an indulgence.

Smoking is something that would've upset Lizzie. Hell, will probably upset Bethan. And while I consider this as I request a packet of Marlboro filters from the cashier, I realise that I'm grasping at a flimsy barrier to protect myself. Because yes, there's a nasty little part of me that wants to find out what it's like to fuck Bethan. Despite having attracted the ire of not just one but two hostile Houses. Of all the times to have lascivious thoughts. Didn't stop me last time, did it? And look where that got me. A father at age twenty-two. I grimace.

She joins me, armed with the food and the coffee, where I'm pacing far from the fuel pumps. I draw a deep toke and let the smoke coil into the sky, to be lost among the stars. The taste of the cigarette revolts me, but I know by the time I light up the next one, it won't bother me as much. In fact, I'll look forward to it. And right now, I enjoy the nicotine wriggling its nasty little fingers through my veins.

Bethan seats herself on one of the flat-topped rocks that form part of the landscaping, places the packet containing our food down next to her, then sips her coffee. She holds mine out to me.

Wordlessly, I take the proffered cup from her and sip carefully at the hot liquid.

"Two sugars?"

"You remembered." Somehow this doesn't surprise me. We're falling into our old patterns.

"If you think I'm going to complain about you smoking, you're going to be disappointed."

I raise my brow and take another long drag so the ember crackles. "You're bitching now. Just trying to make out like it doesn't bother you." Damn. We should be talking about everything else. Not these stupid little inconsequentialities. Like whether Alex is okay. Whether we should turn back and try to figure out whether we can fetch Marlise. Instead we're running. And I'm going along with her plan because it seems like the easiest option.

"Aren't they going to be looking for you? House Thanatos? By now they know you've betrayed them."

Bethan offers a one-shouldered shrug. "Or I could be infiltrating House Alba, using you as my cover." Her smile is chilling. She isn't lying.

I choke on a gulp of coffee that threatens to go down the wrong way. I'm using her as much as she's using me.

She laughs. "Your expression. It's priceless."

"You know, that's just the problem. I don't know

whether I can trust you." I'm angry and grind out the butt of the cigarette, then immediately light another.

"Getting lung cancer or emphysema isn't going to help your cause."

"So? I'll die. Then what? Who wants to come back to this shithole anyway?" I sound like a petulant child, but I don't care.

"Calm down, will you."

"How the fuck am I supposed to calm down? It's all fine and well for you because something tells me you can crawl back to brothers and sisters in your fucking zombie creep House, and they'll welcome you with open arms if you lick the right feet. I don't have that luxury. I don't even know what sort of reception I'll get on the other side if I end up taking an inadvertent shortcut back through the Black Gate."

"Will it make you feel better if I say that I'm the only member of House Thanatos here in South Africa at present?"

"Then who took Alex?" Or is she trying to tell me that Alex isn't even in the country anymore?

"Don't concern yourself with Alex. He's safe."

I feel my eyes bulge as I glare at her. "Don't concern myself with Alex. What? Are you on drugs? He's my fucking *son*."

Bethan casts a glance into the medium distance before making eye contact with me. "Wow. Well done. Now the whole world is privy to this conversation. Your voice carries, and you're pretty much almost shouting." Her tone is bored but holds an edge to it.

My only response to that is to hiss and to commence pacing again while I drink my coffee and smoke the cigarette down to its filter. All the while she watches me, daintily nibbling on the toasted sandwich. Toasted fucking cheese and tomato.

Which reminds me of the food Marlise used to serve me those times when we stayed at her parents' house. If there were any way I could kick myself for stupidly going there I would. I should have grown a pair and stuck things out with Ashton's parents rather, and put up with that disagreeable uncle. I haven't wondered about the Kennedys for a long, long time—yet another damning mark against my name.

"You need to eat something, Ash," Bethan tells me. She's standing next to me where I'm facing the National Road. An eighteen-wheeler roars past and disturbs the otherwise still Karoo air.

The damnable woman nudges the greasy packet containing my sandwich against my hand, and without thinking too hard, I allow my fingers to close around the paper. Mechanically, I go through the motions, all the while keeping my gaze unfocused, half on the road, half on the stars.

Next to me, on my left, Bethan shivers. She must be freezing, but she keeps me company while I eat. Only when I crumple the packaging into a tight ball in my left hand does she touch my arm.

"You ready to go now? Reckon we push through to Beaufort West. I'm sure we'll find a motel or something. You're right. I need to rest."

I don't protest and meekly follow her back to the SUV. Anything is better than standing here for the rest of tonight like the dumbfuck I am.

The Voortrekker Motel is situated on the outskirts of Beaufort West. The ugly, flat building stands right next to the road with a gravel driveway out front. Skinny pepper trees will offer little shade during the day. The replica of a Voortrekker wagon out front stands crippled, the front axle broken, its canvas covering tattered to expose the ribs of the canopy's curved framework.

We wait in the cold and dark for ages before someone answers at the reception area door. By this stage I've threatened at least three times that we should rather pull into the parking lot of a service station, push back the seats, and try get some shuteye.

Bethan wants a bath and a real bed and rightly points out this is possibly the last chance we're going to have to get proper rest for a while. She's right. We're going to need it.

The man who lets us in after the umpteenth time Bethan has rung the bell is pretty much lost in the old khaki army coat that's patched at the elbows and full of unidentifiable stains. He gives me a leery eyeball but focuses all his attention on Bethan as she speaks. Her daimonic power is a subtle whisper of forgetfulness.

I half-listen as she requests a room. The man doesn't input any details in the register, and the transaction is over quickly. Tomorrow, apart from rumpled sheets, there will be no sign of us having been there. By this stage I can only think of a bed. A warm bed. Inkarna mind tricks. We could make a fortune doing this.

The room itself is average as far as motels go. Yellowed photographs of sheep—this is Merino country, after all—adorn the walls in frames that have been badly repaired with glue. A small television is bolted into a casing that can swivel—ostensibly so guests can watch telly in bed. Classy. Not. The floor is linoleum, but by this stage I couldn't care if it was bare cement. I collapse onto one of the two double beds with a groan. The springs squeak alarmingly, and Bethan sniggers from across the room.

"Any harder than that and you'd have broken the bed."

"Fuck off," I murmur into a pillow that smells faintly

of mildew. Those two words give me an almost savage pleasure as I try to imagine whether Bethan's shocked.

She doesn't dignify my curse with a response, and while I try to relax enough to doze off, I hear her running the bath. Bethan's brought a small overnight bag in with her. I have nothing, and I can smell that I should be thinking of getting cleaned up.

By the time she exits—dressed comfortably in matched navy-blue pyjamas, no less—I take my turn in the bathroom. This entire situation is wrong. She's all ladylike, me the one looking and behaving like a thug. But the hot water in the shower does much to erase a measure of my tension. I don't have to think too hard, can concentrate only on the sensation of heat on skin.

Though I know there's no chance of the clothing being dry by the time we leave later this morning, I wash my T-shirt, underwear, and socks, then hang them over the towel rail. Damp and clean is better than dry and sweaty. I wash my hair as best I can with the contents of the puny little shampoo bottle. I can't get a lather going, but it's the act of cleaning that matters more. Dressed in only my jeans, I head straight for my bed.

Bethan, a dim figure now that only one of the bedside lamps is on, sits up in her bed and watches me, a small smile quirking her lips. "That's quite a lot of ink. I'm sure Lizzie would have had a shit fit if she'd known."

"Yeah, well, I didn't exactly have a choice when I punched through again." I slide under the covers and pull them up under my chin.

"It's not a bad-looking *Kha*, despite the ink."

My face grows warm, and I close my eyes. "I do not want to be having this conversation right now." Uncomfortable thoughts stir, knowing that Bethan is considering my physique in terms other than merely platonic.

"Does it bother you that I still find you attractive?"

I groan and turn over onto my side, my back to the woman. Nevertheless, my flesh betrays me, and I can't help but wonder what it must feel like to give in to the physical temptation. After all, we were married. In a past life.

Marlise. I can picture her face crumpling when she figures out I've betrayed her. Not if. *When.* Because there's no way in hell she wouldn't wonder and ask all the questions I don't want to answer. And I hate lying to her.

"We need to get some rest, don't we?" I ask. Just leave me alone. Please just leave me alone.

Bed springs creak then a weight displaces my mattress. I clutch at the bedding, my stomach roiling, yet my traitorous cock stiffening despite my misgivings. Bethan smells honey-sweet as she lays herself down next to me, mercifully not beneath the covers. I keep my face resolutely towards the door.

"Come on, you can't admit that you're not curious, to see if the old chemistry is still there?" She strokes back a damp tendril of my hair, and I shudder.

"Why are you doing this?" I turn around to face her. Big mistake. I can't help but notice the swell of her breasts pushing up against her top.

Her smile is positively wicked. "Because I can."

Then she kisses me, and all rational thoughts flee. Bethan's mouth tastes of mint toothpaste, her tongue sly and insistent as she teases the seam of my lips. Silk-soft, she straddles my hips, shoving the covers down to expose my chest. This is my invitation to touch, and I slide my hands over her thighs and up to her breasts.

For a moment a sense of wrongness nudges at

me. Her breasts are not as large as Marlise's, but then Marlise isn't here now. Bethan is. Siptah. Who supersedes Marlise by many years. Surely this isn't wrong? A love spanning centuries. We were husband and wife once. Death is not the end for us.

And there was Meritiset. Another stab of guilt, but it's tempered by the way my cock presses against my jeans and the warmth of her crotch mere inches from my own. The pressure makes me writhe beneath her.

Bethan rocks back and smooths her hands down my chest, wicked fingers tugging at the silver rings through my nipples. She's smiling, and her eyes glitter. Tears? I can't tell in the low light. "Did you have these put in before or after?" Each tug sends small pulses racing through me. I wouldn't exactly describe the sensation as painful, but in this aroused state it's hard to tell.

"I'm not going to answer that," I reply as I try to sit up.

Bethan has the advantage right now and shoves me back down. "Oh no you don't." Before I can protest, she kisses me again, hungry as she slides slightly to the side of me, her leg hooked over my thighs as she works the button and fly of my jeans with her free hand.

I sneak my fingers into her top from its collar and roll her nipple between thumb and forefinger so that it stiffens into a peak. She moans and rides my thigh even as she succeeds in her task of freeing my cock.

Her hands are…sheer bliss as she grasps the shaft firmly, thumb massaging the head and pumping all the while. I gasp as I try to buck into her motion, but her thigh keeps my legs pressed down.

Even during the times when I indulged in onanism I did not quite manage the push and pull, the right squeeze.

Bethan's smile is broad, her mouth slightly parted as

she nibbles on her lip.

"Sweet Amun, woman!"

Her kiss silences me before I can say any more, and she crawls back on top of me, somehow managing to tug off her pyjama bottoms in the process while she positions my shaft. Her thighs are smooth and warm beneath my hands, and I hiss as she teases the head of my cock with the lips of her cunt.

I try to flip her over, but my balance is wrong, and she keeps me on my back, her smile growing wickeder by the moment as she rubs her wet folds against me. Bethan settles on the tip, then brings her mouth down for another punishing kiss, her pussy contracting partially around my cock. She holds me, rides only a little on the tip, no doubt enjoying the way I twist beneath her ministrations.

I want nothing more than to slam into her, manage to get a hand there where her slick heat meets the hardness of my erection. It's her turn to hiss in pleasure when I encounter the nub of her clit and rub at it with a finger.

That's when Bethan thrusts herself down on me, and I have to grab quickly at her waist so I can push back against her. She is hot and tight around me and settles so that she can take all of me in before she starts to rock.

Her breasts are perfectly in reach, and I knead at one with a hand while I grip her arse with another. She moves with determined assurance, her breath hot on my neck as she tilts forward, somehow squeezing harder with her cunt. I want more, all of her, and the soft skin of her shoulder is within reach, so I bite down where the tendons of her neck muscles are exposed.

Bethan cries out a little and stiffens, but then our efforts become more frenzied, and I am able to flip her over onto her side and thrust in deeper. She twists while I fuck her, her breathing becoming short, truncated screams she muffles in the bedding. Her warmth, depth and wetness consume me while I grip her thighs and sink myself deeper, over and over again until our efforts fuse into a singularity.

The orgasm rips through me, and I thrust long and hard, emptying into her, then finish with a few short, sharp motions. Slowly, the context of this entanglement bleeds back into awareness, and I withdraw and roll over with a groan.

"Fuck." I cover my face with my hands, the guilt rapidly replacing the thrill of spent lust.

"That felt good," Bethan says. "I haven't gotten laid in weeks."

I spare a glance at her blissed-out expression then sit up so I can pull my jeans back up. My T-shirt is wet, but I grab my leather jacket and slam out of the motel room. Fuck this shit. I'm such a heartless bastard. Somewhere, tonight, Marlise is no doubt being held in a strange place by people who'd happily kill her, and here I am screwing around. And Alex is probably on a plane flying to fuck knows where with people who have dubious interests in his future.

I extract a cigarette and light it, drawing deeply of the smoke while I watch the passing traffic. I can smell Bethan on my fingers.

Beaufort West is always busy. It's one of those towns everyone passes through, but hardly anyone stays for more than one night. The cold creeps into one's marrow, congeals the air in lungs.

Standing outside with wet hair is hardly the brightest thing to do, but at present I need to feel like I'm getting a slap through the face. Marlise doesn't need to know. I don't have to tell her. But this betrayal will hang over me and weigh me down so that eventually I will tell her. The entire situation's complicated. I'd like to say it's not my fault, but I know damn well I didn't put up much of a resistance once Bethan had my cock in her hand.

Oh, so rich of her to go off about the frailties of a woman's body when she knew exactly how to catch me at my weakest moment.

"Ash?" Bethan calls from inside. "Will you close the door? You're letting in the cold air."

I growl deep in my throat and snick the door to then curse the fact that my jacket's zip doesn't work. Instead I wrap the thing around my body and pace awhile, the gravel biting into the tender flesh of my bare feet.

The cigarette does little to calm me, but I light another one immediately after. I don't want to go inside. Don't want to face that witch who just seduced me.

Because I can. Those were her words.

So, I'm just a conquest, to see if she can dig her manipulative nails deeper. Was Lizzie just a conquest to Richard? There was a dowry. Lizzie's father had been old-fashioned that way. A bitter taste lodges at the back of my throat, and I don't think it's just the tobacco. Richard used a portion of that money as a down payment on the new chapter house in Simon's Town.

What's worse is the that I'm now dependent on Bethan, just like Lizzie was of Richard. And once again, I have something of value. Only I am the secret weapon. Or, rather, the not-so-secret weapon, since everyone currently incarnated in the material world either wants me dead or wants to control me.

Somewhere deep inside me is someone small and scared, who'd dearly love to break down into ugly tears and rail against the unfairness of it all. I can't do that.

Lizzie thought she was secure, and where did that get her? Nowhere. She was stagnant, and she failed when it came to preparing Leonora for the worst.

Are we ever secure? That's the thing. I've been walking the knife edge since my return, and if I am completely honest, it's that I only know what it is to be truly alive when I'm running under the shadow of death.

If I consider the people who live their sedate lives in this small town that's so isolated in the country's desert, I know theirs is not the life I'd choose for myself. Not again.

By the time I'm done with the cigarette, my teeth are chattering, and I can no longer feel my feet. Bethan's curled up in my bed, and I pause once I've locked the door to consider whether I'll join her or slip into the other bed.

"Hey there, stranger," she murmurs sleepily.

She's so delicate. I estimate her *Kha* to be in its late twenties, but with her hair all mussed she looks to be much younger. Who's the stronger one right now? But my head's buzzing with exhaustion, and the lure of simple human contact is too much.

With a sigh I drop my jacket on the ground, switch off the remaining bedside lamp and crawl under the covers with the traitorous bitch who's done a pretty good job of stealing what's left of my heart. If I dream, I don't remember a thing.

I wake before Bethan does. Sunlight streams through the vertical blinds and reflects off the nowhere dust suspended in the air. She doesn't even stir as I slide out of the covers and make my way to the bathroom.

I wince when my still-wet T-shirt comes into contact with my skin, but it's either cold, wet, and somewhat clean or warm and stinky. Ditto for underwear and socks, but I don't know when I'll get another chance to make myself presentable.

And I'm sure as hell not going to face the unknown on the other side of the pylon looking like something that's crawled out of the bushes. I scowl at myself in the mirror before I head back in to grab my jacket and boots. I want to use Bethan's hairbrush to untangle the snarls in my hair, but I resist the temptation. At this moment I need one thing, to get outside.

Bethan's still dead to the world, for which I'm grateful. Her curves, while pleasing, feel wrong. She's taller, skinnier, and more angular than Marlise, and I hate myself for making the comparison. After I pull on my jacket, I slip outside and blink in the weak sunlight, which does little to warm me. My cellphone tells me it's nine thirty-six. We've slept way longer than we intended to.

Where to from here? Beaufort West is an ugly little dilapidated town that looked like its boom found it then deserted it in the 1960s. Slate-sheathed walls are *de rigueur*. Big trucks roar past outside, the ghosts of their slipstreams tugging at my hair as I light up a cigarette. The nicotine hits me hard, and I have to sit on the front step, the cold seeping up from the cement while my smoke-laden breath fogs before my face.

What would Lizzie do? The old lady was birdlike and stooped by the time she croaked it. Hung on until she was deep in her nineties. Eyesight still fine, despite years of reading, though a strong breeze might've shoved her over. White hair in a soft perm. Yuck. She'd probably lecture me. Then take me home to feed me. That's the way things were with my past self.

Lizzie wouldn't cope in my present predicament. Fuck it. Who'm I fooling? I'm not fucking coping, and no matter how many times I say "if only", it won't make things better.

If only I never allowed Marlise close. If only I'd never followed up on my impulse to accept the note from that old man who'd given me directions to meet up with Leonora—then I'd still be a barman working at The Event Horizon. And I might still be living with this *Kha*'s parents. Or not. I don't know anymore.

Bethan finds me with my head cradled on my arms, my hair a black curtain almost trailing in the dust.

"Jesus, Ash, was it that bad last night?"

"I'm a fuckup," I mumble into my jacket sleeve. "One colossal fuckup."

Her laugh does little to improve my mood. So light, as though there's not a care in the world. "When did you become such a self-pitying fool?"

"I should destroy myself. Then this can end." My words sound petulant and pathetic even as I speak them, and only serve to make me feel doubly the blithering idiot. "Every time I try to fix things, I just make them worse."

"Such melodrama. I really did expect more of you, but then, looking back, Lizzie did have it so easy, didn't she? The pampered daughter of a farmer, then a little bit of teaching before Richard waltzed in and swept her off her feet into a life of pampered luxury. And now, that the crunch comes, you whine and moan like the little princess you are. Grow a pair, Ash. Did you think it'd always be so easy?"

Bethan's words bite deep. They're true. All true. But it doesn't mean that I'm not angry. I raise myself so I can glare at her.

Her fucking makeup is perfect. Lips a lovely shade

of coral gloss. She's had time to apply mascara, and her hair is pinned up. As if she's going to a business meeting or something, dressed in no doubt designer jeans and a dark grey, V-neck jersey that shows off her cleavage.

A wordless moment passes between us before she snorts laughter. "You're such a dick."

I clench my fists but let my hands drop to my sides. I'm powerless, emasculated. "Fuck you too," I murmur then stare out at the road. People. Going places. With purpose. Me. On my butt in the dust.

"We gotta go. I'm not joining you for your pity party, so get your shit together. It's another five hours to Cape Town, barring complete chaos." With that she leaves me where I am.

The woman has a point. It doesn't mean that I have to like it. All I can do is go along with the flow because I'm out of options.

I pretend to sleep most of the way back to the city. Through half-lidded eyes I watch the scenery pass, but it's all much of a muchness—the aquamarine sky meeting the khaki hills. The trucks and buses are scary, playing chicken with each other on this busy highway, and the times when Bethan overtakes strings of vehicles, it goes better for me when I squeeze shut my eyes completely. I find it all too easy to imagine an oncoming vehicle when there's no place for us to give way.

We stop once in the town of Worcester, at yet another big petrol station. Bethan buys us burgers and fries, and a cup of coffee each, then we eat in silence, and she has the good grace to wait so I can smoke.

"Are you done sulking now?" she asks as we hit the road again. "We don't have the luxury of you behaving like a five-year-old that had its favourite toy snatched."

"And your bitching at me's going to help?" My voice is thick from disuse and the emotions tangled in my throat.

"Sugar coating ain't gonna help, baby," she drawls.

I turn to look at her, but she keeps her gaze firmly on the road.

"So, you think I'm a fucking joke? But I'm good enough to fuck, just so you can show me who's boss? Is that it?"

The bitch laughs. "Get over yourself. So we had sex. We got it out of our systems, and now we can move on. Don't lie and tell me you didn't at least fantasise about fucking me before we did the dirty."

I bite the inside of my cheek to keep myself from saying something stupid. I have no idea how to respond to her, but I know damn well I'd have dropped something colossally facetious. Lizzie never won any of her arguments with Richard either.

"I didn't hear anything," Bethan says. "C'mon. Admit it. You liked it. And given half a chance you'd do me again."

I suck in a deep breath. "Don't you think this is a bullshit kind of argument to have when we should really be worrying about whether Montu's going to find us and kill us? Or that we're running with our tails tucked instead of going to rescue Marlise?"

"Marlise means very little in the bigger scheme of things. She can't furnish them with the information that they're looking for, and we both know they're only using her as bait to lure you into their clutches, so we're going to be cleverer than them by not doing what they expect."

"And if she dies?"

"We all die sooner or later."

"I didn't want for her to get hurt."

"Then you shouldn't have expected her to keep up with you. But this is not going to be a lecture about all the stuff you did wrong. We all do stuff wrong. We all do the best that we think we do under the circumstances, based on the information we have at hand. Survival of the fittest, sweetheart. I know I sound like an evil bitch for saying it, but you know it's true. Either she survives or she doesn't. You can apologise later once you have your white horse and tin sword." This time she spares me a glance, and her compassion is a slap in the face. "It's not your fault, Ash. But please believe me when I tell you we need to be clever about things. If you've trained her to the best of your abilities, like you trained your initiate Leonora, then there's a chance that if the worst happens, Marlise will pass through the Black Gate and attain her *Akh*. If not, then you tried your best. There's no sense in you beating yourself up because events transpired the way they did."

And the real Ashton Kennedy? The one whose *Kha* I stole, who now dwells in my son's body? I've failed him too.

"I know you're wondering about the kid. If it's any consolation, he's the primary reason House Thanatos is involved. Though the book would be a pretty sweet cherry."

"Why?" The shock is sharp.

"He's an anomaly, an aberration."

"Meaning?"

Bethan's grip on the steering wheel changes and she keeps her attention focused dead ahead. "He's earmarked for House Thanatos. Those of us whose coming into being is tainted by inconsistencies. Those whose souls are abnormal. You're not that squeaky clean yourself, you know. House Thanatos would welcome you, too."

I try to digest that information and fail. "So, you were like a pack of jackals following House Montu, waiting for the morsels. Why not deliver me and Alex both to your faction in House Thanatos and be done with it?"

"We're going to end up talking in circles this way. Let's focus on the matter at hand: keeping you out of House Montu's clutches and staying one step ahead of the rest who'd like to see you ended. Yes, you're my ticket to making contact with House Alba again. Once we've got that all sorted, you can berate me for being the evil seductress leading you astray from your delectable damsel in distress."

I don't have anything to add to that, so I stare resolutely out the window. To amuse myself, I snatch at whichever echoes of the Blessed Dead I can call up, but after I tune into the three separate deaths of pedestrians struck by vehicles, I quit.

I must've dozed off again because the next I'm aware, we're parked by a thick wild almond hedge, and the light's fading. My muscles cramp, and when I stretch, the tendons click loudly.

"I let you sleep," Bethan says. "We're both going to need it."

"Where are we?" The display in the dashboard reads quarter to five.

"We're parked near the top gate at Kirstenbosch Gardens."

"What the fuck are we doing here?"

"The pylon's in the garden."

The nicotine withdrawals send their insidious little fingers tugging through my blood vessels, and I unclip my safety belt. I should never have bought that pack of cigarettes. How easy it is to fall into old habits. "I need a smoke," I tell her. I won't stay in the car with her unless I have to.

Bethan joins me outside, then digs in the trunk of the vehicle for a long, dark trench coat. She succeeds in looking sleek, ready for anything. Me? I'm a complete and utter mess. Under ordinary circumstances, a gorgeous woman like her would not be caught dead with some arsehole like me. Then again, this is not an ordinary circumstance.

She finishes by tucking a few items in her sling bag, then watches me without speaking as I pace and smoke. Thin drizzle spits down, and my extremities are soon cold. My stomach growls, reminding me I should've eaten more, but I ignore the hunger pangs. Even if I could eat right now, I'm too on edge. I'd mostly likely puke my enemies to death.

"What?" I ask as I grind the butt into the gravel.

"We go." Bethan turns smartly and strides from the parking lot. The area is completely screened from the road by the wild almonds. I vaguely recall some history lesson that identified these as trees planted in the late 1600s or something to that effect. These trees are old, and I'm almost tempted to snatch out for whatever echoes of Blessed Dead memories remain. No. Focus.

We make an incongruous pair as we approach the pedestrian crossing on Rhodes Drive. A pair of joggers waits for the cars to stop—two women—and they give us the eyeball as we pass them. I don't turn around to look, but I'm sure they'd paused to watch us approach the garden's gate. Bethan and I must look like we've stepped out of one of Marlise's favourite supernatural films.

Leonora and I came to the gardens often, many years ago. Lizzie was a member of the Botanical Society. She used to grow indigenous orchids and meet her fellow enthusiasts for tea. None of those old folks would be alive now. Snatches of older times return, the conversations trite considering my current circumstances. This only serves to remind me how adrift I am in this time and place. No wonder so few Inkarna jostle for the "privilege" of returning to the material world.

I barely pay attention as Bethan speaks to the woman in the ticket office, but the barest whisper of her daimonic power is enough to tell me the official will not remember our entry, nor do we pay the entrance fee.

So close to nightfall, the garden holds a sense of mystery, cloaked in mist and shadow. I can still make out the verdant lawns that stretch up part of the way of the mountain's flanks. Small frogs pipe near the watercourses while guinea fowl rasp in the distance. The ever-present rumble of evening traffic is muffled the moment we cross that border from suburbia to garden.

"Hey." Bethan nudges my arm then leads us, along the brick-paved path headed up the mountain.

What can I do but follow? "Where exactly are we going?" I hurry to keep pace with her.

"We need to go down to the Dell. There's a spring that feeds a pool there. That's where the pylon is."

"And you're sure this is going to work?"

"In theory, yes." Bethan laughs.

"That's hardly reassuring."

"I used one of these types of pylons while I was still in England. It linked a spot in Scotland with London. There's no reason this one won't work."

"And if it doesn't?"

"Not the foggiest. We might end up in New Zealand. Or Timbuktu." She grins at me but keeps walking.

"Ha-ha. Very funny."

"Trust me on this, all right?"

"I don't really have a choice."

"You always have choices, Ash."

I growl deep in my throat and turn her words over. She has a point, but I'm not about to admit that while within earshot.

Presently, she indicates that we take a path that segues into the garden proper, and we soon find ourselves on cobbled walkways that meander through a collection of succulent plants. Venerable naboom, which remind me of organ pipe cacti, lean crazily with lichen-clad trunks. Many aloes are still in bloom, their inflorescences like living flames in bright hues.

Bethan stops so abruptly I almost knock into her. She lifts a hand to indicate that I keep still, and I see no reason to dispute her order. Since entering the garden we've not seen a single soul, but that doesn't mean that we aren't alone.

Movement catches my eye across the way. Not long now and it will be fully dark, but three figures cross one of the large lawns near the restaurant about five hundred metres from us, then vanish into a thicket where one of the streams runs down to the green belt. The men move with purpose and pause before they vanish into the screen of foliage.

"House Montu. I'm almost certain of it," Bethan says in a low voice.

"How would you know?" I ask.

"Gut feel. I didn't want to alarm you, but we were followed for a short while between Worcester and Paarl. Or I thought we were."

"And we've led them right here."

"They won't know why we're here," Bethan says.

"But they know we're here," I reply. "Which amounts to the fact that they're after us."

"Cloak yourself. Carefully. I'll draw first. You

follow my lead."

I stand, fuming silently, while she snags skeins of daimonic energy. Bethan works subtly, so that it feels as though an errant breeze tugs at me, a whisper. I've never watched another engage the "here-not-here" of cloaking, and while Bethan doesn't exactly disappear, I find it incredibly difficult to focus on her. My gaze keeps sliding to the side, with small details like a peculiar pattern in the cobbles, or a particular aloe bloom, snagging my attention.

Her hand finds mine, and she squeezes my fingers. I take that as my cue to draw more powers to myself. Now that I'm aware that there are people—enemies—here with us, it just makes things worse. We've had it easy up until now, haven't we? Though Samuel Forrester would disagree. Then again, if all's gone well, he's about to find out whether his training will stand him in good stead in the Hall of Judgment.

Apart from the random House Montu operatives we've spied, the only other visible sign of life is a lone grey mongoose that slinks across our path. The critter pauses before he dashes into the undergrowth, his beady little eyes casting about as though he knows full well something is amiss.

We don't dare speak, and I allow Bethan to direct me towards the cover of the forest that follows one of the streams. Signs point us to The Dell. The scent of moisture hangs heavily in the air, and I can hear the fall of water. Pretty sounds, for prettier times.

Cycads radiate their prickly foliage, and we descend by stone steps at the bath, neatly tucked away behind stone banisters beneath a dense canopy of trees. The water is clear, crystalline, unlike the rivers in the area that are normally tea-stained. Large tree ferns on long stems lean drunkenly, their fronds quivering in the stir of air. Tadpoles the size of my thumbnail wriggle about—dark shapes against the pale sand at the bottom of the pond. Little enough light remains, but it's as if the water carries its own bioluminescence.

"What now?" I murmur.

Bethan shimmers into view, and I let go of my own shield.

"We go into the water, and I'll say the right words." She leans on the balustrade and peers into the pool. She sounds about as convinced as I feel about this situation.

"As in get physically wet?"

"Uh-huh."

"Then what?"

"We'll find ourselves in London. Hopefully."

"I don't like the sound of 'hopefully', woman."

She turns, holds out her hand. "Come."

As I reach for her, I hear the scrape of a shoe on a loose pebble and glance diagonally to my right, to where a man ducks behind a tree on a terraced pathway above us. There's no time to think. The telltale whine begins in my ears—the sound of another Inkarna powering up.

I pluck at Bethan but succeed only in jerking her.

"We gotta run!" I yell. Beneath my hand, I feel the hum of her daimonic power. The water in the pool next to us begins to bubble.

We're trapped, and I turn so Bethan and I stand back to back. Better to make sure no one approaches from the other side. I breathe deeply, then drag at the tatters of daimonic essence around me, but it's like snatching at fronds of kelp when the tide's going out. The power slips between my fingers, and it's almost impossible to hold onto the bits I do trap.

I do the maths: me, Bethan—and three others. All

of us dragging at the same source of power. The water in the pool thrums with its own signature, so I borrow from it instead to build a protective shield so that whatever blow I'm expecting to smash into us doesn't from my sphere of influence.

A memory smacks me out of the present: a man stands almost exactly where we are now, hands in the air, tiny blue-green motes of daimonic power scintillating between his fingers, illuminating his features and gleaming off the darkened lenses of his pince-nez.

Then a blast accompanied by an actinic flash and scorching heat catapults me against the stairs from which we just came, and I lie there, dazed, at first unsure of which direction the attack came. My ears are ringing, and my head feels as if it's slowly expanding and contracting to the beat of my heart. Idiot. They got me from behind. Where Bethan stood only moments ago is empty space, like she's been vaporised.

"No!" I groan as I stagger to my feet, trying to figure out what went wrong. Bethan's got several lifetimes' experience to draw upon. She wouldn't shield incorrectly. Unless...

Betrayal. Then why go to all the trouble of bringing me here? Why not deliver me straight into the arms of House Montu? Why give me false hope? Factions within factions... I stagger up the stairs. Need to get out of the trap. At least if I reach open ground I can see where the attack comes from, draw them out. Maybe.

How is it possible that everything can go so pear-shaped in a mere twenty-four hours? Bethan dead. It seems so unreal, but my eyes don't lie. Blank sorrow wells up even though on a rational level I understand that Siptah is a survivor. The fates of our *Akh*s are intertwined. We'll meet again. Though the sorrow at our parting after such a brief reunion makes my throat tight.

My body protests as I take the stairs three or four at a time, then hit the terraced walkway that leads back to the gate. What the hell will I do when I get to the road? Flag someone down? Make a mad dash to the car park to a car I can barely drive even if I wanted to? Behind me comes the slap of feet on stone, the hoarse grunts of men in pursuit.

At least three Inkarna. I don't have the luxury of time to feel sadness for Bethan's passing, even if she is dead, though any other outcome seems unlikely. I felt the force of that strike. I'll have bruises all down my side later. I pelt down, towards the bigger lawns near the visitors' centre across wide swathes of green. Running. I'm always running.

A loud crack is followed by a dull thunk ahead of me as a small section of turf explodes. Great, now they're shooting at me with guns. Let's kill the motherefucker, won't we? Each breath sears frigid air into my lungs. Not much farther now. Someone shouts behind me but the words are unintelligible, and I don't know if the speaker is berating his companion or ordering me to stop. I'll get to the visitors' centre and take a left down the old section of Rhodes Drive that's been enclosed in the gardens, somehow get down to the main road from there then disappear into Newlands, with its big houses and lush gardens.

Plus, there's the greenbelt—part of the same system in which I managed to shake off pursuit the last time. Run. Hide.

And then what?

More hiding, like we've done for the past year.

Someone's powering up for another strike. The air around me coalesces, so I turn, make a stand. Stupid, really. They've got me three to one. Didn't stop me the last time, my conscience nags, reminding me of the carnage I caused when I wiped out Binneman and his cronies. But then, of course, I went at the Inkarna one at a time. Now there're three.

And they're after my sorry arse.

I shove all my heart into shielding, visualising a shimmering wall warped a hundred and eighty degrees before me. The garden appears to me as though through a heat haze. Three figures stroll towards me across the lawn, the one on my left holding an object pointed down, the gun. They're classic Men in Black, how typical. Stupid really. I mean, who wears suits to hunt down a fugitive? This isn't some fucking American FBI crime thriller.

Stereotypical bastards. Then again, there's magic for sure in presenting an intimidating façade—close-cropped hair, stern expressions, and shoes so polished folks can see their reflections in the leather. I grimace. Fuckers.

Bethan's *Kha* vaporised so callously, all because they want to get at me. So what if she was a member of House Thanatos. She was still a person. The old anger stirs, and a low growl begins in my throat. I'll send their fucking *Akh*s howling into the Sea of Nun. Better yet, I'll destroy—

Someone behind me snakes an arm around my neck, and a familiar static punch fries my nervous system. Well shit.

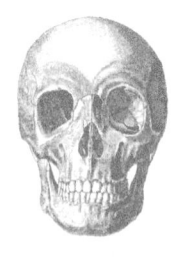

CHAPTER FOUR
Dissonance

SO, I SHOULD'VE expected there to be more of them. But should-haves are always awfully good advice in hindsight. And should-haves won't help me now. My hands are pulled tight behind my back, and I'm lying on my side in the rear of a car. Though it's futile, I try tugging at my bonds, but from the bite of pain in my skin I can tell they've used cable ties. As it is, my hands have gone that awful cold-numb that's going to hurt like hell when the blood gets flowing again. If I thought Binneman's henchwoman Cynthia had a deft touch with the whole incapacitating powers thing, the arsehole who zapped me in the garden was at least a hundred times worse. I feel as if I've been trampled by an angry bull elephant.

Then again, they weren't exactly gentle dragging my body to the parking lot and into the waiting vehicle. The discomfort to my hands and shoulders is nothing compared to the throb of my head, dull and insistent like the world's worst hangover magnified to the scale of a nuclear holocaust. My stomach contracts, and I dry-heave but hold back the sickly bile.

I should be glad I'm not dead. If I were dead, I'd feel no pain, right?

They've covered me in a blanket, so that casual observers won't look into the vehicle and see there's some guy being manhandled fuck knows where. What now? Samuel's dead. Marlise is being held hostage. House Thanatos have spirited Alex away for their own nefarious reasons. Bethan's likely dead. The Neteru know when I'll see any of them again. *If* I'll see them again.

Now's not the time to get bitter about how those who're close to me get ripped away again and again. Wishing for Leonora won't help either. I'm on my own. I can well imagine the old Ashton telling me to grow a pair in his usual brusque manner. Just like Bethan told me earlier.

Slowly, carefully, I quest out with my daimonic senses, with the barest whisper of my ability. The three Inkarna in the vehicle create a fog of power, their daimonic selves overlapping with the sense of a metaphysical iron tang. My *Kha* appears faded the way it's crumpled in the back of an SUV. The vehicle gleams in the nebulous otherwhere in which my daimonic senses perceive the world, perhaps charged by its magical occupants.

We're headed towards the centre of town, weaving in and out between the other cars on the road. Another vehicle tails us, and judging by the muted glow from those within, I'll be dealing with at least four initiates. One versus seven. Didn't stop me the last time.

But the last time I had my angry ghost to help me

and warn me.

Now it's just me.

They must've flushed me out and herded me to their initiates, and I'd been so focused on my pursuers that I hadn't thought to expect an ambush. Stupid.

I trickle back to my physical self with a sigh then blink open my eyes. The men are talking quietly among themselves. I could stall the car, and they'd be forced to get out, but then they'd set a guard. I'd still have my hands in cable ties, which would hamper my escape.

Or I could play their game for a short while, gauge their weak points, then make a break for it. Any serious attempt to drag in enough daimonic power would be noted, however, and if they're headed to town, it means they're not going to the airport, or taking the roads, like I'd have expected if they were trying to drag my sorry arse up to Joburg.

Or they're taking a break or...

Factions within factions.

Should I hear them out at the very least? They'd just want the same thing as all the others. Who'm I kidding?

This is all just a high-stakes game of chess. What are the chances of me breaking free right here? If I succeed in powering up to my full capacity, they'll be onto me before I can release. Sneaking about is one thing. Trying to break up the party, so to speak, is quite another. If I try something drastic while still in the car, the driver might cause an accident, and if I damage this *Kha*, I won't be able to help Marlise or Alex in this lifetime.

So I wait, keep my breath even, and try not to thrash about to relieve the ache from having my arms restrained. As things go, it takes nearly all my concentration not to cry out against the rising panic of being bound. We take the free movement of our arms and hands for granted. Honest. I clench my teeth and stifle any groans.

The men in the car talk in low voices about people I don't know and situations so out of context they might've well been speaking a foreign language. They're listening to Aerosmith, of all bands. The previous tenant of this body I now inhabit didn't like that band. Bunch of cock-rockers, Ashton would have called them. Sweet Amun, they dress like bloody TV FBI agents and listen to Aerosmith, for crying out loud!

Every once in a while, one of the guys in the back seat turns around and flicks up the blanket to check on me, and I lie very, very still, as slack as possible to give the impression that I'm out cold. If they haven't killed me yet it means I still have a chance.

Eventually, after what feels like an eternity, the SUV pulls up.

"Ian, you create the illusion. Donovan, you keep him tractable. I'll do any talking that needs to be done."

"Sure, right, you're the boss," another answers, but a shade of contempt underpins his tone.

No sense in playing dead. I stir as they open the back door. The blanket is whipped away, and I'm convinced the prick who grabs my jacket to haul me into a seated position snags my hair on purpose. I stumble onto my feet, blinking against the streetlights in the gloom.

"One false move, you bastard, and you'll be sorry." I'd estimate him—Donovan, if I'm to believe the earlier instructions—to be only just on the wrong side of forty, with a long face and a receding hairline, and his power thrums through him, the energy arcing between us.

I summon my best glare and stumble to my feet. The movement triggers sudden nausea, and hot-cold flushes which almost bring me to my knees if it weren't for the man holding me upright. His shoes are so shiny. Wouldn't it be a lark if I puked on them? I can't help but snigger before I'm jerked straight. My head thumps horribly.

"Hurry up," the one who would be boss says.

A low hum shimmers around us, so heavy the thrumming sets my teeth on edge. Whoever these guys are in the House Montu hierarchy, they're smooth. And experienced. And used to operating as a team. On top of that, it's clear they're accustomed to handling recalcitrant Inkarna.

Our little party makes its way into marble-clad hallway of a grand building with high ceilings. Where the hell am I? Some really top-notch hotel. Crystal chandeliers. Brass fittings gleam. Massive flower arrangements including a veritable fortune in lilies. Is it even the season for lilies right now? Incurious gazes of hotel staff slide over us as though we are of no concern. Well, that trick isn't new.

I reach out with my own powers to find out whether I can snag any stray echoes of memories in this place, any hints left behind by the Blessed Dead, only to have Donovan's grip tighten on my upper arm.

"I can feel that, bastard," he whispers into my ear. His words are accompanied by an electric jolt so hard and sharp I can only grunt, half-doubled over.

Donovan doesn't allow me to slow them down, and our small party hurries down a hallway to a narrow lobby where a waiting lift door slides open to swallow us.

"He try something?" Ian's bark of laughter is ugly.

I glare at the man. He's at least two heads shorter than me, his eyes narrow in a too-round face and his hair cut in an unfashionable step.

"Ooh, look, he's trying to give us the evil eye," Ian says.

"Cut the crap," the boss man says while he punches buttons. "Not where the muggles can hear you."

I resist the temptation to roll my eyes. Spare me the Harry Potter references. Marlise may have forced me to watch the films, but I refuse to apply the terms to what we do.

Donovan sniggers, but his grip on my arm remains tight. The lift doors swish shut, and we ascend. I'm going to have to wait for a moment when they're not so vigilant, and I don't really want to think too hard about the various methods they could employ to keep me under control. I'd prefer to avoid tranquilisers. They dull my edges for hours even after the effects have worn off.

The rooms we enter are so grand we can only be staying in a presidential suite. Large plate glass windows face Table Mountain, which gleams eerily in the light reflected from the city bowl. We've got a bird's eye view over the city centre—one that I've not seen for ages—but I'm not here to admire the eclectic architecture or the lush furnishings of the living area.

Donovan drags me upstairs to a small bedroom then bids me sit on the bed. Small mercies be praised, he reaches behind me to cut the cable ties. "I wouldn't do anything stupid, if I were you," he says almost conversationally, then gestures out the window. "Also, that's quite a drop, and I have my sincere doubts that you can levitate or that you are skilled in rock climbing. And, besides, Ian's got first shift. He's sitting right outside your door maintaining awareness. He'll enjoy fucking you up after what you did to his uncle."

My arms won't respond properly and flop uselessly into my lap when I move them.

"The slightest bit of draw of daimonic powers and you're going to hurt, okay?"

"His uncle?" Surely...

"Binneman."

"I'm sure they'll be reunited some day," I say. "I didn't destroy him. Permanently." I bare my teeth at him. Always good to remind them I have one advantage. Slender as it might be.

"Fuck you," he mutters and exits the room. Donovan leaves the door ajar. All the better to keep an eye on me.

I allow myself to fall back on the bed. The mattress is springy and firm, the linen white and fresh-smelling. I can almost forget everything but have to bite back curses once the feeling returns to my hands with vengeance. On top of this, my head is still throbbing. Ah, well, I'm sure the previous tenant got beaten up as bad. This *Kha* is resilient.

A sliding door opens in the next room. Now what?

"Must you smoke now?" the bossman yells. I still don't know his name.

"Fuck you," Donovan replies.

The mere mention of smoking elicits my own need to light up, but I tamp down on that desire. A cigarette now would just be...and besides, this is such a kak time to engage in this habit. My recent upheaval is a really lame excuse to get started on it again.

And yet I could lie here all night, and I know I won't go to sleep, not when these fools next door hold my life in their hands. Back in the car, no one noticed when I slipped from my body. That's an exhalation of power, not a sucking in, and I figure they weren't so stupid to not monitor me. Now while dear Ian might be sending out feelers sensitive to the drawing of power, there is a good chance he might not notice me slipping out. At the very least I can gain his measure.

I draw a few deep breaths then let go. At first it feels as though I'm bumping my head against a solid surface. I can't quite separate my consciousness from my physical awareness, but then I slide free.

In the shallow aethers this apartment is spare. Too clean, almost. Ian is a ghostly shape seated on an armchair with his arms folded in his lap, his head lolling. His signature is bolder than the others, suggesting he's aware on more than just the material plane. I watch him for a while, observe snaking tendrils that modulate octopus-like from his chest. But the only way I can explain my situation is that I'm on a different frequency to him. Nevertheless, I give those tentacles a wide berth.

Donovan leans on the railing. I'm half tempted to give him a shove, but that would require drawing attention to myself. I'm a whisper, not a storm right now. Bossman's busy scrolling through messages on his phone.

When Donovan speaks, his voice sounds tinny, like I'm hearing it through a thick curtain of water. "We should phone Joburg, let them know."

"Shut the fuck up," Bossman says.

"Philip," Donovan warns.

"Who's in charge here?" Philip says. "I thought Stefan made it perfectly clear you weren't the decision-maker here. Now shut the fuck up, I'm trying to check my messages."

Donovan paces a bit and draws on his cigarette. Oh, this one's agitated, all right. His signature is static around the edges, his entire being a buzz of animosity.

Presently, he comes inside and slides shut the door, rubbing at his arms before he flings himself down in the couch. "I don't like this. We should let them know we've caught the renegade."

Renegade, hah. I have a name, you twunt.

Ian remains perfectly still. He's in trance, and for all I know, the building could go up in flames around us, and he'd only notice if there were a surge in the daimonic levels. Wrong frequency, dude. I allow myself a small smirk.

Philip looks up from his screen, straight at Donovan. "We're going to NYC. And that's final. Going to the big cheese in the Big Apple is far more beneficial for us in the long run." His satisfaction at dropping this particular factual bombshell is oily to my daimonic senses. The bastard's been holding that information to himself awhile now, and he's evidently enjoying his colleague's discomfort.

Donovan sits up like something's bitten his arse. "That's crazy! If I'd known that—"

"You whine like an old woman. Go order us all something to eat. Even for that dumb cunt next door. No point in bringing him there half-dead."

The man does as he is ordered, gets up and makes his way to the phone. I judge it prudent then to slink back to my body. Not all is as it should be among these fiends, and perhaps I can force some of the situation to my advantage in person. Because one thing's for sure, I have absolutely no desire to be visiting New York City unless it's on my own terms. New York. No fucking way. This is going higher up than I ever imagined.

I have a pressing engagement in Joburg, to rescue Marlise, and if I play my cards right, I might already have an ally. Donovan just doesn't know it yet. Factions within factions. Philip's selling out to a higher bidder by the smell of things.

The room I'm in has decent-sized en-suite bathroom, and when no one comes to investigate my movements,

I go there to take a piss. My reflection tells me I look like shit—rough is an understatement—but I feel better after I wash my face then drink a few glasses of cold water. My stomach growls ominously, and the liquid only aggravates my hunger.

Nice of you to invite me to dinner, would be a choice way to start a conversation, and I snort at the ridiculousness of it. Then the amusement gives way to dread. I sink to my butt on the cold bathroom floor, my back to the sink's cabinet. Bethan. Siptah. Dead. Funny how the grief comes and goes in waves, pulsing to the surface. Just when I think I get a handle on things.

I haven't had long to process this, and the pain strikes me afresh. We didn't have enough time in our previous lifetime either. Am I deluding myself in hindsight? True love is a pile of bullshit sold to us in soppy romcoms and romance novels.

What about Marlise? She deserves better than me. I've behaved exactly like the previous owner of this *Kha* did. Gotta do right by her. Gotta save what I have, not hanker after might-have-beens.

"Stop it, stop it, stop it," I murmur to myself as I pull my hair back from my face, simply for the sake of having something familiar and solid. I'm paralysing myself.

First things first. Find the girl. Kill the bad guys. Then find the kid. Together, Marlise and I will stand a better chance than me acting on my own. If I'm so important to House Alba, they'll send another operative to find me, but I can't sit about beating myself up over my failures. So I rise, straighten my clothing, and do my best to make myself look as presentable as possible, considering the circumstances. I'm done with this dark teatime of the soul.

They're expecting me to keep to my room. If I take the initiative...

I'm about to knock on the door separating my bedroom from the lounge when the handle is depressed, and I step back in time to not get myself bashed by a surprised-looking Donovan.

"You're up." He narrows his dark eyes, and the whip-tight power he holds near the surface whispers against me.

"How about stating the obvious." I smirk and hold up my hands so he can see I don't mean any harm. "I was about to ask whether I can have a smoke. You have my word of honour that I won't try anything inordinately stupid like hurl myself off the balcony."

He stares at me for a few heartbeats, and I worry that he'll refuse me, but then he waves me through.

Philip watches us from beneath hooded eyes, and I get my first proper look at the fucker. He's an older man with a narrow face, crow's feet and faded red hair cut short at the sides. He purses his lips but says nothing as Donovan tails me to the balcony. The air outside is completely still but moist, and only thin wisps of cloud remain—not that the stars are bright or numerous here in the city centre, with all the light pollution.

I busy myself with the cigarette, horribly conscious of how I'm being scrutinised, and Donovan, perhaps in sympathy, or to have something to do himself, lights himself a cigarette as well.

We smoke in silence, with only the rumble of traffic below as accompaniment, and I grow gradually more uncomfortable. What the hell do I say to these people? And if I do hurl myself off the balcony? I peer down and the thought of killing this *Kha* before I've exhausted all other opportunities of escape doesn't appeal. No telling what the repercussions would be on the other side of the Black Gate.

A death curse exists, for severing the *Akh* from the *Kha*, and to let fly the souls back to Per Ankh unscathed, but it is one I've only ever heard mentioned, with the dim recollection that such behaviour is unworthy of Inkarna. What? So there's more honour in taking a knife to the gut like a samurai?

When I look down at the toy-like cars on Wale Street, I know for a fact I'm not ready to die again. For a moment I envision the rush of air, an eternity of falling encapsulated in a few seconds' plunge. Then the impact with the earth. Surely some must have mastered the art of moving, of bending the laws of physics to their command in order to defy gravity?

This is a tempting thought, but I'm not of a mind to try, so I turn to regard Donovan.

"Why're you guys taking me to New York City and not Joburg?" I pitch my words quietly, so only he can hear. Might as well cosy up to him since he's the best bet of the lot of them.

Donovan grimaces and brushes a lock of hair behind his ears, but it slips out again—not long enough to be tied up. He had it severely gelled back earlier. Now he just looks slightly scruffy—and more than just a little bit tired.

"I..." He palms his face then takes a drag of his cigarette. "I am not in a position to discuss this kind of stuff with you. You'll find out as we go along."

"You seem reasonable. You're just doing your job," I tell him quietly.

Donovan snorts softly. "Listen, Mr Kennedy. This is not open for negotiation. You're going to finish that smoke. You'll go back to your room. We'll bring you something to eat, and you'll go to sleep, you hear?

We'll have you under watch the whole night, so there'll be no escape attempts. Of *any* kind." He looks at me meaningfully. "Now I do believe we're both aware exactly how messy an...altercation can become. We don't want that."

I laugh. "No. You don't want that. I never asked for any of this. I don't particularly enjoy the fact that I've had your House meddling in my life." That old, nasty anger stirs, restless and ugly. "So cut me a little slack here if I at least want some answers of my own. I should be going to Joburg. Why New York City? What about my girlfriend? Where is she?"

Donovan swallows reflexively and casts a glance over his shoulder to where Philip sits, his gaze searing the air between us. Donovan and I would be roasted by now if the guy put a bit of daimonic oomph into that glare.

"I don't want to discuss this, okay? Now finish up that cigarette so we can go inside. I'm freezing my nuts off out here."

I flick a scrap of ash over into the abyss, and watch it float in tight circles as it descends. They aren't expecting me to be so compliant. The Neteru know I'd like nothing better than to smash my way out of this predicament, and I'm damned glad they've extended the courtesy of not leaving me hogtied in the bedroom. My edgy appearance is at odds with my behaviour. Good. Let it keep them off balance. Donovan's nervous. And this bunch isn't at all as close-knit as they'd like casual observers to believe.

"You know, I could make it easy for you to take me to Joburg," I murmur. "And I could make it excessively difficult to go anywhere else."

"Don't." Donovan's expression is pained, and he pulls open the sliding door as if to signal that this conversation is over.

I shrug, take one last drag of my cigarette then flick the butt over the edge into the void. The object spirals into nothingness, and while I watch it plummet, I stretch then follow the man back inside.

I'm almost halfway across the room before Philip speaks, his words filled with quiet menace. "You could tell us where you've hidden the stele."

I freeze in my tracks and let out a huff of breath. "No."

"We'll get the information, one way or another."

I give a soft snort then turn to face him. Next to me, Donovan straightens with an indrawn breath.

"You won't. I'm the only one who's got any idea where the stele is, and the very land offers a protective shroud."

"They'll hurt your woman." Philip's smile is predatory.

I keep my face a mask of arrogant unconcern. Just the way the old Ashton would've been callous when it came to the way he treated Marlise. Or the dozens of other women he trampled. "She was a good lay but hey, you know, a man's gotta move on." I give a slight shrug for emphasis, though inside I'm groaning in agony at the thought of this seemingly casual betrayal.

They've said nothing of Alex so far, and I'm going to keep my mouth shut about the boy in the vain hope that they're clueless about his existence. Unless, of course, Marlise has spilled that information. I get the feeling they'll use the kid as leverage the moment they sink their claws into him.

The man watches me, but he's equally adept at not showing any emotion. Or at least I hope I'm good at bluffing. Lizzie always was a shit liar. "There are ways for us to gain that information, Ashton, ways you do not wish to dwell upon. Consider your *Kha*, a form of exquisite commingling of sinew, bone, muscle and blood. Electricity. Water. Daimonic synthesis of *Akh*-hood made flesh. Your *Akh* is defined and finds expression in this form. There are ways we can manipulate the *Kha* so as to…" He smiles and pauses for what I'm assuming is dramatic effect. "Push the *Akh* to its limits, with physical death being delayed indefinitely, and perhaps twist the component parts in such a way that they might be…damaged. Irreparably."

A wave of cold slushes through me, and I swallow hard. The mere thought of physical violence to my person isn't appealing. The *Kha* is our living temple. While we might kill or injure each other in conflict, to wilfully damage—torture—each other is anathema. It is like spitting in the face of Khnum, the Divine Potter.

Words fail me, but before I can stumble over my tongue, Philip waves dismissively at us. "Donovan, put the young man to bed. He can stay in his room." He doesn't need to add, *Like a naughty boy*. The omission is abundantly clear.

All the while, Ian sits perfectly still, a statue. Hands palm down on knees, eyes closed and breaths even. He's younger than I thought. Dark eyebrows drawn in concentration. Thin wisps of fluff on his upper lip not quite ready for him to shave.

We mightn't even be in the room, but Ian's awareness of me brushes against my daimonic senses as I step over the threshold into my room, and Donovan closes—and locks—the door behind me without saying a thing.

"Fuck." That simple little word has no force to it, and I collapse on the bed.

Options. I need them, and I don't have any. I could try go out all daimonic guns blazing, so to speak. Find a way to incapacitate Ian or wait for the changing of the guard, for there's no way the guy can keep his vigil the entire night. I might get past Ian, but that would give Donovan and Philip a chance to charge up. There're still the four initiates to contend with. They'll happily use guns. By then hotel security would have the cops alerted, who'd be here in five minutes... Or I could pretend I'm Spider-Man. Yeah, right. Even some idiot trained in advanced parkour would be stumped by the sheer glass sides of the hotel's upper storeys.

A phone shrills inside—Beethoven's Ninth. A man swears. My drop into the shallow aethers happens without effort, like my *Akh* is eager to figure a way out of the mess. Ian's still oblivious to my more subtle frequency. I've found one weapon against these goons that they don't have—my daimonic stealth.

Philip speaks in clipped tones. "No. No. Not yet. I assure you nothing's gone wrong. We will catch the first flight to OR Tambo in the morning. A small complication, that's all, nothing to be concerned about. Didn't want to trouble you for the private plane. Right. Okay. Later then."

A nasty patch of silence hangs in the next room—expectant, with wicked barbs—and I stretch and uncoil from my physical body beneath Ian's net of awareness.

"That was HQ up in Jozi, wasn't it?" Donovan sounds tired.

Philip doesn't answer. Gradually the room swims into misty focus, and their shadowy, smoke-filled figures billow—mere ghosts in the room next to mine.

"We're sitting ducks here." Donovan's standing with his back against the wall separating the lounge from my room, a beer bottle clasped loosely in one hand, half-empty. My own *Kha*'s thirst and hunger nudges at the edge of my awareness.

"The longer we sit here, the more chance that the other Houses will move. Alba knows we're up to something. As do the Death-walkers. We simply don't have enough intel about who's out there." House Thanatos, for starters.

Philip scrubs at his hair—not that fingers will do a thing against the military cut. "You don't think I don't know that?"

"We need to at least do something to ward. Something more than our individual efforts." Donovan gestures loosely to Ian. "If I take the next shift, Ian's going to be out of it, which leaves you with our handful of initiates, and you know none of them are ready for full-scale conflict. I suggest a proper warding. Then we can all get a night's rest before we move out."

Philip sits very still, and, judging by the set of his shoulders, is filled with tension. "Fine, it'll give those idiots downstairs some practice. We'll host the working in the main lounge. Get them to prepare it."

Donovan's relief is like the loosening of strings. "I'll go get something for our guest. There's no point bringing him to headquarters half-starved." He begins to walk across to the staircase.

Philip raises his hand. "Don't tell those idiots downstairs that we're not going to Joburg, all right? Loose lips and all the rest. We'll be leaving them behind at the airport tomorrow in any case."

Donovan gives the slightest twitch of his head but doesn't disagree with Philip. Nearby, Ian's awareness stirs, almost brushes up against me, and I retreat—a hermit crab into its shell. In the time that I've been AWOL, my limbs have grown leaden, my body chilled, even though the room isn't cold. But I won't remain on the bed. That suggests too much passivity. Instead I seat myself in a gold brocade-covered armchair, a lush thing with a rococo finish detailed with little cherubs' heads on the armrests. Yuck. Even Lizzie would've found the chair distasteful. For once Ash and Lizzie are in agreement.

Better for them to see me seated, alert and watchful than sprawled like a slob.

A warding then? Before I have more time to consider the implications of this, the key turns in the lock, and Donovan brings me a plate of pizza slices, as well as a beer.

He places these items on the bedside table then backs out, watching me. I don't so much as twitch a muscle, keeping my eyes half-lidded. Only once the door is locked do I move, and fuck, I'm starved. One thing's for certain, I can't complain about the food in this hotel. The beer wouldn't hurt, but I wouldn't put it past these twunts to slip me a little something to make me sleep, because the beer bottle has been opened. As much as I want that damned beer.

I'll take my chances with the food rather. It's cold, but it helps line the hole in my belly. Better than my stomach digesting itself. I drink water from the tap in the bathroom.

After that it's a case of sneaking about without my *Kha*. My consciousness slips free with the merest whisper. Ian still sits at his post, small beads of sweat standing out on his brow the only indication that he's experiencing any sort of tension. His fingers twitch, once, twice, then lie still, his hands folded over each other. For a moment I'm reminded of one of those memento mori, the way the photographers would sometimes pose a corpse to give the semblance of life.

A prickling of potential leads me on, something that can best be described as a spiral galaxy turning on its axis, its arms throwing out sparkles of daimonic essence. What are they doing? I drift down the stairs, a leaf caught in an eddy, until I halt on the bottom step. Another reason why it's not advisable to go gadding about on astral jaunts. Reality is not as immutable as our physical selves would have us believe.

Six figures stand in a circle. They've moved the furniture to the sides of the lounge area, and they keep each other at arm's length, fingers almost touching with their palms facing inward. They waver as though viewed through a heat haze, displaying a curious duality. On one level I can see the men in suits, some stripped to their shirts with the sleeves rolled up. Here and there a few sport tattoos—mainly hieroglyphs and names enclosed in cartouches. Donovan stands to Philip's left. A large silver *udjat* eye pectoral hangs from a thick chain around his neck. His eyes are closed, like the others', and he follows the call-answer format led by Philip.

To my daimonic senses, this sextet is vastly different. In the aetheric, they appear as men in white robes, their features glowing, evened out and eerily similar. If I didn't know any better, I'd think them angelic, though that's what they'd like others to believe, that they have divine right to be arseholes. As of yet, they're unaware of my presence, but that doesn't mean I should get careless. I move on a slightly different frequency from them, and so long as I maintain that variance, they might not see more than a slight ripple, a kink of shadow to betray my passage. It's like running across the surface of a water droplet, this tension that I must maintain. One slip and I'll cause a ripple, and they'll detect me.

Philip's and Donovan's signatures, though ascended, are incomplete. Their *Akh*s have not been attained, but they are close. The not-knowing must lend them additional desperation. Until one has passed through The Black Gate, there's no way of telling whether any of the training has been worthwhile. Or indeed whether one has been lied to the entire time. No women either, or rather not many in House Montu, which means their work is essentially a dick-measuring contest. With this comes the realisation that all the Houses I've encountered thus far have been highly aggressive. If only I knew more. If only I could remember more of what transpired in Per Ankh.

And they're all after me, because I'm the one walking around with the recipe for the thermonuclear device that can turn the tide of a centuries-long cold war, so to speak. This eternal conflict of ours. Why is it that we can't all get along then? Surely that's not impossible? After all, we have an eternity to play with, infinite time. Infinite resources. This may merely be naïveté on my part. Not everyone has had the benefit of a gentle upbringing the way my previous incarnation had. Or went into the Tuat without the expectations of politics. Complications. Damn Richard for keeping Lizzie so sheltered.

All the while these six men chant, and their words vibrate from them in pulses of blue-green into the aethers. Libations have been poured onto the white marble floor—red wine spilt like blood and caked with a more than generous handful of salt. Smoke rises from these offerings to flow upward into a miasma of swirling essences. But not real smoke. Twists in the fabric of these realities superimposed on top of one another, with snatches of light leaking through in bars.

Should I make a run for it? Damn, these guys are so occupied with their business I doubt they'd notice an elephant stomping past. In a blink I shoot back upstairs to hover before Ian. The man's twisted to one side, his eyes twitching beneath the lids. He gapes, fishlike, and his eyes shoot open gazing into some point in the distance. Gone into deep trance then? No doubt an aftereffect of the business downstairs that's turning everything a touch weird.

I slip back a step, an almost involuntary action to a lower frequency because, damn, I am getting tired. Does he see me yet? I need to get past him, return to my body. I've tarried too long. Enough of a recon. It's time to work in the meatspace.

Ian twitches, blinks, and straightens, then shakes his head, as though to dispel a fog. A superimposed image tears itself away from him and grows solid as it rises to its feet with the buzz of a thousand winged insects. This aetheric double is garbed as one of the Egyptian pharaohs of old, in a linen kilt with a lapis lazuli- and carnelian-inlaid gold collar resting on a muscular chest. Very little of the somewhat dour mortal reflects in this idealised version.

Well, shit.

His skin glows with an inner fire, and Ian's smile is blinding. He is crowned with a uraeus serpent coiled about his brow, small tongues of fire flickering from its mouth. Oh shit. He's awake. Here, on my level. Like an idiot, I've misjudged the entire time. Grown sloppy.

"You think you're being sneaky?" He ogles my astral form while leering. "I'd not expected this."

"What?" My puzzlement and annoyance dawns into realisation. I might wear a man's body but my *Ren*, my true name, is that of a woman. And it stands to reason...

I raise a hand before me, consciously willing the idea of a hand, and the fingers are fine-boned—a woman's hand. Oh shit. How I remember Lizzie's hands from when she was young. I'd be amused by my oversight if it weren't for the fact that I've tripped into the very trap I'd been so careless about. Or maybe Ian's been toying with me all along, allowing me a surfeit of rope. This doesn't please me.

Ian's laughter rings hollowly in the aethers, as though we stand in a vast, empty room. He advances by a step. "A mere slip of a girl. Hiding in the body of an oaf. How is it that you can cause so much chaos?" He cocks his head, his gaze speculative.

My *Kha* is slumped over in a chair just on the other side of the door. So close but so far, because to reach it I need to get past Ian's double. And if I try to make a run for it, leaving my body behind, what then? Clearly, he has the upper hand here. I could easily spend the next century wandering about like an angry ghost. I take a step back.

A different frequency, perhaps? Deeper into the aethers? I might not be able to find my way back. Our state of being is but a fitful existence on a narrow band, and travelling without the *Kha* already stretches the limits. Horror stories exist of Inkarna who've fallen prey to body snatchers themselves. Like the original tenant of Bethan's earthly *Kha*. I must return to my *Kha*.

A quick feint to the left but the man's ready for me, his arms snaking out to catch me around the waist and lift me from my feet.

"Not so fast." He laughs while I struggle, my skin aflame at points of contact. He is fire to my ice.

We exist in the aethers, partially in the realm of the mind. What does this shape of me as a young girl tell me about myself? I don't like what I see in the mirror. This form is mutable, I can shift. Even as he drags me upright, I draw upon my inner reserves and will this fragile form to change. Ian wants to tangle with me? Well, I'll give him a shape that can tangle to its heart content.

My limbs fuse to my sides and my form elongates even as a drawn-out hiss escapes my mouth. A snake, yes. I spiral and wrap around the strong man whose grip loosens and slips as he tries to control my flow. Tighter and tighter I spiral and squeeze, muscles undulating as I press his arms to his chest and constricting.

Ian's form grows thinner and his face distorts as his mouth opens but no sound comes out. Then his shape attenuates, hardens, and branches out. What the hell? Dozens of thorns pierce me, and I'm impaled on a tree, each piercing burning with a cold fire that drains my essence. The more I struggle, the deeper these thorns bite, tearing, sapping my strength. But the game is not over yet. Not by a long shot.

I wriggle, then loosen my hold on my physical shape. Trees burn nicely, and I visualise my form melting into flames that eat at my opponent's fabric.

An unearthly scream rips from Ian as I consume him, the entire tree bursting into an inferno as I absorb his daimonic energy along with some undefined essence. My being flares, and his strength feeds mine before he can gather himself and retaliate.

When my vision clears, I'm once again viewing the lounge as though through a heat haze. Of Ian's double there's no sign, and my spirit form glows, its shape indistinct until I visualise a hand to raise before my face. Ian's *Kha* has slumped to the floor and lies there in a boneless heap. No telltale sparkles are visible, and he doesn't move, not even to breathe.

His souls are fled, their tether to this flesh snapped now that I've stolen his life force. I've killed him. These facts are plain, but I can't bring myself to feel any emotion. The atmosphere vibrates, with a tension from downstairs. Chanting. The voices well up in a chorus, the syllables latched together so that the words no longer make sense, stripped of their meaning to create a barrage of rhythms that ripple through the fabric of the aethers.

They're doing their warding, reaffirming their connection to Montu. Which means they're distracted, for now. But if they can finish, they'll seal me in here with them for the rest of the night. I have no doubt that Ian's death will make this a very uncomfortable next few hours. I need to move quickly before they figure out what I've done. I approach my *Kha*, but it's like wading through syrup. The tug of my flesh is strong, but not so that I can reach it.

Panic flutters through me as an inexorable tide drags me away, like water running down a plug hole in a bathtub. What the hell? Of course running about in the aethers when someone else is conducting a ritual of this magnitude isn't advisable, but I've never felt this much drag before. Such an overwhelming power sucking at me. They're warding. Which means they'll be blocking off this area, changing the pressure so to speak. Then again, I've never been dumped in this sort of predicament before. How the hell was I supposed to know?

The room stutters then the world of matter turns into a blur that orbits sickeningly. One moment I can see Table Mountain picked out in its customary spotlights. The next a light fitting bleeds into its reflection on the white marble floor. Around and around I spin, until all colours and all sense of dimension compress into a singularity, and I blink out of this existence.

For a moment their chanting follows me, something about the light of Ra burns from my eye as I step forth into...

Darkness. Utter darkness accompanied by the absence of all sensation. No sight. No sound. Nothing. No sense of time either. I'd whimper if I could, try to form the words, In the beginning…

Nothing.

Get a grip. This is not the sucking Sea of Nun with its grey limbo to wrap me in a fuzz of unknowing. I'm very much aware here and now, wherever that might be. I tune up and down the scale of resonation until the blackness turns pearlescent at the edges, morphs into static snow then snaps into sharp focus. A large, vaulted chamber. Pillars inscribed with hieroglyphs and painted with bright pigments create a vast forest stretching on either side as far as the eye can see. The ceiling, high above me is so distant, the writing upon it is a blur. But that's fine. I don't intend staying wherever the fuck here is long enough to be reading anything.

I'm evidently *somewhere*. At that I laugh and am gratified to hear my voice. The tone is a light alto. A woman's voice. That's all right. No surprises there. The hands I hold up before me are slender, fine boned. Thanks be to Amun not a little girl, then. I can deal with that. Here I'm Nefretkheperi. Not Ash. Not Lizzie. I'm good. This will work, wherever the hell this is. This is the *I* from Per Ankh.

I walk, but this scene creates an optical illusion, the pillars marching ahead and those small rectangles of blue sky never getting any closer. This place is a clever trap, designed to keep those captured within it moving ahead indefinitely. Infinity.

I stop, lean against the nearest pillar. The stone is reassuringly solid against my arm. The textures of the carvings press into my skin. Too real. Things here shouldn't feel so definite if this is a permutation of one of the realms of the mind.

What was Per Ankh like? I snatch at memories of the afterlife, but they remain skittish. Opal walls shimmering with the light of nebulae. Ageless faces lifted to a starry void. Dreamlike reality.

Not this. I've heard it said that if I'm dreaming, I should mindfully study my hand, and in that way take control of the scenario, break away from passive dreaming to a lucid experience. I peer at my hand once more, take note of the small details such as the whorls of my fingerprint. Too much detail. Not a dream.

I taste dust, and the slightest breeze wafts through this crazy hypostyle hall of madness. The air is warm and raises pinpricks of gooseflesh. I want to cry. Smooth planes of my cheeks beneath my palms. No stubble. Warm, elastic skin. Delicate cheekbones. Longer lashes. Hair cut in a bob. Damn, this is so frustrating. If only I had a mirror. I want to know what I look like, to gain a solid appreciation of my identity. Who am I really? That timid widow? That oaf who cheated on his girlfriend?

With a sob I sink to my haunches, my back to the stone and my head cradled on my arms. The sheer cotton shift I'm wearing barely reaches my knees. Fine, translucent hairs on my legs, my arms. The tears won't come, however, but my chest is tight, and it's with great effort that I suck in each breath. In the distance, I can hear their chanting—those six members of House Montu who've opened that portal to inadvertently trap me thus.

I can't stay here. Some way to escape must exist. Surely.

A movement in the corner of my eye has me lift my head. A vaguely humanoid shape walks backward and forward diagonally to my right. The same set of movements are repeated, over and over again. Two steps. Pause. The figure turns around and takes five paces across my field of vision, pauses, then returns to the initial position.

Mesmerised, I watch. The figure is filmy, indistinct, but present. As I watch, a bunch of others filter in and out of view. I rise to my feet with a startled oath as the realisation grows. This location is a halfway house of sorts that sucks in spiritual residue—and holds it. Possibly for eternity.

A very real tremor of fear has me spin about. I'll be stuck here for goodness knows how long. Eventually my body back in the hotel will starve and die, a mysterious sleeper who'll never awaken. And I'll remain trapped in limbo, almost worse than the primordial chaos that is the Sea of Nun. At least there, in Nun, I'd lose all consciousness. Here I'm bounded by the limitations placed on me by aeons of Inkarna who've reinforced this particular vision to the point where it is near unassailable. Aware. Forever.

These poor fools must've slipped into madness by now.

I peer at my fellows, but they remain smoky shades, impossible to define. Some appear to walk on a treadmill, trudging eternally towards a freedom they can only wish for. I'm not like them, though it can be argued that I'm an idiot that I put myself in this position in the first place with my snooping around.

"This is bullshit," I say as I close my eyes. I draw in a deep breath and tug, feeling at first the structured resistance, a latticework of power initially rigid to my intrusion.

House Montu expects me to be blinded by the illusion, to willingly go along with the pretence. I might not be physically stronger than my enemy, but I'm small and flexible. Like a needle pulling through fabric, I slide, feel the individual threads try to constrain me while I push myself to an area where there's less pressure.

A current snatches me up, and I dare to open my eyes, only to find myself dragged along through a vortex of blues and greens that twist towards a brighter point. A small voice at the back of my mind wails on and on about how the hell I'm ever going to find my way back. There's no point in worrying at this stage.

The light grows brighter and brighter. Have I somehow died again? Am I about to pass through the Black Gate?

The light explodes, and I fall, only to land on my hands and knees upon a sandy floor in a large, domed chamber. The area appears as though a giant has taken an enormous ice cream scoop and bitten out a perfect hemisphere from the palest marble. No definite light source exists yet the very stone gleams with an ivory glow.

The sand is warm and runs through my fingers as a fine powder. Tiny glints blink back at me as the grains settle. Like miniscule diamonds. I could play like this for hours, but then I rise to my feet and dust off my hands against my shift. Now's not the time for games. Where the hell am I now?

A trapezohedral onyx stone plinth stands in the midst of this chamber, upon it a khopesh sword. The sickle-blade gleams with the same undefined luminosity as the stone and emits the faintest of hums. I shouldn't be here, should I? This must be an auxiliary ritual space that exists to complement House Montu's practice. I don't need glaring neon-lit signs to tell me that.

I know the theory behind this well enough. House Adamastor never possessed the combined daimonic strength to create its own parallel realms with any true permanence. This chamber would be a shared space, common grounds but dedicated for House Montu's Inkarna to meet to practise, though their physical *Kha*s might be geographically separated. And I'm an infernal trespasser.

The khopesh lures me. I really should look for a way to get the hell out of here rather than indulge my curiosity, but hey, I wouldn't have signed up for this Inkarna business in the first place if it weren't for my damnable curiosity. Damn you, Siptah, for bringing me into the fold.

About the length of my arm, the weapon gleams dully. Black titanium? Does it even matter? Then again, this could be glass in this place for all the laws of logic that would apply. Even as I wonder how heavy the damn thing is, I stretch out my hand so I can heft the blade. The grip is cool to the touch, and the edge makes the air sing.

I've never held a sword before. Even for ritual purposes. We always used a staff. Marlise would've made lightsabre noises as she whooshed the thing through the air. I smile.

The severity of my situation comes crashing down again. Here I am, in the midst of House Montu's daimonic territory, and I'm cooking up trite scenarios. Somewhere, in the material world, my *Kha* is languishing while my *Akh* is stranded. I need to get my arse back. I don't want to consider the fate of my *Akh* if its constituent parts are scattered. There's no way I'd be able to pass through the Black Gate unscathed if bits of me are missing.

I move to put the khopesh down but then pause. What if I hold onto this obviously ceremonial weapon? This would be an ultimate way to cock a snook at House Montu, akin to scrawling I was here in faeces on their metaphorical bathroom wall.

Right.

But then of course, this very weapon is quite clearly an object of great value. Like the ankh symbol so beloved of ancient Egypt. An item only has so much value as one places on it. What were the chances of me blundering into their holiest of holies? Slim, perhaps. I'm giving them a big fat metaphorical middle finger by taking their toys. Or maybe I'm nicking a trifle. Does it matter?

Khopesh in hand, I make my way to the perimeter. The stone is smooth beneath the fingers I trail idly as I walk the perimeter, my feet sinking into the soft sand. Great. Now what? I'm a bug trapped beneath a cake dome, and I can spend an eternity wandering circles until someone cottons on to my presence. Also, I've got no way of figuring out exactly how much time is passing here. Around and around I go.

Bloody hell. How did I get in? There must be a way out. Some obvious trick I'm overlooking, just as I shoved my way out of the illusion of the vast pillared hallway filled with trapped ghosts.

I take a deep breath and turn to face the stone. The curve is gentle, rising to its apex in the centre of the room, about ten metres above; my skin rasps slightly against the surface, tiny crystals glittering. I close my eyes and imagine pushing through this barrier with the silent hiss of my daimonic powers. Nothing. The rock doesn't yield, remains deceptively solid.

"Fuck!" My voice echoes back at me, the single syllable refracting in the space.

Small whispers of panic rise from my belly and tangle with my spine. I need to get out of here. With a yell I swing with the khopesh. I don't fucking care if I shatter the blade on the stone. Serves House Montu right for having such a stupid construction anyway.

Much to my surprise, the sword sinks into wall as though the rock were no more than butter. I stare stupidly at the weapon and the tear it's made.

"Okay," I whisper then continue with the downward motion. The action is as simple as slicing sticky Styrofoam, and I cut a doorway. Bright light bleeds round the edges, and once I'm done, I shove hard with my shoulder. My makeshift doorway collapses outward, and I stumble out into what feels like a furnace.

Once I'm done squinting back the brightness, I'm struggling ankle-deep through scorching sand where a trio of dunes several storeys high meets. The heat haze makes the air shimmer, and the sun, at its zenith, blazes down, scorching my exposed skin.

When I turn, the doorway's gone, and I take a few drunken steps before I lose my balance and fall. Hot air bakes my lungs, and I gasp like someone who's drowning until the pain from the searing sand registers, and I lurch to my feet again.

Like a fool, I still cling to the khopesh, and start climbing the nearest dune. Each step has me slide back almost as far as I've tried to ascend. Slippery. Impossible to get a grip of. Fortunately, the sand just beneath the surface is a little cooler. Maybe if I can get to the top, I'll be able to see where I am, in whichever nightmare sea of rusty sand I've been mired. Thanks to all my sliding progress, my legs are aflame, the skin on my feet most likely blistering.

"Got...to get...the...top," I say for no one's benefit but my own.

When I halt to glance over my shoulder, I'm disheartened to see how little progress I've made. My tongue feels swollen, the inside of my mouth parched. By Set's testicles, the heat. I have died, and I am in Hell. Really. The Sea of Nun and its primordial chaotic soup be damned. I'm going to spend the rest of eternity here, slowly roasting beneath a naked, unforgiving sun.

But the most peculiar aspect of my attempt at summiting this wave of sand is the sound my progress makes, a baritone groan with each step. Very peculiar. Eerie even, making the small hairs on my nape prickle. The sound falls into a rhythm every time I sink a foot into the ground. Some bizarre ritual chanting. Like I can almost discern words at the edge of my hearing. Or maybe I'm becoming delirious.

What happens if my *Akh* withers here? Where exactly is this place? Or am I trapped in my own mind? My entire existence narrows to the fine point that I need to reach the top of this mountain of sand even as the inferno from above threatens to suck all the moisture from my body.

The khopesh's metal grows too warm in my grasp, and I'm tempted to cast it away, but some dim, stubborn whim forces me to hold onto the thing. Each step requires effort, and I swing my arms to help me overcome inertia and the slow slide that promises a descent to my starting point.

Those damned voices. Ahhh... Ahhh... Ahhh... the sand cries with each step, the sound reducing to a dusty sigh even as I drag up the next step. People should climb dunes instead of going to the gym. Good cardiovascular workout. But oh, sweet Amun, I'd kill for water right now. My chest is on fire, dark spots swim before my eyes, and the fucking summit isn't any closer.

I try to swear, but the expletive gets stuck in my throat, and the only sound I make is a raw whimper. Eventually I sink to my knees in the scalding sand and slide a few metres backward. My lids slip shut and I wonder what would happen if I collapsed now. Would a soft avalanche bury me, given enough time? Would anyone ever find my desiccated corpse? Can an *Akh* have a corpse at all? Will it break up into *Ba* and *Ka* and shrivel?

But I can't give up. I need to get back to the material world. Marlise is out there somewhere, a prisoner of House Montu, and I have a responsibility towards her. I'm the one to blame for having dragged her halfway across southern Africa to such an unremarkable little town, far, far away from all that is familiar to her.

Alex. The damned little sprog. My kid.

Here, removed from the realities of being Ashton Kennedy, arsehole deluxe, I'm cut off from the guilt, and can behold the secret wonder. I'm a parent. Despite all the twisted shit in the world, I somehow share a bond of love with someone. A being who exists because of me. No matter the crap that's been happening of late, I can't renege on that bond.

With a gasp I throw myself back onto my feet. For an awful moment I'm afraid I'll overbalance and tumble down to my starting point but regain my balance and continue the ascent. The sand groans with each step, but I push on. I close my eyes and am conscious only of the scorching sun and how my lungs work like bellows, to suck in air.

A journey in the realms of the aethers should not feel so real, so solid, but for now my entire experience is summed up in this challenge.

I let loose a jubilant shout once I crest the dune. The muscles in my legs are thin strips of wire, and a terrible pain grinds in my side—the mother of all stitches—but I'm here at the top. A sea of sand rippling towards the horizon all round, as far as the eye can see. Beautiful yet it fills me with crushing despair.

"No." The enormity of this vista swallows that one word. What now? I can walk forever in any direction and still not escape.

This is yet another hypostyle hall.

Deep within my heart that old anger stirs. What gives House Montu the right to mess with my life? I didn't ask for this. The pressure builds in my belly and forces its way up my throat. "No!" I channel that anger, grab that khopesh in both hands and thrust down with the blade.

I fall to my knees, my chest heaving as I breathe, still holding the sword embedded to its hilt in the sand. The metal grows warm, brighter. Then it becomes transparent and begins to glow. A sudden gust of wind sweeps up grains of sand into my mouth, and a low groaning begins as the particles sift into the air. Sandstorm.

From isolated chants, the sound grows and thrums, with two distinct tones at counterpoint to each other until my collarbone buzzes in sympathy to the unearthly song of the sand. The volume increases as the wind picks up, the sky dimming with its burden.

The khopesh glares into brightness then, with a soft implosion, draws itself into my flesh. Fire sears its way up the tendons of my arms to lodge, gleaming between my breasts. The heat spreads through my chest and ignites serpentine coils that twist in my belly and explodes out of my throat in a scream.

A column of light impales me, a falcon-shriek of agony blazing through the core of my being. I am a cinder adrift in a sea of ash as all existence sifts to nothingness.

I am the raging one who prevails over the serpent Apep.

I am the strength of Ra, and my enemies are crushed beneath my feet.

I am he who lends dominion to…

The words fade, and the sun goes out. My world becomes moist and heavy and dark.

☥

My lungs spasm, and I inhale a shuddering breath that sticks in my throat. Then I'm convulsed in a fit of coughing that dumps me onto the tiled floor of the bedroom. In the hotel. In the material realm. My flesh is alien, each movement unfamiliar. Small blue-green motes sparkle about my hands, but the visual disturbance vanishes after I blink a few times. My pulse is a frantic snare drum.

Where? What the hell? I'm fucking freezing, and I shiver as though I'm about to have a seizure. My body feels as though it swarms with a multitude of electrical charges, my chest and belly as though I've swallowed a small sun—verging on exquisite agony. Something tickles the skin beneath my nose, and I swipe at my face only to reveal a smear of blood. Great. A nosebleed. It's been ages since I've had one of those, though the ache in my body is so polarised I'm not sure how my head feels.

The room is unfamiliar. High ceilings with fancy pseudo-Victorian styled mouldings. A watercolour painting of Table Mountain. My legs are numb, and when I try to stand, I collapse. Warm tiles. Underfloor heating.

The hotel room. The Taj, of course. The room tilts, my stomach spasms, and I retch weakly. My semi-digested meal makes a bid for re-emergence, but I swallow it back down. My extremities tingle, and I half-drag myself onto the bed while I recover a measure of physical coordination.

Nauseating flashbacks remind me of the hall of pillars, the subterranean chamber and the desert. The disparity between the body of my blessed *Akh* and the *Kha* I inhabit are so striking I'm almost revolted by the obviously masculine hands and the snippets of tattoos sticking out beyond the sleeve of my jacket. What the hell happened? Visions of that khopesh sliding into me stutter behind my closed lids.

That dreadful pressure in my chest spreads through the rest of my body with a feverish glow. I need to get out of this place. Distantly, I can still hear my captors' chanting, and I'm reminded that a corpse is sprawled on the floor just outside the door to my bedroom. A corpse I made, that will no doubt cause me a whole world more trouble if I don't act soon.

Urgency brings me to my feet, and I stumble to the door. Locked, of course, but the mechanism yields to me with absolutely no trouble. I barely have to push. How come it's so simple? I don't recall my daimonic powers ever coming this easy? I hold a shaking hand before my face. The tiny motes are frantic, twisting like gnats between my fingers before I will my eyesight more fully into the realm of matter. I don't need daimonic double vision here.

From the stink of it, Ian's corpse has released its bowels, and I gulp back a reflexive need to gag as I pass the pitiful remains. People look so small in death, their flesh shrunken without that which animates it. I pause before I take the stairs. They're in full chant in the big room below, and I recognise the last few stanzas of the Hymn to Atum, a standard closing for most of our ritual work, no matter what the House, or so I've been told.

But with all the daimonic energy coiling about, and with my doorkeeper dead, I doubt anyone's about to pick up a slight warp in the overall effect, a bubble of oil to their water slipping past their awareness. I drag on the illusion of invisibility with an indrawn breath. So easy and barely a flicker in my attention. It's never been this easy. I've changed, and I'm not quite sure how. There's no time to figure out why.

Without a backward glance I descend to the hallway. Unless these dumb twunts are actively looking for me, they'll not see me. Their gazes will slide elsewhere should they turn in my direction. At least I hope that's the case. I unlock the front door and step into the plush, carpeted corridor. A 'do not disturb' sign hangs on the door and, oddly, I cannot hear their chanting through the door. Some sort of daimonic sound barrier? I shrug. I couldn't care less. I need to get the fuck out of here, preferably before these idiots finish their warding ritual and make the unfortunate discovery of their buddy's untimely demise.

The Opener of the Way must be smiling on me, because the lift door yawns a half-second after I press the button. I could take the stairs, but I prefer to err on the side of speed. The lights are dim in the lobby, and two night managers chat quietly behind the desk, oblivious as I pass them. They only look up when the door opens seemingly of its own accord. I resist the urge to smile and wave.

I suppose I'd still show up in the CCTV footage. Best not to tempt fate too much by being cocky.

But I'm outside. Unfuckingbelievable. The cold is marrow-deep and sears my lungs. I dig my hands deep into my pockets and stride away with purpose. Friday night in the Mother City. I'm back home, some small part of me thrills. Must be past midnight now, but the cloud cover's torn ragged to reveal dark patches blinking with stars. A chill wind teases me, but it's not wholly unpleasant. Yet. I can still appreciate the taste of freedom.

How long before they pick up my trail and try to drag me back into their clutches?

I take a right into St George's Mall, the paved, pedestrianised street that runs all the way down to the Foreshore. Most of the shopfronts here are closed for the night. No nightclubs or restaurants open, and the only folks I see are, like me, hurrying to their destinations with purpose. For a moment I experience that weird dichotomy of having known this street in the days when it wasn't paved with redbrick, and of walking where cars would roar along. The trees are skeletal hands grasping the sky, and a large rat skitters from a trunk the same shade as old bone. The creature pauses to glare at me before it gives a sharp squeak and hustles into the shadows.

A gaggle of teens crosses my path. They don't see me and have eyes only for each other's smiles. They're eighteen, if that. Not much younger than me, but of a sudden this twenty-two-year-old body feels positively ancient. One of them clutches a smartphone. He's extolling the virtues of the electronic rubbish the tiny speaker is spewing, tinny beats and synthesised sounds. They laugh.

On a whim, I tail them, since they're headed up Shortmarket Street anyway, and my feet are following a route this *Kha* of mine knows all too well, to The Event Horizon. Too predictable, but right now any touchstone of familiarity seems better than remaining out in the cold and the dark.

Just over a year ago, Ashton Kennedy and his girlfriend, Marlise, dropped off the face the planet so far as all the regulars at this den of iniquity were concerned. I can hardly imagine the owner, Gavin, or even my erstwhile manager, Lisa, taking kindly to my prodigal return. What sort of rumours must be circulating? Perhaps a story that we'd been running guns over the Congolese border. Or maybe I'd hanged myself in prison after Marlise got raped by the wardens. Fuck knows. This'd be funny if it weren't for the fact that I've heard stories like that before, relating to others in the scene who'd pulled a vanishing act. People like to talk over their beers and spliff.

Maybe that's why I keep myself cloaked as I approach the building on the corner of Shortmarket and Long, and I linger awhile on the pavement opposite to watch the entrance. Time enough to smoke a cigarette and decide what my next move should be. Memories of Ashton's past bleed back through our connection. He really loved being here at The Event Horizon. To him it was a palace where he was lord. Home. To my eyes it's tired, the neon lettering flickering and thick dust coating the once-bright purple of the windowsills.

By now my captors must have made their grim discovery. They'll rightfully blame me for Ian's death. They'll be looking for me, and they'll expect me to try hightail it the fuck out of the city, which means they'll mobilise the cops, set up roadblocks, and keep tabs on the airport, buses, long-distance taxis, and trains. They saw for themselves how desperate I was.

Would these fuckers know enough about my past to come knocking at The Event Horizon? Would they even expect me to be stupid enough to return and try to hide in plain sight?

What Gavin and the rest are unaware of can't hurt them, and I have intimate knowledge of this building, enough to know of the unused offices on the second floor that Gavin has purposed mostly for storage. His doors and locks will present me with no problems, and no one will be the wiser. Tomorrow, once things are calm, I'll have had some rest and formulate a better idea of how the hell I'm going to get to Joburg, save Marlise, and figure out how to go about rescuing Alex from House Thanatos's clutches. All in a day's work, really. I suppress a hysterical snigger.

One last drag of my cigarette, my invisibility still cloaked about me, I grind the butt beneath my boot heel. Viking, the aptly named blond bouncer, doesn't even glance in my direction when I shoulder past him and pad up the stairs.

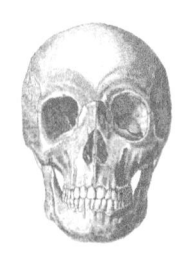

CHAPTER FIVE
You're Lost, Little Girl

ONCE I'M on the second floor, the groaning beat of the music from downstairs is muted to a dull thump that rattles the sash windows in their frames. My view overlooks the roofscape and the back of the big art deco hotel that faces Greenmarket Square—the side the tourists don't see, with clumps of grass clotting the gutters and sleeping pigeons huddled on the ledges.

A threadbare carpet muffles my footsteps as I make my way down the passage to one of the smaller offices. Without meaning to, I tap into a memory belonging to the Blessed Dead, and for a moment a vision of the past is superimposed over mine.

The woman pauses to look over her shoulder. A small string of freshwater pearls gleams on the cream leather of her fitted coat. Her lips are as scarlet as sin, her eyes heavily made up. Spanish eyes. Then she unlocks the door to step into a room beyond. A musky jasmine scent escapes accompanied by the faint strains of psychedelic rock.

This place used to be a brothel. Why am I not surprised? I'm left blinking in the dark passage, momentarily disquieted and weighed down by delicious sorrow. Nostalgia. So many lives passed in the blink of an eye while it's my doom to live and die and be reborn. Not that I'm complaining too much to number among the quick, mind you. If I could sort out this nonsense with Montu, then life would be much sweeter.

Yet, what if I turn the words encoded on the *Book of Ammit* on myself? Is that even possible? I shiver at the implications. To simply not be at all? I can't follow through with something that would be the ultimate in selfish acts. To leave all these loose threads behind me. Oh, hell no. I'm cursed with terminal curiosity.

I choose the second-last office before the door that leads down to the back staircase and the service entrance—a good escape route, should the proverbial excrement hit the fan. Judging by the heavy padlock on my side, the staff don't come up here from the back, so that's fine with me. Less chance of discovery.

The office door's lock clicks at the slightest daimonic nudge, and I step inside a small room looking out over Long Street. I daren't risk flipping on the light, but enough illumination from the streetlights outside reveals stacks of cardboard boxes—the type used to file documents. There's that, as well as what appears to be a pile of old curtains folded neatly beneath a rickety steel-legged table with a scuffed linoleum top. An office chair missing two of its casters leans against the wall. Behind me, tacked to the door, is a poster of a naked woman, reclining suggestively on a red couch. She fingers herself while brushing her lips into the receiver of a hot pink telephone. Her poodle perm hair suggests this image dates back to the 1980s.

A wave of exhaustion has me slump against the door. I could sleep wrapped in those curtains, though I shudder to think how dusty they are, and how long they've been forgotten in this depressing little room. Dusty or cold? It's my choice, and I opt for dusty, so I drag myself back onto my feet so that I can lock the door from the inside then shake out the curtains.

The fabric is fuzzy, synthetic wool—the kind I'd expect in someone's home rather than discarded in an old office. But such is the nature of The Event Horizon. People and things wash up here with nowhere else left to go. I create a half-decent makeshift bed, grateful that I'm not freezing my arse off waiting at the train station, or trying to keep myself warm by walking until sunrise.

Though I'm physically exhausted, sleep won't come. Over and over again I replay the crazy series of events that uprooted me and dumped me here. All of it seems too unreal, like I'll blink and find myself back in our little cottage in Nieu Bethesda. I'll take Alex's constant screaming any time over this madness of having to run while I keep looking over my shoulder.

Lay on the self-pity, will you?

Somewhere between my worries and trying to filter out the ever-present drone from downstairs, which is occasionally punctuated by shouts, I slip into a fitful half-doze.

☥

The sky is so dark it might almost be carved from lapis lazuli. When I look up, I fancy that I see the slightest sprinkling of stars, though the sun is halfway to its zenith. How peculiar. *Look at your hands. You're dreaming. Look at your hands.*

I raise a fine-boned hand so that I can examine the fingers. A woman's hand. I really am dreaming. My bare feet sink into warm white sand belonging to a dune field that stretches into infinity, but I turn towards the direction where I can see the distant profile of what I assume to be a pyramid. And yes, this is a dream, because if I really were standing in the desert, I'd feel the heat. I don't feel hot or cold. Nor do I feel the stir of air. I'm here, but I'm not here.

The piercing shriek of a falcon has me spin in a half circle, and I shade my eyes to catch a glimpse of the raptor. At first I am dazzled by the sun, but then I lock onto the bird, its wings angled sharply as it stoops, growing larger, and more defined by the second as it approaches me.

The gesture seems to me the most natural—I hold out my left hand for the falcon as it flares its wings, talons outstretched as it lands on my offered wrist. The pain as the claws dig in is real, however, and I give a small shriek at the blood that flows.

A peregrine falcon. How I know this, I'm not sure, but I'm mesmerised by the bird's topaz stare as it seems to look right into me. The bird opens its beak and shrieks, its wings arched over its back as it pins me with its mad glare. Its eyes are tiny suns that burn right through me.

☥

I jerk into a seated position with a strangled yelp, my left arm on fire and the sleeve of my jacket wet. Enough light from the streetlights outside filters in to reveal that the liquid trickling down my wrist is blood. I hiss and jerk off the jacket so that I can pull up the sleeve. Thin slits in my skin leak blood, and that dreadful dream involving the bird goes into instant replay.

What the hell? Downstairs the party still groans on, but I'm buggered if I'm going to get any more sleep. My chest is tight, and my pulse thunders. Outside sirens paint the air blue as cop cars scream up Long Street. But they don't slow down or stop, and I sag a little in the realisation. No one knows I'm here. Yet.

Then again, holing up here is stupid. The gesture is futile, a last-ditch attempt to hold onto the past. Yet out there, on the streets, they'll be looking for me. I've nowhere to run, nowhere to turn. No allies. No resources but my own wits, and see where that's gotten me.

The wounds on my arm weep more blood, and I clutch the sleeve tighter as I pinch shut my eyes. Stupid dream. The ache of the wound drags right into my bone marrow.

Remaining here feeling sorry for myself means my enemies will eventually discover my location, and I'll be trapped. A not-so-wily fox brought to bay. What can I do to get one step ahead of House Montu?

One plus point: I'm free. For now. I grimace at the thought. The 'for now' is the big fat disclaimer on that fact. Let's try to keep it that way, hey?

Some of Gavin's friends run a clothing shop on the first floor. I can raid that for clean gear. Gavin's safe won't present much difficulty, either. He always has a ridiculous amount of cash on hand—the kind of money he won't be in a position to bitch about should a particular amount go missing.

All I need to do is wait for the dead hour before dawn to help myself to what I need, then steal forth. Let's not fall back on clichéd comparisons about candy and babies, shall we? I try not to smirk, but hiss instead at the pain in my arm, which goes beyond the flesh wound. Here, in the murky orange light I'm all the more aware of the hundreds of wriggling sparks of power that flash like blue-green tadpoles around my hands and forearms. That dream. It was more than just a dream, wasn't it? My stomach twists at the thought. Falcons are a symbol of House Montu. Does that mean they've found me?

You should know better, my logical self states. When dreams bleed through to the world of matter... I'm too tired to feel fear. There comes a point when you simply can't take on a bigger portion of terror.

Dim memories belonging to the previous tenant of my body recall acid trips, of the ways light would split into its constituents of red, blue, and green at the edges. This is exactly the effect I garner when I move my hands slowly before my face. What the hell?

Heat flares in my chest, over my heart. I can no longer write this off as another batch of adrenaline-induced sensation. My body feels as though it's over full; my skin is too tight, and I might somehow spill over in an explosion of power.

That nagging sense of dismay crawls through me again. Something's not entirely right. Actually, this entire situation's fucking wrong. It's been wrong since I fell into House Montu's warped little playground. I groan and drag a hand through my hair, most of which has come loose from its band. I'm a fucking mess. Who'm I kidding? And knowing my luck, I'm liable to disintegrate catastrophically and leave a bloody fucking mess all over the walls.

Then I have to laugh, picturing a self-combusting Inkarna. Now that's impossible. I'm sure it's impossible. It must be. Please, dear Amun, let that be the case. But the gaping eye sockets of some of my victims return to me, their grey matter liquefied and oozing out of eyes, ears, and noses. What's stopping the entire body from going that way off its own bat?

"Fuck it!"

I wish I knew what the time is. The ringing in my ears is the loudest sound apart from the lone cars that rumble up Long Street. Enough time has passed during this hallucinogenic threnody that the club's closed downstairs, and if there're any people they'll be in Gavin's office by now, counting the night's takings.

Money. I need cash and a game plan.

"Stop being fucking pathetic and grow a pair," I mutter to myself. That's something the old Ashton would've told me. Sweet Amun, I miss the bastard, even if there were times I'd have happily obliterated him. I hope he's happy and safe, if that is him in Alex's *Kha*.

My entire body aches but I can't hide here indefinitely and wait for House Montu to find me. I'm reminded of the leopards the farmers used to shoot. The men used to brag to Lizzie's father over their glasses of sherry. The big cats would always follow the same pathway, even if they'd taken over another feline's territory. This made it easy to set traps for them.

I'm doing exactly that—returning to the path of least resistance. The best course of action would be to behave how they don't expect me to. A fact: they can be fairly certain my next move will be to make my way up to Jozi to find Marlise. I might not know exactly where she is, but, given a little time or luck, I can find her. We have a bond. If I'm closer to her, I can lean on that connection and find her. It's just going to take a little time, that's all.

The roads won't be an option, and neither the

airports. The most anonymous—and uncomfortable—method will be to take the train. If I book a sleeper carriage, I can barricade myself in a particular cabin. They won't expect me to have the resources to do this, and I can garner a degree of anonymity. No roadblocks, either. Yes.

Or I could try for that portal that ended Bethan, and lay the entire problem at the feet of House Alba, who won't know who I am.

"No," I murmur, and shake my head.

A wave of dizziness assails me as I make my way to the door, and I have to pause and lean my aching forehead against the splintery wood. My world spins and drifts as though I've drunk too much wine, and I gingerly feel at the back of my head to find out whether I've injured myself without being aware of it. Nothing.

I gulp back at the nausea, then unlock the door with the barest whisper of my powers. The tiny motes wriggle at my fingers, little gnats of power, and I stare at my hand, mesmerised. These little telltale signs should not be so visible. What in the hell happened to me back in the aethers? Things were as normal as they could be before I went under. And now? I wouldn't be surprised if mere mortals see me glowing in the dark.

A light gleams from the stairwell as I make my way there. Shivers wrack my body, and a cold, slimy trickle runs down my left nostril. I wipe at it. Blood, of course. The mother of all nosebleeds because as fast as I swipe at it, the seep returns. Annoying. I can taste it on my lips. Fuck it. I can't go into public looking like I'm haemorrhaging.

I pause on the turn of the stairs and cast out with part of my awareness. Three people are downstairs on the ground floor, the low buzz of their life force tired, their movements jerky. Closer to me, on the first floor, there's a man in Gavin's office. Most likely the royal douche himself counting his money. With a sigh I drag on my powers and make it so that I am all but invisible. Clothing first, then the money. If I'm lucky, Gavin will have gone home by the time I'm done getting something to wear.

Lady Bathory's Parlour is a small shop run by a lesbian couple who used to frequent The Event Horizon happy hour every evening without fail. I don't remember their names, only that the pair looked almost identical. They could've been sisters with their black bangs and wasp-thin waists invariably constricted by all manner of intricately stitched corsets. Two sisters who drank enough for four.

I'd kinda figured out they were not sisters the day I'd seen them snogging. Lisa'd caught me staring and had a good chuckle at my stricken expression.

"God, Ash, you sure you're not from the Victorian era?" she'd said.

I hadn't had the heart to break it to her.

In a way I feel bad about stealing from them, but I don't currently have better options. Maybe one day I can make it up to them. Like I could make it up to the old Ashton's parents. I huff out a sigh then pop the lock.

The shop's interior is, predictably, painted black. I have no qualms about switching on the lights here as a veritable queen's ransom in black velvet has been draped artfully over the window. The red crystal chandelier must have cost a fortune, too, so maybe the two ladies aren't so badly off. I start when I catch sight of my reflection in the mirror. Just as well that I'm doing something about my appearance. I look like shit with the rusty smear of blood running down my face and my hair a rat's nest of snarls, and I gaze about as I run my fingers through my hair. Better a finger comb than no comb at all.

Band posters have been used as wallpaper on one of the walls. All the usual suspects glare back at me with kohl-smeared eyes. An anorexic-looking Peter Murphy, Siouxsie with her signature liner, as well as a postapocalyptic Carl McCoy. Funny how the names come easily here, whispers of other people's memories surfacing as though I am a sponge. Old school.

I could make a killing setting myself up as a television psychic and magician. No sleight of hand involved. Wouldn't that just mess with people's heads...

Then I catch sight of myself—the old Ashton and his band, Anubis—and shock thrills through me. I've hardly given his—*my*—old band much thought lately. Marlise had posters in her room back home before we ran off to hide in the Karoo, but the idea that someone else might find me attractive enough to decorate their personal space still strikes me as odd. And there I am, topless, with my tattoos bared, screaming into a microphone with my hair obscuring most of my face. A fucking savage. The memories of that night are sluggish, fish struggling against a frigid current. Bright lights. Too much coke and red wine. A magic combination.

If I delve deeper, I could retrieve specifics, but they really did happen to someone else.

Oh, Ashton, please don't fuck up Alex's life. My mind bends when I tried to consider the present outcomes.

Sometimes I dream about what it was like to be on stage, the music a sonic assault of deep bass tones and the crash of the snare. Faces are turned up towards me juxtaposed with the inevitable heaving of bodies in the mosh pit. Lizzie's somewhat delicate sensibilities struggle to grasp why youngsters would want to risk permanent damage to their hearing, but by now I understand some of that excitement and the sheer thrill of being able to be master of the situation, to enrapture others.

All eyes focused on me, the centre point of the vortex, the song starting somewhere deep within my belly charged by the dark flame in my chest to be amplified and distorted electronically.

What could I do now with this talent? Some evil little voice suggests that the Ashton as I am now could do far more than my predecessor. As much as I can make it that people's gazes slide over me and un-see me, I can do the opposite. I can draw them to me—make them fall irrevocably in love with me.

If I were to abandon the path of Ma'at, that is. Just because I can do something doesn't mean I should.

It's so ridiculously easy. This alternate future could work, if it weren't for the fact that I have the ravening hounds of House Montu snapping at my heels.

This sobering thought snaps me back to the cold, rather unpleasant reality facing me, and I busy myself going through the rail that holds the men's clothing. I find a decent pair of denim pants—black, of course, and a little tighter and flashier with more buckles and shit than I'd like, but serviceable. Then a black long-sleeved T-shirt and hoodie I can wear under my leather jacket. My jeans and old shirt I bundle and slip into a sling bag, but before I get dressed in my stolen threads, I first wash as much of the dirt and grime off me as possible at the small sink behind a lacquered Chinese screen. Sweet Amun, I can smell myself despite the clogged-up nose. I can't do anything about the stubble, but I can at least try to make myself come across less like a bergie. The way I figure it, I'm going to draw enough attention with my height and brooding looks, I might at least do the best I can about the rest. I feel better after cleaning up, but if I'm honest about my appearance, I'd still scare small children and old grannies.

Some dumb curiosity has me look at the women's clothing—all corsets, velvets, lace, netting, and some latex and PVC. Marlise loved this shop, if I recall correctly, though she never had the cash to buy anything beyond that one corset she sometimes wore out. The fabric is like a dream between my fingers, and I'm transported to a few of the nights working here at The Event Horizon before everything turned to shit, when Marlise would be dancing at just the right angle for me to watch her from the bar. She'd be unconcerned with the looks she'd receive from the other guys, but she'd always position herself so that she could watch me watching her.

The pang of guilt stabs me. I cheated on her—with Bethan, who's dead, because of me. That old, familiar claustrophobic sense of being hunted tightens my chest, and I check that I've got all my things. With luck, the shop owners won't figure out stuff's missing for a few days and by then, I'll be long gone.

Now, for money.

The corridor is deathly quiet, and I snick the door shut behind me then I stand absolutely still while I stretch my senses. No cameras on this floor, but there's an alarm set in Gavin's office. Of course. And it's armed. While I was engaging in a spot of shoplifting and drifting down memory lane, whoever was still left behind locked up and went home. I'm all alone in this building, and that knowledge sinks into me with the sense that the walls breathe around me.

Three heartbeats and I find frequency that disarms the alarm in Gavin's office with a resonant beep. The door swings inward with a slight groan, and I flick on the switch to reveal the chaos that hasn't changed in years.

Gavin's desk is covered in papers and manila folders. A pile of pizza boxes creates a leaning tower in one corner, while crates are stacked and overflowing with all manner of shit, from what looks like power cables and old boots to a deflated blow-up doll and a disco ball with most of its mirrored tiles missing.

Here, too, the walls are pasted over with yellowing, dog-eared posters of the bands that must've played at the venue over the past decade. More than one poster for Anubis adorns the walls, though by now a few of them are half covered by posters of other bands whose names I don't know. Gavin has a habit of pasting one on top of the other. A cork board has been stuck full of photographs, and idle curiosity leads me to scan the faces—mostly people I've seen and whose names I'd know if I tried hard enough. What's the point, though?

A bunch of drunks or drug-addled punks. I'm way past that. There's Ashton, arm in arm with Gavin. My mouth twists in a sneer. Whatever we took that night, we're so wired in that shot, and our nostrils are pink. Probably speed, coke. Or a combination thereof.

A phantom medicinal tang rises in the back of my throat, which I swallow down with a grimace.

Never again.

The safe hulks in the corner, a bulky thing with its once-cream enamel paint badly chipped and peeling away in large patches to reveal blooms of rust. I crouch before it, place my hand over the lock, then close my eyes and shove with my daimonic powers.

This is slightly trickier than the alarm or the usual locks—a series of tumblers, a bit like a Rubik's cube that I have to twist in different combinations until the clatter and click of some hidden mechanism unlocks deep within the door. My hand tingles and so does that badly banked fire in my chest, and the temperature in the room plunges so that my breath plumes wisps of vapour. I've been leaning on my powers far more than usual, and it's taking its toll on me. Must pace myself.

I need a moment to steady my breathing, then I open the safe door to reveal the rolls of notes secured with elastic bands and wadded on the shelves. And a bunch of flat, plastic-sheathed packets about the size and shape of paperbacks.

Curiosity gets the better of me, and I slide one of these out. Whatever's inside is compact. Curious, I slide a fingernail under the duct tape that's been used to seal them only to reveal more plastic inside. White powder. I sniff and detect that unmistakable chemical odour that creeps through the plastic. Vacuum packed. Cocaine. A veritable fortune in Bolivian marching powder. And Gavin's sitting with three of these packets in his safe. The recognition of what I've just found triggers an ancient memory. Cocaine is one of the reasons a Russian mafia boss got him all nicely riled up over Ashton enough to run him over with a big shiny SUV. That, and the fact that Ashton had knocked up his kid sister.

An engine roars, and I look over my shoulder too late to see the metallic sheen of the BMW X5 as it roars down the street. No matter how fast I try to twist, I know with a sick kind of inevitability that I'm not going to throw myself out the way in time. Tinted windows reflect a flash of late-afternoon sunshine. I don't want to die. Not—

The memory of that blankness after impact shudders through me with that instant on loop. A strangled cry escapes—my own—and I clutch the packet for a short while, then consider my situation. Fuck it. Gavin can take a hit on one of these. Maybe some mafia boss'll take care of his sick predilections. He's an oily bastard. I, however, don't know where I'm headed or whether I'll need currency. So what if I fall back on some of Ashton's old tricks while I try to gain my feet.

I'll never take the stuff again, but it's valuable currency, nonetheless.

I snort softly. Sure, I can try to justify my slow slide to the wrong side of the path of Ma'at as much as I want to, but I can't see any other options open to me at present. I have absolutely no issues taking the money. A good few grand vanishes into the pockets of my jacket before I shut the safe.

Out of being in a fuck-you mood, I light a cigarette, which I smoke while peeking past the horizontal blinds. A disconsolate wind whistles through a gap in a pane where the putty has fallen out and rattles the sash window. This is a cold sound and matches the chill that has my flesh in its grips.

What I'd give to be back in the small house Marlise and I were renting, screaming baby and all. That illusion of domestic bliss, even with its squabbles, is preferable to this diminishing sense of direction. When Lizzie had been alive, she'd been content, upholding the chapter house, stuck in her little routines. But Ash? What the hell does he want? I don't even think the previous Ashton Kennedy knew his own mind.

I was never ready to return to the material plane. I should have fought harder to stay in Per Ankh and ingratiate myself with the elders. Now that I know what I do of Siptah, he's safe, no doubt flown back to our sanctuary and free of this mortal existence. For a while.

He's another who holds the forbidden knowledge of

the *Book of Ammit*, but I draw cold comfort from that knowledge. My responsibility now lies with Marlise, to get her out of House Montu's clutches. We can run; work our way to Botswana, then maybe farther where we can lose ourselves in Nigeria among the seething masses. Always running, but hey, that means we're getting somewhere, right? Maybe we can forge an alliance with one of the African Houses. Surely they have little love lost for Montu.

Only when my fingers sting with the burn of an ember, do I realise I've smoked the cigarette down to its filter, and I grind it out in the overflowing ashtray on Gavin's desk. Time to go.

An athame with a rusted blade catches my eye as I turn to leave. The damn thing looks like it was purpose-made for Wiccan rituals, complete with a resin hilt shaped like a dragon, with a stone that looks suspiciously like labradorite gripped in its mouth. About twelve inches long, and possibly quite blunt, it will still puncture guts. Knowing Gavin, he's probably used it to open letters and pick gunk out from under his fingernails. I slip the thing into my bag and exit the office.

From there it's a case of disarming the alarm and stepping out into the night. I pause at the doorstep and feel outward for any of the cameras in the city. No more taking chances with the CCTV cameras the police or security companies are watching. I should have thought about this when I fled the hotel. It's only a matter of time before they think to hit up the CCTV system.

Sheltered in the shadow of the doorway, I try my most ambitious stunt yet—knocking out the camera network in the CBD and Foreshore.

In theory, this sounds a lot simpler than what I

initially consider. Following any thread back to its source is tricky beyond hell when a thousand such filaments exist, an insane network of electrical wires and signals that blend into static.

In the end I have to walk a bit down Shortmarket Street before I get one of the cameras within my range. I take a deep breath, close my eyes, and flip my awareness to the higher frequencies, all the while maintaining enough consciousness to keep my *Kha* upright. Dimly, I'm aware of beads of perspiration breaking out on my forehead, and a slight tremor that courses through me with each heartbeat.

That alien part of myself begins to hum, a black sun lodged in my chest sending out its negative radiation to build up a hiss of static in my head until the entire world roars.

Millions of electrical impulses flow, but I'm looking for one, specifically, spread out across this area. A shining net. Then a nexus of power, a brief flash of dozens of screens followed by the buzz-crackle of frying circuit boards, a blue flash and the ghost of burnt plastic in my nostrils.

I stagger back on the uneven cobbles of Greenmarket Square, dizzy and horribly nauseous. My sinuses ache as though I've inhaled freezing air, and although a sharp pain chews through to the very centre of my brain, I don't feel the telltale trickle of blood. I honestly do feel as though someone's taken a nine-inch nail and slammed it through my skull. My eyes water.

Something must've happened now. My body feels light, and the little blue-green sparkles are back, whizzing about my fingers. Dare I continue? Greenmarket Square is deserted this time of the morning, and a glance up at the clock on the façade of the big art deco building tells me it's half past four.

Almost on cue, my stomach grumbles, and I figure I'm dizzy not so much from overextending myself, but from hunger. Pure and utter fucking hunger.

It's too early to go to the station, so I wend my way down to the Foreshore. The first of the city's cleaning trucks—the ones with all the flashing orange lights and the big-arse brushes and jets of water—are the only vehicles moving, apart from the occasional cop or security company van parked in strategic spots.

A few pedestrians, as furtive as me, and some clearly done clubbing for the night, walk in a similar direction, to the station. I must look like any other bloke. At least I hope so. I've no way of telling whether I've been successful in blowing all the cameras, but by now House Montu must have some sort of alert out for me, and I work on projecting the image of me not being there. Cape Town Station is a vast, semi-deserted cavern. The lights are glaring, and I need a few moments to adjust. Giant white tiles are laid out and polished to a high sheen, except where pigeon shit has spattered horrid green splotches. Fortune smiles on me because there's a small diner of dubious standards at the far end, near the entrance where the long-distance buses stop to collect and drop off passengers. A number of tired-looking folks hunch at the plastic tables over Styrofoam cups of no doubt watery coffee. One man clutches a quart of beer as if his life depends on it. Maybe it does. Bleary serving staff lurk behind the counter with its display of cling-wrapped hamburgers and pies that may or may not be riddled with salmonella or some other dread disease.

My stomach flips at the thought of steak and kidney pie, and the ghost of that taste teases me. But fuck, now just looking at food, I'm starving, and I let slip my anonymity long enough to place an order. I pray a large order of greasy fries won't kill me. To be safe, I douse it in enough vinegar to cure a corpse and settle in the most convenient corner I can find, my back to the wall so I can watch the early morning idiots who've got better places to go.

Despite my initial misgivings, the food tastes like heaven, even if I have to shut up my inner critic who voices intense displeasure in me feeding my body fast food. One meal isn't going to kill me. I slug back on a cola so cold the blood in my body sends chill fingers outward from my throat as the liquid goes down.

I hunker down, wrapping myself in my power while painfully aware that I am isolated and most definitely hunted. Montu will be on high alert. I might've blinded their mechanical eyes temporarily, but I'm not falling prey to the same mistake that possibly got me caught the last time I was on the run from them.

I curse Ma'at for having me fall into my current *Kha*. But then, how differently would things have played out had I ended up in that little girl's body? I'd be nine now, and possibly sunk deep within the particular nest of vipers I rooted out only a year ago. But a little girl is far less conspicuous than a muscular, tattooed bloke who stands more than six feet tall. Little girls could most likely not run about this godforsaken hour without drawing almost as much attention.

I can't win, can I?

It's still dark when the movement out in the big hallway shifts. I assume the first trains arrive from town—workers spilling in to town from goodness knows where, but since it's the weekend there aren't that many—just a trickle. That's when I take my cue to visit the ticket office. Economy class means I'll be seated with half of Africa. Tourist class, which costs considerably more, will at least assure me the privacy of my own space. This is by far the better option, but since cash flow isn't exactly an issue at this point, I can't help but smirk when I use Gavin's ill-gotten gains to pay for my comfort.

The train departs later this morning, at ten, so I have quite a bit of time to kill, but I use it well. First, I purchase a few toiletries and extra clean clothing, and freshen up. This alone makes me feel almost human. Then I find myself a restaurant on the Foreshore where I can lurk in yet another dark corner—this time with a newspaper to while away the time. I'm almost civilised. But that packet of cocaine I have hidden in my bag seems heavier than what I'd expected. I'm painfully aware of its mass, and of the fact that I'm skirting dangerously close to the kind of lifestyle in which the previous tenant of this body used to engage.

☥

The train slips out of Cape Town without any complications. Thank fuck. Surely House Montu will be watching the roads, looking for a lone hitchhiker, though I shouldn't discount them trying the trains, either. The most reasonable course of action would have been to coerce someone to drive me up. And, while the creation of my own, personal chauffeur would not be difficult, the anonymity of the railway is preferable.

After I lock my compartment's door, I seal it with a strong ward. Then I stretch out on the crisp white linen of my bunk and allow the motion of the train, and the *click-clack* of the wheels to lull me into a kind of half-doze. A cold wave of exhaustion sweeps through me, and I don't linger in that half-limbo of not being quite asleep for long.

Such dreams that do come are a confused mash-up of the cottage in Nieu Bethesda somehow transposed over the old chapter house in Simon's Town. Leonora is trying to tell me something, but the wind is blowing too hard for me to hear her words. And, besides, my vision is dim, as though I'm viewing the world through a misty veil. I scrub furiously at my eyes, but my vision does not improve.

I jerk awake with a gasp, my heart threatening to tear through my ribs.

For a moment I can't quite place where I am; the motion of the train compartment and the muted clatter of the rails. The light streaming in through the window is dim, and when I press my face to the glass, all I can see is the stretch of the Karoo landscape, endless hills rising and falling like an ochre sea of scrubby bushes. Occasionally, a wind pump flashes past, or a stand of prickly pear. Sheep in the distance pick their way across the stony ground and then they're gone. A leaden sky presses down, and judging by the chill even inside the train, it's freezing out there.

A foul taste lingers in my mouth, and I'd dearly love to know what time it is, save that I'm reluctant to leave the compartment so that I can ask a fellow passenger or one of the train's staff. But I need to take a piss, and those wriggly little nicotine demons tug at my veins and beg for another fix. That uncomfortable pressure remains lodged in my chest, like I need to break wind but can't. The only difference is there's less discomfort, as if I'm getting used to feeling this way.

Smells are unusually acute. Faint traces of a woman's perfume linger—heady, too much rose. I pluck up the courage to enter the corridor that leads down to the bathrooms. Children's laughter sounds from behind the door of another compartment, followed by thumps. The little tykes are probably jumping about, and I have to wonder about parents who smoke with small children around. Great. That means no one's going to look askance at me breaking the no smoking rules despite the stickers forbidding the filthy habit.

Thankfully, the passage is deserted, and I'm able to do the necessary in the bathroom then duck back into my compartment without seeing a soul. The brochure I picked up at the station tells me there's a dining carriage I could visit, but the idea of rubbing shoulders with strangers is not my idea of fun while I'm a hunted man. Hunger wins out, however, but only once I allow myself a cigarette—blowing smoke out the window just in case my breaking the rules is detected.

This trip will take a day if there aren't delays en route, and the compartment seems to close in around me, the walls squeezing. An entire day. Unbidden memories of the Blessed Dead squeeze past my defences. Shadows of souls. Hollow whispers and the interminable waiting. An ashen shade paces from window to door, door to window then back again. Staring out of windows, restless. I dig the heels of my hands into my eye sockets in a vain attempt to stop the psychic bleedback. How much better would things have been had I coerced someone to drive me up? Or sought the relative anonymity of playing hitchhiker?

Fuck knows.

The coffee in the dining car is the watery instant kind. But it's hot. An old black man with tired eyes is my waiter, and he brings me a burger and fries swimming in so much grease I can almost feel my arteries constrict before I take that first bite. Grimly, I keep my gaze focused on what's going on outside my window, wrapped in my silence. Although a few folks pass my table, no one tries to sit here. Whether it's brooding looks alone or my projected aura of avoidance, I'm not in a mood to wonder.

Every minute brings me closer to my destination. And then what? The food clumps in my belly, and I swallow it down with a gulp of too-hot coffee. *Clickety-clack, clickety-clack* goes the train, and I stare dully ahead. It's going to be a long night.

☥

Boredom is a terrible thing, yet I'm too keyed up to sleep. Every time I try to meditate, I'm distracted. My leg starts cramping, or the wail of some dumb brat in the compartment next door yanks me back into the here and now. The couple in the other carriage are having noisy sex, judging by the thuds and squeals. Would they be so vocal if they realised how much sound travels? Do they even care? Then there's the slight sway of the train carriage on the rails. A faint metallic grinding just beyond the stretch of my hearing. Or the ever-present hiss of my tinnitus begins to annoy the shit out of me.

I can't relax.

All the while that sick flare in my chest sends its tentacles down my spine. I'm seated cross-legged on the floor, my head nods, and the half-imagined screech of a hawk tears through me. Nightmarish. This entire experience. My entire being is off, but the sickness is daimonic, not physical, and I'm incapable of fixing it here.

I could go to the dining car and get something to drink. Beer perhaps. Fuck. Even whiskey. Anything. But I need to stay sharp. Every time the train stops at some small, nameless station, I press my face to the glass and stare out at the platform, casting outward with my senses and searching for any telltale smudges of power to betray my enemies.

What if they're cloaked? What if they're already on the train, waiting for me to slip up on my vigilance? Every face that happens to turn in my direction could be someone hunting me. Vendors run up and down the platform with their laden baskets, selling fruit, chips, sweets, and chocolates. I keep my window closed, my power barely leashed; an invisible bubble protects me and repels unwanted advances.

How many hours still of this hell?

I set wards on the window and the door and prop myself up on the narrow bed with its clinically white linens. The chemical stench of the detergent is sharper than it should be, and that damnable slow burn in my chest makes me gulp for air.

A man and a woman are locked in a furtive embrace. She drops her beige overcoat on the floor in her urgency to allow the man access to her body. With a groan he pushes her against the door, his hand sliding up her corduroy skirt. An oval-cut smoky topaz winks from a silver chain at her throat.

I jerk awake, my jeans uncomfortably tight. Nothing more than an echo of the Blessed Dead. And I hate the way it's made me horny. But that creeping daimonic malaise has me twitchy and nauseated, and it takes me a moment or two to figure out why.

The train isn't moving, and it's so damned quiet I can only hear my own breathing and the everlasting goddamned hissing in my ears. I slip into a crouch, lean a hand for support on the bed, then close my eyes and stretch out with my daimonic awareness, spiralling up and outward from my compartment.

Predictably, the train's stopped in the middle of fucking nowhere. Fucking South African Railways.

An arid landscape punctuated with the swell and ebb of flat-topped hills bedecked in a fuzz of nondescript scrub stretches for many kilometres in all directions, pallid in the moonlight. Slowly, I sink back to ground level and travel the length of the train, probing. The buzz of so many hundreds of people on board is dull, much more than it should be. How is it that everyone can be sleeping? Their signatures modulate along, blended along a single wavelength.

This sort of synchronous behaviour isn't natural, but as much as I rush to and fro, anxiously searching, I cannot find an anomaly in this pattern to betray the presence of another such as myself. How can this be? The train's lights pierce the darkness ahead of it with a bright beam, and the driver is slumped at her seat, her head resting on her arm draped over the console.

And my body is empty, vulnerable in my compartment. Even as I think of the danger, I am snapped back into the heaviness of my flesh, and with a low cry, I propel myself to my feet. Fuck this train. I grab my bag, withdraw that pathetic letter opener of Gavin's, and release the wards.

My breath plumes before my face as I step into the corridor running the length of the carriage. Stars gleam coldly through the windows, and the quiet presses in from all quarters. A woman snores two doors down, but other than that, my footfalls are the only sound, and they're pretty damn fucking loud.

On a whim, I peek into the compartment next to mine. The family of four is asleep. Nothing unusual about that, but that ill-ease prickles. The entire fucking train asleep, save for me. A reverse fucking Sleeping Beauty. Not normal. I withdraw, then hurry to the exit, where the lock disengages at the slightest touch. I stand at the edge waiting, listening, my heart thudding wildly.

Where are they? I'm reminded of old fairy stories about the Hand of Glory cut from the body of a hanged man, that supposedly possesses the power to send all souls into such deep sleep they cannot be roused. Such a trick wouldn't be impossible for the savvy Inkarna who has a strong will. Strong enough to send hundreds of people to sleep simultaneously, though? Give me the right reason and the perfect opportunity; I could work something out. Shit. Gotta get out of here. Get out of the fucking train. *Now*.

The carriage door's lock clicks without any problem, and I shove the doors open with so much force they try to snap back. With a grunt I wedge them apart with my shoulders, then wait for a moment to check whether there's anyone already out there. The leap to the ground jars my knees, but I'm clear of the train and stand still awhile, listening, breathing, scenting the air. Nothing but the slight creak of the mechanism and the wind soughing through the bushes. The slightly bitter, dusty scent of the Karoo fills my lungs. The cold sucks all the warmth from my flesh. A man can die out here, and I take those first steps away from the train, looking back every few steps.

That feeling of the jaws of certain death snapping shut behind me is all the prompt I need to get my arse moving. This not knowing what the fuck is going on is worse than being able to see who's after me. Not one whiff of another Inkarna's power. Just this disconcerting deadness. My enemies could be waiting to ambush me just around the next hill, or even worse, I could get lost in this trackless wasteland. The farms here consist of many hundreds of hectares. I could go days without seeing another living soul. I might not find water.

Bullshit. It's not like I'm stuck out in the Western Desert halfway in the middle of nowhere between Libya and Egypt.

A light skidding across the upturned bowl of the sky catches my gaze. A shooting star, so bright, an actinic flare of green that burns bright then fades almost as quickly. So many more stars are scattered here. They look like ash strewn in a broad band, the sky itself darker without the light pollution of the city.

Now's not the time to marvel. I need to keep moving. The moon's not up yet, and I stumble over rocks. The brush might only be knee-high at most parts, but I can't see the stones and other obstacles that lie in wait for me.

As soon as I'm behind the first hill, the light from the train is gone, and I don't see the barbed wire fence into which I stumble until it's too late. Fabric tears, and cruel thorns bite into my flesh with searing pain. I wince at the warmth that soaks and immediately freezes against my skin. Consequently, I'm careful about lifting the top strand and easing through to the other side. This, at least, I manage to do without snarling my hair.

Great. I'm on the other side of the fence. Now what? But twin strips of sand gleam in the starlight, and my eyes have grown accustomed to the dark. A road going where? A rough estimate suggests that it runs parallel with the tracks, but for how long? I don't even know where I am right now. Nowhere near fucking Joburg and still in the Karoo. If there's a road, however primitive, it does mean I'll arrive somewhere. Eventually.

What about snakes? Night adders? Scorpions? Nah,

it's too cold, right? My boots are thick, the soles sturdy. I'll be fine. My breath rasps, and I push myself hard.

I choke back a dry snigger. This entire situation is just fucked up, but only days ago I was bitching about stuff being so crap at home. Now, look at all the excitement I don't want. On the bright side, I'm walking in the direction the train would've taken. How long 'til I get to Joburg? Half a week? I draw skeins of power closer to me and wrap myself in a blanket of shadow. It's just me and the fucking semi-desert.

An ear-splitting scream that tapers off to a wavering note spikes right through me. To my left. About half a kilometre or so away, maybe. What. The. Actual. Fuck?

It's only a jackal, Lizzie's memories inform me. I heard these exact same calls when she was at Sabi Game Reserve with Richard. She was scared and clutching at a laughing man, who explained this was the call of the black-backed jackal.

"It's sounds like the Tokoloshe or something," she'd said.

I'm tempted to agree. While this might be a small canid yowling and yammering, its call still sounds like some fucking undead thing. I shiver, and it's not just from the cold. Old memories stir, just beyond the veil of my previous death, and nostalgia squeezes my heart. The jackal continues its plaintive cry, and I feel so fucking alone beneath the shelter of the naked sky. The universe is so big and empty while I stumble along in the dark.

Self-pitying Ash. Enough. If I stop moving, I'll freeze to death, so I pick up the pace. For how long I keep this up, I don't know, and at first I don't recognise the rumble of an engine. There are no convenient thickets where I can hide, only the swell of those ubiquitous flat-topped hills on either side. The one on my left seems a better option since it has more of a ridge than the other, so I make for that, mindful of any surprise fences—which there aren't, thank fuck. I stumble a few times on the uneven stony ground on my ascent and hiss a few choice expletives when I wrench my ankle.

The idea of being out in the open when the vehicle passes scares me more than worrying about whatever snakes or venomous critters I'll disturb, and it's better not to think too hard about what might lie in wait for me as I blunder forth. Once at the top, I press myself to the side and wait, my muscles protesting, my breath ragged gasps—far too loud by my estimation.

If I'm hiding, it doesn't mean they won't find me. Oh, and they'll certainly be looking.

The wait is interminable. That's the problem with it being cold—sound has a particular way of travelling in low temperatures. Things that are far away have a habit of sounding a helluva lot closer than what they really are. Lizzie might've remembered what this effect was called but now my memory of the particular terms remains unclear. Fuck it. Who cares?

How much will I forget as the years go on? And my next incarnation? That's if House Montu doesn't succeed in its mission to erase me? My feet grow numb, and I shift to alleviate the cramp starting in my thighs. A thorn bush prickles on my right leg's muscles, and I shift yet again and send a small avalanche of pebbles rattling down the hill.

Damn, I'm too loud.

The first stab of headlights slices its beams through the night. Diesel engine. Someone's driving deliberately slowly. What are the chances that this is just some ignorant farmer out checking his livestock?

I huff a silent cough of laughter. Hell no. As if I'd ever be that lucky.

I'm only on the most-wanted list of one of the most hardcore bastards known to Those Who Return. I must've been high when I thought I'd be able to slip out of Cape Town without them finding some way to trace me.

Or maybe this is just a dumb farmer. Let this be some dumb farmer.

That alien heaviness in my chest expands, and I struggle to draw breath again, and it takes all my willpower to keep from passing out—painfully conscious of the way the sharp edges of the rock bite into my palm, of the way I have to continually shift to stop myself from sliding down the slope.

Every sense screams at me to run, but I hold. My pursuers want me to run.

What if it's not them? What if I'm just paranoid as all hell?

A frustrated hiss escapes, but I cling to the ridge like it's a lifeline. Think logically. If I were hunting a fugitive, and I knew he was running ahead of me, I'd cast my attention on the road ahead. I'd do everything in my power to flush him out, make him this paranoid as fuck so he'll break cover.

Whatever tatters of self-control remain, I draw my daimonic power around me into a blanket so that I reflect an absence—just another patch of rocky ground punctuated by brush. Eyes must slide off me. I'm unremarkable. Not here. Not there. This is not the fugitive motherfucker you're looking for.

I grit my teeth, and a terrible trembling shudders through my limbs. So. Cold. Ice is lodged in my belly, turning my blood to liquid that sludges through my veins.

When the SUV rounds the corner, its arrival is almost an anticlimax. My eyes are closed, and I press my cheek against the rock as the blades of light cast by the headlights pass dangerously close to my hiding place. Then the car rumbles past, the engine a cheerfully familiar sound signifying civilisation, the occupants no doubt comfortable in the interior with the heater going while I freeze to death out here in the open.

Just like that, the red taillights vanish behind the next hill, and I'm left shivering against the ground. In movies, that car would slow down and grind to a halt, the reverse lights coming on. This is not a movie, and whoever is in that car, whether they're just some civilian in the wrong place at the wrong time, or one of my pursuers—it doesn't matter. They're gone.

I sag half onto my knees and draw a deep, shuddering breath before I right myself and stumble down the hill, almost tripping and falling face-first before I reach the bottom. Damn rocks. I'm still free, though, and that counts for something. My hands jammed deep in my jacket pockets, I resume walking, and let slip some of the tension.

"Ashton Kennedy," a man says behind me, his tone matter of fact, as if he's expected me here all along.

Nausea spikes right through me, and I whirl around, but there's no one there—just the empty jeep track.

A hand clamps down on my shoulder, and a crippling pain buzzes through me, bringing me to my knees. How in the hell? My attacker presses his face so close to mine I can smell the iciness of the mint he's been sucking. His grip on my shoulder doesn't relent— the old House Montu trick of jabbing me with just the right amount of daimonic power to seize up my muscle control.

"You've given us quite the runaround. I'm almost impressed. And I'm pretty sure that blackout with the closed-circuit cameras was your doing. A stroke of genius. Some of the elders who've returned haven't kept abreast with technology. You've been trickier than most." Old, craggy-faced Philip. Dismay sours the back of my throat.

I open my mouth to speak, but the only sound I make is a croak.

He leans close enough for me to smell his woodsy aftershave. Something named after a celebrity, no doubt. "In case you were wondering how we found you, because I know this must be a burning question, have you ever considered how the noble Verreaux's eagle hunts?" Philip pauses for dramatic effect, as if he expects me to answer, but I'm frozen. "What? You're rendered speechless. Oh, dear." Mock pity stains his tone, and another jab of his power frazzles my nervous system with cold fire. "Well, I'll tell you. Usually they hunt in pairs, and one raptor will fly out in the blue sky so the whole world and his wife can see him. The partner, well... He'll be flying against the sun, really high up so the stupid prey animal will be so fixated on the predator they can see, that they'll miss the one that really was the clear and present danger."

In the distance, the rumble of a car engine becomes louder. Philip's grip on me loosens a fraction, and I try to twist, but he's faster than me and digs in deep, this time with both hands. The world blanks out in a burst of static. A man cries out. Me, I suspect, and I'm brought to my knees. A terrible buzzing starts up in my ears, accompanied by the thunder of my pulse. My extremities have gone numb from the pounding of my assailant's daimonic power. He's not stupid enough to let up until they can incapacitate me.

"Stubborn bastard, aren't you."

I can only grunt in response. The world's gone grey through a haze of pain.

"I suggest you play along now. You've wasted enough of our time."

Philip had better pray I don't get loose because when I do...

Blinding headlights immerse my world in brightness, and I have enough motor functions to blink back tears. All that trouble, only to have had them zero in on me after all. A small, petulant part of me wants to gnash its teeth over the unfairness of it all.

The vehicle stops, and a door slams. Boots crunch gravel as a man approaches. "You sure as hell took your time," the man comments. Donovan.

"Says he who lost him in the first place. Let this be a lesson as to how things get done around here," says Philip. "Have you got the tranquilisers?"

Oh, sweet Amun, not again. Not the drugs. This seems to be House Montu's fallback when brute force fails. I draw hard on my powers, and try to struggle to my feet. My tongue is heavy in my mouth, and a low moan escapes.

The twitch of Philip's finger is almost disdainful as he finds a pressure point and zaps me again. Donovan closes the distance between us and pulls aside my shirt long enough to press a needle into the flesh of my upper arm. Mercifully, the sting is brief before the coolness of the drug takes effect. Tiny little ants nibble up my neck, and my eyes grow heavy. The ground rushes forward, but strong hands keep me from dropping. My stomach lurches, and I retch, again and again as I gulp for air, but only a thin stream of bile comes up.

From a distance, someone says, "You sure you didn't fuck up and overdose him?"

"Do I look stupid?"

"Must I answer that?"

"Help me get him to the car. He's a dead weight."

My eyes slide shut. Strong arms yank me into a vaguely upright position, but my legs don't work properly when they drag me to the car.

"You've given him too much, you twit. If he pukes in the car, you're cleaning it up."

"You want him at full power so he can fry you, then you fucking underdose him. You seem to conveniently forget that he fried Ian."

"Ian was weak."

"Ian was my brother, you wanking fuck."

I collapse against the car, my arms slack. Even when I try to open my eyes, I can't. The metal is blessedly cool against my skin.

"Help me get the bastard into the car."

"Do it yourself, Philip."

"This isn't some episode of *Supernatural*. You can't afford to be sentimental. Besides, you'll see Ian in Per Ankh. That's if he makes it past the Hall of Judgment." Philip's laugh is nasty.

"Fuck you. Just one less to compete against, isn't that it? To show how the rest of us fail?"

"You want to carry on like a baby, and cry foul at every perceived injustice, you're welcome. But as I recall, you're not the one who's in charge of this mission. Which means you're supposed to do exactly as I tell you. Insubordination won't go down well with the council. Suck it up."

Another wave of nausea grips me, and this time I do puke, violently, all down the side of the car. Only Philip's firm grip on the back of my jacket, and the fact that he has a more than generous handful of my hair, prevents me from becoming intimately acquainted with the dirt.

"Set's balls! Don, get your arse here! This is your fault. He's gotten puke all over my shoes."

Dimly, I'm aware I should find this latest turn of events hysterically funny, but at present I can barely stand upright and still deal with the waves of hot and cold sweeping through me.

A hand is clamped over my forehead. Philip, I think, says, "He's sweating. You've given him too much. Bosses aren't going to be happy if he ups and dies on us before we get him to NYC."

Donovan's sharp intake of breath cuts through my mental fog. "What do you mean, NYC? I thought we had this out already?"

"We don't have time for this now. Let's get this fool into the car."

Donovan's hiss of annoyance cuts through my hearing, and my awareness fades to black.

Such dreams that do filter through are abstract, weird things involving repetitive actions, of opening doors and entering room after room. Always trying to find an object of value, but I keep opening the same door. Only once reality filters back, with the steady shake of a car's progress along dirt roads, am I able to crack open an eye.

My mouth tastes like a dog's shat in it, not that I'd know what dog shit tastes like, but it's the vilest substance I can think of. The faint, acrid stench of my own vomit burns my sinuses. When did I get sick? I'm in the back seat, slumped against the right passenger door. Every time the vehicle goes over a bump, the side of my head klonks against the glass. No pain. My entire body is leaden, unresponsive.

Donovan's riding shotgun, and Philip's driving. A stab of headlights from behind informs me of another vehicle bringing up the rear. I try to draw on my daimonic power, but if my physical body is reluctant to function properly, my ability to wield my finer abilities is severely curtailed.

"He's awake," Philip says without turning to look.

"Want me to dose him again?"

"No. Watch him rather, at least until we get to the tar road. We can't afford to have him up and die on us."

Donovan shifts in his seat, and I'm vaguely aware of how he turns around to face me. "You doing okay there, buddy?"

Buddy? The guy's just drugged me up to my eyeballs, and now I'm his buddy?

I groan, and Donovan flips on the interior light. What I can see of his facial expression bulges and distorts. I can't seem to focus on any one point, and small swirly shapes bloom at the edges of my vision.

"Phil, I think he's going to get sick again. His colour isn't good."

So good of you to notice.

But Philip, bless his soul, slams on the brakes. "You've got five minutes. Hit his nervous system if he acts up. Walk him up and down so he can get a bit of fresh air. Then we're out of here. We've got a plane to catch in Kimberley."

I don't complain when Donovan comes around to my side of the car and helps me out. I lean heavily on him, and he keeps me upright. The cold Karoo air is a slap through the face, and I suck in great chilly gulps. Some of the nausea dissipates. Should I feel grateful that they care so much for my physical well-being?

Donovan keeps me propped upright then walks me a few dozen paces away from the vehicles. Behind us, doors are opening and slamming, men trading banter.

"I'm sorry things have come to this." Donovan

pitches his voice so low I know he's meant the words for my benefit only.

Why's he sorry? I've killed someone he named as his brother.

Loudly, he says, "Want a cigarette?"

"Donovan, what the fuck? We don't have time for a fucking cigarette!" Philip yells at us.

"I want a fucking cigarette," he calls back. "So you can stop getting your knickers in a twist, you cock-sucking douche. I'm smoking, and if I'm smoking, it means we can at least offer our prisoner the same courtesy."

They're playing good cop, bad cop. The knowledge somehow seeps through my sluggish brain. I'm being manipulated, but I don't complain when Donovan lights two cigarettes and pops one between my lips. He hasn't uncuffed my hands, but then again, I don't expect that much leeway. Cuffs, though. If I can just clear my head, I'll be able to gather the power needed to jimmy the mechanism. As much as I try to be unobtrusive about reaching for my powers, they're impossible to catch, like droplets of mercury.

"I want you to listen very carefully," Donovan says to me. He speaks so quietly I almost can't hear him. In the meanwhile, he makes a big production of checking his phone. "If you leave for New York, you're as good as dead. Philip thinks I'm going to drug you again, but I'm going to inject you something that will help alleviate what I gave you earlier, and you're going to help me. Philip must not take you to the States. Under no circumstances. If you play along with what I want, you'll get your girl, and everyone will be happy. Got it?"

"Let me go," I whisper. What garbage is he spewing now?

"I can't do that, but I can promise that you won't be hurt if you play along with what I want."

Okay, maybe not good cop, bad cop then. I'm dealing with two alpha dogs fighting over a bone. And if Philip gets to take me to the US, he'll get the pat on the head. Ditto for Donovan if he foils his rival's plans and gets my arse hauled to the original destination. Donovan also knows exactly which reward to dangle in front of my face.

I draw on the cigarette and wince when smoke curls into my eye.

"Are you going to play along?"

"Donovan, hurry up!" Philip shouts. "We're sitting ducks out here."

Men murmur their assent. How many are there? If I can shove aside the effects of the tranquilisers, I'll have to face off two full-blown Inkarna and maybe the five initiates who've followed us in the other vehicle? The odds aren't great. I won't get killed, but that won't stop them from kicking the shit out of me.

"I'll do what you tell me to do," I mumble around the fag.

Donovan doesn't say anything to that but then makes a show of walking me up and down the road, ostensibly to sober me up a little.

He pushes me so I almost stumble, then makes a show of shaking me into a standstill. It takes all my willpower not to fall over.

"He's getting a little frisky again," he tells Philip. "I'm going to dose him again."

Philip eyes us warily once I'm brought back to the SUV. "He's not going to fucking puke again, is he?"

"No worries. I'll give him a smaller dose this time. Wouldn't want to fuck up the upholstery of a rental car, now would we?" Donovan answers even as he directs

193

me into the back seat. Only now he makes a great show of shooting me up but then surreptitiously uncuffs me as well. What a relief to feel the blood flowing to my hands. Even if my extremities hurt.

I oblige by pretending to slump against the seat, grateful for the slow, creeping sense of being a little less foggy. What the man has planned, I have no idea, but I guess it's a case of having to go with the flow on this one. I want to laugh at the thought that they'd have drugged me again despite my adverse reaction to the chemicals the last time. What if I'd started convulsing or something? No mind.

As it is, I find it difficult to remain awake despite the supposed antidote now that I'm out of the cold air. Little tendrils of sleep snake out to snag my awareness, and I doze fitfully, waking every so often every time the vehicle hits a rut in the road. Some of the woozeinss has lifted, and I snag at the smallest tendrils of power. Not so much that Philip would be aware, but since he's driving, I'm banking on his attention being on the road.

The atmosphere in the SUV is tense. They don't even listen to music or anything. It's just their breathing, and I'm pretty sure Philip grinds his teeth every once in a while. I don't need to be a brain surgeon to figure that these two fools aren't putting up a united front. The way both men sit, Donovan barely leaning against his seat, his hands clenching his thighs. Philip's shoulders are squared, as though with some supreme force of will he'll rip the steering wheel from the column. A poorly maintained truce, then.

I can assume then that Donovan's the second-in-command? Does he mean for me to make the first move? So he can then turn around later if this plan fucks out and say I somehow got the better of the drugs? Maybe.

So, what does he want me to do?

Slowly, so as to escape notice, I draw harder on my daimonic powers. At first it's like trying to grasp smoke coiling in the air, but I snag a whisper, then reel it in. A little power from the ambient environment jumpstarts that furnace within me, which flares into life—a small, bright sun. Heat travels through my veins, purging the last of the chemicals from my system. I'm instantly, painfully awake, my pulse thundering in time with the bass drum of the inferno in my heart.

"You sure he's out?" Philip rasps. "I thought I felt something."

With a mental shrug, I plunge daimonic fingers into the heart of the SUV's engine. These modern cars all have computers, which makes my job so much easier. An automatic cutoff when I force the device to reboot. The engine obliges me by dying quietly.

"Fuck!" Philip hauls up on the hand brake. "Check on our passenger. He's—"

I don't give the bastard a chance to try anything further. All my anger and pent-up frustration for this entire damned situation flow through me the moment I bring both hands down on Philip's shoulders. I've learnt all too well how House Montu inflicts its pain and draw deep on the potential that sings through my *Kha*. A torrent of agony is concentrated through my fingers. Payback, bastard.

Philip's scream fills my head, vibrates through the aethers. Take that, you arsehole. That's for Samuel Forrester, who'd probably intended to knock around this material plane a bit longer. And more, for Bethan, who deserved that second chance after being trapped for so many years. All my fears for Marlise, for Alex— these terrible emotions sink deep into Philip, burning him from the inside out. My chest aches, bursting with an inferno lodged where my heart used to be.

"Ashton!" Donovan is shouting, but his voice comes to me as though I'm listening for his words over the rumble of a massive waterfall. "You can stop."

The need to punish is strong, and I struggle to wrench my hands free from the man's shoulders. He slumps the moment I let go, and the stench of cooking pork fills the interior of the car. Oh, sweet Amun, I'm going to get sick. A glance at Donovan's features informs me of the horror of our situation—far, far worse than he'd expected, for sure.

We lurch out of the car instantly, and I hate the way that cooked-meat stench lingers. I fried the bastard, and the greasy aroma clings to my hair and clothing, and I'm perversely happy I couldn't see his face. What did his face look like? Donovan's busy tossing his cookies on the other side of the car, and though I retch too, I heave up nothing but painful belches of dry air. I'm never going to scrub this smell out of my clothing, my skin.

The car that was following halts a few metres behind us, and I recover quickly when I figure out the occupants won't stay inside like good little initiates. The first bloke raises a gun at me but only the barest twitches of my power knocks him off his feet. Within me, the furnace of daimonic energy roars, a vortex of anger that already has me barrelling towards number two.

The man gives a short, sharp scream when I knock him into the side of the vehicle with a wall of energy. A tingling of power behind is all the warning I have to spin around and haul up a shield. My attempt at defence is clumsy, and Donovan's blow sends me flying sideways. I fall hard, on a prickly bush—

unhurt but winded.

But four guns are trained on me when I stumble into a crouch. The initiates' fear is a solid thing, leaving bitter traces in the air I can somehow taste at the back of my throat. Four guns... Could I spread my awareness and jam all four at the same time?

The guy on my left has such a tremor in his arms he can barely keep the gun steady. Donovan stands behind them, a trickle of blood running down one nostril, which he wipes away carelessly, his gaze never once leaving mine. "Stand down, Ashton. This is not worth Marlise's life."

I could take them, knock the initiates down with a rolling wave of daimonic force and hope to make Donovan stumble. He'd be too busy holding his position, but then I'd be vulnerable to his attack. Do I want to risk that? A groan from one of the downed chaps suggests the guy isn't quite as dead as I suspected he'd be. I blow at a tendril of hair that lies across my face but don't dare move my hands to take care of the annoyance. That fire within begs for more bloodshed, a dark voice chanting at me: *You've got all the power you need, all the power, just trust me. You can make them burn, you can make them pay...*

And I could make my own way to Joburg, could figure out how to find exactly where Marlise is located, on my own, with these tenacious fuckers' friends like bloodhounds on my trail.

Or... I could give up the fight, hand myself over, and get a free ride, albeit in chains until I decide to make another bid for freedom.

"Ashton, be reasonable." Donovan's eyes are wide and staring in the harsh, contrasting glare cast by the headlights. Five versus one. I have a fair chance. Then again, I might end up getting shot.

Free ride or more bloodshed? Truth be told, people are going to die later anyway.

That power within me threatens to surge down my veins, but I rein it in and lower my hands. "I'll come with you," I murmur and drop my head.

The initiates move quickly to bind my hands behind my back, though I want to tell them this isn't necessary.

A man cries out, "Sweet Amun!" and retches. I guess one of the other initiates must have recovered enough to luck out and discover crispy-baked Phil. That's my cue to start laughing, and I don't stop until they've got me wedged between two nervous initiates, with a grim-faced Donovan casting dirty glances my way once we get moving again. Pity the youngsters who have to drive the car in which I cooked Philip.

CHAPTER SIX
The Price You Pay

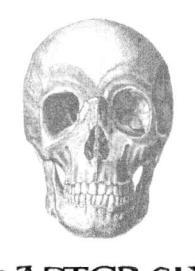

THE RIDE NORTH is subdued. Actually, that's the fucking understatement of the week. We skip the airport and opt for the road, which takes longer, but they're choosing secondary routes. Which suggests they're trying to evade detection. I should at least feel a more than healthy dose of fear, but my emotions are blunted. Instead my body settles into a state of half-awareness. Maybe it's a dissociative effect of the drugs. Maybe I've exhausted all my physical, emotional, and daimonic resources. Maybe it's this new power that's at my fingertips. None of this matters.

My backpack with the wads of money and the packet of cocaine is examined without comment, though the younger initiates trade glances. The money they keep, but the coke they dispose of. The powder is so much dust in the wind, and it's difficult to remain impassive. Poker face, Ash. That's my meal ticket they're destroying.

It totally sucks being at someone else's mercy.

The SUV grinds along the black scar towards the madness of the City of Gold, and the realisation that each kilometre brings me closer to the certainty that nothing from here on in will be any easier.

Sure, I try to look on the bright side, that I'm letting these folks do all the hard work, but some proud, stubborn part of me wails on about how I should've been doing this myself, that I've failed somehow.

Donovan is solicitous and buys me coffee and a hearty breakfast at some roadside diner once the sun is up. My bonds are removed, but I'm too tired to try anything stupid. Yet. For all intents and purposes, our little party consists of a bunch of blokes on the road home after a conference. We're all a little rough around the edges, our gazes hollow from lack of sleep. No one speaks much beyond "Pass the salt" or "Can we order a refill, please?" I can't help but wonder about Philip's corpse rotting, forgotten many hundreds of kilometres behind us in the wilderness. No one mentions him.

I do my best impression of a moody bastard, which isn't difficult since that's exactly how I feel. But I'm quite happy taking Donovan's cigarette when he indicates that we duck out to the smoking area near the restrooms.

Sparrows chirp in the eaves beneath the thatch, and the sky is already a delirious shade of blue sharpened by a wind so chilled it slices the skin. My lips are sore and chapped, and no matter how often I moisten them, they continue to ache as though sunburned.

Donovan rests his butt against the outdoor table, watching me while I pace the length of the courtyard.

"What's it like?" he asks. "Per Ankh, that is?"

His words bring me up short, and I turn to face him.

"You mean you've— Never mind. Is there some sort of global conspiracy to create an army of Inkarna? I don't ever remember there being so many new..." Then again, Richard hadn't exactly gone out of his way to encourage me to meet that many of the other Houses, and after his death, we'd had precious little contact at that.

"We're preparing for the war." Donovan's stubble rasps as he scrubs at his face with the hand not holding his cigarette.

Not a war. *The* war. Like I've been living under a rock all this time and should know better.

"War?" I fumble for any of Lizzie's memories, and those from Per Ankh that suggested a war. "We're always at war, aren't we?" I'm beginning to see a pattern here—keep me in the dark so I can't make informed decisions of my own.

Donovan grimaces. "I forget you're not in touch with all the rest, but I'll fill you in." He sighs, takes a drag of his cigarette, then fixes me with his gaze. His expression is especially mournful, and he makes me think of Eeyore. "That little incident involving Binneman in Constantia, before you pulled your year-long vanishing act. Well, our House construed it as a declaration of war here in Africa. House Alba, a few of the others... You're a wanted man, though we've been instructed to bring you in alive because of the location of the artefact."

"You can forget about me telling any of you where it is or what's written on it."

Donovan laughs quietly, shakes his head. "That's not for me to decide. Personally, I'm of the opinion that there's some bad mojo out there that can stay unknown as far as I'm concerned. Sometimes it's better not to know stuff. Then people won't come looking for you when they've called your number."

His admission floors me, and I gape at him—that's not what I expected of him. Granted, I'm a fool for even thinking that all the House Montu Inkarna might show a unified front.

The man smiles, takes another drag of his cigarette. "You look surprised."

"I'm gobsmacked."

"I follow orders. I didn't ask for any of this, but it happened. I got recruited, and by the time I figured out what the hell was going on, it was too late to turn back. Might as well ride this carousel to the end. Good little soldier. It's either that or die because I know too much."

"Only there isn't really an end," I say. Dare I hope I've found an ally? "And, to answer your question, by the time you come back, your time in Per Ankh will seem like a dream. You'll be able to tap into forgotten snatches, just a shade more confusing than your average Blessed Dead memory."

The man raises a brow. "You can tap into the Blessed Dead?"

"What of it?"

He shakes his head and gives a soft snort. "You are one hell of an unusual guy, Kennedy. You look like there shouldn't be half a brain cell to rub together but you talk like you've actually had an education. And now you tell me you've got priestly abilities, too."

"What's weird about this? All those who've returned can...or can't they?" Now I'm the one who's confused.

"It's probably a House thing."

His phone rings and he gets up, turns his back to me, and begins to pace himself, leaving me standing like a fool. Two of the initiates lurk near the only exit, and when I head towards the bathrooms, one of them follows. I swear the guy would've entered the stall with me if he'd had half the chance, but he needn't have worried about me escaping.

The windows in the bathroom are all so narrow a three-year-old wouldn't even be able to squeeze through, and I'm too tired and out of ideas to bother. Richard would've been on my case, but I'm not in a fighting mood anymore. Maybe it's the aftereffects of whatever drug they gave me earlier, but I simply don't possess the wherewithal.

By the time I'm done in the bog, they're all waiting for me by the car. My escort of two tails me through the fast-food outlet where folks queue to pay for their overpriced coffees and deep-fried breakfasts. I try to see myself from others' perspectives and figure it must look pretty darn strange for some scruffy alternative type to be so obviously tailed by two guys who look like they might be secret agents.

The pair almost visibly sag in relief when I get into the car without giving them hassle, then our little convoy hits the road again. Donovan doesn't speak to me again. I don't know if this has to do with the call he received or whether he's embarrassed by his show of interest when he should be playing the bad guy.

In order to avoid some of the tension in the vehicle, I close my eyes and pretend to sleep. I'll be delivered to the head of House Montu in Joburg now, handed over like some sacrificial goat. Marlise had better be all right. Would they hurt her in any way? Old, barely scabbed wounds in my conscience are scraped raw again.

I cheated on her. I'll have to tell her. This is not the sort of thing I can hide. Of course, Siptah, Bethan, or whatever I struggle to name him/her isn't here anymore. In a way this is a relief. Bethan's dead, and

Siptah's flown back to Per Ankh. He will be able to speak on my behalf once he arrives. I've cleared my name with the elders. That part of my quest is at least fulfilled.

Then why do I feel like I've failed? Because no one bothered to tell me the real reason—to guard the stele—and now I'm unable to do even that. Things would be so much simpler if I could walk away from this all and just be Ashton Kennedy, to subsume myself so fully into a life where I'm not plagued by Blessed Dead or nosy Inkarna who want to know how to destroy souls. How would it be to live just this one, finite life?

Perhaps, if I were given the opportunity, I could fall into such dissolution that I'd not be able to keep my *Akh* from disintegrating into its component parts upon passing through the Black Gate again. But that is the way of failure. That is not the way of Ma'at, and even if Lizzie had never met Richard, if Lizzie had somehow become what I am now, I'd still balk at giving up. So long as I draw breath, hope remains. I own my failure.

I must tell Marlise. Everything. My stomach contracts.

Let me first face the figurative dragon.

☥

I'll be honest. I can't tell my Highveld from my Lowveld. All I know is that the compound that serves as House Montu's headquarters here in Gauteng or the North West or wherever-the-fuck this place is, is situated somewhere to the north of the City of Joburg, somewhat to the east of Pretoria. We travel for a while along dirt roads, between thick stands of acacia, and once we surprise half a dozen kudu—and I understand why they are referred to as the "grey ghosts" of the bushveld. The proud kudu bull has seven twists to each of his horns, and he stands, ready to bolt while his cows vanish into the thick underbrush. Liquid eyes are bulbs of obsidian. Then he is gone, and it's only us and the dirt road that is a bright red-ochre slash, heavily corrugated, not that this matters much to our vehicle. We drive past a porcupine carcass, a mess of black-and-white quills scattered in a profusion and the rusty smear of gore soaked into the sand.

In the time that we've left the service station what feels like half a century ago, Donovan's taken three terse phone calls. Each time he finishes, the tension in the interior of the car grows worse. His words are so muffled, and pitched so low, I can't hear what is said over the rumble of the tyres on the dirt road. From what I can make out, something really bad is happening, a turn of events that has my seemingly unflappable captors' feathers more than just ruffled. The men sitting next to me keep darting glances my way, as if to make sure I'm not going to try some crazy, last-minute stunt. A war, he said. What's waiting for me when we reach our destination?

I can't tell them I actually want to go here, wherever here is, that I have obligations, responsibilities. Instead I breathe deeply and try to keep my hands still. Not much longer now.

An overhead sign scribed in hieratic, that reads "Akhet" is all indication that the turnoff leads to some place remotely related to Those Who Return. Another sign, its lettering burnt into wood, spells out "Van Rensburg Wildplaas"—a decent enough cover for this region. Most of the fencing running alongside the road seems fit for game. I'm in no mood for a safari, however.

We drive through several camps, but the last has

electrified fencing. This gate opens automatically, and we drive through quickly and wait for the gate to close behind us.

"Lions," Donovan says to me with a smirk.

A man dressed in khakis waves us through from his perch in a pillbox—à la Afrikaner Weerstandsbeweging—complete with a high-powered rifle. He speaks into a walkie-talkie, mostly likely warning the folks at our destination. Great stuff. I've never been enamoured with military aficionados. For all I know I'll be heading right into some bullshit racist nonsense. Well, what do I expect if the bloke's surname is Van Rensburg? I've never much been enamoured with the folks I've encountered in the Ou Transvaal. They're almost as bad as the Whenwes from the old Rhodesia. Richard told Lizzie enough stories about the colonial mentality that prevails up north. And Ashton's older memories recall the children of those same, embittered folk washing up at the bar at which he used to serve. Somehow, I don't think things have changed much over the past century or so. Farmers are as tenacious as pit bulls when they're driven to protect what they consider their territory. Even if their forefathers cheated it off the indigenous population.

Might doesn't make right, fuckers, but you sure know how to piss people off.

Our road curves through the acacias in a way that teases that it will continue like this infinitely, like a wicked cosmic joke. The men let out a collective breath of relief when we round a bend and approach a massive set of double rough timber gates set in wall more than six feet in height and topped with sharpened wooden staves. The overall effect is more than just a little bit forbidding. Not even one of Marlise's fantasy film heroes would readily scale that.

The gates swing inward and we roar through. The late afternoon sun is slanting between the trees.

Donovan offers a muttered, "Thank fuck," then we roll onto a redbrick driveway towards a sprawling gabled home. A wraparound veranda extends all around the ground floor, decorated with a vine-choked trellis. Massive trees cast shade that's undoubtedly more than welcome here in summer. Even as we roll to a halt before the front door, two massive red-gold mastiffs gallop out of the doorway to greet the cars.

These beasts are easily the largest of their breed I've ever seen, and it's with some trepidation that I climb out of the car and allow first one, then the other to nuzzle at my legs with saliva-flecked muzzles. Oddly, they show me little interest but growl ferociously at the initiate I now know as Duncan.

"Bring him in," Donovan says over his shoulder even as he strides into the house.

The black guy whose name I still haven't caught, who sat on my left for the last leg of our trip, inclines his head and motions for me to walk next to him. I shrug and follow. No point in delaying the inevitable.

A chill, like outside the car, prevails inside the building. It's like walking into a fridge. We follow a long passage with a few closed doors running off each side, but then we arrive at an inner courtyard surrounded by a colonnaded walkway. We take a left, but I've long enough to rubberneck at what looks like a mean ritual space. A large fire pit is surrounded by a paved area, and a carved stone pylon creates a doorway towards what I presume to be north.

Then we enter a darkened office, where it's warmer thanks to an altogether cheery fire crackling in the hearth. The walls are almost completely hidden by row upon row of bookshelves stuffed with leather-bound tomes as well more than a handful of cylinders that can only contain scrolls.

Thick Oriental carpets with stylised floral patterns cover most of the stone-flagged floor, and a wrought-iron chandelier hangs from the centre of the ceiling. To complete the picture, this space boasts two over-sized sofas upholstered in zebra skin. A glass-eyed lion head trophy gazes at us from one of the walls. How quaintly colonial. I try not to sneer. I've never really had much fondness for the taxidermist's profession.

The man seated at the desk moves, and I can't help but jerk in surprise. He'd been sitting there all the time, and I didn't notice him. In his late fifties, and completely bald, he nonetheless suggests that he possesses plenty of youthful vigour, because he rises quickly and marches directly to me without offering a word of acknowledgement to my travel companions.

"You must be Master Kennedy, lately of House Adamastor." The man speaks with a slight lilt, and I can't quite place his accent.

He holds out a hand, and I stare at it dumbly until the black guy nudges me in the ribs. I look askance at him before I return my attention to my host, whose eyes have not left my face once. Although every instinct screams that I need to get out of here now, and fast, I reach out and shake hands with the man.

Dry desert sands crumble underfoot, and a naked sun blazes. My sandals disintegrated hours ago, and now the scalding ground roasts my feet. The pain is such that it sings through my blood and bones, and each step I take brings me no closer to the shimmering mirage tantalising me, just out of reach.

A man cries out and I stagger back, knees buckling, only to realise I'm the one who's screamed. A terrible pain sends bolts of iron through my brain, and the world fades to darkness for a heart-stopping second. Strong hands keep me from collapsing.

A memory, belonging to the Blessed Dead. Attached to this man. Shit. He's powerful.

"Who are you?" I manage to say.

His expression remains genial. "Adriaan van Rensburg. How terribly amiss of me." He cocks his head. "You look a trifle pale, Kennedy. Do take a seat." Adriaan gestures towards the couches.

I don't get a chance to argue, as the black henchman all but drags me to the seat, where I'm shoved back into the striped hide.

"Arrange some refreshments for our guest. He's no doubt famished. And ask Essie to serve our supper early in the dining room." Isis' tits, what century is this guy from? He speaks like a bad caricature of an English lord.

I try not to choke on my laughter. Hysterical laughter at best. Donovan casts me a warning look but Adriaan doesn't give any indication of noticing my attitude. What would Lizzie do? Good question. Not speak until spoken to, for one. Of course, now I'm way past that sort of circumspect behaviour. Evidently.

Adriaan makes a show of inspecting papers on his desk, his back turned to me. I fucking hate it when people play these games. I grit my teeth.

"Where's Marlise?" I ask. "I want to see her."

Donovan, who's hovering near the door, stiffens. Adriaan gives no indication of having heard me and lets the moment play out that little bit longer.

I'm on the verge of rising when he eventually turns and regards me coolly. "I do believe the weather in Cape Town is miserable this time of the year. Quite the runaround you've given my colleagues, Kennedy. I'd bet you're glad to get out of the cold now, aren't you?"

The black guy presses a hand on my shoulder, and a faint warning buzz runs down my spine. Barely suppressed daimonic power, on the verge of zapping me a big one. I fall back into the seat and glare at Adriaan.

"You try so hard to put on a sense of bravado, pathetic, really." The man's eyes glitter with malice, at odds with the slight smile curving his lips.

"Well, if you'd cut the crap and let me see my girlfriend, then maybe I'll be a little more tractable." Sweet Amun, I pray they haven't hurt her in any way. It's all my fault if they have.

"The question is, my dear boy, what makes you think Marlise wants to see you? Especially considering how abominably you've behaved towards her and your son."

He's talking crap. At least I hope he is. "Bullshit! Where is she?"

Adriaan makes a placatory gesture with his hands then perches on the armrest of the couch opposite mine. His movements are dainty, almost like that of a dancer. A weird thought seeps to the fore.

"You were a woman in a past life, weren't you?" I blurt, then immediately wish I'd had the forethought to just shut the fuck up.

The man jerks upright but then curtails the jaggedness of his response to make it seem as though he's stretching a crick out of his neck. The black guy's fingers pinch on a nerve, hard, and I have to bite the inside of my cheek to stop myself from crying out.

Adriaan's smile is lazy. "We know all about your past life as Mrs Elizabeth Rae Perry. Do not consider that your situation is unique. By now you must agree that the male physique is eminently more suitable to wield these powers."

Sure, ask Siptah all about that. I choose to remain silent and merely glower at the man. I damn well hope I've discomforted him somehow. Dare I hope that this juicy snippet of information isn't common knowledge? What little I know of House Montu, fair undercurrents of general misogynist tendencies flow through the House's elite.

"Where's Marlise? I need to speak to her before any of this goes another step further."

"You're in no position to make demands, Kennedy." Adriaan rises and begins to pace the length of the room. "The matter remains whether you will be compliant, but first I do believe we shall have coffee."

A busty black woman bearing a tray enters the room. She eyes me with detached boredom as she places her burden on the table. A French press is filled with coffee, but there are only two mugs. A small plate of biscuits looks damned inviting, but I'm damn well not in the right space to calmly go about having coffee and biscuits with this madman.

Adriaan stands perfectly still until the woman leaves—Essie, I presume—then returns to the couch opposite mine. This time he seats himself comfortably, and Donovan approaches. I watch, incredulous at how my former captor fills the role of butler and fixes his superior's coffee.

I shouldn't be so appalled. After all, didn't Leonora do the same for me, even when I possessed my current incarnation? But for some reason it just seems so wrong. Like every person around this man is obligated to serve him, whereas with Leonora it was a sign of affection. She *wanted* to serve me. It was a sign of love, trust, and respect. This situation? It's obligation. Pure and simple.

He smiles at me over his mug. "Aren't you going

to help yourself? You know it's rude for travellers to refuse hospitality when it's freely offered. We would not want to injure the delicate situation between our Houses any more than it already is."

I don't like the way he watches me while I go through the motions of pouring coffee. The not-so-subtle snub is apparent, in me having to help myself, but at present I'm grateful to have something to keep my hands occupied, though I spill the sugar and the milk. Not quite stage fright, but close enough. The small blessing is that the coffee's hot, and if he's drinking from the same pot, there's slim chance that I'll be drugged. Nothing's stopping them from coming at me with one of their damnable drugs, in any case. When it's convenient. Right now, they don't seem at all worried, and I try not to distract myself by considering ways in which I'd escape with enough time to find Marlise.

Shit, and isn't it fucked up that I'm thinking along these lines?

The bastard waits for me to take a sip of coffee before he speaks. "*The Book of Ammit the Devourer*. We've got our teams scouring the Graaff-Reinet area. Where did you hide it?"

I smile into my cup but keep my eyes lowered. No need to piss him off. His tone of voice is firm, but there's an edge to it. "What makes you think I still have the thing? That I haven't destroyed it?" I pause dramatically then force myself to stare unflinchingly at a point about nine inches on the other side of his skull.

Perseus must've felt pretty shit facing the gorgon Medusa. My smile might be strained, but I hold it there for an instant before I sip at my coffee. An ashtray with butts in it is a centrepiece on the coffee table, so I take that as permission to reach for my cigarettes.

I'm stalling. I know it, and so does everyone else in this goddamned room. No one says anything or moves a muscle while I go through the routine of lighting my smoke. I lean back in the chair and gaze slightly to the left of Adriaan's head. All the better to avoid his maddening stare. Bastard's trying to feign nonchalance, but I'm pretty sure he's pissed as all hell. Impatient.

"We're pretty aware of your movements since you quit Nieu Bethesda with the Thanatos operative. We've traced the route you took. The stele never left Nieu Bethesda. Where did you hide it?"

"I don't have it. And, even if I did, what makes you think I'd give it to you? Marlise doesn't even know where it is. Isn't that just so frustrating?" I blink at him, smile, then take a drag. The smoke curls slowly into the air between us.

The man's features are impassive. If I'm annoying him, he covers his emotion by drinking more coffee. Those eyes burn into me with the same intensity my last opponent possessed. I have a habit of making enemies. How will this sorry dramarama resolve? Will I end up employing those accursed words again?

"You forget that you are at our mercy," Adriaan says.

"What are you going to do? Kill me?" I ask. "That's not going to help in the long run. You'll have to wait a few generations before you can continue your search. How frustrating."

His flinch is microscopic, but it's there. A slight tightening around the eyes. "We don't have to kill you. There are ways and means, and you are foolish to bait the lion in his own den." Adriaan's smile is chilling. His expression shifts to that of cool geniality, and he downs his coffee before setting the mug down on its coaster. "Come, drink up. We must go enjoy our dinner. I'm sure you are keen to refresh yourself. Marlise has been most anxious to meet you."

My mouthful of coffee almost goes down the wrong way, and I try not to cough and make a fool out of myself for having lost my composure.

Too late. Adriaan watches me with evident amusement. Languidly, he rises and makes his way to the door, where he waits while I kill my smoke, then stumble to my feet. Donovan falls in behind me and purposefully doesn't make any eye contact with me, like the past few days haven't happened and we're total strangers. Like he wasn't the one who betrayed Philip.

The damn bastard's used me. Of that I'm sure. Typical House Montu politics. I was merely a convenience for him to rid himself of a rival while currying favour with his superiors. What else should I expect from this House? They're noxious weeds. Cut down a sucker, and three more spring up to take its place. What's his game?

"Like our little compound?" Adriaan asks as we make our way down the colonnaded walkway.

I grunt in response and glance about as though I'm interested. Yes, the place is ostentatious, as are most of the dwellings this far north that belong to the wealthy. The old farmers had money, and then some. This was the case even back in Lizzie's day. Adriaan's property is but one of many I've seen over the years that belong to erstwhile colonial powers.

We make our way back into the main wing of the house into the stone-flagged reception hall, then cut a left immediately to a large dining area. Here a twelve-seater table runs the length of the room, ladder-backed chairs accompanying the crisp white linen. A large floral arrangement of pincushions, in bright yellows and various flame-shades of orange and red, takes pride of place in the centre. Soft music plays over a hidden sound system. Vivaldi, I think. Not *The Four Seasons*. I'll give him that much.

Adriaan naturally seats himself at the head of the table. This chair of his is carved of dark wood and stands almost throne-like, crested with a massive gilded sun disk flanked by outstretched wings inlaid with a veritable wealth of lapis lazuli. The man sinks back into the red leather upholstery, a self-satisfied smile tweaking the corners of his lips.

He watches me awkwardly seat myself to his left, as directed by the black guy. Should I care, even, that he remains anonymous to me? The way they treat him—not a fully fledged Inkarna yet—suggests he's only one step up on the rung from Essie, who brought tea. His presence behind me is fitful, like an alternating current in wave form. One false move on my part can result in goodness knows what sort of repercussions from him.

Donovan sits opposite me, on Adriaan's right. He snatches up the napkin from his side plate in one practiced sweep and places it on his lap, but his gaze doesn't leave mine. If I narrow my eyes, I can almost see his readiness to strike, the coiled power humming in the air around him and leaving little glowing motes around his fingers.

I turn to Adriaan and allow my smirk to the fore. Time to needle my foes a little. Maybe the cracks will show. "You are aware that Philip was planning to sell me out to your colleagues in the States, right? We were bound for New York City." I shift so that my gaze meets Donovan's. "That's until Donny-boy here set it up so that I'd do his dirty work for him."

Donovan's complexion pales, and his eyes bulge. No poker face for him today. He swallows hard then recovers, but he slumps back in his chair. Didn't count on me spilling his dirty laundry out for all to see, did he?

"Oh, really?" Adriaan says. "I'm all ears."

"He's bullshitting you," Donovan says. "Kennedy tried to escape, that is all. Until we sedated him."

"You've always been an awful liar. Since your days as an initiate." Adriaan's smile is a razor. "No need to be coy. We knew this was coming. Just why you had to resort to underhanded methods is beyond me. This is not our way."

I snort, and they glance at me for a moment before resuming their staring match. So, my assumptions about House Montu's unnatural selection process are most likely not unfounded.

Donovan keeps his gaze pinned to his plate and draws breath as though he's going to speak.

Essie bustles in at that point and places a basket of bread on the table. "Shall I bring the meisie in, baas?" she asks Adriaan.

My heart gives a little squeeze. Marlise.

"Please do." He sits back, his attention riveted on me, and I try my damndest not to show any reaction.

Marlise. I try very hard not to think of Bethan, and a sudden flush of guilt suffuses me. I'm going to have to tell her. There's no escaping that.

Adriaan smiles at me as though he's well aware of everything that transpired, and he's only too happy to oblige by sharing every last, juicy detail.

The woman leaves us, and I reach out for the bottle of wine on the table. Might as well take the edge off the unpleasantness, though by all rights I should stay dead cold sober in this nest of vipers rather.

Fuck that.

"She thinks the world of you, you know that, right?" Adriaan says.

"What's that to you?"

"More than you know. Your dedication to each other is...commendable."

I don't like the direction this conversation is going. "Are you threatening her in any way?"

"Oh, not at all." That smile again. Too knowing, like he's got some nasty surprise waiting for me.

"What have you done to her?" I try to keep my hand from shaking as I pour the wine, put the bottle down, and take a sip.

"Nothing. But she was most agreeable once we explained the situation in broader terms."

As I open my mouth to speak, I catch a movement from the doorway opening onto the entrance hall. Marlise hangs back at the threshold, one hand clasping the lintel. Her eyes are huge, and she's biting her lower lip. "Ash?" she says in small voice.

All the words I want to say flee from my thoughts, and I shove the chair back so hard as I rise that it almost clatters over. We meet each other halfway across the room, and I surprise myself by lifting her in a ferocious hug. Her hair smells so good, so clean, and I press kisses on her mouth, her cheeks, her forehead. Her arms tighten around my neck as she buries her face in my chest.

"I'm sorry," she says.

"It's okay," I murmur. "We can talk later." I'm all too uncomfortably aware of the arseholes in the room watching our little public display of affection.

Carefully, I unwrap her arms from around my neck and steady her as I lower her to the ground. She fits perfectly in the curve of my arm, and I don't want to let her go.

Adriaan's expression is blank, and he indicates with one hand that Marlise is to take the seat diagonally opposite mine so that she sits next to Donovan, whose face is unreadable. Meekly, she obeys, though she unclasps her small hand from mine with great reluctance.

"As you can see, she's perfectly hale and hearty," Adriaan says. "Now please, take a seat. Dinner is about to be served, and I do believe we were discussing matters of great import."

Marlise stares at me, her mouth drawn in a tight line. Gods, she is beautiful. Doll-like. She shouldn't be here among these wretches. They've given her a dress in a style she'd never have chosen to wear herself. The fabric is a midnight blue, which suits her, and contains sparkles that catch the light subtly every time she moves. The neck is a deep V, which accentuates her cleavage. Beautiful breasts, and I drag my gaze to a more neutral target—her eyes.

"You've missed her, haven't you?" Adriaan inquires, and I'm forced to look at him.

"What do you think?" I ask. "Of course I've bloody missed her."

"It thrills my heart so to see new love. Such…devotion in a pair of young lovers is so…refreshing, don't you think?" The man's smirk suggests he finds us childlike, pathetic even.

"Just because your cold, dead heart withered the last time you passed through the Black Gate doesn't give you the right to pass judgment on us," I tell him.

The temperature in the room plummets, and both Donovan and Marlise stiffen, their indrawn breaths not quite masked. If Adriaan is annoyed, he doesn't let on. The damnable man sips from his wine glass, his attention not deviating from me. Heavy silence thickens the air then he turns abruptly to the black guy.

"Andile, please see to some music to lighten the mood. I'd like to suggest one of the Brandenburg Concertos. It should be more suitably uplifting than the Vivaldi, don't you think?"

Andile dutifully rises, and I feign interest in my cutlery, and place my napkin on my lap.

"I see you've not forgotten some of your manners. Appearances can be so deceiving, don't you think?" my dubious host asks.

"I don't want to play fucking games with you," I spit at him. "We're here, we're evidently both completely at your mercy, and now you've got us sitting here at this dinner table engaging in this farce of a formal dinner. For what?"

The Brandenberg concerto comes on, but Andile doesn't seat himself just yet, and positions himself behind Adriaan's chair. His face betrays no emotion, but he watches me warily, and the taut buzz of daimonic power from him suggests he's holding on in case he needs to strike.

Adriaan speaks, "My, my, so much vitriol. Patience, Kennedy. By now you should know it's a virtue."

"Patience got me nowhere in my past life. I don't see why I should waste time now." I don't even bother trying to disguise the disgust in my tone.

A warning glance from Donovan keeps me in my seat; I pointedly don't look in Marlise's direction because I'm sure she's silently pleading with me not to do something stupid.

"You should at least calm down long enough to enjoy your meal. You'll give yourself indigestion otherwise. We are not here to torture you. In fact, we wish to make a proposition. But we will not discuss business on an empty stomach at the dinner table." He turns to Andile. "Go ask Essie to bring in the starters. Donovan can pour the wine."

The men rise and do Adriaan's bidding, and I take the opportunity to make eye contact with Marlise. Her smile is tremulous, and the fingers of her right hand twitch as though she'd like to reach across the table but daren't. Unbidden thoughts of Bethan resurface, of her hungry mouth on mine. I've cheated on Marlise, and the shame burns through me.

Conscious of being under scrutiny, I speak first. "Are you well? I'm sorry about the other day." Osiris wept, I sound like an idiot.

"I'm fine, Ash. I was so worried about you. They said—" She darts a nervous glance to Adriaan before she licks her lips and focuses entirely on me. "I was freaking out, Ash. They said you and Alex were kidnapped by a member of House Thanatos. Adriaan told me all about them. They're evil."

Oh, so now he's Adriaan to you, is he?

I disguise my choking by taking a sip of wine. "That's only a matter of opinion. Point is, they've got Alex, and we need to find some way of getting him back." How do I tell her that the wee lad is probably better off with Bethan's bunch for the time being? That they've laid some perverted claim on him I'm not sure I can argue against? She doesn't even know about my angry ghost and that he has become her son.

What about the soul of the real child? Shoved aside? Assimilated?

"Ash? What's wrong?" Marlise asks.

I come to myself with a sharp intake of breath. How long have I been staring vaguely at her face? "Nothing I can discuss in present company."

Marlise glances at Adriaan, as though for reassurance. "Adriaan says he can help us get our son back."

What the fuck? Did I just hear right? I suppress

laughter. "So, this fucker gets his goons to kidnap you less than a week ago, and now you reckon you trust him because he says he'll help us get our baby back? Fucking hell, woman, are you daft? He'll use anything at his disposal to get what he wants, and I'm sorry, Alex is just a convenient lever. Van Rensburg wants the stele, or failing that, he wants what's in here." I tap my forehead.

Her features grow pinched. "This is our son you're talking about. He's not some *thing* to be used. Right now I'll do anything to get him back."

"Anything?" My laughter is bitter. "Evidently. So, you'd believe any cock-and-bull story that man"—I gesture vaguely in Adriaan's direction—"feeds you because you want to believe him. Despite the fact that he just plucked you out of your car when you went shopping. What the hell was I supposed to think, huh? That they've gone to so much trouble to keep us safe. If they had our best interests in mind, why didn't they just approach us like normal people would?"

Wow. We must be creating quite the mini soap opera around the dinner table. Inwardly, I cringe, though right now I'm so angry I could spontaneously combust.

Marlise stabs in the air with her butter knife. "We should have approached them sooner. Made a bargain. I don't know, Ash!" She gives a small wail of frustration. "We were cowering there like criminals waiting for the cops to find us. We did nothing wrong. That thing Leo asked you to take, it wasn't even hers to give you."

I sit back in stunned disbelief. How the hell can she believe this bullshit they're feeding her? "What do you know?" I sneer at her. "So, you'd rather believe these fucktards than me." A whining starts in my ears, more so than usual, and I flex my fingers to rid the sensation of static building. I'm drawing daimonic essence, without even meaning to.

"Kennedy." Adriaan's voice is laced with power. "We will not discuss business at the dinner table." Like I'm some child chewing gum or talking with his mouth full.

I offer the man a withering glare before focusing on Marlise again. "We'll speak about this. Later. *In private.*"

She juts out her lower jaw and furrows her brows. Oh, I know that look well enough. Marlise aims to give me a dressing down once we're on our own.

Essie wheels in a *bain-marie* and Andile passes around bread rolls. Adriaan is all smiles again and inquires as to whether I follow the rugby. The dumb fucker. He probably suspects I hate fucking rugby. Donovan chips in with some helpful comments about the latest match between the Stormers and the Blue Bulls, and I'm grateful that for now some of the attention has been shifted from me and Marlise.

Andile settles next to me with a massive plate of food, and gestures for me to get up and go help myself to a meal. The mere thought of eating anything beneath Adriaan's roof sickens me to my gut, but my body betrays me. Eat, damn it. Play along with this charade of a dinner party so I can cut to the chase once Adriaan finally deigns to allow us to discuss "business".

Marlise shoves her chair back hard and follows me to the *bain-marie*. Donovan shadows us, and hands us each a plate, as if this were of no more consequence than a casual gathering among old friends.

"What the hell is this?" I mutter at him, but the damned man makes as if he hasn't heard me.

Essie watches our interchange without the faintest flicker of curiosity. Is she an initiate? Definitely not Inkarna, though after my last misjudgement I don't want to fall into the trap of making any assumptions about folks who are supposedly the hired help. For all I know, this woman's second in command here.

The food looks good, and considering that we're all eating from the same dishes, it's not drugged or poisoned. Roasted impala, Essie explains in thickly accented English. Green beans, roasted potatoes. Sweet pumpkin cubes served with cinnamon sticks. Good, wholesome boerekos. Marlise tries to catch my eye when I return to the table, but I keep going. What, so she doesn't think I'm not pissed with her too?

She's not in a position to pass judgment on me. I've gone through hell and back to rescue her, and now she wants to make outrageous suggestions? I was a stupid fool to bring her into this.

You should have checked that she was using birth control, idiot.

Then again, Lizzie was no better than what Marlise is now when Richard brought her into the fold. Why? What made a schoolteacher material to become an initiate? Back then women could only become nurses, teachers, or secretaries. Or a housewife. Lizzie's mom was so overjoyed that a man of substance courted her daughter.

An awkward daughter, who'd wanted a career, then had ended up marrying anyway. Had Richard wanted to amuse himself by indulging professional curiosity, or had he actually wanted an equal to stand by his side? Lizzie never did get to find out, and I'm pretty darn sure Richard hadn't planned on contracting malaria either. A wrench in the works, so to speak. Which makes me wonder what the hell he'd been playing at in the first place. Lizzie had believed in true love, with all the trimmings. Ashton's been kicked in the teeth one too many times.

Then again, it wasn't every day that someone founded a new House. Richard could go on to have carved his own sanctuary in Per Ankh.

Those memories are so distant, dreamlike. How is it for the Inkarna who've returned again and again? Siptah's claim that he's loved both me and Meritiset.

You never told him your Ren.

I need to stop thinking of Siptah as Richard, but as Bethan. Only Bethan's most likely been blasted to molecules or into another dimension, for all I know. Does this mean I don't have to tell Marlise about my casual betrayal? Siptah never told me about Meritiset.

He loved her before me.

These ugly thoughts twist the rusted, serrated blade deep in my chest, making it difficult to draw breath. So easy to repeat the patterns. I don't want to hurt Marlise.

The food barely has any flavour yet I eat mechanically, intent only on feeding the body.

"Show me your tattoos," Andile says to me between bites.

I almost choke then swallow a mouthful and stare at him, incredulous. "What?"

He gestures at my arm with his fork. "I've always wanted tattoos, but I've just never gotten 'round to it."

They're keeping me prisoner, and now one of them wants to discuss my tattoos? "I beg your pardon?"

"Did it hurt when you had them inked?" Andile comes across as being genuinely interested. Not a trace of nastiness. He's just some dude. So far as things go, he's perfectly at ease among these people. To him, House Montu's the good guys.

"Um." Vague recollections of the previous tenant's times in the tattoo studio return, but the memories are so faded they slip from my grasp. "I don't really remember. I wasn't in possession of this *Kha* when the guy had the tattoos done." It feels weird being able to explain this to someone who'll understand what I mean.

Andile's barely out of his teens. I don't want to get to know him, especially if it means I'll have to kill him later. The previous time it was so easy to go in all metaphorical guns blazing and see my opponents as enemy. Not individuals. No names to go with the faces before their souls winked out. *Didn't stop you from offing Philip.* I miss my angry ghost's presence keenly, but my conscience seems hell-bent to make up for the first Ashton's absence.

Geeze, lock me up long enough and I'll start babbling to myself.

"Can I see?" Andile points at my jacket sleeve.

The conversation at the table has lulled, and the others are watching me. The bastard thing to do would be say no, and to tell the guy he can go fuck himself, but he's just a kid.

With a sigh I shrug out of my jacket. The room's warm enough anyway, and I roll up my sleeve to let Andile inspect the ink. Hours of sitting in the tattooist's chair. Silently howling demon heads and bits that look like dragon skin morph into biomechanoid shapes embellished with occult symbols and bad knock-offs of Enochian script. Once again I have to wonder if Ashton didn't inadvertently open himself to possession through this preoccupation with the occult trappings.

Andile gives a low whistle, but I draw the line at letting him see my chest piece. I have my limits, and cringe inwardly at his enthusiasm and unmasked awe.

He's so young. And I'm going to have to kill him later. I'm sure of it.

"Have they taken care of you?" I ask Marlise now

that most of my anger has subsided. Anything is better than talking to Andile.

"Very well. They've got lions here on the game farm. You can hear them roar at night." Her enthusiasm is childlike and transforms her face.

"That's... That's just great." The words won't come, but I force myself to ask Marlise about trivial, inconsequential things, and she obliges by spilling out a story at odds with what I envisioned. We refrain from discussing Alex.

I'd expected them to keep her locked in a secure room, yet she's been given the run of the property, so to speak. She gushes on about the people she's met, and the fact that there's a school for some of the local Tswana kids where she's going to start helping soon. All the opportunities I could never give her. Her about-face turns my meal into a lump in my stomach, and some of my sourness must show, because eventually her conversation dries up, and she refuses to meet my gaze. Instead, she pushes her food around her plate, and hunches her shoulders as though expecting a verbal lashing.

For a moment I entertain visions of us accepting Adriaan's offer, becoming turncoats. No more running. Safety. Some semblance of a life. It's tempting. If I could stomach the man's casual, condescending authority.

All the while Donovan and Adriaan discuss strangers, as well as matters pertaining to the running of this property. I might not even be in the room, and all I can do is fume quietly. Dessert passes in a haze of spongy malva pudding with melted ice cream, and I dutifully swallow down every last bite while watching my captors surreptitiously. Their lack of interest in me is a calculated insult aimed to remind me of my place—*we'll deal with you when the time is right.*

They're not in the least bit concerned that I'd try anything. Then again, I have no idea what sort of defences they have in place, and to nudge at the aethers now would be considered rude.

"We'll take our coffee in the voorkamer," Adriaan tells Essie when she comes to remove our dessert bowls.

I take my cues from my captors, only too glad to shove my chair from the table so I can rise. Mute, Marlise walks just behind me as we traipse through to an adjoining room I can only describe as colonial-era safari chic. Three large leather-upholstered couches are arranged in a semicircle facing a slate-paved hearth. A veritable bestiary of stuffed wildlife gazes at us with glass eyes, complemented by an assortment of African sculptures—demented things carved to resemble an uneasy union of human and other.

Without even trying to, I pick up a buzz emanating in this room—a low-level current of daimonic energy. Unsettling. Uncomfortable. If these walls could speak... I keep my arms folded across my chest and seat myself on the side of a couch that will place me as far away from Adriaan and his henchmen as possible. Marlise seats herself next to me, but it's quite clear she positions herself so that we're almost but not quite touching. Her hands remain clasped on her lap, and she keeps her head bowed so that her hair partially obscures her face.

Damn it, woman. My viciously keen guilt washes through me, reminding me I'm the one responsible for dumping her in this nest of vipers. I need to stay focused. Get the girl. Escape. Sounds simple if this were an action adventure movie carefully scripted for Hollywood.

They're using her to get to me, holding her hostage.

Adriaan settles himself on the couch almost opposite mine, his self-satisfied smile broadcasting that the games are only just getting into full swing after the overture. Now we can talk shop, is what he's telling me.

Andile's absent, but that doesn't mean he's far—should the need arise. Donovan settles on the central couch, one arm flung casually over the armrest nearest us while he scrolls through his phone.

Essie brings in the coffee things, and I swear her gaze lingers on me a few heartbeats too many. Dare I test my theory that she's full-blown Inkarna? I keep my awareness close, much as a child wary of being beaten would keep his grubby fingers to himself in a store full of glassware.

Ever so slightly horrified, I sit back and watch as Marlise pours the coffee for us. She keeps her eyes downcast, and only the briefest nod acknowledges my murmured thanks. Good little Afrikaans girl. What have they done to her?

"I trust the meal was to your satisfaction?" Van Rensburg asks me.

I glare at him over my mug. "Am I supposed to be grateful?"

"A simple thank-you would do. You are our guest, after all. But, no mind. We can get down to the bones of what's at stake. After some…dialogue, House Montu has a simple proposition to offer you. We will offer you and your partner an opportunity to align yourselves with us."

Woo-hoo. No surprises there. Try the easy route first.

"In exchange for the stele, no doubt." I can barely control my need to spit the words.

"Everything has its price. Surely, you don't think you can keep running? In addition, we will help you retrieve your son from House Thanatos's clutches. Your family will be reunited." The man sounds so reasonable.

Too goddamned reasonable. Next to me Marlise sneaks a hand into mine. She's shaking, but I don't look at her. Instead, I stare into my coffee mug—too sweet and milky. She always puts in too much sugar and milk.

What are my options here? These crazy bastards will hound me through many lifetimes. The prize is that valuable, and I'm already exhausted. What of Siptah? He'll hunt me down in future incarnations if I go over to House Montu. He is also privy to the secret, and he'll destroy me utterly if he believes it will keep this terrible secret from spreading.

But to know peace? Adriaan watches me, leaning far back in his seat with his legs crossed, a finger pressed thoughtfully to his chin. A faintly amused smile flickers at the corners of his lips.

"I'm afraid of what House Montu will do with the knowledge you seek." Might as well be upfront.

"And you think it doesn't bother House Montu that mere a handful of individuals is privy to such a devastating secret? Your fears cut both ways. We are most anxious to level the playing field. Think of this as nuclear technology. If all sides possess the knowledge, then we can at the very least enjoy the stalemate of a protracted cold war rather than fear that the wrong group gains the upper hand."

"Houses Alba and Adamastor have done nothing with this knowledge," I point out. "We have kept it safe. By all rights, we should have destroyed the stele and allowed the knowledge to pass into forgetfulness. I can't imagine that House Montu would put this to any good use. Your House has an expansionist attitude I'm not all that entirely certain I'm comfortable with."

"Ah, Kennedy, your naïveté makes me smile. Librarians are notoriously bad leaders. We have the entire world at our fingertips. Why should we waste our gift of immortality peering into forgotten scrolls? Humanity is seething in its blithering ignorance, its leaders distracted by partisan politics. Let them stay that way. It's for the best. Think on the role of the pharaoh, who rules with the crook and the flail. He is a shepherd and a warrior. Humanity is simply not fit to rule itself. Consider the mess they're making of the Middle East and the United States, with their pathetic notions of submission to their Abrahamic delusions. Let's not forget Europe. Democracy is a dismal failure. Who will curb China? Lift Africa out of its vassal state?"

The man's a megalomaniac. I snort. "You're the one who's delusional. The age of pharaohs is over. If you think I'm going to hand over any secret as dangerous as the one I have the misfortune of carrying, you are sorely mistaken."

Next to me Marlise's indrawn breath is a hiss, and she stiffens. "Ash." My name is the merest whisper.

"House Alba's days are long gone, despite all their best efforts to arm themselves. You'd best reconsider your stance, Kennedy," the man says.

"I'm not doing this for House Alba. I was tasked with keeping the book and its secret out of enemy hands, and my past and current experiences with your House haven't done anything to make me change my mind."

Adriaan tuts quietly. "So much bile, dear boy. You must learn to overcome your knee-jerk reactions and try to see things from our point of view. We're trying to pick up the pieces after your patrons brought the West to its knees. Don't you think two world wars were enough? Not to mention countless skirmishes exacerbated by attempts at 'quiet diplomacy' and the failure of globalism and its neoliberal capitalism?" He crooks his fingers to suggest the quotation.

Oh gods, he's spewing exactly the kind of language that is guaranteed to get my hackles up. Under ordinary circumstances I'd avoid him. If he thinks he's going to win me over with his attitude, he's seriously misjudged my character.

"That's bullshit, and you know it," I say. "Montu is a House of warfare and destruction."

"And rulership, which is exactly what this world needs at this time. What do you think will happen if everything is allowed to continue as is, the populations multiplying, to breed like the vermin they are? A plague of locusts descends upon the green wheat fields and strips the living earth of everything that promotes life. We have a great gift. We must use it."

His words sicken me. "So, you'd see us enter into a dictatorship then." I turn to Donovan. "You brought me here for this bullshit?"

Donovan's expression remains bland as he glances up from his phone. "You wanted to be reunited with Marlise."

I offer him what I hope is a chilling smile, then swivel to make eye contact with Adriaan. "You are aware, of course, that your minion here had me murder one of his colleagues. He conspired against one of his own House. How am I to trust any of you if treachery abounds within your organisation?"

Adriaan doesn't so much as flinch. In fact, he returns my smile with what appears to be genuine warmth. "We put Darwin's theories into practice here, young man. I'm sure you'd know that by now. After all, what better way to learn when one is faced with the severe consequences of failure?"

Young man? "That's barbaric," I spit at him.

"Oh, so now we must all play nicely? Really now, if I recall, *you* haven't been playing nicely at all. What was your body count back in Cape Town?"

He has me there. How many have I killed? I never counted, and of late I've simply stopped caring. That morning up on the mountain returns to me—scarlet spatters on lichen-encrusted boulders.

"Oh, you can't answer that question, can you? Now, who's the barbarian here? Who's *Akh* is stained with the deaths of others?" He leans closer. "And you know what? You haven't even given those poor bastards a second thought since you left the city, have you? You've got blood on your hands, Kennedy. As much as I do, or Donovan. Even your little woman here. You are no better than the rest of us." Adriaan glances at her before fixing me with his gaze.

The need to turn to Marlise is great, but I don't break eye contact with the man. My pulse hammers, however, and my throat has gone dry. Marlise has killed? Poker face, Ash, poker fucking face.

"So what's your point?" I ask, feigning indifference.

The man raises a brow then sinks back into his chair, his fingers steepled. "It's very simple. I suggest you relax for the rest of today. Spend some time with your companion. You can dine in your suite. Tomorrow morning, after breakfast, we will reconvene, and you can give me your answer."

CHAPTER SEVEN
Salt in the Wound

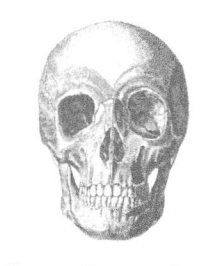

THE BASTARD WASN'T bullshitting me when he said we had an entire suite to ourselves. From what I can tell, we're in the east wing of the building, of what used to be storage but has been converted into accommodation. High ceilings and exposed beams reveal thatch. Terracotta quarry tiles on the floor with the prerequisite Nguni skin sprawled across the expanse. The four-poster bed is a monstrous affair complete with a pale froth of ornately draped mosquito netting. The suggestion of a bridal chamber is not lost on me. One end of the room is dominated by a widescreen television and a gargantuan oxblood leather sofa.

My prison looks more like it has fallen out of the pages of some décor magazine for a fancy private game lodge rather than the not-so-humble abode of the big cheese of an Inkarna House. Then again, what was I expecting? To be tossed into a dank cement cell with only a bucket for my waste? There are more exquisite ways to torment a captive.

Marlise's presence in the room is a fizz-crackle of agitation. Bastard that I am, I ignore her while I make a show of examining the pictures on the walls—bland prints dating back to the colonial era. Distorted giraffes and fanciful representations of indigenous people. How fucking clichéd.

"Ash, are you going to talk to me?" Oh, so she's doing the little-girl-lost voice.

There, the first clue that this is even vaguely the home of a practitioner of the daimonic arts; the print of a leopard has a particular zing to it, and when I reach out to touch the gilt frame, I get a zap of static.

A dark chamber, chanting. Tart smoke of herbs at the back of my throat. Vigilance. An udjat symbol scribed with red ink on a square of papyrus.

Of course we're being watched.

"Ash?"

I round on her. "What?"

Marlise is standing about two metres from me, which suggests she's followed me on my circuit around the room. The way she's clutching her arms suggests that she thinks I'm either going to bite her or smite her.

"We need to talk." Her lower lip quivers.

"Hhhhm, no shit." With a weary sigh, I drag my feet over to the couch where I collapse noisily. The leather is cool against my exposed skin.

How do I explain to her that she's betrayed us by listening to the rot Adriaan's been feeding her? Exhaustion turns my limbs leaden, especially considering all the food we've eaten. My *Kha* wants sleep. Scratch that, I'm craving the temporary oblivion sleep offers.

"How have you been?" I ask her. Might as well extend a figurative olive branch.

Marlise takes this as her cue to seat herself on the couch's armrest, perched as if she might fly at a moment's notice. "I've been all right. All things considered." She offers a tremulous smile. "I spoke to my mom yesterday." Her bottom lip starts quivering, and the tears run freely down her cheeks.

"My dad's had a stroke. I wasn't there."

Shit fuck.

"Is he okay?" I scrub my face with the heels of my hands so hard my stubble rasps.

Marlise starts crying in earnest, terrible wracking sobs. Only a douchelord would leave a woman who's obviously hurting sit on her own when she needs comfort. The old Ash would have told her to suck it up and stop looking for sympathy, but it's her dad, for fuck's sake.

I uncurl myself up into a seated position and drag the woman into my arms so that she can cry herself out. Like a great big fool, I whisper soothing nonsense while I smooth her hair. What else can I do? All the while, there's a nasty, evil side of me that hisses about how these people are manipulating my emotions.

Once she's calmer, I go make her a cup of tea in the kitchenette and even fetch her tissues from the bathroom. Marlise's complexion has gone all blotchy, and she swipes at her nose.

"Thank you," she murmurs then blows her nose noisily.

"So, is he going to be okay? I take it he's not dead."

She shakes her head. "He's having physio sessions. He's had to resign. They've sold the house and moved to a place in Diep River. Robert's taking a gap year and he's got a job at a computer store in Plumstead, so he's helping them cover the rent. Trevor's working part-time at the Spur, but the school's understanding about the fees, Mom says. All this time that we never made contact. All this has happened."

"Man, that sucks." And I was the one who enforced the months-long radio silence. My guilt gnaws and gnaws.

Marlise sniffs loudly then sips her tea. "Adriaan says they'll help sort something out. There's a property in Noordhoek where they need a caretaker. Mom and Dad could handle that. He says he'll also sort out the medical expenses not covered by medical aid."

"Gee…" *Fuck*. "That's…very…kind of him."

Her expression hardens. "You don't approve."

I can't help my sharp bark of laughter. "You're forgetting that a year or so ago these people kept you drugged up to your eyeballs and locked up, for surety. They were prepared to *kill* you. And now you're just letting them walk roughshod all over you. After all we've been through to be free?"

"I want what's best for my family, Ash."

Amun wept, I hate it when she says my name like that.

"In case you haven't noticed it, so do I." I try hard not to clench my fists.

"Well, you have a funny way showing it, keeping us living like degenerates out in the middle of fucking nowhere, without being able to even contact *my* family. It's not my fault you're not arsed to give a shit about blood ties."

"All my family died more than a hundred years ago," I grit out.

"What about Mr and Mrs Kennedy? Don't you care that your little accident cost them everything?"

That's it. I'm on my feet, towering over her. "They're

not my fucking family. It's not my fucking fault that they didn't do a good enough fucking job raising that idiot. Do you think I asked to end up like this?" I slap my chest. "Do you think I wanted to be this...this oaf? I'm making the best of a bad situation. I'm trying to do my best. To keep *us* safe."

"Then what about Alex, hey?" She's on her feet too, not cowed by my presence. "You left him so that the Death-walkers could take him."

I'd like to take her and shake some sense into her.

"He's probably safer there with House Thanatos than he is with us," I say.

Marlise's response is an inarticulate scream, and she flies at me, pummelling me until I'm able to capture her wrists. This little tableau must be ridiculous to our captors: me holding the small woman at arm's length while she attempts to kick the shit out of me. This tantrum lasts for about half a minute until she's clearly exhausted herself.

"Are you quite done?" I ask.

Her only response is to go limp, and I let go so she crumples to the floor then pace to the double doors leading onto the veranda. Locked, of course. I growl and give the handle a solid shake, briefly toying with the idea of blasting the lock.

"They don't want you going out," she mumbles.

"Fuck that shit." Instead I reach for my smokes and light up.

"You shouldn't do that in here."

"Now's not the time for me to give a fuck about social niceties. If I were a pyro I'd have burnt this fucking shithole to the ground already. The only reason I'm holding back is because I need to figure out how to get us out of here without getting you killed."

Her glare is venomous, but it doesn't stop me

from lighting up.

"Or maybe I should just fucking leave you here," I say. "You'd like that, wouldn't you? You've just traded in your old daddy for a new one who'll buy you all the pretty ponies your heart desires." Okay, that last bit is just plain fucking evil.

My words have the desired result, and her eyes start tearing up again.

"Oh yeah, that's just the way to get me to feel sympathy. Go on. Cry." I turn my back on her and stare out the window, at the winter-brown lawns where a gaggle of grey-and-white geese are wandering about.

Her sobs wrench at me, and I hate myself for having stooped to this all-time low, but what else can I do? Play along with this little charade? More than ever, I'm furious with Adriaan for exploiting my weakest link. If I were half the bastard the old Ashton Kennedy was, I would've left both Alex and Marlise to their own devices and looked out for myself. I could be in London this very moment, without a care in the world.

I'm not that bastard.

What are my options? We could try right now, break down this door and try to walk out. But I have no idea how strong these people are. Adriaan has about a dozen or so battle-hardened Inkarna at hand, no doubt proficient in a number of different weapons, not to mention unarmed combat. And fuck knows how powerful daimonically.

Or we could wait until the dead of night and try subterfuge. Possibly the best course of action that would result in the least amount of potential bloodshed. How far would we get? Especially walking through a camp filled with lions. Sure, so I could maintain awareness and keep us out of harm's way, but potentially dealing with a pride of big cats on top of a tag team of Inkarna doesn't appeal to me.

Unless we steal a car ...

But that's hardly making a quiet getaway.

I was such an idiot to allow myself to be taken captive so quietly.

Then again, would I even have gotten this far if I'd not? No, I need to find another angle, and fast. I need help, but from whom, I have no idea.

What are my strengths? Damn it, I'm not thinking along the right channels. I take yet another drag and burn my fingers—the cigarette has gone down to its ember. I grind the butt out on the floor, then pick it up and toss it in the bin.

Mercifully, the woman's sobs have subsided, and I turn to face her.

"You done crying?"

She's moved onto the bed, where she lies on her side with her head cradled in her arms.

"Lying there unresponsive like a petulant child is not going to endear you to me, woman. There's no need to play this game."

She sits up with a huff and scrubs at her face. "You're such an arsehole."

"And your taste in men is appalling. Now let's be adults about this situation. We need to get out of here so that we can go rescue Alex."

"Didn't you hear what Adriaan's offering? You want to throw away everything?"

"For fuck's sakes, we're going to go around in circles on this. House Montu are not our friends. Think of them as the Borg, if you want to stick with your stupid sci-fi movie references. They're going to take over everything, given half a chance. They've made power grabs in the past. Can you imagine if they could permanently obliterate their enemies? The only thing that's keeping them in check is the fact that we keep coming back for another round if we get knocked out of the game. But then I don't expect you to understand that. Yet."

Her glare is venomous. "I've been doing my studies, and I've been doing the exercises. Don't underestimate me. I've a better idea of this whole Inkarna business than that night when Leo gave me that book. But I'm looking at the bigger picture here. I have people I care about. I'm not a heartless monster who can blithely go on and trample people. House Montu is offering us the better option. We might be able to effect more change for the good from within the organisation."

"People allow themselves to be trampled, and House Montu is a den of vipers. You're more likely to be killed trying to move up the ranks here," I spit. "Some people think they can get their way by manipulating others' emotions."

"Then why did you come back to me if that's the way you feel?" Marlise's face has gone chalk white.

"Because it's the right thing to do."

"And that's supposed to make me feel grateful? A year ago I followed you into exile voluntarily because I loved you, and I thought it was the right thing to do. Now..." Marlise squeezes shut her eyes and shakes her head slowly before she dares to regard me again.

"You were in danger. Your family was in danger by default. Can you imagine if they'd come to fetch you after I was gone?"

"My parents thought I was lying dead in a ditch somewhere," she says. "*For a whole year*. I did that for you. For a whole year."

"So you could do *what* exactly? Prove how much you love me?"

"Doesn't the fact that we have a child together mean

something?"

I gulp back a laugh. "What fucking planet do you live on? To think that getting yourself knocked up would make me love you?" Then I step back, the horrible realisation sinking in. There. I've finally said to her what I've always held back on all this time. *I don't love you anymore.*

To give Marlise some credit, she doesn't start crying. She sits motionless, a wax doll with mussed auburn tresses. "So I was basically just a pity fuck?" she murmurs.

"I care about you, deeply. You've helped me when no one else wanted to, but I'm not *in love* with you."

She rises, her hands clenched at her sides. "So I'm just a friend with benefits, right?"

Okay, she's ticked off, all right. How the hell to respond to that, because it's true. I hold up my hands to try placating her. "It's not what I mea—"

Next thing I know, an invisible force slams me into the wall. My awareness cuts out before the pain kicks in.

☥

Those moments of waking after some unforeseen trauma are always the worst. A serious case of what-the-fuckery as I gradually gain an impression of what my surroundings are.

A woman's sobbing, calling my name out repeatedly while pleasantly cool hands cup my face. Glass crunches beneath me, and my back throbs. It takes me a few moments to flex fingers and twitch my legs— the synapses are fried, like I've just had the world's greatest electrical shock.

A key grates in a lock, men talking rapidly to each

other, but it's difficult for me to follow their dialogue. All I want to do is sink back into the welcome nothingness of sleep. The woman starts crying in earnest, but her wailing recedes, followed by the tingling warmth of daimonic presence that starts at my head and works its way down to my feet then back up again, to hover above my heart.

"He's slightly concussed, nothing more," says a man. "No bones broken. Organs are intact."

"Good," says another.

I try to ask what the hell just happened, why I'm lying on the ground, but all I manage is a dry croak. My lids are heavy, and even when I do manage to crack them open, all I see is a blur of faces peering down at me.

More frightening is the realisation that my thoughts are jumbled.

"Bastet's dried-up cunt, what did she do to him?" one man asks.

"Some sort of neuro-daimonic shockwave, I think. That's what it feels like anyway."

"Fuck me."

"You said it."

"Is he going to be okay?"

"We'll have to see. He's lucky his brain's not jelly."

"Boss isn't going to be amused. We'd better get him to the clinic."

One of them helps me into a seated position, and I'm limp. It's easier to allow them their way with me, but then a blistering pain crawls up my spine and unplugs my brain.

☥

The desert stretches out in an undulating dune sea that vanishes to each horizon. The sand is orange, and my feet sink ankle-deep as I trudge along the crest of a dune. The sun has burnt the sky as white as bone, and I keep walking. My throat is dry, my tongue stuck to the roof of my mouth. No matter how hard I swallow, there simply isn't enough saliva. If I don't find shelter soon, I'll shrivel away to nothing, and eventually the relentless dunes will bury my desiccated corpse under tons of sand.

My hands are fine, woman's hands. My arms are smooth. Why do I expect to see a swirl of ink? A large faience scarab decorates a silver ring I wear on my left hand. I've seen this ring before, but where? None of this will matter soon when I die.

Just as I am about to fall to my knees, I reach a clearing in the trough between dunes. A red granite outcropping stands upon a small, quartz-strewn plain curiously free of the dunes' progress. The temple constructed out of pale limestone has been built into the outcropping, and its trapezoid pylon stands in contrast to the ruddy cliff behind it.

My certainty of death evaporates. I stumble and slide, and almost roll down the dune as I make my way to this sanctuary. Anywhere to be out of the sun. Anything.

The pebbles hurt my feet, but not as much as the baking-hot sand that blistered them only moments before. I run to the rectangular slot of an entrance, my skin smarting from the brilliance. Cool dark beckons. Relief, no matter what lies ahead of me once I step across the threshold.

The wind laments its eerie sorrow down here, and I almost cry for joy as I stumble up the ramp that leads to the entrance. Giant figures have been carved in relief on either side—strident, falcon-headed men. My thirst lacerates my very *Kha*.

The passage is long, and its end is a small rectangle of luminescences ahead. My breathing echoes in the enclosed space as I approach my goal. Like a child, I trail my fingers against the walls, for the reassurance that there is a surface to remind me that I am not about to tumble into nothingness. Each step doesn't seem to do much to deliver me to my destination, and fear digs in its talons. What if I spend an eternity trudging along, going nowhere?

A buzzing begins at the edge of my hearing, that vibrates in my bones and sets my teeth on edge. The ground shivers, and the stench of ozone floods my sinuses. When a tall figure steps into that rectangle ahead of me, I almost fall to my knees in fright. A man, no more than a silhouette, but there is no denying the broad shoulders, the well-muscled limbs. The head is oddly proportioned with regard to the shoulders, a bit too large and most likely due to the man wearing some sort of headdress.

"Greetings!" I call out. "I'm sorry. I might've become lost."

The man stands, arms akimbo. Waiting.

"Enter, and be welcome." His voice reverberates, both within this passage, and inside my head.

As I begin walking, the distance between us closes much faster than expected, and soon I stand before him. The man has the head of a falcon, His eyes fierce and His beak wicked. Instant recognition brings me to my knees before Him.

Montu.

Deep-rooted fear has me sobbing, for there is no escape from this, one of the most warlike of the Neteru. He could smite me by barely lifting a finger, yet He allows me to remain before Him, naked in His brilliance.

"Rise, stand before me, daughter," He says.

Montu grips my upper arm and helps me to my feet. With great difficulty, I tilt my face so that I can look up at Him.

"Why you?" I ask, and immediately hate how trite my query sounds.

He takes my left hand and turns my arm so that my wrist is exposed. There, emblazoned and glowing faintly beneath the skin is the outline of a khopesh, and the thrill of recollection hits me hard.

A rectangular onyx stone plinth stands in the midst of this chamber, upon it a khopesh sword. The sickle-blade gleams with the same undefined luminosity as the stone and emits the faintest of hums.

The weapon I took from the chamber, which has somehow become part of me.

"What do you want from me?" I ask.

"The Kha is a living temple. I walk before you. I stand behind you. I strengthen your arm and straighten your spine. When you bring down your hand to strike your enemies, it is My hand that guides you. When you throw a spear, it is My power that causes it to fly true. You see with My eyes, and when you shout, the heavens will roar and the earth will tremble," Montu says. *"Together we will slay Apep."*

He grows brighter, yet for some reason I don't need to shield my eyes as I'm enveloped in His brilliance. I'm engulfed in flames, yet I'm not consumed. Every atom, all aspects of my daimonic self are raised to infinite splendour, and for an eternity I know the secrets of the Universe, the totality of being, how every small thing is defined by entropy.

There are four beds in the room—the kind you'd find in a hospital—and for a heart-stopping moment I believe that I've somehow returned to that time just over a year ago where I woke in hospital, in the wrong place and time, in the wrong body.

It's not the same room. Instead of vertical blinds, cream-coloured curtains filter light through. Grey loeries are calling their maniacal *khwê-khwêee* outside. My thoughts are sluggish, and try as I might, I can't seem to retrieve anything concrete. A small town in the Karoo. A woman with auburn hair. Some secret… I know time has passed. Months. But the memories are mercury.

Lizzie's old life unfurls easily. Even Ashton's. I know exactly what brought me to this *Kha*. Visions of my time in Per Ankh tease me, of great halls and soaring voices. But of the past year or so? Not much.

The man has the head of a falcon, His eyes fierce and His beak wicked. Instant recognition brings me to my knees before Him.

The dream-vision blazes through me with terrible clarity, and I start to shake, reliving each word, each moment etched indelibly on my *Akh*. I can't help myself. I'm stricken. Teeth chattering. My vision segues violently between that moment in the dream-temple and the ward, and a high-pitched whining starts in my left ear. A sharp chemical stench floods my sinuses, washes my—

☥

A man stands by my bed. He's tall, well tanned. Completely bald. His eyes are dark, and he's frowning, clearly troubled. He confers with another man, who's holding a tablet that they both study. After that one, blurry glimpse, I keep my eyes closed. Listening.

"Vital signs are fine. ECG shows his brains are basically scrambled, especially if you look at that point. Grand mal seizures," says the younger man.

"Any idea what's causing this?" asks baldie.

"I don't want to try anything involving daimonic effects, unless we trigger another seizure. We'd have to take him to Pretoria for an MRI."

"Out of the question," the bald man snaps.

"Thought as much. I'd say just keep him quiet, keep him sedated until he's had a few days to rest."

"We don't have a few days." Bald man sounds agitated.

For some reason Baldie's discomfort amuses me vastly. Though what the hell I'm doing here, I don't know. Pretoria? Surely there are MRI units in Cape Town. Fuck. The last I knew, I was standing in the road outside The Event Horizon, and that SUV was heading straight to me. Obviously, I got hurt real bad. Experimentally, I flex my muscles. All fine. Nothing broken. Just stiffness, especially in my lower legs, neck, and jaw. Like I snorted too much charlie and was grinding my teeth overnight. What's more worrying is the realisation that I've been strapped to the bed, and a cursory tug and a kick informs me that my bonds are pretty much industrial grade shit.

I open my eyes and glare at the men. "What the hell happened? Why'm I tied to this bed?"

Baldie breaks into a relieved smile. "Ah, Mr Kennedy, so nice of you to join us. I trust you are feeling better?"

"Who're you?" I ask. And why the hell is he talking to me like he knows me? I try to thrash about a bit more, but my skull feels like it's about to implode, so I quieten. My breath wheezes, and a cold sheen of perspiration has filmed my brow.

A shadow of unease flickers over Baldie's expression before he reasserts a pleasant demeanour. "Haha, that's amusing, Kennedy. You're not going to get out of this so easily." He turns to the other guy. "Sedate him so he can't do anything with his powers. We'll see him at the meeting room at twelve."

"Sir?" the other man queries. "There might have been memory loss..."

Baldie pauses by the door, turns and smiles evilly. "I'm sure that's what he'd like us to believe. I'm not fooled."

The dude with the tablet shakes his head then turns to me. Even as he busies himself with various vials and shit on the bedside table, it's clear he's troubled.

"You're not going to shoot me full of kak are you?" I ask. "Which hospital am I at?"

The man's gaze is full of pity. "You're not at a hospital. You're a guest of—" He shoots a glance toward the door. "Adriaan van Rensburg."

The name means nothing to me, and I stare at him blankly, waiting for him to fill in more details.

"Where. Am. I?"

"You're on a game farm, about two hours outside of Pretoria." He regards me closely.

"What?" How the hell did I get from Cape Town to Joburg? "What day is it?"

"Wednesday, June six."

Hang on, that's not right. "It's January," I tell him.

Fuck. Gavin's going to kill me. Because something in that man's expression, his entire bearing, tells me that he's right, and I'm wrong.

"What year is it?" I ask him in a small voice. For some reason this is highly important. *Why* I ask this, I don't know.

He tells me.

Fuck. Somewhere along the line, I've lost more than a year. I can't even. I don't argue when he shoots me full of drugs. Better that than to try figure out what the hell happened to make me lose a large chunk of my life.

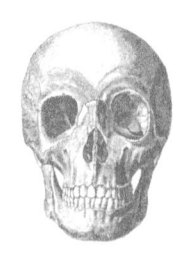

CHAPTER EIGHT
Ghost of the Past

SLEEP DOES LITTLE to restore my memories, nor do I have any recollections of dreams. I wake chained to a bed and needing to take a slash bad so bad it feels like my bladder's swollen to the size of a football.

"Hey! Hey! Let me go!" I yell for what feels like a gazillion years.

A sad-looking man enters the room after I'm nearly hoarse. Slightly thinning hair, long nose. He would've been good-looking if it weren't for the bags under his eyes and his pallor.

"Relax, Ashton. Please."

"Who're you?" I shoot back at him.

"Please, you can drop the bullshit memory loss thing with me, okay? I'm not your enemy."

Should I laugh or scream? What the fuck is everyone on about? Like they've got some sort of secret history with me I'm totally clueless about. I yank at my bonds, but they remain resolutely secure.

"Listen, buddy, I don't know who the fuck you are, nor do I care, but you've got my word I'm not going to try jack shit so long as you untie me so I can take a slash."

He hesitates then approaches the bed. The air around him seems filled with static. Creepy. A small spark shocks me when his fingers accidentally brush my skin. I jerk back. The dude just looks confused for shit.

"You really don't know who I am, do you?" he asks as he unties my feet.

I glare at him then swing my legs off the bed.

And immediately wish I didn't sit up so fast. My head swims with dizziness, and I have to breathe deeply until I stop feeling like I'm going to upchuck. Jesus fucking Christ. I prod at the tender spot on the back of my head. Whatever happened, I got seriously fucked up.

Once I'm sure I'm not going to puke my guts out, I stagger over to the en-suite bathroom. Fuck me, I look like hell. No muscle tone. Lost about twenty or so kilos. And seriously? This crappy hospital gown? I look like a moffie. What the fuck has been happening to me in the meanwhile? I can't have been in a coma or something.

"Get me my fucking clothes, you moron!" I shout at the dude in the ward. He's obviously in with the people who're in charge of this joint. Least he can do is get me something half decent to wear so I don't look like a lunatic escaped from the asylum. But fuck me, it feels good to piss, and afterwards I splash my face with water and drag my fingers through my hair.

My body feels alien to me, unused, and I rest my forehead against the mirror and allow myself to unfocus. Get clothes, get dressed. Find a fucking cigarette. Hopefully by then these fools will tell me what the fuck is going on, and I can go home.

Jesus, and all my stuff? Who's been paying the rent? George's probably been helping himself to anything of value.

I need a fucking phone.

At least just call Mom, let her know I'm still alive.

Fuck, she must be worried sick. That last argument we had. A vague sense of guilt nags at me. She's most likely convinced I'm buried in a shallow grave next to a highway. No doubt Marlise would've played the tragic ex and arranged the memorial service to end all memorial services where they play all my favourite songs, and everyone gets totally wasted afterwards. And the blokes from the band will stand around, beers in hand, and make shitty jokes about all the stuff we did.

Fuck, who'm I kidding? Marlise no doubt danced on my grave.

Gavin's probably thinking the Russian mafia finally got hold of me. His expression when I walk into The Event Horizon more than a year later, whole and alive, will be priceless. I allow myself a small chuckle at that scene. Though there's going to be hell to pay for that shipment of charlie I was supposed to handle…

Ah well, it's not the first time I've had to dig my way out of the shit. I'll figure it out, as soon as I get away from these freaks of nature.

My clothing is unfamiliar—a pair of recently mended pants covered in way too many buckles, zips and shit, like I've seen the cyberkids wear to the psytrance parties. I haven't seen the shirt before either—it's not the sort I'd go for: long-sleeved and obviously handmade with seams on the outside to make a feature of the needlework. Where's a good Slayer T-shirt when you need it? The jacket is familiar, and I go through the pockets to see if I can find clues. A few till slips from Graaff-Reinet. The fuck was I doing there? A soft pack of cigarettes that has two crushed fags in it. A lighter that works.

Sad Man watches me as I pop a cigarette in my mouth and light it, and I almost dare him to tell me I'm not allowed to smoke inside. I check out the till slips. Grocery items. Nappies? What the fuck?

Nauseous, I crumple the paper and slip it back into the jacket pocket.

Why in god's name was I buying nappies?

My guardian's expression remains puzzled, perhaps with a hint of pity.

"What?" I ask him.

He shakes his head. "You really don't remember anything, do you?"

I look at him blankly. "What is it that you want me to remember?"

Sad Man narrows his eyes at me. "What can you tell me of House Adamastor and *The Book of Ammit the Devourer*?"

A weird, prickly feeling washes over me. "Dude, seriously. Are you on drugs or something?" The man's spouting gibberish at me like I'm supposed to know something about it.

He goes pasty all of a sudden and sags against the door.

"You okay?" I ask.

Sad Man shakes his head then seems to gather himself. He peers at me, and yet another prickly sensation washes over me. Then he starts laughing as he walks out the room. His cackles follow him down the passage. Mad. Absolutely fucking loony.

Righty then. I finish my cigarette, pull on my boots

and lace them, then see about getting out of this shit dump. The corridor outside the ward-like room in which I woke looks like it belongs to a farmhouse—terracotta tiles on the floor. Old prints in heavy gold frames on the walls. Exposed rafters and thatch. The window overlooks a pool.

I exit into a hallway that's all larny, with antique cupboards and huge oil paintings of old dudes in military getup. Probably dates back to the South African war. Uniforms very British. Next to a grandfather clock is a painting of a sad-eyed woman dressed in black. Her hands are folded over what looks like a scroll of some sort. There are pyramids in the background viewed through the arched windows.

The man has the head of a falcon, His eyes fierce and His beak wicked.

The vision hits me like an acid flashback, but the importance of the vision is lost before I can figure out its meaning. Instead I'm swamped by dizziness and have to sit on the armchair beneath the painting.

That's where they find me, my head in my hands. Sad Man is back, and this time he's brought his crew—three similarly dressed dudes in suits, like they're the FBI or some such.

"Mr Kennedy, will you please come with us?" Sad Man asks.

I'm tempted to walk right out and see whether they'll stop me, but a faint stirring of danger prickles. No visible weapons, but that's not to say these guys aren't dangerous. I could run, but I won't get far. Best to play along for now and see what they want.

We march through a courtyard with a real outdoorsish fire pit. It's easy to imagine the inhabitants of this home all relaxed around their braai with their Klippies and Coke in one hand, braai tongs in another. Jesus fuck I just want to get out of here.

The room they bring me to is some larny lounge with those huge leather couches you see in houses on *Top Billing*. Fuck me, this whole place could be on that TV show, complete with whoever the botoxed presenter is. They all look the same anyway, with identical cheesy white smiles and hairdos that cost more than a secondhand Fender.

No one sits, so I go over to the fireplace to warm my hands, 'cos there's no other way I'm going to get rid of the residual chill in the air that seems to have invaded my bones. The dudes stand by the door, Sad Man closest to me, like they're waiting for someone.

"What now?" I ask.

Fuck me, the stuffed buffalo head on the wall is huge. I'd hate to be tripping off my tits in this room. Fuck that shit, I already feel like I've dropped a cap or two.

Sad Man clears his throat and looks toward the door. "We're waiting for Mr Van Rensburg."

"He the bossman?" I ask.

The two henchman trade worried glances. What the fuck is wrong with everyone?

"In a manner of speaking, yes," Sad Man says.

"Can you explain to me what I'm doing here? Or even tell me who you people are?"

Sad Man takes a deep breath, and his buddies watch him expectantly. "I'm Donovan Binneman. These guys here are Andile and Duncan. We're all part of House Montu."

"House Montu." My memories itch, the same way I'd run a tongue over a missing tooth.

Donovan stares at me expectantly, but my mind remains blank. Weird name for a club or a business.

"What the fuck did you guys do to me?" I ask. Okay, I'm getting pissed. These fuckers tampered with my brain in some way. Fed me drugs or something. Mind-wiped.

Another man speaks, his accent oh-so proper, like he's attended some fancy schools in the past. "We didn't do anything to you, Mr Kennedy. What we'd like to know is what did you do to yourself?"

As one, we turn to face the newcomer, an old dude who's completely bald but well tanned, and self-satisfied. He makes me think of pictures I've seen of our president, only this guy's white, and there's something oily about the way he oozes into the room.

"You must be Van Rensburg then," I say to him and bare my teeth at him like a dog that wants to bite. I'll be damned if I call him Mister the way all these twunts do. The fucker is a whole head or so shorter than me, but he seems to fill the room with an undefinable crackling presence.

Without meaning to, I take a step back, even though the bald fuck stands four paces from me. Andile and Duncan flank him, their hands close to the firearms they carry by their sides. Donovan merely watches me from beneath hooded lids, and I can't figure out if he's amused or annoyed by this interchange.

That bizarre, static feeling passes over me again and a frown of puzzlement mars the Van Rensburg dude's forehead. He turns to Donovan. "You were right." He sounds surprised.

"*Akh*'s gone... The *Sheut*'s running on the template provided by the original *Ka*."

What the hell are they talking about?

"Do you guys mind?" I ask. "I'd like to suck off into the funset, if it's not too much trouble. Whatever bullshit it is that's going on here, I'm so over it."

They both turn to me, Van Rensburg with his eyes narrowed.

"I don't know," says Van Rensburg. "The *Akh* could be dormant." He snaps his fingers at Andile. "Go fetch the girl. Bring her out to the courtyard. We'll meet you there." Then he heads over to his desk where he flips open a small, leather-bound chest.

"Mr Kennedy. You are proving to be far more difficult than expected. Believe me, this precious little ruse of yours isn't fooling me. Hiding behind the *Sheut* of your present *Kha* is certainly a novel approach, but do you honestly expect us to believe that your blessed *Akh* has somehow fled?" He snorts with amusement.

"What the fuck bullshit are you spewing?" I shoot back. "Shit and Ach." Jesus, I don't even think I'm pronouncing the words properly.

He shoots a withering glare in my direction then raises a blade that looks like it's been lifted from the Stone Age. I've seen historical documentaries where dudes have carved different types of stone to create tools, but this makes those items look like toys. The knife is easily as long as my forearm and has been shaped from a black material that might be glass.

"Obsidian, in case you're wondering," Van Rensburg says, smug. "The Egyptians discovered that this holds an edge quite effectively. Naturally occurring glass with myriad uses within a ritual environment."

"What the hell do you intend to do with that?" I ask, but I'm starting to put two and two together and getting a nasty, crawling suspicion.

The girl, out to the courtyard. Violence.

"Who've you got?"

"I'm sure you'll be pleased to see her again."

Van Rensburg's smile is filled with so much malice, I take a step back into the bookshelf.

"Sir, with all due respect—" begins Donovan, but Van Rensburg silences him with one glance.

"Bring him." Van Rensburg gestures at me with the blade then turns his back on us and stalks out.

Oh hell no. I need a weapon, something.

Donovan and Duncan approach, and a wave of static smashes into me and sets a vicious, electric hum going in my head. Now or never.

I charge Duncan, because he's the younger of the pair. Figure I can knock him over and shove past. Only it's like I run full tilt into an invisible brick wall before I've taken two steps. Next I know I'm lying flat on my back with bright, silver spots wriggling across my vision. My lungs feel like an elephant is stepping on my chest, and judging by the pain, the back of my skull's caved in. The two guys peer down at me.

A few seconds must've passed with me being unconscious, because they give the appearance of having had a conversation about my condition. I don't argue or fight them when they lift me to my feet. Duncan then pinches a nerve by my shoulder and zaps me with a taser or something that sends a low buzz of sheer agony through my nervous system. It takes all my concentration just to put one foot in front of the other to allow them to guide me out the door and to the courtyard.

Though I'd dearly love to cuss the ever-living crap out of them, I end up biting the inside of my cheek so hard blood fills my mouth with a burst of iron. There's nothing but to allow them to bring me exactly where Van Rensburg wants us.

That's when I see who the girl is for the first time—Marlise, ashen and with Andile gripping her wrist in such a way to suggest that she's not running anywhere. She's lost weight since I last saw her, and is pale, almost sickly so.

"Ash!" she calls, but whatever it is that Andile does

to her, she's brought to a quick standstill from her attempt to rush at me.

"What the fuck?" I ask Van Rensburg, who has seated himself on one of the benches, that blade still in hand. "What is she doing here?"

Marlise is ancient history. If this douche thinks he's got some sort of leverage over me, he's sorely mistaken. Conniving little gash and her trying to guilt me after that whole episode with that Russian slut. We weren't even dating at the time.

Van Rensburg smiles, like he's holding a royal flush. "May I present the mother of your child. Surely you do care that she is well, Mr Kennedy?"

That crumpled till slip from the Spar in Graaff-Reinet. Nappies. Now this.

An absent year. My stomach clenches horribly at the missing chunks of time. Anything could have happened. Wouldn't it just be divine fucking justice?

Marlise's expression is stricken, but she's either unable or unwilling to say anything to confirm or deny Van Rensburg's assertion.

I sneer at her. "There's no way the kid could've been mine. I'm not an idiot. I wouldn't have fucked you again even if you were the last woman on this planet and the survival of the human race depended on me knocking you up."

Grasping, manipulative little bitch.

I turn my regard to Van Rensburg. "What's the point of this? You bring my ex to me, wave that funny knife of yours around like I give a fuck. I don't take kindly to motherfuckers who threaten me." I try to take a step in his direction, but Duncan zaps me with that taser thing, and brings me to my knees.

Van Rensburg rises and approaches Marlise. Tears are running down her cheeks, and she tries to pull away when he trails the blade along the tear tracks.

"You sure she means nothing to you?"

Even from where I'm standing, I can hear the rasp of glass on skin. That blade is fucking sharp. Marlise whimpers.

"You're a sick fuck, you know that?" I spit at him.

"Then you won't be surprised when I do this?" Van Rensburg moves so fast it's easy to mistake the way he brings the blade across her throat as a joke.

But there's no mistaking the truncated cry and the whistle of air nor the flood of scarlet that soaks the front of her grey tracksuit top. Andile holds her up for a few seconds, but when her knees buckle, he allows her to fall and steps back.

A sensation like a curtain of icy water drenches me, and all I can do is watch, held in place by Donovan. My voice is strangled in my throat, and make choking noises and half reach out to Marlise. Okay, I didn't like her much but for fuck's sake, she didn't deserve this.

With all my might I try to fight against the bonds that hold me, but my body is unresponsive. Every twist brings a fresh stab of electricity until the ground rushes up to greet me, and I discover that I'm sprawled on the slasto, at eye level with Marlise's corpse. She gazes into eternity, her lips parted, and some undefinable part of me is screaming, No, I never meant for this to happen. I never meant this to happen. No-no-no.

This isn't the first time I've watched someone die due to being in the wrong place at the wrong time. I've been party to enough bad shit over the years. But it's a little too close to the bone when it's someone innocent like Marlise. All those days when I walked her home from school or when she trailed after me. A large chunk of our childhood. She was always there, and I took her for granted.

That knowledge bites deep and draws blood.

Tears are on the edges of my vision, but I blink them away, my chest too constricted for me to do more than draw ragged, wheezing breaths while I watch the blood pool and spread.

This entire sick picture is missing important pieces, and I can't put them together. I give a strangled cry and shove myself onto my knees, my body weak. I'll carry Marlise's empty stare with me to my grave, but that sick fuck is going to pay. An animal growl escapes me as I stagger to my feet and round on the man, but they're ready for me.

They don't even touch me. An invisible force slams into me, and I fly across the courtyard and crash into a pile of firewood. For a few moments my world is slashed into agony, and it takes me precious moments to try figure out how I've managed to become airborne without anyone laying a hand on me.

Someone's shouting, Donovan I think. "Leave him be, master. Can't you see, there's something wrong. You're dealing with the shadow. *The man you want is not there.*"

A prickle of static washes over me followed by a meaty thud. What does he mean by me not being here?

No one says anything, but a man groans.

"Take them both to the clinic," Van Rensburg says. "Clean up the mess. The lions will eat well tonight."

The fuck?

I'm too hurt and in too much shock to argue.

Marlise. Dead. It's my fault. Yeah, I know I was a dick about the way I've treated past lays, but the fool woman could've used birth control. She should've known better. Ditto for Marlise. But fuck, what I said to her.

My body is limp when I'm manhandled up, and

it's Andile who gets me stumbling back to the ward where I first woke. I concentrate on simple stuff, like breathing, like putting one foot in front of the other, because if I think too hard on what's going down here, my brain seizes up, and I can feel a scream building up in my chest.

Do not want. Do not want.

"I'm sorry," Andile murmurs to me once I'm seated on the edge of the bed.

"Fuck you," I say, but there's no power in my words.

Andile's eyes are white-rimmed, and he fetches a trolley with medical supplies.

"I didn't know, okay?" he replies. As if that will make any difference.

Then he's dabbing my scratches with disinfectant, and it's all I can do not to drop more F-bombs because holy hell those abrasions hurt.

"You're not pretending, are you?" he asks.

"Pretending about what?"

He pauses mid-dab. "About forgetting who you are."

"Okay, there's a whole lotta weird shit going on." I suck in a breath and try to squeeze the last view of Marlise dying out of my mind. Not now. I need time to process. Then I regard him evenly. "Please tell me what the hell is going on."

Donovan stumbles in at this point and collapses on the bed opposite mine with a groan. "Don't tell him anything, Andile. You can go help Duncan, okay?"

"Sorry," Andile mutters but puts down his swab and obeys Donovan.

I scrub at my face and immediately wish I didn't, because I encounter myriad scratches, and my hands come away with a smear of blood.

There's a squeak from the bed Donovan's lying on, and when I glare at him, he's propped himself up. He's pale, with a thin trickle of blood running down his left nostril. "I've gotta hand it to you Ashton. Whatever stunt you've pulled, it's a master stroke. No one should be able to do it."

More rubbish. Why can't anyone speak in terms that I can understand?

I continue to glare at him. Maybe he'll implode or something.

Instead, he gives a wry chuckle and pushes himself fully upright.

"Amun's balls, this is a cock-up," he mumbles then starts examining containers on the trolley until he finds what he's looking for.

"Want some codeine and muscle relaxants?" he asks. "You gonna need it later." He tosses me a plastic container which, I catch—a surprise in itself considering how shaky I am.

I pop four of the green-and-red capsules and wash them down with water from the glass next to my bed. Give me about ten minutes, and I'll have a pleasant little buzz going, and these fuckers can run me over with an eighteen-wheeler, and I'll not feel a thing.

"Now what?" I ask my new best friend.

"Van Rensburg's gonna want to examine you under formal conditions, I'm afraid."

That doesn't sound encouraging. I grimace. "And if I refuse?"

Donovan gives a soft snort of amusement. "You won't have a choice."

"Bullshit." But I don't get up, don't move.

"I'm sorry about your girlfriend."

"My *ex*." The lettering on the pill container blurs.

"I had no idea. Really. If it were up to me. If it's any consolation, there's a chance she'll make it to Per Ankh. She'd come into her powers."

More fuckery and terms I don't understand. The plastic of the pill container creaks when I clench my fist.

Donovan gets up and sits down next to me, careful to keep space between us. "We don't have much time. I'm sorry that things have come to this. Whatever's gone wrong, I didn't expect this to happen."

"What. Happened?"

"I know this is going to sound like... Like some sort of weird, made-up story, but you must believe me. You and I, as well as everyone here, are members of a type of being known as Those Who Return. Inkarna. When we die, we are reborn into new bodies. You and I belong to rival sects, Houses, as it were. You have... information...that we need."

This is too much. I start laughing, because I really don't know what else to do. Because if I don't start laughing, I'll cry or throw a tantrum, or punch his sad, ugly mug until his nose is nothing more than a mash of cartilage.

My reaction is clearly not what he desires, and he watches me in stern disapproval until the last spasms of laughter die away.

"Are you quite finished?" he asks.

I wipe at my eyes. My chest is burning, and my head feels like it's about to implode. Any moment now I'd dearly love to wake up in bed. Hell, even like that time when I woke in the gutter outside my digs in Obz. Anywhere but here, now, with Marlise's dead eyes staring at me accusingly. I will never forget that.

"This is a waste of time, whatever it is you're planning," I tell him.

"I realise that," he says. "But please, if...if whoever it is that you were before the...glitch. If you're still there, I am sorry. I know how much she meant to you. I just want you to know that I'll do my utmost to retrieve your son from the people who have him."

Donovan might as well have punched me in my gut, and some of my stricken expression must've gotten through to him.

"Yes, you have a son. His name is Alex. He's a few months old."

I'd love to tell him to fuck off, that he's talking kak, but he's not.

That's when I reach for my last cigarette, and Donovan even lights it for me, because my hands are shaking too much.

"How did I get into this mess?" I ask. "I'm telling the goddamned truth. I don't know anything of what you want."

"I believe you. Your mannerisms, your... lack of...the souls I could read before this... Everything is different. But that's not going to stop him."

He means Van Rensburg.

"He's calling up a ritual this evening. He's going to invoke Montu. That's our... Patron...for lack of better description. He's going to peel back the layers and take what he wants by force, even if it damages you. It's not something that is done lightly. It goes against most of our tenets. It might even have repercussions...for him, *for us*, if it goes wrong."

"Then why do it?"

"What you carry inside you is too important. We'd hoped that you might see reason, that you would give the information willingly. That method didn't succeed. Now we're having to resort to more extreme methods."

"Why try to take the information in the first place?"

"If we didn't, someone else would. In fact, there were already those searching for it when we... retrieved Marlise."

"She wasn't just some object." A bone-deep weariness makes me lean against the headboard. The nicotine wriggles through my veins, and I wish I could make the slight feeling of drunkenness last. I'm a man on death row.

"I'm sorry. I know it's cold comfort, but she was being groomed to join our ranks."

"Can't you just help me get out of this place?" Kinda stupid asking, but I feel compelled to.

"You wouldn't get far. Even if you manage to evade us, there's still the fact that you've got about ten kilometres of game farm to get through without the lions tracking you."

"And if you helped me."

He gives a humourless cough of laughter. "It's not worth my hide."

"So you're just going to sit back and watch your arsehole boss give me a lobotomy so that he can scratch around looking for information that I don't have."

Donovan sighs. "We don't know whether the information is there."

"You're wasting my time."

His expression is pained, and I suspect he wants to say more, but then two guys I haven't seen before enter the room to fetch me. Donovan watches as they take me down the passage. I'm tempted to kick up a fuss, but they're both openly carrying guns, and besides, who knows what other methods they could employ to control me. Weird shit is weird, and all that.

I wouldn't call it giving up exactly, but most of the fight has gone out of me. What's the point? I'm more than a thousand kilometres from home, everyone most probably thinks I'm dead, and even if I do break out, these fuckers have me outnumbered. And there's the lions. I don't disbelieve him on that. This Van

Rensburg dipshit looks the type who'd happily stand back and watch while I get mauled.

Not to mention the fact that they've gone and fed Marlise to—

I shake my head to dispel that image and fight back nausea.

When I was little, my mom took me to Tygerberg Zoo, and one of the neighbouring farmers had goats wandering near the lion enclosure. Those lions immediately sat up and took notice when the livestock approached. The intensity of their sudden regard was terrifying, how the big male sat up, followed by the two lionesses—their flat, yellow gazes pinpointed on the fence where the goats were grazing.

It won't be any different here, and it's almost impossible not to imagine Marlise's still form tumbled out of the back of a truck for the waiting cats. Or maybe the hyenas. Surely they'd have hyenas here, too, if there are lions.

Don't think about it.

The men guide me through the house to a structure out back—a lapa with circular stone walls and a conical thatch roof. The air is thick with incense, and my nose prickles uncomfortably. What the hell? It's dark inside, and when I balk, I get prodded in my spine with a sharp object.

"What are you guys planning with me?" I ask.

No answer. Instead they grip my arms on either side and force me over the threshold. It takes me a moment or two for my eyes to adjust, and what I discover is hardly encouraging. Some sort of fucked-up ritual space, complete with an altar. Heavy, fragrant smoke rises from incense burners placed at strategic spots and creates a stinking fog that makes my eyes water.

I struggle and kick against being dragged forward,

but one of my captors is armed with a goddamned taser, and I'm nearly senseless from the pain that jags through me. After that it doesn't take them long to drag me before the altar, where they force me to my knees, tie my hands behind my back, and shove me down further so my forehead comes to rest against the slasto.

Even as my muscles recover, I wonder at the merits of trying to struggle to my feet, but one of the fucking bastards zaps me again, and all I can do is drag in deep, ragged breaths. They must've put some sort of narcotic in the incense, because bright fractals begin to swirl at the edge of my vision. Oh wait, I did drop all those fucking pain pills too. Shouldn't have done that... But I guess hindsight, twenty-twenty vision...

Then the chanting begins, an unearthly chorus of male voices that reminds me of the recordings of Tibetan monks that I've heard. The sound rattles right through me, a baritone rumble that thrums in my bone and blood, throbbing an urgent rhythm. Frequencies expand and contract, and my skin grows cold.

Nausea creeps up my throat, and I dry-heave, but nothing comes out. My stomach twists on itself, like the times I've taken bad MDMA, and I gulp at the soupy air.

A man begins to speak, but his voice speeds up then slows down, each oscillation of every vowel, each sibilance resonating. Whatever language he's speaking, it's not one I understand.

The pressure builds.

Then I'm falling.

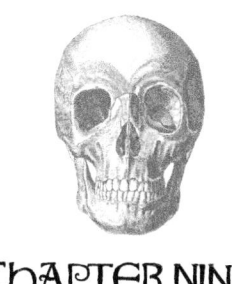

CHAPTER NINE
Flame War

"WHAT HAVE YOU done?" I ask Montu.

He never gives me a direct answer. Instead He shows me a fragrant, cypress-crowned bower or a chamber inlaid with precious stones.

I've been trapped here in His temple for what feels like days, nights. He has garbed me in filmy vestments spangled with stars. He has gifted me with a *nemes* headdress laden with lapis lazuli and a golden headband.

"You are my queen, my chosen consort," He tells me.

The woman who looks back at me from the reflecting pool is foreign to me, her eyes heavily outlined with kohl, her skin like raw sugar. Her eyes flash like fire opals.

My entire being is daimonic flame, insubstantial yet vital.

Even now my life in the world of matter fades. This is

Per Ankh, or some such reality much like it. Surrounded by an endless dune sea of roaring, moaning sand. Of desert winds that scour the landscape, of a sun that is a flat disc that traverses its stations.

I struggle to make sense of time, but there are occasions when smoky apparitions arrive in supplication at the temple pylons. My role is simple, to walk at the Neter's side, to be beauteous and in every sense a queen.

You need to remember.

Here I am Nefretkheperi, becoming perfect, beautiful. What I've always been meant to be.

Remember what?

At night, when I stare up at the silvery disc of the moon that is always full, and a bone-pale reflection of its solar companion, I am troubled by vague recollections. A man, who's angry and bitter, who carries a great burden.

Yet it's as if some vital aspects of my self have been sheared away, separated.

Once a day, Montu departs to do battle with the serpent Apep. His chariot flashes with the fire of the sun, and his horses' hooves are burnished with flame. Khu and Nakhti stamp and snort, and their eyes roll, foam drenching their jaws as they ride with my Lord.

I am the Lady of the Sanctuary, who sings the hymns to Montu and lights the incense at the prescribed hours. There have been others before me, of that I am certain, because I find small traces of previous servants—a comb inlaid with mother-of-pearl discarded in a corner behind a pillar; beads that lie scattered in a corner; and a sandal strap beneath my bed.

Each day my Lord returns, and I take his spear from him and clean the foul blood that tarnishes the bronze head. I bathe his brow with cool waters and bring him the beer that I brew to refresh him.

In all my years I understand that I have never brewed the stuff, yet in this place the knowledge comes to mind unbidden.

Some dim memory rages against this order, this routine existence with each action prescribed and premeditated. Time is irrelevant here.

Occasionally, my Lord sees the concern writ on my brow, but then He rests his cruel beak gently against my forehead.

"You are safe here. Do not concern yourself with matters that are beyond your ken. I have chosen you above all others."

For a while I am reassured.

Sickle-wing swallows dive in the blue rectangles of sky that are visible from the courtyards. Sparrows chirrup in the eaves. Once, I glimpse a fierce falcon glide into the sun and vanish. These are our only guests, other than the supplicants who visit and bring their gifts, be it freshly baked breads, sides of beef, or fresh water. My duties require that I store these in the appropriate places until they are required. Nothing spoils in this haven.

I eat, though I do not hunger. I drink, though I do not thirst.

I am allowed to wander at will throughout the sprawling temple complex, from the gleaming hypostyle hall to the myriad courtyards and their colonnaded ambulatories. Many hours are spent in silent meditation as I ponder the scenes carved in relief on walls and painted in scarlet, blue, gold, and verdant tones.

Djehuty weighing the heart of a deceased pharaoh. Temple singers giving praise to Hathor, the Mistress of the Heavens. Diligent servants tending vineyards of the Duat. Other, stranger scenes impinge themselves on my senses, but as soon as I try to penetrate the mysteries, those thoughts flee like a murmuration of starlings.

"You are not ready for those truths yet, my daughter," He tells me. "Some other time. Patience."

I have His permission to wander everywhere, but for the inner sanctuary at the heart of his temple. Twice a day I may bring libations of beer and bread, which I place before the door. Twice a day, I return to find the cup and platter empty. When the Neter takes His fill, I do not know. I am never there.

One morning I comb my hair by the reflecting pool, savouring the sweet scent of lotus in full bloom. Dragonflies skim across the surface and leave the barest ripples. The tune I hum under my breath is an old lullaby, of the kind mothers have sung to their younglings for eons in the ancient land of Khem and recalls nodding papyrus heads and the inundation of the Nile that lays a layer of fertile earth down for the next season's planting.

My eyes begin to slide shut gradually, until my reflection in the water's mirror-like surface becomes a silhouette. A blur of static mars this, and unease crawls its finger down my spine. A man with long black hair has his hands tied behind his back, and his head is pressed against the ground. He is surrounded by figures dressed in white robes, and a flame-eyed high priest stands above him with a drawn blade.

Bitter myrrh reaches me for a fraction of a moment, and two jagged heartbeats pass where I can feel the strain in his muscles, the sickness roiling in his belly. Bitter bile forces its way up his throat, but he gulps it down, his lungs thick with smoke. His veins are sluggish with drugs.

Fear slams me out of this dream-vision, and I fall back from the pool. It's as if the vision of Montu's temple wavers, becomes superimposed over a void. Then reality solidifies, and I am conscious of the sun-warmed stone beneath my splayed palms, of the way my chest rises and falls with each ragged breath.

Sweet Montu, what was that?

Were they going to sacrifice him?

The ritual is none that I have known in Per Ankh, and at once a flood of memories assails me, of the opalescent halls where I resided with those of my House. Ageless faces raised to the stars in adoration, of the many hours spent recording the passing of the Blessed Dead. Immortal librarians we were, bearing witness to countless lives that have passed into the Sea of Nun.

I remember.

Richard and Lizzie.

Nefretkheperi passing through the Black Gate.

The Hall of Judgment.

Anpu takes me by the hand and leads me to Djehuty by the scale. My heart weighed against the feather of Ma'at. Or at least the closest approximation of this occurrence that I can recall, because in truth the images are vastly different from what actually took place. No mind, human or immortal, can truly come to terms with the enormity of the experience of the potential for the complete dissolution of being. The Opener of the Ways and The Scribe of Ma'at are forms of being, and our paltry attempts at framing them, clothing them in easily digested symbols in order to understand them, do not even come close to the task.

I am inconceivably small, but a flyspeck for them to take notice of me. To suffer their regard is almost more than what my small heart can bear, but I have no choice but to subject myself to the weighing of my heart.

The Forty-Two Negative Confessions roll off my tongue. I'm babbling, almost sobbing, but I am so afraid that I will be found wanting.

I gaze into a mirror, and a man stares back with stormy grey eyes and a scowl to frighten even the Sebau fiends.

"I know your name," I tell Ashton Kennedy.

And I understand what has been done to me.

Montu has captured my *Akh*, so that all that remains animating the *Kha* that I took a little over a year ago is an echo, the *Sheut*. That which is vital, has long fled. So far as I can tell, the *Ka* and *Ba* have reunited in the unholy creation that is the son of this body in the mirror.

The wrongness of this makes me gasp, but there is nothing I can do here, like this.

The man growls soundlessly then in an epic, futile gesture, lunges back with all his force and smashes the glass into a thousand fragments.

Phantom pains dance across my knuckles, and when I hold my shaking hands before my face, the skin is split, and a faint ooze of blood runs down my palm. Even as I watch, the bruised flesh becomes whole.

Yet I remain irrevocably lodged in this reality, the temple complex of the last of the Neteru I ever imagined would take an interest in me. I get up and run, and the passages empty into hallways, or courtyards with burbling fountains or gardens where trellised vines hang heavy with grapes. I need to escape, find that entrance that leads into the desert, but where to from there? I lose my sandals and my veil. I smash into a pillar and nearly brain myself in the process.

My heart constricts painfully, and I must escape,

but none of the places where I end up look familiar. Eventually I sag to my knees, my forehead pressed to the sandstone in a gesture very similar to Ashton's. I fancy I can hear the men's guttural chanting of the Invocation of The Ruler of the Two Lands.

Shadows ripple across my vision, and I want to vomit. The bile of Ashton's fear is bitter on my tongue, and I understand on a deep, primal level that they are seeking not so much to rule Ashton, but to reach me, and to find that one, awful secret that I hold locked away as deep as possible. They are coming for me. They are coming for the book. The obsidian blade burns bright.

The Book of Ammit the Devourer.

So much as I try not to think about those cursed, words, they spring to the forefront of my mind, along with a wicked plan. Through my own actions I have brought myself here, into the very heart of my enemy's stronghold. Not only has their Patron tolerated my presence, but He has welcomed me. A snake into His bosom.

When aligning to a particular Patron, those who serve tie themselves to the essence of their Neter. While House Adamastor is small, we recognise the Titan Adamastor, the sleeping Guardian of the South, of the Cape of Storms. Likewise, those who follow the tenets of Montu are inextricably linked with Him.

Granted, it means that my Patron might not be as ancient as those who persecute me, but it does give me a distinct advantage—my Patron is harder to define and more difficult to find. House Montu may possess the might and the strength borne up by hundreds if not thousands of years, but they might as well have posted a massive billboard above their heads saying, "Here we are!"

The sanctuary, where the souls find nourishment. The one place that I was forbidden.

Though my body aches, and the fear hasn't abated much, this option is an almost tangible possibility. What if?

What lies behind that door? What happens when I open it?

A fierce wind screams between the pillars, and my Lord's displeasure vibrates through the stones and echoes on the edge of my hearing, but I don't allow this to halt my progress. That door beckons, and even as all attempts to exit the temple complex are met with failure, all routes inevitably do lead to the heart of the matter.

Nefretkheperiiii...

The wind moans my name, or perhaps my Lord does. It matters not. With trembling hands, I pull on the door, muscles straining against the resistance. It's not going to budge.

"Come on, you bastard," I say between gritted teeth.

My arms feel like they're about to be yanked out of their sockets, but I don't stop pulling. My strength is not equal to the task before me, but the ghostly whiff of fear and stale incense goads me to try harder.

"Set's balls," I grit out.

Stone squeaks on stone, bringing with it the slightest shift of the door.

I drag again, and whimper when something in my arm snaps and the pain sings through my veins. With a yell, I summon the dregs of my strength, and the door swings open.

The sanctuary is nothing worth mentioning. A narrow slot leads into darkness, and I pad down the passage where immeasurable quantities of stone press down onto me from all sides. My breath rasps in the close confines until I'm squeezed into a chamber filled with row upon row of shelves. Shabti figures. Hundreds, if not thousands, of shabti figures done up like small mummiform men and women, each inscribed with a name inside a cartouche.

Some *Ren*s have only a few shabtis. Others have dozens, each representing an incarnation. The only differences are the names of the *Kha*.

Time is irrelevant.

I find the shabti representing Adriaan van Rensburg eventually. Meritsekert. A woman. She was once a temple singer, the daughter of a pharaoh. All her shabtis over the centuries are women, until this last one. What happens if I break all the shabtis?

I hold Adriaan's form. Baked clay is so brittle, and I almost feel remorse when I drop the shabti on the ground where it shatters into a thousand pieces. Adriaan's should be enough. I don't want to destroy the *Ren* by working my way down the incarnations.

Who's next?

At random, I draw a few more that are clearly incarnate in the present times.

Their cartouches glimmer faintly. The sound of them breaking thrills me even though I know my behaviour is that of a petulant child. I'm destroying the movers and shakers of House Montu.

This is for the chapter house in Simon's Town. This is for Leonora's initiates that you arseholes murdered. This is for the grief you caused me when I returned to the world of matter, and you hounded me, threatened me, and tried to force my hand.

Donovan's shabti fits neatly into my hand. That's when I stop and reconsider.

He's in service to an enemy organisation, but is he really my enemy? If my suspicions prove correct, destruction of these figures results in the destruction of the *Kha* of the owner, not the *Akh*. Not that I've been counting, but I assume less than twenty have died so far, including Adriaan.

No amount of restating The Forty-Two Negative Confessions will quite erase the sin that stains me now, for I have destroyed wilfully and harmed others. But damn it feels so good. The amount of mischief I've just wrought rivals that of Set in a moment of hubris.

Could I destroy Donovan? Having one's life truncated before its time is more than just a small inconvenience, even for one who is almost certain that they'll pass into the Duat and reside in Per Ankh. This is his first shabti. His *Ren* is Sekhemib. His *Kha* is in its forties. I don't even know if he has kids. He could quite easily have a wife or a girlfriend. Parents somewhere who're still alive. Perhaps a brother.

My shame blooms in my chest, and I put down his shabti. I've done enough.

The shabti of a woman is right next to Donovan's. With trembling, almost reverent hands I read the inscription. Nebty-tepites. The name of the *Kha* belongs to Marlise. That knowledge echoes in my heart of hearts. I want to weep and crush the figure to my chest. Joy and sorrow are at war within me, for here is evidence that she will live. Another immortal enemy if she hates me, and she has good cause to do so after all I've done to her.

Destroy her before she can destroy you, my rational mind whispers.

Enough.

I place the figure next to Donovan's. I might come to regret this in the future, but for now I shall cease in my wanton desecration.

A gleam of gold catches my attention, and that's

when I see the prize above all prizes.

The sacred figure, in this holiest of holies, is a strident figure of Montu, no more than a foot tall that stands on a plinth. The hawk-headed man is crowned with a sun disk surmounted by two plumes, and resplendent with two uraeus serpents. In his left hand he grasps a was-sceptre surmounted by the head of Set; in his right, a khopesh sword.

I grab the figurine almost without thinking. If I could smash it... The metal is cool to the touch, but rapidly warms, and even if I want to fling it from me, I can't, for it has fused to my flesh, burning and slithering up my veins. I scream and flames belch from my mouth, and the statue glows with a white light that blinds me. I can only compare it to stabbing myself in the eyes with needles that drag their thread through my nervous system and stitch up my lungs so that I cannot draw breath or give so much as a twitch. A chorus screams at the limits of my hearing, the agony of thousands incinerated in a lake of fire. The conflagration chews the flesh from my bones, until my *Akh* is laid bare, and I exist as a singularity. Then wink out.

CHAPTER TEN
Aftermath

SWEET AMUN. Everything hurts. I'm lying on my side, and it's like a herd of buffalo have stampeded through my head. Light slants through gaps in the thatch above me. People are groaning, and a vile stench of burnt pork taints in the air.

That can only mean...

I retch, but my stomach muscles hurt too much.

My vision blurs and doubles with the floor of a temple in another place and another time, but then shivers back to the present, to an obsidian blade that lies discarded inches before my nose.

Row upon row of shabti figures.

My brain is doused with scalding fire, and the memories pour back in vivid Technicolor, of the statue of Montu melting into and melding with my flesh. As if in response, a banked ember within me flares. A falcon's scream echoes in my ears, and I have to lie still for a few heartbeats until the dizziness passes.

What I'm certain of, however, is that I'm back in the material realm, locked in the meat and bone of my familiar form—Ashton Kennedy. With that, I'm slammed with a rapid ratcheting of visuals.

She's dead. By Sekhmet's fury, *she's dead*.

That blank gaze—dark, startled eyes staring into nothingness from a spreading pool.

I didn't mean to. I'm sorry. I wasn't myself.

Useless fucking excuses. She needed me, and all she could depend on was a shadow, an empty ghost of my old Self, the one who by all rights should be dead. Maybe it's a mercy that she doesn't know about Alex, that the old Ashton's cobbled together an *Akh*, and it brings small comfort knowing that she has a *Ren*, that she's residing in Per Ankh by now.

I'm sorry, Nebty-tepites.

When I reach out for my daimonic powers, they are immediately accessible, and I snap my bonds as though they are but a thin skein of silk. With a groan, I rise into a crouched position to survey the damage.

Set's ballsack. What the hell happened? What I assume to be the charred remains of Adriaan van Rensburg lie about two metres from me, supine. His once-white ceremonial robes are blackened, and his skin has been cooked to crispy crackling to reveal the shock of white dentures clenched in denial of his mortality.

Donovan's crouched not far away, and shakes his head repeatedly, as if he's trying to dislodge an irritant. The moment he sees me watching him, he freezes. The whole deer startled in headlights thing.

"You look like a real idiot in those robes," I tell him.

And he does look foolish. If I ever have the misfortune of getting involved in any heavy ritual shit with my kind, I'm so not opting for natty costumes like wise men at a primary school nativity play. Fuck that. I straighten fully, then stride towards him. He flinches, no doubt expecting me to blast him.

Instead, I hold out my hand and help him up.

The relief in his expression is almost pathetic.

"Ashton?"

"I'm fully here. Don't you worry."

I let go of his forearm, and he takes a few steps back.

Andile and two others rush in, guns drawn, but Duncan gets to his feet, motioning for them to step back.

Donovan inclines his head, as if to say, All's well.

All had bloody well better be well, and I quirk a brow at him. "Am I still under arrest or whatever it is you'd like to call it?"

"I can't answer that. I don't have the authority."

"*What*?" I'm too tired to be angry.

"We have to arrange with the Nesut-Bity here in SA."

"You mean?" I cut a glance at Adriaan's smouldering corpse.

"No. He was the vizier of the north." But he walks out, shoulders slumped.

Guess I should follow. "Which makes you?"

He mumbles something that sounds like 'lieutenant'. But who cares anyway? I'm glad to be out in the weak winter sun that doesn't quite chase away the chill. Judging by the angle, it's late afternoon.

Donovan shucks that stained white robe and rubs vigorously at his arms while he paces about in slacks only. The skin on his chest pimples with the cold. Almost immediately, Andile rushes up with a blanket he's fetched from who knows where.

While I'm not exactly left to my own devices—at least three initiates are posted at strategic positions with guns pointed in my direction—I'm too exhausted to argue. What's important is that no one is doing anything to me or forcing me to do anything I don't want.

"I could use a drink round about now," I say to Donovan.

His hand gesture suggests I should follow him, and we make our way back to Adriaan's study, where two teenage boys are building the fire. No one speaks, but they all watch me with wide eyes. Except for Donovan. He's gone all pasty and collapses onto one of the couches with a loud sigh.

Only then do I realise exactly how cold I am. My arms feel weird—too big-boned and well-muscled, and I'm reminded of Nefretkheperi in the temple complex of The Lord of the Two Lands, as Montu is sometimes referred to.

Coffee laced with a more than healthy dollop of brandy is brought.

Only once he's had a sip, and he's lighted a cigarette—and passed me the box—does he speak.

"What did you do?"

I blink at him. "What do you mean?"

An initiate hurries in, and because Donovan appears to be the most senior remaining member, he bends his head and is in immediate, urgent conversation with the man. I hadn't thought it possible for Donovan to pale further, but he does, and he accepts the phone that is offered to him.

"Yes?" He places a hand over his face, like he wants to block out the light.

"What?" Donovan sits bolt upright, but his expression is stricken.

"I... Um."

It's not every day that I get stared at as if I am

a plague carrier, but this is pretty close. Donovan swallows hard. "I see." He must be getting the bad news that most of his higher-ups are all suddenly and catastrophically deceased, and it's pretty clear this has something to do with me.

Several times he tries to get a word in edgewise, but whoever's on the phone doesn't give him the opportunity. He holds the phone slightly away from his ear, and even from where I'm sitting, I can hear the tinny tirade aimed at him.

Eventually, the person loses steam, and Donovan assures them that everything is under control and that no, Mr Kennedy will not be a problem, that we will hasten to Montu's private lounge at the airport as soon as humanly possible.

The conversation ends, and Donovan makes as if to throw the phone across the room before evidently thinking better of it, because he places the device down next to him on the couch.

"We don't have much time," he tells me.

I laugh. "Where have I heard this one before?"

"We need to leave. Immediately. It is in your best interest to not make yourself difficult."

I shrug and offer him the universal gesture of helplessness. "What can I do?"

Because, really, what can I do? The whole point of me being here had been to rescue Marlise. They could try to pry the secret of *The Book of Ammit* out of me, but judging by the catastrophic results of their most recent attempt, this appears to be ill-advisable, due to the small fact that their Patron seems to have taken a shine to me. Not to mention the fact that I trashed their holiest of holies.

Marlise made it. There is that small relief. I can still apologise to her and try to explain that she was dealing with my *Sheut*. Surely, that must count for something? Though it will bring her cold comfort at present, and I can only hope that her sojourn in Per Ankh will lend her the perspective she requires to view the events that played out today with a degree of objectivity.

Yet another doubt gnaws at me and whispers that I'm fooling myself, but I can't chase down this line of thought yet. There are too many loose ends. Like what is House Montu going to do with me now?

"You can behave like an adult, surely," Donovan says. "I will say this much, that for now you are under no threat of coercion. We will not force you to give up any information. An emergency hearing has been called in London, and it will be decided what we will do with you, and how to deal with the repercussions of what has happened."

He makes me sound like a particularly devious problem.

Then he leans forward. "What did you do?"

I light my next cigarette off the one I've just finished and take another sip of my brandy-laced coffee. A pleasant, mellow feeling has crawled up from my belly.

"I don't think you'd believe me even if I told you."

How can I tell him about that temple complex? How can I tell anyone? My time there is mine alone.

☥

What follows is a blur. I wouldn't exactly call it receiving the VIP treatment, but it's pretty close. I'm harried through a clean-up routine, dressed in a suit that's slightly too tight across my shoulders. They can't find shoes the right size for me, but I draw the line at letting go of the boots and the leather jacket. That's all the reminder I have of my *Sheut*.

The Ashton Kennedy who grimaces back at me from the mirror looks better for having shaved and showered. Still a thug, but the hair's tied back neatly, and though I have dark rings round my eyes and I'm horrifically pale, I don't look like I'm about to keel over.

Then we're hurried into a black BMW X5 with tinted windows, and I find it easier to sit back in the seat and allow myself to shift into a semblance of sleep. The disconcerting thing is that whenever I do drift off, I find myself in Montu's temple complex. My experience verges on a lucid dream, because when I examine my hands, they're mine—Ashton's—and I can discern the ink of my sleeve work clearly.

Out of curiosity, I wander the passages and sit by the reflecting pool, but it's like the essence of the place has fled. The sun shines, but its warmth is reduced. The scent of ashes hangs on the air. Ashes and blood. My boot connects with a soft bundle of feathers, and when I pause to investigate, I discover a sparrow gone stiff in death.

With a shiver I yank myself back into a semi-doze, conscious of the rumble of wheels over gravel, and the low discussion going on around me. Andile's driving, and Donovan rides shotgun. Duncan sits next to me, and considering the way he shifts continually, he keeps cutting glances in my direction.

They talk as if I'm not in the car, and I can't help the small thrill of shock when the enormity of my actions sinks in. Within the past two or so hours—or so far as we can figure—during the time that my *Kha* had been dragged into that awful ritual chamber and my *Akh* fled, fourteen Inkarna of House Montu spontaneously combusted. The synchronicity is too tidy for them to ignore that I'd been threatened in the ritual chamber when it happened.

I'm too numb to feel much guilt. My mass-murdering spree wouldn't have been so much of a problem if it weren't for the fact that I took out the Nisut-Bity of the United States and the European Union, and at least four prominent viziers, among the others. Nothing they won't bounce back from eventually, but they're severely chastened.

What's more telling, however, is the global failure of their daimonic defences. They simply ceased to function. And the sacred flames in their most important temples have been extinguished.

As if their Patron has simply abandoned them.

With the Lords Council of House Alba now demanding that they hand me over, they really don't have a leg to stand on. So, we're bound for London, and somehow I'm hustled through the airport security with hardly any hassle, my lack of passport and appropriate visa immaterial.

Donovan flashes the officials a document, and before I have a chance to cast a last glance at the airport buildings, I'm ducking into a small, private jet. No promised private lounge with its free drinks even features on my journey. I don't know whether I should be pleased or annoyed.

The shit thing about a twelve-hour flight is that you can only pretend to be asleep for so long. At some point you need to get up to take a slash, eat, or drink. The jet's more like a lounge, with seats that fold down into daybeds. A flat-screen TV at one end shows some dumb action movie that has Andile and Duncan occupied. I'm paging through a suitably bland travel magazine when Donovan seats himself across from me.

"Coffee?"

"What, you're an air hostess now?" I ask.

He winces. "I see you're back in top form. We need to talk."

I sit back and regard him evenly. "Really?"

"If you think you can just walk free after this, you must be mistaken."

"No, I'm just some juicy bone everyone can fight over. The way I look at it, I've got something I can hold over all of you. And I can go back any time I want to, and finish what I started." I say this last bit with a slight measure of forced joviality.

"We can take steps," he says. "Eventually, with a little bit of effort."

"Do you know where your Patron is?" I ask him as sweetly as it's possible for some six-foot-tall dude with tattoos can. I sound like some sort of infomercial.

"A temporary…glitch." Donovan fiddles with his tie.

I narrow my eyes at him. "Really? Have you looked at me? As in good and proper. I dare you."

He blanches, but when he relents, I'm ready for him. And I show him, as simple as it is for me to open a figurative window and allow him a glimpse.

A shabti, lying flat in my hand, and clay is so brittle. I could tilt my hand…

"Sekhemib," I murmur, so only he can hear.

"Bastard," he says and gulps audibly.

"It's in your best interest that I'm allowed to go."

"You can't hold me to ransom."

"I can do many things—things you haven't even dreamt of," I say. "Things that will make you wish you never existed."

"We should end you."

"And then what? Have that secret slip through your fingers. Houses Adamastor and Alba find new and more inventive ways of keeping *The Book of Ammit* out of your grasp. Or the fact that I've done something to separate you from your Patron, and only I can undo it. So ja, sure, go ahead and kill me. What will happen when I die? What will happen to your Patron?"

He licks his lips and darts his glance about the plane's interior as though looking for help from his mates. Whether they fully realise the seriousness of this conversation or are ignoring Donovan's predicament for their own sakes, it matters not. The man's on his own for this round.

"I'm sorry about your girlfriend," he tells me.

"Right you are." I breathe deep to keep my expression bland, even though the rusty blade digs in deep.

We're at a stalemate, and that suits me fine. The plane has a minibar, and I figure now's a good a time as any to drink myself insensible or make an attempt to dull the agony of mind that has me in its grips. At least if I drink, I can't think straight. The booze prevents me from slipping into that cursed chamber where I fear I'll drive myself mad trying to resist smashing all those figures.

What's stopping you?

I can't tell myself to fuck off now, can I?

What would Lizzie do?

Problem is, I can't answer that question anymore.

☥

I don't get to see much of London. We arrive at some ungodly hour and hurry straight from the plane to a pair of waiting Mercedes sedans that gleam black like giant alien beetles. The windows are heavily tinted, and surprise surprise, we're in the midst of a torrential downpour, so the lights smear in rainbow hues down the windows. My head feels like it's stuffed full of sodden cotton wool, and there's a foul taste in my mouth.

Remind me not to drink again.

No one bothers to explain to me where we are or where we're going, but we end up in a dimly lit underground parking garage. Half the strip lighting doesn't work, and there's a huge puddle that takes up a goodly quarter of the area, no doubt runoff from outside. That can't be good, but then again, it's not my place to worry about these idiots. Instead, I allow myself a slight sneer and let these same idiots guide me along.

What have I got to lose? Not much, really.

This is the end. Death holds no fear for me. What's the worst they can do? Kill my *Kha*? I have a more than nagging suspicion that I'll end up at that temple complex, and that thought seems worse than hell instead of Per Ankh. Still, it isn't all bad, is it? Of course, it will do them no good to have me there, will it? Able to destroy them from their holiest of holies.

We're brought to a waiting area in an echoing passage. Ladderback chairs with hard seats line the wall, and there aren't enough for all of us to sit—myself, Andile, Duncan, and Donovan, as well as four others in dark suits who're local. They're pasty-faced men who seem to strive for a pseudo-military approach. They're fully primed, with their powers barely held back, and much like one wouldn't want to provoke an angry dog, I don't make eye contact and try to keep my body language as unthreatening as possible. Hands visible at all times. Slow, measured movements.

No trouble for me, thank you. I've done enough already.

Oddly enough, I'm calm. Deadly so. Could be weary resignation. Could just be plain old exhaustion. The events of the past few days seem to rattle past on repeat. What would have happened differently if I'd gone with Bethan and been able to use that portal? What if I'd not let Marlise go to the stores on her own? Okay, that's an easy one—we'd both be up in Joburg or NYC by now. We'd both be alive. Maybe. And Alex? If we'd taken him with, what would these people have done to him? Would Thanatos have slid their cold, dead hands further into this snarl of trouble?

With all this comes the knowledge that, ultimately, none of this matters. We've moved along the timeline. Marlise is dead, and when I next encounter her, she'll no doubt want to end me, and Ashton's proved himself to be the A-grade arsehole that everyone's always said he is. On top of this all, two of the biggest Inkarna Houses are poised on the brink of open warfare.

Now, that latter fact I can almost entirely guarantee because House Alba wouldn't like the tasty morsel that I am to fall exclusively in the hands of its greatest rival. The only question is when they will make their move. In the movies, round about now, there might be a dramatic rescue, with all guns blazing, but I'm under no illusions of something that significant at present.

Before I have more time to bemoan the fact that I haven't had a cigarette in more than fourteen hours, one of the double doors opens, and an elderly woman beckons for us to enter. Old she might be, but she walks with that characteristic self-assurance that so many senior Inkarna possess, and I'm smacked with the certainty that we're in the presence of someone I don't want to fuck with.

The same goes for the crone seated at a massive carved desk. Her hair has been shaved to the scalp, and her eyes are almost lost in a nest of wrinkles, but her gaze is sharp. That she's missing her right arm doesn't matter. She still sits on that giant, throne-like chair as if she's the fucking Queen of Egypt. There's a good chance she was one during a past life.

Four chairs have been drawn before her desk, and I claim one of them without being advised of whether it is safe to do so. The only indication of annoyance comes from Donovan, who gives a huff of displeasure before he takes a seat next to me.

In typical Inkarna fashion, the chamber's walls are taken up with floor-to-ceiling bookshelves laden with an assortment of tomes that rivals most that I've seen. Centuries of serious collecting here, for whomever's pompous arse graces the hot seat. The full suit of armour in one corner takes the cake—a baroque, gold-trimmed and black-lacquered mating of Victorian-era Egyptomania and Renaissance plate armour. I try not to smirk too much when I cut a glance in its direction.

Dried-up Prune in front of me clears her throat, and I try to return her gaze evenly. With emphasis on try, because she's unashamedly examining me using her daimonic senses, which leaves me feeling like someone's goose-stepping on my grave.

"Ashton Kennedy," she reads from a sheaf of papers before her. "Of late of the Eastern Cape, ex-Cape Town; apparent age, twenty-two; occupation, barman." Her mouth pulls in a moue of disgust. "I see a criminal record here for drug dealing. Several arrests for disorderly conduct and assault, but the charges were dropped. A suspended sentence. Police are currently inquiring with regard to your whereabouts relating to the disappearance of a young woman just over a year ago. And that's only the incidents that affect the public."

That gaze locks onto mine again, and I am the first one to look away. Amun's cock, she makes me sound like the worst kind of reprobate. Oh, wait, I am, aren't I?

The woman continues to read off the report. "You're also responsible for the demise of nearly all the senior members of House Montu in the Western Cape region, including the southern vizier. That was a year ago. To date, you have wilfully destroyed House Montu property, caused injury, and been implicated in the deaths of..." She rattles off a bunch of names that have little meaning to me, except when she mentions Adriaan and ill-fated Philip.

The temperature in the room grows frigid, and I'm not certain if it's the tension of the mounting accusations brought against me or if it's a daimonic backlash due to these people clearly being pissed as hell about my presence. I'm so not walking out of here, and I doubt there'll even be enough to stuff a body bag.

When she's done, she tucks the papers away into a manila folder and places her hands palm-down on the desk. Every eye in the room is focused on me, and I can't help but to want to shrivel into the floor.

"How do you answer to these charges, Mr Kennedy? And, more importantly, how did you perpetrate your most recent attack?"

I squeeze shut my eyes and feel how damp my shirt is, stuck to the small of my back and my armpits. One, two...three deep breaths and I summon the courage to return her idiotic glare. She reminds me a little of the way birds of prey have this ability to stare at those who are beneath them.

"An introduction to whom I'm dealing with would be nice, lady. I do believe that in your haste you've forgotten your manners." Oh dear gods, I'm channelling Lizzie at her best, down to the carefully pronounced schoolteacher syllables.

Someone behind me hisses, but the sound is truncated when Henchwoman swivels her head in the person's direction. Sucks to be you, buddy. Then again, I'm the one in the hot seat. I have every right to be worried.

Henchwoman speaks. "You haven't deserved the right."

Dried-up Prune holds up her hand, but she doesn't look away from me. "No mind, Mona. He is right. I am Emily Bracewell, acting vizier of the United Kingdom. My assistant—" She inclines her head toward her henchwoman. "Charlotte Honeyman, our acting general. I do believe you understand that you have done House Montu great damage."

No shit.

I nod and resist the urge to scrub at my face. There is no way in hell they're going to let me walk. No way in fucking hell. I am so very done. May as well do whatever the fuck.

I clear my throat. "I have countercharges to lay on your desk." Might as well come out with the entire sob story. Not that it will matter. "In my previous incarnation, I was in charge of the chapter house of House Adamastor. I know to you we were but a small, inconsequential blot in the bigger scheme of things, but we were once a vibrant House. At the time I wasn't aware of the fact that we were a scion of House Alba, but that is no matter. We had a purpose—one that I only discovered when I punched through in this incarnation."

Their looks of distaste make me want to slap the nearest face really hard, but instead I clench my hands on my lap.

"There is the small matter of *The Book of Ammit the Devourer*, which no one has sought to bring up yet here, which I'm sure you're aware of," I tell Emily.

Next to me, Donovan twitches, which the hell bitch doesn't miss.

Her brows all but shoot to her hairline. She doesn't know.

"You have the book?" she asks. By now a whole bunch of stuff must be falling into place, especially the fact that factions within her House have no doubt been trying to gain an unfair advantage. The mere fact that she isn't in the know—now that is juicy.

"No. I have hidden it."

She turns to Donovan. "Well?"

"We're still looking, ma'am." He sounds resigned, which suggests that my wards have held up.

Emily returns her attention to me. "You might as well relinquish the information. It's only a matter of time, you know. We'll find it eventually. Save yourself the trouble."

"No." I manage a smile, though I suspect it's more like a cornered dog baring its teeth at its attackers.

To Donovan, she says, "Why was this information not brought to the attention of the EU Nisut-Bity? Africa answers to the EU; not the United States, if that's what the brouhaha with Texas was all about."

I hope I'm the only one who catches the slight whimper that escapes him. The woman is ferocious, and I'm glad that I'm not the focus of her attention at this instant. Gives me a moment to regroup.

"Ma'am, if I may. The late general was the one who had an arrangement with the US. I tried to dissuade him but had to resort to extreme measures to stop him."

Oh, nothing much, just use your prisoner to do your dirty work, hey, Donovan?

He turns in my direction for a moment, and I grace

him with my most evil grin. Donovan blanches and finds the shit under his nails far more interesting than what's happening in the room around him.

"You did not report this to your seniors?"

Donovan huffs a breath. "I liaised with Vizier Van Rensburg. He advised me to bring the prisoner to him at his sanctuary."

"Yet he did not inform the United Kingdom or indeed the European Union branches. What was he planning on doing with the information? The book has been a sore topic long enough. It is a disgrace that within this House we lack cooperation. We're like a pack of schoolchildren fighting over a toy from a cracker at a time when we can least afford it. Especially since Alba is actively recruiting. It's only a matter of time before the balance is tipped. And for me to discover now, this conspiracy among our ranks that reduces us to mere factions grubbing for temporal power within a hierarchy when we should be facing the external threat? Unacceptable!"

Her words slice through us collectively, like an arctic wind. If I wondered how a woman had managed to claw her way to the top of a usually male-dominated House, I have no doubts now. Emily Bracewell has bigger balls than all the males gathered here combined. Me included.

Whether this is her age or power, or a combination thereof, I'm not in a position to argue.

"Mr Kennedy."

Oh shit.

"Explain your actions leading up to the attack on our House. And believe me, I'll know when you're lying."

Her force of will washes over me, a tsunami of pure, unadulterated presence. For a few heartbeats I can't draw breath. Her gaze pins me in place, strips away whatever bluff I might've been able to throw in her direction. The briefest vision of her *Akh* blazes through—regal, fierce countenance wearing the double crown of Upper and Lower Egypt, the sun blazing in her features.

I want to throw up my hands to protect myself, but when I blink, I'm faced with just an old woman made larger by her self-righteous anger.

"*Everything,*" she says.

So I begin, right from the beginning, and I spill my entire sorry story. What else can I do? It's not like she's going to change her mind about what a shit I am, or the fact that I will not escape unpunished. If I'm going to go down, I'm going to drag as many people down with me, and I don't spare the details.

Even as I tell my little tale of woe, it sounds like a big load of hogwash to my ears. Ninety-something biddy who's a member of an ancient Egyptian reincarnation cult croaks it and gets reincarnated in the body of a twenty-one-year-old arsehole covered in tattoos. She then tussles with her body's previous tenant, knocks up his ex-girlfriend and discovers that she's got custody of the Inkarna equivalent of a final solution to a recurring problem. Notwithstanding the high body count when she makes immortal enemies with a militant House that would love nothing more than to shred her souls into their component parts while dancing on the suppurating remains of her shrivelled *Kha*.

I try making Bethan's involvement less than a footnote, considering my connection to her that runs deeper than merely this incarnation, but despite my best efforts, I vomit up all the dirty laundry. Emily is relentless. The moment I begin flagging, she notches up that glare. Was this what it was like to face the pharaohs of old? No matter how I twist and turn, she digs her daimonic claws in and draws out the information. Everything up to the point where Adriaan van Rensburg dragged me into that ill-fated ritual. Even I don't know how to explain that. Nor can I explain my time as purely Nefretkheperi. Those thoughts refuse to be fully realised in the Queen's English, for to do so would rob them of all meaning.

As for *The Book of Ammit the Devourer*. Oh, she's a clever one. She discovers that it's indeed a stone tablet, of unusually marked serpentine, but other than that, nothing. Some of the ward that I placed back in the Eastern Cape remains in place, echoing on me. I praise The Divine Potter's wheel that I had the wherewithal to lay down the wards that day that feels like half a million years ago. Warriors House Montu might excel at making, but the scions of Alba are far cannier when it comes to the daimonic arts.

"You can threaten all you want," I tell her.

The air in the office has gone stale and reeks of sweat and fear. I'm wrung out, my throat parched. Next to me, Donovan has slumped slightly.

"We have other methods," Emily says.

"They won't work," I tell her.

"There are several chemical compounds that will lower your resistance."

"How do you know I'll give the correct information under interrogation, even with the drugs? I've placed wards. There's no telling what sort of backlash there might be."

She frowns. "You're bluffing."

Shit. Truth be told I have no idea what will happen if they drug me and try to extract the information. For all I know, I'll get damaged in the daimonic backlash. Or go incurably mad. Or I could spill every last utterance of that spell.

My pulse quickens. If there were any way that I could physically implode my *Kha* and cease to exist in this time and place I would. Instead I'm faced with a deathly silence and too many eyes trained in my direction. The buzzing whine starts in my ears, and the room blurs at its edges. Unbidden, I find myself once again seguing between that room filled with shelves.

I blink. A terrible chemical smell invades my senses, and warm liquid tickles my upper lip.

Mouths open and shut around me, but the sounds are distorted, as if they're moaning at me through great ocean depths. In slow motion, I lift my hand to my face, and the knuckle of my index fingers comes away with a smear of crimson.

Nosebleed. Great.

Is this how it's going to be? Every time I'm under stress, that I find myself in that dusty temple complex?

Reality melts, and my nausea threatens to empty the contents of my stomach. An audible snap, and I'm fully in the sanctuary with its hundreds of shelves. The plinth where the statue of Montu stood is still empty, and the air is musty. This time I'm not even worried about the chaos. Shelf after shelf comes down so that the figurines shatter upon impact.

I'll show them.

The pieces that fall I stomp, gratified to feel the crunch of clay shards beneath my boots, because this time, in this realm, my *Akh* has taken the shape of my current incarnation. I'm Ashton Kennedy here, not Nefretkheperi.

As suddenly as I wreak havoc, I'm yanked back, to where I'm sprawled on a carpet in an unfamiliar room, every muscle in my body cramping like I've been fed a convulsant. The room is filled with a haze of smoke, and the shelves of books are covered by some sort of metal barriers, like roller blinds that have slammed down. A sprinkler system hisses to life, and people are screaming and shouting.

Not that many, mind you. Just a woman and two men, if my scrambled brain makes any sense of their cries. The stench is unbelievable—a mixture of voided bowels and burnt pork. It's at that point that I roll over onto my hands and knees so that I can puke, and not much burns like the predominantly alcoholic stew that returns to say 'hey, howzit'.

By the time I'm able to pull myself into a hunched position over the desk, I can get a better idea of the chaos. Three survived—Emily, Donovan, and Andile. The rest... Well, I try not to look too closely at the blackened corpses scattered on the ground. The three remaining House Montu members pull themselves into a defensive position at the door. The atmosphere crackles with their power. They're ready to unleash. One false move from me, and I'm fucked.

"Do. You. Know. Where. Your. Patron. Is?" I gasp out the words, not breaking eye contact with Emily. She's the most dangerous one. She's the one who calls the shots with these arseholes.

Covered in dust and now sodden with the spray of water, the woman is anything but the dignified madam she carried off before everything went for shit. But she could still blast me into a flaming mess. Donovan, ever the gentleman, has positioned himself so that he covers her body from the brunt of the proposed unleashing of daimonic power. That's if I was primed and loaded—which I'm not. Andile looks like he's about to fall over, but he's trying not to show it.

Emily grimaces. "What are you trying to say?"

That slow-blooming suspicion that's been nagging

at me ever since I saw that empty plinth comes to the fore, especially why I keep getting dragged back to that particular spot in the aethers. I've assimilated their Patron. I don't know how—or why even—but I have. I am an avatar of Montu. He is incarnated. In me.

"Think about it," I tell her. "Just consider, for a little bit, why your people die every time you try put me in danger."

Her eyes narrow, and she grows pale. The waters continue to hiss down. Someone's knocking urgently from the other side of the door.

"*What have you done?*"

"I've become a living temple," I say. Weariness threatens to land me on my butt, and it takes all my effort to remain upright.

"What if you kill me?" I add. "What then? Every time I'm under severe threat, He will take steps." There is no need to name Him.

"You are my queen, my chosen consort," He tells me.

The woman who looks back at me from the reflecting pool is foreign to me, her eyes heavily outlined with kohl, her skin like raw sugar. Her eyes flash like fire opals.

Donovan places a hand on Emily's shoulder. "Ma'am. Let's get out of this room. Get dry. Talk things through."

Andile is there to support her when she sags, and Donovan unlocks the door. He yells at someone on the other side to shut down the sprinkler system, and I'm only too glad to follow them out. There's more carnage in the passageway. Of the two guards who stood outside our door, only one is alive. The other is a carbonised wreck. We stare at each other with wide, frightened eyes.

"Fuck this. I need a cigarette," I say.

Wordlessly, Donovan hands me his pack, and we light up. No one's going to bitch about smoking regulations. Not if they value their life.

CHAPTER ELEVEN
On the Streets

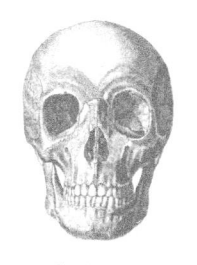

NO ONE STOPS me when I leave. In fact, I don't even have to rely on my daimonic powers to mask my egress. The initiate who meets me as I make my way down to the car park takes one look at me and legs it the other way. Let's just peg it to me experimenting to see whether I can walk out of the place without being stopped—my surmise proves correct, but I'm too exhausted to pat myself on the back.

The House Montu headquarters are fuck-ugly in an obviously expensive neighbourhood. It's at least three storeys taller than its neighbours but is painted the identical blinding white of its Victorian-looking neighbours and has two art deco-era falcons guarding its front door. No one comes crashing out after me.

Looks like I'm in a residential area. I shrug, turn, and begin ambling along the kerb.

I have no idea what time of night it is, except it's

fucking freezing, and a fine misty drizzle rains down. And they call this summer here? Two blocks away from the Montu headquarters, and I'm thoroughly damp, but I can't bring myself to care. Point is, I'm out. Free.

There's something that looks like a park on my right, but then I hear the familiar coughing roar of a lion. A zoo? London Zoo? Cars grumble past, and there's something glorious about being completely on my own in a strange part of town. Why the hell am I grinning like an idiot? Anyone who sees me would think I'm a complete nutter. My prospects are shot to hell. I'm basically an illegal immigrant, in a country where I've got bugger-all currency, and once Montu get their shit together, they're no doubt going to try regain custody. Unless I go back and wipe out the rest of the shabti figures. Which they probably can't stop me from doing.

So, excuse the grin, okay?

Could they move their sanctuary, or if I hold onto this bizarre link to their Patron, does that mean there's no way they can run and hide? Well, talk about having insurance. What now? There's nothing to do but walk, even if my hair is plastered to my scalp and runnels of water are sending their clammy fingers down my spine.

Eventually, I find my way to a river. Here the night life is a little more pronounced, and I can tell by the signs that I've reached Camden Town. Though some folks are clearly headed home by the looks of things, there are still a fair number of revellers out, despite the shit weather. I lurk by the water's edge, contemplating the way the reflections are liquid, like an oil slick. Then my feet drag me along, aimless. My stomach twists on itself, and part of me knows its hunger, the other just plain old sickness for all the dross of the past few days. And it's only been a few days. That's the scary thing.

My grief is a peculiar thing. I should consider myself an arsehole for being so quick to abandon Alex, and as much as I'd hate to admit it, he's probably better off where he is, for now. If I look on the bright side, I'd sooner him be with the Death-walkers than the militant fools I've just had a waltz with. Marlise will live again, or, if she has any sense, she'll remain in Per Ankh. The what-ifs bite harder with regard to her.

What if I'd tried to go it alone after all? Would she just have tagged along after me like a lost puppy in any case? Would House Montu have left her alone at all? This fruitless speculation will do nothing to change the outcome. I can't even justify things by saying I was not myself, for the *Sheut*'s memories of her death are as clear as if I were present when Adriaan drew that blade across her throat.

Bastard.

I should have used the words in *The Book of Ammit* on him, but then I would have been no better than him at the end of the day. Of course, how do I judge who is worthy and who is not? Who has given me the right to balance any hearts according to Djehuty's scales?

Maybe I'll kill him again the next time I see him. That thought delivers much satisfaction. And I can keep on killing him. Again and again. Just like I'll kill any of the others I crossed paths with, until they all just leave me the fuck alone for eternity.

At some point I'll have to figure out what my next step is, but I can't bring myself to care right now. Instead, I stretch my daimonic senses to overlap my usual ones and am carried along by energy lines and whim.

Perhaps that's why when someone calls my name, I'm not surprised.

"Ashton Kennedy!"

I wheel around to see two guys about my own age—alternative types with long hair. One's got a glorious mane of red hair and matching goatee. The other's blond and skinny, wearing a Type O Negative T-shirt.

We're standing outside a pub with the lurid name of The Devil's Parlour, and judging by the crash of music thrashing out from inside, one hell of a loud metal band is in full throes of angry guitars and wailing vocals.

The ginger-haired guy speaks again, "Ash, right? Jesus fuck, we heard you were dead."

Ancient memories stir. These are people from before I punched through—good friends of the old Ashton's. The blond dude is completely unfamiliar to me—he could be any Nordic type. But the other's name comes to the fore, sluggish—the memories are old, and I have to dig deep to extract them.

"Scott?" I say to him.

Before I can respond further, he closes the distance between us and all but crushes me in a fierce bear hug.

My efforts to extricate myself are absolutely no use until he withdraws to hold me at arm's length. His face lights up with such joy at seeing me that I can't help a horrible twinge of guilt. Please, oh, please let me not have screwed this guy over badly in the past like my previous tenant seemed to have done to so many.

"We heard you got hit by a car, then when you woke up you suffered amnesia. We had to go on without you," he says, as if that explains everything. "We didn't expect that you'd ever wake up. Meant to get in touch, but..."

Bits of memory nibble at the edges of full awareness. Oh. Wait. The band. My old band, for which I was the lead singer. A few visions of a slightly thinner and clean-shaven Scott pounding away on a drum kit. Long, lazy afternoons of us working out songs with the other guys.

The blond guy steps forward and holds out his hand for me to shake. "Jason."

I shake his hand.

"I kinda replaced you." He seems embarrassed.

"That's fine," I tell him. "I'm sure you're doing a better job than I did."

Because I recall how many practices I used to miss, because the old Ashton had been fucked up on coke or off with some chick.

"The recordings... Your voice..." Jason gushes. "I had big shoes to fill, man."

"Size thirteens," I say with a laugh. "Kinda awkward finding big-enough boots."

Scott knocks me on my shoulder. "No offence man, but you look like shit."

"Long story," I say. "How's the band going?"

Scott's expression is wry. "Better than when we were in SA. But the scene's pretty kak here too for live musicians. We're scraping by. We've been booked on a tour supporting some acts in the US in the fall." He squints up at the sky before making eye contact with me again. "But what the hell are we doing standing out here in this piss? Come in. We were just packing up. Come say hi to the rest of the guys."

Without anything better to do, it's easy to let them drag me along, to fall into old patterns—albeit a much more sober Ashton Kennedy than they knew. Gerhard and Pieter, the Anubis guitarist and bassist respectively, are at first a bit reserved when they see me.

Nothing a few pints can't solve. The story I spin them is as sketchy as possible. Yes, I'm in the UK. I got into a disagreement with my landlord, and he's taken all my stuff, so I'm sitting without a passport and a place to stay. A little judicious nudge here and there with my daimonic powers, and the guys have sufficient sympathy for my cause.

I hate myself for doing this, but the longer I stay with them, the more I realise this is a way for me to hide in plain sight. By the time we spill into the street and pile into Gerhard's dilapidated van, we're all old mates, and Jason insists that I can crash at his digs until I've found my feet. Who am I to say no?

The entire situation is ridiculous, really, if I consider the bigger picture—the fact that I'm a fugitive *and* an illegal immigrant. No other options present themselves, and within a week, I've been adopted by my erstwhile bandmates as their de facto roadie. The couch in Jason's lounge turns into a spare room when one of their housemates leaves. Within a month I've got a job at a pub in Camden Town. When the manager asks to see my passport, I give him a not-so-subtle nudge with my daimonic powers, and he conveniently "forgets" to bother about those pesky details. I get paid in cash, after each shift, and I'm not on the books.

On my off nights, I play roadie to Anubis.

From time to time I end up on stage, belting out old classics once I get over my initial reticence.

I can live with this.

But I don't ever stop being careful.

Often I pause whatever it is I'm doing so I can scan the people around me. A few times I pick up a whisper of power—witches perhaps—but they're well hidden and seem to have a natural inclination to keep away from me once they notice my awareness.

But I'm a fool to think this lull will continue. Each day might be the last.

I'm walking home from my shift, late one night—or early in the morning, depending which way I perceive it—when a woman falls into step next to me. I turn, half in annoyance, but then jerk to a halt.

"Bethan?" Sudden nausea has me reach out for a lamppost.

We're the only ones in the street. The tenements on either side are mostly dark—people are abed.

Her smile is wicked. "You thought I was dead, didn't you?"

I take another step back so I can prop myself up against the aforementioned lamppost. I haven't an inch of daimonic power at my disposal to protect myself, but I begin to draw—surreptitiously.

Bethan's wearing a form-fitting black leather coat that accentuates her curves, but the thick, burgundy scarf around her neck is the only splash of colour. Her face is so pale she might even be a porcelain doll.

Unaccountably, my eyes prickle, but I suck in a deep breath then distract myself by digging in my jacket pocket for a cigarette—I've had to ration myself here. Smoking's a bloody expensive habit, but right now I can be excused for the indulgence.

She watches me light up.

"What happened?" I ask.

"Contrary to popular belief, rumours of my death were highly exaggerated."

"Evidently." Anger simmers just beneath the surface of my shock. Once again, I've been left to do the heavy lifting.

"I must congratulate you on how you dealt with House Montu," she says. "Your methods were...most unconventional."

I bare my teeth at her. "No thanks to you. Are you going to explain yourself, or are you going to stand there acting all smug and superior because you know more of what's going on than I do?"

"Oh, Ash, always so quick to anger. Are we going to stand out here like a pair of love-stricken teenagers, or are you going to walk with me to my car so that we may discuss things in a civil manner?"

"I've got nothing to say to you!" I spit at her.

"Now, there I disagree with you. I think you've got plenty to say, but your ego's standing in the way of you having a rational conversation. Aren't you in the least bit curious as to what sad state of affairs has transpired in the wake of your successful going to ground? I am quite proud of you. You've led Alba and Montu on a merry chase. They had to eat crow before they came to House Thanatos for help."

I snort. "It's certainly taken everyone long enough to find me."

"Eight weeks, to be precise. And that's come to an end because I was only brought in on the case about a week ago."

"Where have you been all this time?"

"Not in the UK. And that's all you need to know. C'mon." With that she quickens her pace, and I'm forced to hurry after her.

Granted, no one's forcing me to do anything, and if I had any sense, I'd pull another vanishing act. But then how long before someone else comes? I don't want Jason, Scott, and the others to be caught in the fallout with House business. Nonetheless, I draw in my powers, until it feels like all the small hairs on my arms are bristling. If Bethan notices, she doesn't say anything, but I'm pretty sure I detect a faint smirk once we reach her car.

Bethan's BMW convertible—black, of course, with tinted windows—crouches like a predator, and I slide into the passenger seat. One of Schubert's string quartets—I forget which—filters softly through the speakers. One of Richard's favourites, and I don't want to know whether this is a calculated move on Bethan's part to trip me up emotionally, or whether it's the fact that we tend towards some of our old habits when we're out of our depth.

Though I've been doing a damn fine job of breaking Lizzie's mould.

"Where are we going?" I ask.

"You'll see," she says as we cruise down the road.

Despite my promptings, she refuses to discuss business, and instead regales me with some of the sights of London that I should take in while I'm here— especially the museums. They've changed much since the last time we came here.

The 'we' stings. There is no 'we' now. Just this guarded tension, and the knowledge that we are, by all rights, eternal enemies. A ridiculous notion enters my mind, of Bethan and I somehow falling into another relationship and how the dynamics would work. We're still good in bed. That much I can't forget, and my cock grows a bit hard at that thought until I will the desire to ebb. She'll end up betraying me again.

This time of night there aren't that many places open, but it's soon apparent that we're not headed anywhere public, because we arrive at an upmarket area— terraced homes and narrow streets. Take away the modern cars parked outside and add a few carriages, and it's easy to imagine this as a rather sweet part of London during the Victorian era, complete with ornate lamps. Or at least the London that's seen in period dramas. I know enough to understand that this is an area that's beyond the means of the average Londoner.

"What are we doing here?"

Bethan slides me that inscrutable smile of hers as we get out of the car. "We can talk."

"Are you sure that's all you want?"

"Why? Are you offering?" Her dimples make her seem much younger.

I mutter a few ugly words under my breath and enter the building. My heightened senses prickle as we pass over the threshold. The ward laid down here is strong, and I wouldn't want to stumble into this by accident.

"Thought we could have some coffee in the kitchen," Bethan calls over her shoulder as she walks down the long passage.

"That bloody well better be all," I mutter.

The kitchen is modern compared to the dark wood interiors of the rest of the house, or at least the parts I've seen. Brushed stainless steel finishes combined with sparkling ivory artificial stone tops. Bethan busies herself with the coffee machine—one of those expensive Italian jobbies I've still not quite mastered. While she works, she goes on about the coffee blends she prefers. Another habit that's annoyingly Richard all over again. He always did love to overexplain everything to Lizzie—as if she didn't have a brain of her own to formulate an opinion.

The cappuccino she presents me is perfect. She's even gone and doodled a heart shape in the foam. She's seated herself opposite me at the kitchen counter, her metallic black-purple lacquered nails the only thing out of place with the picture.

"So... Now we can talk," she says.

"Gee, thanks." I take a sip of my coffee. It is good, but I don't let any of the appreciation show.

"Plainly put, you've created a bit of a conundrum," she tells me.

"How so?"

Bethan brushes the hair back from her face, but it falls back over her brow. "Let's see, there's *The Book of Ammit the Devourer—*"

"That's not even an issue," I counter. "No one's getting that thing."

"I agree. House Thanatos is satisfied that you've taken enough cautionary measures. For now."

"You've gone over to them, fully now, haven't you? You've given them the secret." Where the hell that came from, I don't know.

"It's not what you think." She holds up a hand. "They are aware that I know the words. They have agreed to abide by me keeping the knowledge to myself on condition that I offer my loyalty."

"What do you know of loyalty?"

"More than you know." Bethan gives a soft sigh.

A cold, hard knot tightens in my chest. "You've got a funny way of showing it."

"Oh, my love—"

"Don't." I scrunch closed my eyes. I don't want to see her face, those lips.

If Lizzie had known better, she'd never have gone out for that afternoon walk with Richard Perry. She'd have stayed in her room to finish reading that Jane Austen novel. She'd never have accepted the invitation to see Richard the next time she visited Cape Town.

Everything that I am now would have returned to the Sea of Nun, to forgetfulness and nothingness, and round about now, that option feels like the most humane.

Chair legs scrape back, and I feel rather than hear Bethan come around the island to my side of the counter. Her arms are warm, and the cloves scent of her perfume undoes me. I should get up, shove her away from me, and leave. Instead, I allow her to hold me and stroke my hair. None of this will last, but while I can drown myself in the illusion, I will. Her daimonic power mingles with mine, and there is unity.

"I killed Marlise," I say after a while. I don't look up.

Her arms tighten around me. "No, you didn't. Adriaan killed her."

"It's my fault."

"These things happen. You don't think I haven't been in a similar situation before? Where I've had to make a difficult decision that has resulted in the deaths of others?"

I straighten and pull out of her embrace. Bethan remains standing next to me, close enough that her thigh brushes my knee.

"It shouldn't have to be like this," I say.

"Life isn't fair. Do you remember the day Richard asked Lizzie whether she wanted to reach for the stars or remain safe, without any chance of falling or hurting herself?"

I nod. Of course I do. They were walking along the Promenade in Sea Point. The sun had turned blood-orange and was melting in a cobalt sea. The sky had burnt to apricot and salmon hues. Almost unconsciously, I raise my hand to the silver pectoral that I keep on its chain around my neck, on the same chain as the Anubis pendant from Ashton's old life.

"Richard showed Lizzie the pendant and told her about House Adamastor, about immortality. Lizzie thought it was some sort of Gnostic sect similar to the Rosicrucians." I manage a bitter laugh. "You created fertile ground, filling her head with all that nonsense beforehand."

Bethan's smile is tight. "We had to start somewhere."

"And now this," I say.

"The time we spent together was such a small

fraction of what I've experienced. We can never go back to those moments. We can only go forward."

"What are we now? Certainly not friends."

"Not enemies. Remember that, no matter what happens." She dabs at the corner of one eye with her index finger. What? She's feeling actual emotions?

Then again, I'm not much better myself.

"Okay. I need a smoke." I rise. Anything to put distance between us.

"Not in the house." She goes to open the back door for me, and I stand in a tiny courtyard where the washing line is.

"Whose place is this anyway?" I ask as I light up.

"House Alba's. One of their generals. Usually reserved for visitors."

"And now House Alba is in bed with Thanatos?" I ask.

"Not quite. Let's just say that a certain General Frost, newly appointed general of the UK, owes us a favour, especially if we remain discreet about what purpose my being here was."

I sigh, take a deep drag. "I guess this means I'll shortly be acquainted with said general?"

"Indeed. Though out of the entire situation, it's not as dire as you think it is. And to lay your mind at ease, it always was my intention that you should return to the fold, so to speak. Until such time that we can re-establish House Adamastor."

"Why? And start the whole sorry business again?" I glare at her. "What's actually going on?"

"There's a truce, of sorts," she explains. "A way to create balance. The deal is that Thanatos and Alba share the burden. We have signed oaths that are binding, upon our Patrons' sacred names, that we shall not share nor teach the words of *The Book of Ammit* with any. Upon our deaths, these secrets return with us to Per Ankh. The stele remains hidden in perpetuity, until the knowledge to read it is eventually gone from this world."

"You and I are not the only ones to know the truth," I tell her.

"That I am aware of, which is why I've taken it upon myself to communicate with the one once known as Leonora."

"That's not possible!" I snap at her.

"You forget our gifts among Thanatos," she says.

The small hairs on my nape prickle with the wrongness.

"Leonora understands that she must hold the secret. She has sworn as well. You and I must swear before the Nisut-Bitys of Thanatos and Alba to not share the secret words."

"And use it?"

"Only if requested by a full quorum."

"What of House Montu?"

"What of House Montu?" Her expression is cryptic.

"How bad is it with them?"

"Oh, they'll recover. Eventually. It's in their best interest to treat you well. I'm sure you can well imagine."

My head hurts as I chase through events, and then I narrow my eyes at her. "You set this up, knowing full well what I was capable of. You walked us into a trap. You knew they'd be there, waiting for us in Kirstenbosch."

"To be honest, I expected some resistance. I just hadn't intended for either of us to be captured."

"What happened to you? I thought you were dead."

"The portal activated in time for me to step through."

Her face is a mask that doesn't betray the faintest

smidgen of a lie. Then again, Richard was pretty damned good at misdirection, too.

"But not me."

Bethan inclines her head. "No. That is regrettable."

"Why didn't you come and get me?"

She huffs out her breath and rolls her eyes. "What the hell, Ashton, is this the third degree?"

"Answer me!" For emphasis, I slap the door frame. I don't mean to, but a small sliver of daimonic power escapes, and a hairline fracture crawls up the door's windowpane.

We stare at it for a few seconds then Bethan laughs.

"Sweet Amun," she says.

"What?" There's nothing funny about the situation.

"You should learn to curb your enthusiasm for rampant destruction."

"Then tell me what I need to know."

"You don't need to know where I was." There. The slightest whiff of annoyance in her tone.

"And the child?"

"Alex is safe. That is all you need to know. For now."

"When can I see him again?" I owe the bastard at least that much.

"When he is ready to see you."

"So, the Death-walkers can have a head start in brainwashing him, I suppose."

"Would you have done any different for him? Especially now that his mother's dead. What would *you* have taught him? How to be an uneducated slob? You don't have money. You're pretty much indigent. You have no paperwork, no hope to return to South Africa. And you don't even want to know what sort of trouble you'll be in when the authorities here catch wind of you. Unless some House takes pity on you, what are you going to do? Play bartender for the rest of your natural life? Be some hanger-on with a sub-par music group? Spend your nights getting drunk when you've nothing better to do? Your daimonic powers are only going to get you so far on their own."

I'd dearly love to smash my coffee cup, but I suck in a deep breath and try to rein in my emotions.

"What do you propose?" I crush the butt of my cigarette under my feet and brush past her back into the kitchen where I take my seat. The dregs of my coffee are cold and bitter.

Bethan closes the door gently, locks it, then turns to face me. "That's better." She says it like I'm some brute of an animal that needs to behave itself. "Thing is, Thanatos was all too willing to take you in. In fact, I lobbied for it. But then you began that unfortunate—for Montu—decimation of their ranks, and that threw everything out of whack. I must have you know that Alba was all for having you put down."

"What's stopping them?"

She smiles. "Us. Of course, there's one small problem. They can't let House Thanatos hold the secrets to *The Book of Ammit*. Hence the trade. While they've got you, House Montu has no choice but to behave themselves. Very convenient. Though they'd prefer to end you, or find some sort of way to remove your rather intimate association with their Patron. We, of course, would, prefer not to have you passing on to Per Ankh just yet."

"Why? Surely, that's convenient?" I narrow my eyes at her, and some idea of what's happening here strikes me. "You're keeping me alive so that you can maintain balance. So House Montu owes you favours, isn't it?"

Bethan shrugs. "I have no idea what the head mambo's up to. I just follow orders."

"Liar. House Montu's brought in check." I stab a finger at the kitchen counter. "They rely on you to ensure that I stay alive because if House Alba kills me, though they destroy House Montu once and for all, they lose the knowledge of *The Book of Ammit*. Dear Aset, my head hurts."

"In other words, it's a bit of a Mexican standoff, but it works better than a cold war, don't you think? Because that's what we had, with House Thanatos the convenient scapegoat for both." She pats me on the shoulder. "There, there. It's not so terrible."

"You say it like it's a good thing."

"For us, yes." Bethan starts trailing her hand across my thigh in a way that suggests she'd like to take things elsewhere.

"Now what?"

"We get some rest. Tomorrow you collect your things from your friends, say your farewells, and we catch a flight to Dublin."

"I don't have a choice."

"Not really." Then she leans in, and I let her kiss me.

I'm fucked. I might as well get laid, too, while I'm at it.

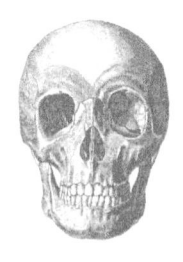

CHAPTER TWELVE
Closure

I LIKE DUBLIN the moment I set foot in the city, which blends old and new in a way that makes me wish I could slip into its streets to explore. And, contrary to what I've been told, it's not raining, and there are only a few clouds. The only pity is that I'm not here to do any sightseeing. I'm whisked along the streets in what I'm quickly believing to be de rigueur accessories for the high-ranking House members—a black, shiny Mercedes-Benz S-series with tinted windows so dark they may as well be opaque.

Bethan's dressed in a black suit that somehow only serves to accentuate her curves, even though she's aiming for a masculine appearance. I can't say I'm enamoured with the suit I've been forced to wear—I drew the line at getting a haircut, the only part of the old Ashton to which I can cling. The suit is certainly not my style, even though it no doubt costs more than what I've earned the entire year. We make a striking couple, though.

Not that Bethan's said much to me beyond briefing me on who we will face and what I must—and must not—say. The closer we get to our destination, which is in the grounds of Trinity College, the more my stomach churns. For Bethan, this is full circle. For me, who knows. We're talking centuries of custom, and here I'm about to traipse in, an uncouth yob in their eyes.

The car draws into the courtyard of an imposing grey building that suggests a Georgian style, complete with columns and a fanlight above the double doors. The only sign of security is the flood of awareness that tickles across my body. The wardings here are old and powerful, and an itch at the back of my brain suggests that they've created a powerful egregore to guard their chapter house. What better disguise could they ask for, on the grounds of this venerable institution? Richard often spoke of the library, and its many precious volumes. I'd much rather be there than about to face the bastards that started this whole sorry business with *The Book of Ammit*.

A young man comes down the steps and does the whole vibe with opening the doors for us. Like us, he's garbed in formalwear, but his entire countenance is bland unto the point of complete anonymity. Is this to be my fate—rendered to the status of yet another minion?

"George," Bethan says to the young man and shakes his hand.

His smile transforms his face, and paints laughter lines, and none of the good humour vanishes as he turns to me. "You must be Ashton Kennedy. Welcome. We've heard so much about you."

There's no trace of irony in his tone, and I allow a grudging smile. His grip is firm. Definitely self-assured, despite me towering over him.

"Right this way. I expect you'd like a pint of the good stuff?"

Bethan trots after him, and neither turns to see whether I follow. For a wild moment I'm tempted to run, but I suck in a breath and stay on their heels. The reality of my predicament is such: I'm stuck on an island in the Atlantic Ocean. How far would I get if I attempted to go AWOL? Not very. Thing is, I've been running, and have been so suspicious of others for so long, that my mistrust has become embedded in my psyche.

Bethan and George trade easy banter as we make our way down an echoing passage. These could be offices, I suppose. The dark wood doors on either side of us are closed, and I don't have time to read the brass nameplates on each.

We traipse upstairs until we reach the fourth floor, where we are brought to a comfortable lounge that gives us a panoramic view of the university grounds. George indicates for us to take a seat on a couch, then busies himself at the bar.

"Isn't it a bit early to booze?" I ask Bethan, as quiet as possible.

She raises a brow and gives me the kind of look that suggests disbelief at my statement.

"It's never too early," George quips as he opens a can. "You need your inaugural taste of Guinness, Mr Kennedy." The bastard actually winks at me.

"Okay then," I mutter.

Bethan gives an unladylike snort of laughter. "He's probably going to hate it, just to be contrary."

"I've managed twenty-two years of not touching the

stuff in this life," I say.

"The face he pulled in his past life when he tasted it was priceless," Bethan says.

"Fuck you," I mumble.

"You already have."

George just laughs and brings a silvery tray with three glasses of that infernal brew which he places on the coffee table before us with a flourish. "Ah, come now, Mr Kennedy. There's surely a little bit of the Irish in you to appreciate a pint?"

"I don't want to be drunk when I go meet your superiors." The glare I give him could strip paint.

Bethan and George both start laughing, and I can't help but sense that I'm inadvertently the butt of their joke. All I can do is sit there while they finish wiping their eyes.

"Oh, Ash, I meant to tell you—" Bethan starts.

"But you didn't."

George says, "I am the superior here."

My heart clenches, and it feels like all the blood in my body rushes to my feet in the space of two heartbeats. "You're the Nesut-Bity of the British Isles?" I almost choke on the words. "But—"

"I'm so young, yes," he finishes then glances at Bethan. "Old Siptah and I here go back a long way. I was the one who asked Richard to do his little vanishing act back in the eighteen-hundreds, and though things didn't quite go according to our intentions, we're satisfied that we've concluded our plans to the best of our abilities. All things considered."

Of all the things... I stare at him for way too long, robbed of whatever I wanted to say. I'd expected some sort of council, a courtroom environment, and interrogation. Not this, whatever it is. "Now what?" I manage to say.

"You're here," Bethan says, then reaches over to squeeze my hand briefly.

"And?"

George shrugs. "We make of it what we do."

"I'm free to come and go?"

They glance at each other; Bethan inclines her head.

"It's complicated," George says. "I think you're aware of that."

"No shit," I growl. "What next, though?"

"We're not sure yet," George says. "But you're safe. For now."

"I'll drink to that," Bethan says.

"Aye, indeed," George flashes me another disarming, roguish grin. "Welcome to House Alba. I trust your stay here will be filled with many wonders." He raises his glass, and Bethan mirrors him.

I have no choice but to participate in this most ancient of rituals. The stuff doesn't taste half as bad as Lizzie thought it did back then.

EPILOGUE

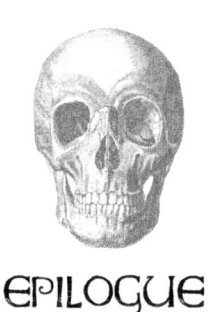

MR AND MRS Kennedy have moved, but I've tracked them down to a cottage in the backyard of a home in Plumstead. Ironically, not far from where Marlise's parents stayed. Up until five minutes ago, I had every intention of getting out of the taxi as planned, and going to knock on the door, but now that I'm here, I'm paralysed.

Call it reparation, but I've a document from an investment firm that I intend to hand over personally. As much as I've established that House Montu kept up their end of the bargain with Marlise's family, I've convinced House Alba to do the same for the two people who suffered the most with their son's dysfunctions.

But I can't do it. Shame plays a large part in it. Twenty-one years of this *Kha*'s life were nothing but trouble, and the short while I've been in charge, hasn't been much better. There's not much to help my situation with Marlise until I meet her again, but this policy I intend to gift to Ashton's parents is the least I can do for them. This is full circle, and House Alba has deep pockets for its scions. I figure they owe me this much for all the trouble I've caused on their behalf.

Yet perhaps I should get the taxi driver to slip this into the post box…

An incoming text message chimes, and I'm of half a mind to ignore my phone, but invariably I swipe the screen to see who's bothered to contact me.

Bethan. Of course.

I'm staying over at the Mount Nelson. Join me for High Tea if you have the balls to speak to your old folks. And trust me, I'll know if you didn't…

Bitch. How she's even aware I'm in the country…but I suspect George has passed on my whereabouts and phone number. Conniving bastard.

I'm smiling, though. Bethan and I have unfinished business, but I doubt she's ready to let me see Alex. Just yet.

"I'll just be a minute," I tell the driver. "Please wait. I won't be long."

Okay, I can do this. Following the way of Ma'at means doing what is right. But that doesn't mean that it's particularly pleasant or easy. If I can face the wrath of immortals, I can master my shame and put right some of the wrongs of the innocents I've harmed.

The promise of a congenial tea afterward should sweeten whatever unpleasantness I face now.

The wind is as cold as the first time I died, but I've got a new leather coat that I can button up against the chill. Three pied crows flap up from the pine trees and are torn away by the wind.

ABOUT THE AUTHOR

Nerine Dorman is a South African author and editor of science fiction and fantasy currently living in Cape Town. Her novel *Sing down the Stars* won Gold for the Sanlam Prize for Youth Literature in 2019, and her YA fantasy novel *Dragon Forged* was a finalist in 2017. Her short story "On the Other Side of the Sea" (Omenana, 2017) was shortlisted for a 2018 Nommo award, and her novella *The Firebird* won a Nommo for "Best Novella" during 2019. She is the curator of the South African Horrorfest Bloody Parchment event and short story competition and is a founding member of the SFF authors' co-operative Skolion, which has assisted authors such as Masha du Toit, Suzanne van Rooyen, Cristy Zinn, and Cat Hellisen, among others, in their publishing endeavours.

Do follow Nerine on Twitter at nerinedorman

OTHER BOOKS BY NERINE DORMAN

Books of Khepera
Khepera Rising (#1)
Khepera Redeemed (#2)

Those Who Return
Inkarna (#1)
Thanatos (#2)

Camdeboo Nights

The Gatekeeper Cycle
The Guardian's Wyrd (#1)

Dawn's Bright Talons

The Blackfeather Chronicles
Raven Kin (#1)

In Southern Darkness (2 novellas)

The Firebird (novella)

The Company of Birds

Sing down the Stars

Aetheria (short story)

Printed in Great Britain
by Amazon